Riley's Pond

a novel by
harley brooks

ISBN: 978-0-9856598-1-3

Editing by Joelene Coleman
Formatting by Bob Houston
http://about.me/BobHouston

Edition: Createspace.

Brooks, Harley
Riley's Pond / by Harley Brooks

Praise for *Riley's Pond*

"Smart, sexy, and sassy...Brooks drives home what it means to be young and in love."
—Kelli Ann Morgan Author of "The Rancher"

"With a colorful cast of characters, this spicy teen romance tugs at every emotion from laughter to tears, and shows the meaning of compassion, forgiveness, and unconditional love."
—J. Cole, author

"RILEY'S POND took me down memory lane, reviving feelings of elation, angst, and the unbridled passion teenage romance is all about. The tenderness and crushing heartbreak of young love are captured perfectly in Brooks' characters. You don't have to be a teenager to enjoy this delightful read."
—K. W. Green

"Brooks created characters that are vivid and believable—hard to do. Great story!"
—Tiffany Helmer, Author of "Impact"

"Harley Brooks shows teen-boy angst so accurately, she should be required reading for anyone (of any age) who wants to understand the adolescent male heart. Witty, edgy, tender and true, RILEY'S POND will draw you in and make you gasp—like plunging into a cold pool. You'll emerge shaking tears from your eyes and envying Taylor as Riley morphs into the superhero her strength and love inspire him to be."
—K. Kelly

"A charming and realistic read through the ventures of a teenage boy who encounters desire, love, and heartache through a journey that will make you giggle and weep. RILEY'S POND is addictive!
—S. Ovard

About The Book

Riley Martin finds being the middle son, standing in the shadow of a wayward older brother and a "baby archangel," challenging. He feels responsible for keeping his parents happy by compensating for his older brother's bad choices, while unable to sow his own wild oats because of his impressionable younger brother. When his rebel brother, Jaxson, turns their family life upside down and Riley's into a personal hell, he escapes to the one place he considers his private sanctuary. The pond he and Jaxson built three years earlier, spending an entire summer bonding together while damming the stream at the end of their property and creating a secret swimming hole.

However, when Riley arrives ready to break in the rope swing for the summer, he hides within the chokecherry bushes. Someone has discovered the secret hideaway and is swimming within the dark waters. Someone beautiful inside a revealing wet T-shirt, who captures Riley's lustful heart immediately.

Taylor Wilson's peaceful afternoon swim is interrupted when a teenage boy slides down the hill and lands on the banks of the pond. Her hopes for escaping her complicated life in Boston by spending the summer with her grandmother, take a sudden twist when she meets Riley Martin.

A steamy late night rendezvous violates Taylor's grandmother's only rule—obey a midnight curfew. Fear of being sent back to a life she no longer wants sends Taylor on a speedy retreat, but red and blue flashing lights halt her in the middle of skid. When the sheriff advises Taylor she's under arrest, her heart stops, especially when she finds out she's charged with failure to give the sheriff's son a proper goodnight kiss. Riley's secret is out.

Taylor's, however, remains hidden and weighs heavy enough on her mind she could sink into a dark abyss and never see light again. Climbing out of Riley's pond and into his life, Taylor realizes for the first time she can be happy, but the monster following her is far more dangerous than any mythical creature hidden in the depths of a dark lagoon.

Dedication

For Jaycee—my exuberant teenage inspiration and one of the greatest joys in my life.

"Never stop dreaming."

Acknowledgements

First, my overwhelming gratitude to you, the readers of *Riley's Pond*. You are the wind beneath my author wings and the driving force in my passion to share the romantic tales my young characters constantly shout in my head.

Second, my heartfelt thanks to Kaye Green, Sascha Ovard, and Karla Kelly, for the endless hours spent editing, reviewing, and basically holding my hand from the moment *Riley's Pond* became more than a thought in passing. I could not have asked for a more dedicated support staff, or dearer friends. Your talents, inspiration, "cyber tissues," and ability to push me forward when I tried to give up, took this from a dream to reality. I'm forever in your debt.

Third, recognition and love for a man who spent a good portion of the past two years taking a backseat to my literary love affair with my characters. Without my husband's patience, understanding, and bank account, *Riley's Pond* would still be trapped on a memory stick.

I could not have succeeded in seeing my dream to be a writer come to fruition without the support, guidance, and kick in the butt I get from my writing colleagues. Being a member of Romance Writers of America (RWA) and Society of Children's Book Writers & Illustrators (SCBWI) has connected me with an awesome group of authors who I rely heavily on for their banter, wit in the wee hours of the morning when I can't sleep, and expertise—many having kicked the stones away to make my path to self-publishing smoother. I love you all.

To the manufacturers of Harley Davidson motorcycles, I owe you for giving me the means to stimulate my muse, while straddling a 103 cubic inch powerhouse engine. Clad in leather, the wind in my hair and sometimes a bug between my teeth, you have made it possible for me to ride the edge of life only the brave dare drive. My imagination soars when I'm racing down the open road.

Riley

Everyone experiences one poignant moment in time they never forget. We remember where we were, what we were doing that very second, and the way our heart ached with overwhelming helplessness when it happened.

*****

She emerged from the sapphire pool almost in slow motion. Her head flipped, sending her wet, golden mane arcing through the air, the thousands of water droplets sparkling in the sun like a shower of diamonds.

She turned my direction. Dark lashes glistened against pale pink cheeks and full lips still hummed the bewitching tune that stopped my world from spinning. Her wet baby blue T-shirt clung to curves my hands longed to touch and when her delicate fingers braided into her hair, the small silver ring piercing her navel shimmered in the sunlight.

All the saliva in my mouth evaporated. My name escaped my memory and my swim shorts suddenly felt tight. I'd never seen her before, but knew immediately I didn't want to go without seeing her ever again. Every teenage boy's fantasy—wet and gorgeous. Swimming in my pond.

What I didn't realize in this defining increment of time? I faced my future. No clues warned me my summer plans were about to be altered. That I could have handled. What I didn't know, nor could have prepared for, was that in the three short months of summer my entire life would be redefined. I embarked on an unknown journey having the potential to destroy everything I believed, and possibly everyone I cared about, in its wake.

No, none of this I knew. The only thing I did know…I wanted to jump her bones.

****

One
THE NIGHTMARE
Riley

Mom's shrill carried up the stairwell and I jerked upright, my heartbeat slamming in my ears. A kaleidoscope of red and blue flashes bounced off the walls of my bedroom. I rubbed the stubble on my chin hard, tearing apart the last sleepy cobwebs, and took in the scene out my window. Charlie's cruiser sat crooked at the end of the driveway and Pete's rested against the curb across the street, his light bar the brightest by far. Our neighbors, the Hendersons, had to be thrilled living across from the local sheriff.

The swirling torrent of orange lights from the wrecker truck, danced with the red and blues. When I made the connection *Dad's* sheriff cruiser dangled from the wrecker, panic swamped me. The front corner of the car crumpled back to the edges of the large star on the passenger door.

Shit.

"Dad!" I yelled, rushing from my room wearing only boxer shorts.

An eerie silence permeated the empty hall. Did I dream Mom's scream? I glanced back through my doorway, the room pulsating with color. No dream. I waited for my heart to settle back in my chest. Years of being a cop's son taught me to "evaluate" my surroundings before freaking out, but staying calm didn't work at the moment.

The door next to me leaned ajar, the pigsty void its occupant, my older brother, Jaxson. The disgusting smell of dirty socks and other mysterious odors attacked when I stepped inside. *Such a gross waste of skin.*

In the room across the hall, buried under a pile of blankets, the small lump consisting of my little brother, Dirk, lay still. The raspy sounds of a half snore confirmed his immunity to the loud commotion that had blared from downstairs.

When I passed Mom and Dad's empty room, my panic re-ignited. The unmade bed changed everything calm, back to chaos. A nuclear bomb could be suspended over the house, and my mother would stop to make the bed before she evacuated. She never wanted a news crew with television cameras giving the world a bad impression of her housekeeping skills. However, the image would only hold until someone opened the doors to either my or Jax's room.

The scratchy transmission of a dispatcher's numeric response echoed from below and I padded down the stairs, not sure what to expect. My dad's best friend and partner for as long as I could remember, Lieutenant Pete Lamb, stood in the entryway writing something on a notepad. The radio clipped to his shoulder chirped again, solving one mystery. The fact Pete didn't race to stop me or hadn't ventured upstairs in the first place, relaxed me a little. Still, I wanted to hide the horror waging war in my gut, edging me to a total meltdown, so I summoned my cocky attitude.

"How's it going?" I asked casually, treating Pete as some stranger selling a magic cleaner only available from a door-to-door salesman. Nonetheless, my voice carried an edge of hysteria, but Pete's wide smile sent relief washing through me. He didn't notice my knees sudden wobble from delayed shock.

"Interesting underwear, boy," he laughed, eyeing the heart-covered boxer shorts my girlfriend thought to be an appropriate Valentine's Day gift. My mother didn't agree, so I seldom wore them to avoid the lecture.

"Laundry day's tomorrow." I flipped the waistband. "Besides, Kaylee's opinion is all I care about."

"She likes her *sweetheart* in boxers sprinkled with tiny red hearts?"

"Depends . . . are the boxers on or off?" I answered, shutting him down. I licked my finger and drew an imaginary, *shaky* #1 in the air. "One for the 'boy,' zero for the 'Copper'." His middle finger gave me a pointed salute. "Nice. Way to corrupt the impressionable minor," I smirked.

"You *impressionable*? That's a crock."

I swallowed the lump in the back of my throat, ready to ask the ultimate question. "Where's my dad?"

"In the kitchen."

The breath I held came out in a rush and I fought to keep from collapsing against a surge of dizziness. I folded, leaned on my knees and willed the wave of nausea to cease. "He's okay?"

"Yeah. He wasn't in the cruiser." Pete stepped closer, placing a hand on my shoulder. "Riley?"

I waved him away and straightened. "I'm fine." My brow puckered. "If Dad wasn't in the car, then who—" The look on Pete's face answered my question. "Shit. Jaxson?"

"Afraid so."

"Damn! What happened? Is he hurt? Where's Mom?"

Pete's radio squawked again and he tipped his chin towards the dining room.

I hesitated outside the doorway. Once I crossed the threshold, I'd be sucked into the drama vortex my older brother created. Jaxson proved a magnet for trouble. When the two collided, my life became a living hell. The pressure on me to be the shining example doubled when Jax's bad behavior threatened to embarrass our family, or corrupt my younger brother.

White glass half-moons covered the glowing bulbs on the fixture overhanging the table, the light way too bright for 3:30 A.M. The kitchen and dining area presently served as the "Martin Family Crisis Control Center." Dad dictated authority on his phone, pacing the length of the kitchen unaware of my presence. I watched him purposely calculate each footstep to land precisely in the center of a floor tile. A perfectionist to a fault.

Charlie Adams, the owner of the other police unit flashing out front, engaged in a conversation with the tow truck driver as where to take Dad's wrecked cruiser. They paused and while neither said anything, Charlie's eyes checked off my shorts and the hint of a smile pulled a corner of his mouth.

"Riley."

"Charlie."

Mom bustled in from the laundry room and dropped a pile of freshly dried towels onto the dining room table. The smell of fabric softener overpowered the aroma of fresh coffee brewing. I'd watched my mother handle many uncontrollable situations over the years and discovered she dealt best with the stress by *doing* something. Tonight's project: folding laundry.

Swollen eyes and cheeks shimmered with tears, transformed her otherwise pretty face. Her cherry red nose rivaled "Rudolf's" and wads of tissues bulged in her robe pockets. My stomach dipped.

"Mom?"

She looked up, surprised. Her bloodshot blue eyes blinked a few times and she gazed about the room as if dropped from outer space, having no idea where she landed. I walked around the table and put my arms around her. She turned into me, laying her wet face against my chest and her shoulders shook when I pulled her tighter.

"Mom, forget the laundry," I whispered, placing a kiss on top of her snarled hair. "Tell me what's going on."

Dad's choreographed steps halted when he saw me. His gaze immediately landed to my boxers. A slight shake of his head momentarily interrupted the conversation with whoever's ear he bent.

His fingers scrubbed the thinning stubble on top of his head and he resumed his pacing…one step per tile.

Mom guided me to the sofa in the small sitting area off the kitchen. Her voice trembled. "It's Jaxson."

"Duh. Isn't it *always* Jax?" I huffed. She pressed a finger to my lips to stop me before I started one of my Jaxson rants. "Where is he?"

"The hospital."

"The *hospital*? Crap. How bad? Why aren't you there?" I asked feeling a niggle of fear at her possible answer.

"Your father wanted to tell me in person and take me himself. It's nothing life threatening, but still, having one of my boys hurt—"

Suddenly, Dad hovered over us, his expression mixed with anger and angst. "Bev, get dressed. We need to go. Jax will be out of surgery soon and I want to make sure *my* face is the first thing he sees when his eyes open. I'd like to kick his sorry ass to the moon," he grumbled walking away. *"Bev! Now!"* he yelled from the stairwell.

My little brother had to be in a coma if not awakened by Dad's loud demand.

"I'll call you with details from the hospital. Take care of Dirk, and make sure you're both out the door in time for school." She paused at the banister, giving me a no-nonsense glare. "You told me you got rid of those boxers, Riley. Cheeky girl." I opened my mouth to argue, but she'd already quickened her pace before Dad yelled again.

**

I never officially went back to bed. Instead, I curled under a lap quilt and settled in Dad's recliner in a dark corner of the sitting room. I played *dead* and listened to Pete and Charlie's hushed conversation as they wrote their report. The gist of what happened, involved Jaxson getting drunk at some party—a favorite pastime, and stealing Dad's cop car. What an idiot. However, the title needed clarification as to who officially had earned it.

Dad apparently left his keys in the ignition and the doors unlocked. He'd taken over a graveyard patrol shift because one of his deputies called in sick, and stopped by the house to use the bathroom. He only planned to take a minute, figuring no sane person would be out at one o'clock in the morning on a weeknight. Especially in the boondocks where we lived. He was right. No *sane* person lurked—just his *insane* offspring. His pride and joy and the neighborhood embarrassment, Jaxson Martin, my dad's favorite jailbird and eldest son.

The whispered report confirmed Dad's "minute" turned into an entire newspaper section of reading. Meanwhile, Jaxson helped himself to the patrol car. Pete and Charlie speculated, based on some evidence, Jaxson played chauffer to a couple having a "romantic interlude" in the backseat, while he probably received some personal attention from his girlfriend. The end result—Jaxson lost control of the car and crashed into the city's new stone marquee.

Chips of granite smashed the cruiser's windshield and those of two parked cars across the street, setting off a melody of alarms and waking the fine citizens of Wellsville. The backseat lovers apparently bailed, leaving intimate apparel strewn across the floor. Jaxson's partner wandered off until she passed out under a tree a few feet away. The paramedics found Jaxson unconscious and gouged by some twisted metal off the steering wheel.

I worried about my stupid brother, whose insides were being rearranged by doctors at the moment. However, this was by far the dumbest stunt Jaxson had pulled. If what Pete and Charlie said proved true, Jax could find himself spending a long time inside a jail cell.

**

Cold water pounded my back before I gathered the wherewithal to shut the shower off. School. I dragged my naked, dripping body across the hall and face planted into the center of my mattress.

"Your butt's whiter than an Albino's," Dirk said.

My head felt too heavy to lift, but I saw Dirk's face, twisted with disgust, reflecting off the glass covering Kaylee's photo on the night table.

"You checking me out little bro?" I teased.

"Ewwe! Gross! No way!" he grimaced.

"Close the door and go get ready for school. I'll be down in a minute and fix breakfast." No matter what crisis evolved, Mom insisted our lives remained normal as possible, and ditching school was never an option.

Inching my body upright, I blinked against what felt like tiny razor slices along my lashes. I stretched a T-shirt over my head, wondering if the naked silhouette covering my chest would earn me an excuse to come home and crash. Pulling jeans up my legs drained my last energy reserves. The socks on the floor passed the smell test to be worn another day before being tossed in the dirty clothes hamper. I yawned the same time I pushed my foot into my shoes and stumbled into my desk.

"Damn," I hissed, shaking the numbness out of my hand. I shoved the math book lying on my dresser into my backpack, snatched my iPod from its docking station, and the sweatshirt off the hook behind my door. I'd need to hide beneath the hood with earphones pushed in my ears to catch some serious ZZZ's in English. Good thing Bruiser sat in front of me. He was big enough to shield me from Mrs. Bornstein's iPod thieving eyes.

I tossed a slice of toast onto a plate and slid it down the counter to Dirk, engrossed in some handheld video game. "Put that away."

"My toast is burned," he complained.

"So? Shut up and eat. You've got ten minutes until your bus comes." I held my own piece of toast between my teeth, refusing to bite. *Beyond* burned.

Dirk started whining and the sound grated inside my skull. "Where's Mom? I don't want to take the bus. Give me a ride, Riley."

Mom didn't give me any instructions past feeding Dirk. Explaining *why* I fed him was another story. I spit my toast into the garbage and grabbed my backpack. "Hey, what's with the list of demands? Mom had to go into the shop early."

"You're lying."

11

"You're a loser. Now get your crap. The bus will be here any minute."

"Why can't you give me a ride?" I glared at Dirk over my shoulder when I locked the back door. He gave me a toothy grin. "*Ooooh*, lover boy's got to pick up his *girlfriend.* Maybe get in some action before school?"

I smacked the backpack hanging off his shoulders. "Geesh, you're *ten.* What do you know about anything, and her name is Kaylee. And yes . . ." I smiled, not finishing my X-rated thought. The bus horn blared out front and I gave Dirk a slight shove. "Go."

"Why do you have to be such a butt wipe?"

I burst into laughter. Dirk wouldn't swear if his life depended on it. Maybe because Jaxson and I cursed enough to cover him.

"I'm telling Mom, 'potty mouth'."

Dirk stood in the doorway, face puckered. "*Paleease* give me a ride."

"Fine," I surrendered. "Besides, there's something I should probably tell you."

I waved off the driver and a cloud of blue smoke rolled up the front lawn when the bus pulled away. Dirk caught the keys I tossed, smiling triumphantly at his little victory.

"I forgot my cleats for soccer practice. Wait for me in the truck, but don't mess with anything or I'll purposely run over your skateboard…then your bike. And, I *will* torture you in your sleep."

**

Taking Dirk to school cut big time into my morning make-out session with Kaylee. By the time we arrived at school, we barely got in five minutes of tongue tagging before we'd be late for first period. Didn't even steam up the windows, but worked me up enough I held my Chemistry book low and close. Girls had it easy. Kaylee ran her fingers through her hair and applied more strawberry flavored lip-gloss. My *situation* worsened, watching. A serious headache would start within the hour, pissing me off. Damn Jaxson. Even from his hospital bed, he messed with my life.

I helped Kaylee out of the truck and eased my arm around her waist, trying to sneak a feel from one of my favorite places on earth.

"Ouch!" She flinched, moving away from me.

"What? Did I hurt you?"

Her gaze fell. "No, I...um, tripped on the stairs this morning and fell." She flipped her head of chestnut colored curls back. "I'm so clumsy, sometimes."

That's when I saw it, in the bright sunlight, out of the shadow of my truck with my mind clear and eyes wide open—the bruise spreading over a lump above her left brow.

"Kaylee?" When I reached out to touch it, she grabbed my hand.

"I told you, it's nothing." Her brown eyes peered from beneath her long lashes, her tongue easing out of her pink glossy lips and licking my palm, slowly . . . seductively. I forgot my name and no longer gave a damn about the mark.

Pressing my Chemistry book tighter, I wrapped my free hand behind her neck and pulled her fruity glazed mouth onto mine. The outside bell rang and we jumped, raking teeth. I hissed, licking "Strawberry Delight" off my lips. Carefully, I tucked the loose curls covering her cheek behind her ear.

"Baby, I'm sorry. It looks sore." I pressed a gentle kiss to the shiner as if that would erase it and the pain. "Be careful. I love you."

She pulled the curls back over her face. "I will, I promise." She didn't say *I love you* back and my brows folded.

"Kaylee, is everything okay?"

"Yeah, silly, but we're going to be late, so get your horny ass in class before we're both in Detention." She backed away, blowing me a kiss before crossing the parking lot to catch up with her girlfriend, Shar, waiting by the doors to the main building. I turned on my heel and headed in the opposite direction towards the gym. A dull headache already thumped in my brain.

**

A call from my mother summoned me out of second period to the principal's office.

"Riley, did you get Dirk to school on time?"

"Yes, *Mom.* Seriously, is that why you called?" She sighed hard and guilt kicked my gut. Being our mother and the wife of the Sheriff brought her nothing but grief and many sleepless nights. "Sorry, I'm tired." I blew a long breath. "How's Jaxson?"

14

"Surgery went well. His nose is straight again, and he only needed a few stitches for the cut on his stomach. The spleen is the main concern. It will be another twenty-four hours before he's is out of the woods. The doctor said he's in remarkable shape, considering."

"Great. A perfectly shaped nose. Just what he needs," I sneered.

Jaxson looked like one of those guys sculptors used to pose for bronze figures of Greek gods. He inherited the best genes, leaving me and Dirk with leftovers.

"Riley!" Mom snapped. "Your brother is lucky to be alive and all you can think of is how jealous you are of his *nose*? Shame on you. And for your information, young man, you are every bit as handsome as your brother."

"Geesh, enough already. So when will you be home?"

"Well, that's why I called."

Damn. Here it came…*responsibility*. "I know. Pick up Dirk. Order a pizza. Do my homework. Make sure Dirk does his. No TV after nine. Anything else?" The secretary sitting at the desk across from the counter glowered.

"You make me sound like a prison warden, Riley. However, yes. All of the above, plus one you forgot. No friends, which specifically means 'no Kaylee'."

I pulled my head back to my shoulder blades, squinting against the fluorescent lights. "Yes, Master," I answered in a tight voice.

Mom laughed, lightening the conversation. "Thanks, son. Hopefully, I'll be home before you go to bed. Be good to each other, please. I love you."

"Love ya, too. Bye." I held the phone out to the disgruntled government employee still glaring with dagger eyes. "What? You want the phone or not?"

She rose from her desk and snatched it from my hand, trading it for a tardy excuse.

"Back to class Mr. Martin." My hand barely touched the doorknob when she vocalized her next threat, "And turn off that iPod, or I'll have it confiscated."

The door slammed loud enough to rattle the glass insert when I walked out.

**

Dirk was my parents' dream child. Jaxson and I were switched in the hospital, according to Dad. Someone else had their *real* children. If I didn't look so much like my mom and Jax the spitting image of my father in his teens, I might have believed him.

After unloading the dishwasher, Dirk's one and only chore, he settled at the kitchen table with his spelling book, copying his word list—the one I'd have to quiz him on later. He'd wait however, until I became engrossed in my favorite TV program, or worse, when I'd be attempting to convince Kaylee phone sex would have to work tonight because I had to babysit.

Pizza arrived promptly at 7:03, two minutes before it would be a "freebie" according to the stupid advertisement. I decided both of Dirk's legs were hollow when I lost the fight for the last piece of pizza. He managed to inhale almost all twelve inches of cheese and pepperoni.

"Dirk, you're such a pig."

"You're a bigger pig. A humongous, gigantor pig dork," he laughed, spitting Oreo cookie crumbs across the table."

"Yell, well this *pig dork* is Master and you are my slave. Get your butt in the shower while I clean up the gross mess you made."

"I took a shower last night," Dirk argued, snatching another cookie before I could grab the bag.

"Really?" I turned my nose up, sniffing dramatically. "Then why do you stink?"

"I don't stink."

"Sure you do. You smell like a wet dog. A *dead* wet dog. One covered in maggots...disgusting, rotting flesh smell—"

"Stop before I puke!" he screeched, holding his hands over his ears.

I scooped him under my arm in a football hold. "You hurl, you lick it up." Fighting to keep his squirming body in my grip, I carried him up the stairs and dropped him in front of the bathroom door.

"I hate you, Riley."

"Yeah, well the way you smell, I hate being around you. Ass in the shower."

He slammed the bathroom door and I swear I heard him call me a name worthy of a week's grounding, but I didn't push it. I had a more urgent agenda. Once I heard the water turn on, I barreled down the stairs to take advantage of ten minutes of privacy alone with my cell phone. It would have to be *speed* phone sex.

Kaylee sounded sleepy when she answered and my heart sank, as well as other body parts with the realization my fantasy might not come true.

"Hey baby. How's your head?"

"Sore," she answered through a long yawn. "How's Jaxson?"

Her question threw me and I couldn't hide the irritation in my voice. "*Jaxson*? What about Jaxson?"

"Oh…uh," she stammered, making me suspicious, "I heard he got in an accident. Practically everyone in town knows. You know how fast gossip travels."

True, except the details of the accident, especially those involved, hadn't been released. No one at school said anything either, but the neighbors may have spread rumors based on Jaxson's previous antics and the crumpled car hanging off the wrecker.

As much as I wanted to tell Kaylee about what happened this morning, I couldn't. What I overheard remained confidential and Dad probably already drowned in hot water, not to mention embarrassed that the whole department knew the sordid details. He didn't need me spouting my mouth off and making things worse.

"Actually, no I don't. What did you hear?"

She cleared her throat a dozen times. Her voice came out too high to be believable. "That he wrecked your dad's cop car and broke the stone marker on the edge of town. My brother said he didn't see Jaxson at work last night, either." Her brother worked on the loading docks at the train yard, too, but not on Jaxson's crew so my own lie worked.

"I know nothing about the accident, and Jax had last night off."

Kaylee yawned again and I decided to let it go. I didn't want to ruin the mood by arguing, although the *mood* faded fast. I made a desperate move to salvage the last five minutes of our call.

"So…you want to uh, talk about something like….you know…?" I asked in the deepest voice I could contrive.

"Not tonight, Riley. I'm too tired."

"Can't you give me anything to dream about? Come on, I'm alone with the 'baby archangel'. I need some devilish thought to keep me from swaying to the other side."

Kaylee laughed. "You're crazy, you know that? Tell you what, pick me up ten minutes early tomorrow and I'll make sure you never see the 'pearly gates'."

"You're evil girl." Upstairs, the shower shut off. "Gotta go. Love you, babe."

"I know. See you tomorrow."

She hung up the phone without repeating "I love you" back to me for the second time today. The prickle of hair standing on end warned me something bad was about to go down.

**

Mom called just before nine to check in. She took over the daunting task of drilling Dirk on his spelling words while I finished cleaning up dinner. Paper plates and cups inside the empty pizza box, and then into the trash. Dishes done. I carried a scoop of dogfood out to the patio to feed Lucky while Dirk repeated the words he missed. When I walked back inside, Dirk rolled his eyes, verbally repeating his bedtime routine to Mom.

"Night, Mom. Love you." He handed the phone to me, "Your turn, *loser*." He took off running for the stairs when I lurched forward, pretending to attack. His scream however, brought my mother's voice shrilling through the phone.

"Stop teasing Dirk," she scolded.

"Hi, Mom."

"You're going to make him have nightmares."

"Not until I creep under his bed and shake the mattress."

"*Riley.*"

The only person more fun to torment than Dirk, was Mom. "Chill. I'm joking," I laughed, realizing after a couple of seconds Mom remained silent. "So how's my fine example of an older brother?" A sudden thought entered my mind. "Mom, what about Ally? Did she get hurt?"

Fused at the hip, as well as a few other significant places, Jaxson and Ally had dated constantly for almost two years. Naturally, I assumed she'd been his partner-in-crime.

A heavy sigh traveled through the receiver. "I'm not sure about Ally. Your father didn't say anything and you know he would have, given his, well, mild dislike for the poor girl."

"*Mild dislike?* Dad hates Ally. He blames her for half of Jaxson's problems."

Mom breathed a long *hmm*. "Riley, your father wants to ask you about some of Jaxson's friends. I guess there were others in the car, but the paramedics found Jaxson alone. He's worried they might be hurt, but got scared and ran off."

I played stupid. "Why does Dad think that?"

"*Clothes* were found on the floor in the front and backseats. Jaxson was dressed, thank God." Mom did that nervous clicking in the back of her throat. "*Underwear,* Riley." I could actually hear her blush and needed to stop her before she started explaining her ideas on what happened. Some things I did *not* want to hear told by my mother.

"Okay, enough details."

Mom wasn't naïve, in particular to Jaxson's behavior. He told me how she came home sick from work one day, finding him and Ally going at it like rabbits on the family room floor in the basement. Apparently they'd skipped school, thinking they had all day alone.

According to Jax, Mom heard noises in the basement and flipped on the lights. Jaxson and Ally sat up surprised, but not as much as Mom. There's still a hole in the wall of the stairwell where the baseball bat she held, went through the sheetrock.

Thanks to his two week grounding, dinner conversations every night during Jaxson's "house arrest" centered on topics related to sex: the consequences of unprotected sex; psychological babble about sexual relationships at a young age; the emotional needs of girls versus boys. And my personal favorite…*abstinence.* Dirk spent so much time across the street at the Hendersons during those talks, I wondered if they considered adopting him.

Mom never spoke of Jaxson's "indiscretion," but ever since, if he or I remained downstairs alone with a girl for longer than thirty minutes, Dirk would be commissioned to come downstairs for some useless errand in order to "spy." The back of the couch could be viewed from the fifth step, but the second stair had a built in alarm. The loose boards squeaked loudly when touched, giving you time to sit upright. As long as the TV blared and we appeared to be engrossed in whatever streamed across the screen, nobody ventured further. Grandma's afghan folded over the back of the couch came in handy. She died years ago, but Jax and I had mentally thanked her numerous times.

Two
FAMILY MATTERS
Jaxson

I wished for death. Trapped between scratchy sheets that shifted during the night into a wadded knot at my lower back, and a blanket small enough to count as an infant's, I'd barely slept. Machines beeped behind my head, paging units from patients in other rooms dinged constantly, followed by the grating squeak of rubber soles skidding against tile floors. The nurses' station outside my door served as the social gathering place, where I'd been unwillingly privy to conversations on everything from cheating spouses to menstrual cycles. Anyone who thought hospitals were *quiet* never slept in one.

The throbbing between my eyes pounded unceasing, worse than any hangover I'd experienced since my drinking rampages started five years ago. My first alcohol binge happened at summer camp at the age of fourteen. The memory remained so fresh I swear when recalled, I could taste dirt on my tongue.

Three bunkmates and I slipped out after curfew with flashlights and backpacks holding beer, Wendell, the devil's right hand partner disguised as a fifteen-year-old computer dweeb, managed to steal from the refrigerator in the counselors' lounge.

We sat on the banks of the lake making up drinking games starting with intelligent substance like word trivia, moving to who'd gotten the farthest with a girl, slowly demeaning ourselves to who could belch the loudest, and the grand finale—farts.

I knew nothing about word trivia and my experience with girls remained limited to kissing a cousin under the mistletoe to please a twisted grandmother. When the belching contest started, I'd definitely drank too much. I couldn't say "burp," let alone force one without bringing stale ale with it. When "farts" rolled around, I'd passed out in the cold mud.

When I didn't show up for breakfast, my counselor set out to find my dead body. Of course when he dragged me into the medic station, my cohorts, all suffering various stages of leftover inebriation, denied my existence.

**

The ugliest nurse in the hospital had been assigned to me and last night when she leaned over to check my bandages, her breath reeked of garlic. I'd wrinkled my *broken* nose to ward off the stench and screamed from the pain. Startled by my yelp, Mom, half asleep, jumped on her metal folding chair and tipped a tray of half eaten food onto the floor.

She stood between me and a puddle of chicken noodle soup, not knowing what to do first—rush to my side, or clean up the mess. She chose mopping up soup. I pushed aside the pinch to my heart and blamed her choice on the fact she couldn't get around the medical Neanderthal restraining me, not that splattered food could be more important than her own son.

"Get the hell away from me!" I barked yanking my arm from beneath the stethoscope pushing my inner elbow. The sudden movement tugged the IV needle on top of my hand, and a smug smile wandered over my medical warden's mouth when I sucked a sharp breath.

"Shit!"

"Jaxson!" Mom gasped.

Unbelievable. *Tears* leaked from the corners of my eyes. *Nineteen year old boys don't cry*, I commanded my inner child. I hadn't cried since I was a kid. What I'd give to be six years old and curled up on my mother's lap listening to a bedtime story.

Mom looked over at me, dropped the dripping towels into the garbage can and muscled around the nurse. Her floral perfume overpowered the "vampire repellent breath" smell, competing with the aroma of chicken broth.

"Leave him alone. Can't you see he's hurting? And you better get someone in here with a mop before my husband comes back." The nurse "hmfed" in disgust, but left the room.

Mom smoothed my brow with comforting strokes. She pushed the hair from my face and pressed light kisses to my cheek. "Shhh, baby. It's all right."

"Nothing's ever going to all right again."

"Yes it will, Jaxson. Everything's going to work out. The important thing is you're okay."

"But, Dad—"

25

"Loves you," she punctuated. "He loves you, regardless of all the 'stuff', got that?"

A feeble "sorry" tumbled awkwardly out of my mouth. I loved my parents, but constantly stressed them out with my asinine choices. The worry lines on my mother's face deepened the past year, and my father avoided me whenever possible. Dirk acted like he feared I'd murder him in his sleep and Riley hated my guts. Or soon would, when he discovered the truth about the accident. Smashing Dad's sheriff cruiser would pale in comparison to the crushing blow I'd serve my brother's heart.

This time, I really fucked things up. The damage I caused could create a rift in my family that may never be fixed and I had no one to blame but myself…and my good friend, "Jack Daniels."

Three
TRUTH OR DARE
Riley

The grandfather clock in the living room chimed out the eleven o'clock hour. Still no Mom or Dad. Dirk had been asleep since 9:30. I even did my homework out of boredom, channel surfed the satellite, finding nothing but infomercials and old sitcom reruns. I lingered for a moment on some soap opera relayed in Spanish, amused at how the voice track missed the lip movements.

What's taking so long?

I checked my cell. No missed calls. Finally, I decided to go to bed with the belief that sometime before morning, parental supervision would return to our house again. Someone who could cook a decent breakfast.

I locked the doors, put Lucky in the laundry room, and set the security alarm. I left the front porch light on, even though my parents would come through the garage. Something about the way the light shone through the leaded glass window and lit the entry, gave me a needed sense of security.

Dirk was well on his way to healthy snoring rage by the time I made the last stair. The glow from a lamp in my parent's room sent a ribbon of gold light across the hardwood floor. They must have forgotten to shut it off in their rush to get to the hospital earlier. I stepped inside, freezing at the foot of the bed. My world righted just a bit. Even in their hurried frenzy, Mom managed to make the bed, perfectly arranging the stupid lacy pillows Dad hated. They made great fabric bricks to throw and wake him on Sunday mornings.

When we were little, we could get away with jumping on the bed while pulverizing our parents with pillow bombs, but when you're closing in on the six foot mark, jumping on a bed could send you through the floor to the basement.

My thoughts whirled back to present and I reached out to shut the lamp off, tipping over a picture on the dresser, knocking another, until several frames slapped the wood. The last picture I lifted to arrange was of Jaxson, who now had a new nose. Just what he needed—another physical *perfection* added to his credits.

Jax could have any girl he wanted…well, actually he had. I hated admitting *my* girlfriends drooled over him. After spending an hour at our house under Jaxson's dazzle routine, when it came time for some serious kissing, I didn't doubt his face replaced mine. Couldn't complain, though. Make-out sessions always seemed hotter *after* Jaxson cast his spell.

"Riley? What are you doing in here?"

My skin slammed the ceiling and my skeleton flattened on the floor when Dad's voice suddenly perforated my thoughts. All the pictures I'd just re-arranged flew across the room when my arm jerked. Jaxson's picture symbolically hit the bedpost and shattered.

"Shit you scared me!"

"Watch you language, son."

Dad wore his uniform, his sidearm resting in the holster. He didn't remove the gun to put in the safe, nor did he shrug out of his jacket.

"You on duty? Where's Mom?"

"I'm filling in on another graveyard with Pete. I left your mother at the hospital with Jaxson, but promised to come home and check on you boys. You didn't answer my question. Why are you in our bedroom?"

"Turning off the lamp someone left on."

Embarrassed, I picked up pictures and haphazardly placed them on the dresser. Dad bent on his haunches, carefully plucked shards of glass out of the carpet, and set them on Jaxson's face.

"How is Jaxson?"

"He's out of the woods. They were able to save his spleen. He'll be coming home in a couple of days." Dad set the broken picture on the nightstand, easing onto the edge of the bed. He patted the mattress to his side. "Riley, sit with me. There's something I need to tell you."

Cautiously, I lowered myself a foot away, hugging the bedpost for support.

"Riley, we've determined there were others in the car with Jaxson. Unfortunately, one came as a surprise." He regarded me. "Son, Ally didn't ride in the front seat with Jaxson."

"That figures," I scoffed. "Was she in the back doing Brandon while Jaxson drove?"

"Honestly, I don't know where you boys get such a crass attitude. My old man would have paddled my butt for talking like that and your grandmother would have fed me hand soap for a week."

"Sorry, but believe me, I'm nothing like some kids I know." He had no response, so I went back to the accident. "Okay, so Ally wasn't in the front seat, but did I get it right about her being in the back?"

"Ally wasn't in the car, period. Brandon and his girlfriend, what's her name…?"

"Jamie."

"Yes. Those two were in the backseat fooling around, I suppose, by the undergarments left on the floor. But someone other than Ally rode next to Jaxson, who also left intimate apparel behind."

The hair on the back of my neck tweaked. "Okay, so Jaxson has a new girlfriend. Ally will take care of that. Be ready for the chick fight."

"Ally's not the one I'm stressing about over-reacting. It's you, Riley, I'm worried about."

"*Me?* Why should I care who Jaxson's screwing this week?"

A brow rose in disapproval, but Dad didn't chastise me. Instead, he pulled a long, breath, letting it out slow. The words he spoke hung in the air, having nowhere to go—too heavy to float away, but too light to be within reach so they could be taken back.

"Because Jaxson's date was *Kaylee*. She wandered off after the accident, disoriented. We found her unconscious under a nearby tree."

"Kaylee." I didn't ask, just confirmed.

"Yes, son. Kaylee. She admitted to being in the car at the hospital."

I swallowed several times, trying to pick which emotion to deal with first. Betrayal, anger at Kaylee…at Jaxson, or the ugly monster rising quickly—jealousy.

"What clothes did she leave in the car?"

"Riley, that doesn't matter…"

"It matters to me!" I blared over him. "What clothes?"

My father lowered his eyes, his voice almost a whisper. "Her shirt…and bra."

"But not her panties?"

"Riley, I've already told you too much—"

"Were. Her. Panties. On?"

"Whose panties?" sounded the sleepy voice from the doorway.

Damn. We woke Dirk, who diverted my father's attention and left my question unanswered.

Four
CONFESSIONS OF A CHEATER
Kaylee

My heart smashed my spine when I shut the locker door and found Riley fuming on the other side.

Pull it together Kaylee. He can't know.

When I reached out to touch him, he grabbed my wrist, his fingers constricting so tight, I felt my arm numbing.

Damn. He knows.

"Riley, you're hurting me."

He yanked me close enough that on any other occasion my bones would have melted. Riley's eyes narrowed to angry slits and I felt tiny puffs of air against my face from the words he quietly, yet firmly spat.

"Tell. Me. What. Happened."

"I don't know what you're talking about." Stupid reply, but then most everything I did lately bordered "stupid." Riley kept my wrist hostage, placed his free arm around my waist and towed me to the parking lot. "Riley, I can't miss first period. My parents will kill me."

"They're not going to get the chance, because I'm going to beat them to it. You *owe* me an explanation, Kaylee," he shouted loud enough to get a couple of students' attention. Riley turned to the few witnesses of my possible demise. "Mind your own damn business." His popularity gave him absolute power and they scurried into the building like spineless cowards.

Except Shar. She held her own against Riley and followed us to his truck.

"Martin, what the hell do you think you're doing? Do you want me to—"

"What Shar? Call the *police*? Go ahead. In fact, ask for my dad personally. After all he's the one... Never mind." Riley clamped his anger, softening his tone. He glanced at me cowered against the door of the truck. "Does *she* know?"

My eyes darted between Shar and Riley. She knew all right. But Riley couldn't know *how*. Shar's dad was the mayor. If he knew about her being in the car—in the backseat with Jaxson's nineteen-year-old friend, her sixteen-year-old butt would be shipped off to a private school. Possibly a nunnery. Good Catholic girls supposedly didn't do what Shar did to Brandon.

When the sheriff cruiser crashed with a little help from "yours truly," Shar jumped from the car and Brandon followed, pulling his shorts over his bare butt. When I saw Jaxson bleeding and heard the radio squawk "officer assistance *stat*," I knew the police would swarm the place any minute.

Jaxson appeared lifeless, slumped over the steering wheel, face down in the airbag. I honestly thought he was dead. My stomach swirled. Somehow, I managed to climb out the passenger door and staggered across the lawn away from the car. The cold blast of air on my skin reminded me I'd left my shirt and bra on the front seat. I turned around, took in the crumpled car, smoke billowing under the street light. The squeal of car alarms echoed everywhere. Sirens wailed in the distance and I decided to take my chances sneaking in the back door at home. When I whirled back around, something hit the side of my head, hard, turning the world black.

When I woke in the hospital, Sheriff Martin sat next to my bed, holding my clothes, demanding to know what happened. I confessed to being in the front seat with Jaxson. *My* panties were still on, but Shar's apparently, remained on the floor in the car. When he asked who else rode in the car, I added another lie to my list of sins. I said Brandon was with his girlfriend Jamie, which hopefully spared him from jail, and Shar from her father.

I blinked away the vivid nightmare and stepped around Riley. "Shar, it's okay. This is between Riley and me." Worry clouded her gray eyes. I winked and forced a smile. "We just want to go somewhere private and you know, *talk.*"

Her shoulders relaxed somewhat, but a doubtful expression showed she didn't believe me. "I'll meet you for lunch," she said and turned back toward the school.

Riley wrenched the truck door open. "Get in," he demanded. I didn't argue and climbed over the console into the other seat. Permanent black streaks marked our retreat. A few silent minutes later, he pulled into the library parking lot at the edge of town. The city's granite marker at the end of the property looked like some large creature took a bite out of the corner.

"Why are we *here*?" I asked, playing coy. He didn't answer and climbed out of the truck, coming around to my side. I almost dropped to the pavement when he dragged me out.

"Okay that's enough, Riley. If someone sees you acting like some abusive lunatic, you'll get arrested."

His cheeks puffed in and out. He reached around my shoulders, gentler, pulling me to the middle of the small, tree-dotted park to the side of the building. We stopped at a picnic table in the far corner hidden by a clump of scrub oak.

Riley perched on top of the table, resting his feet on the bench. He twisted the strings of his hoody mindlessly around his finger. "So. Which tree did they find your half-naked body passed out under?

I gasped. "Riley, I'm tired of this game. I have no idea what you're talking about."

"Tell me it isn't true." He pointed at the broken marker. "Deny it to my face that you weren't with Jax when he hit that."

We played out an optic tug-o-war. I crossed my arms in defiance over my chest. Riley flipped elm seedlings into the air, letting Nature's "helicopters" flutter to the grass.

"It's going to be in the paper, Kaylee, so you may as well fess up."

"They can't! I'm a minor!"

With a big mouth.

Riley hopped off the picnic table nudging my shoulder as he walked past me. "We're *so* done, bitch."

35

The world bubbled behind watery curtain when I suddenly realized I watched the better of two brothers disappear. I ran after him, throwing myself in front of him. "No! Riley, don't say that. I'm sorry, *really* sorry. Jaxson means nothing to me. I love *you.*"

Riley squared my shoulders. His eyes glistened. "Really? *Love* me? I doubt you know the meaning of the word. Face it. If you really *loved* me, you wouldn't have gone after my brother." He kissed my forehead, and continued to his truck.

"Hey, I need a ride back to school." He kept walking. "You can't just leave me here!"

Riley spun around, hands facing out. "Call somebody who cares, Kaylee. There's someone more important than you I need to see, one who's new nose needs rearranging."

Five
RECKONING
Jaxson

I needed to pee, but couldn't wake up enough to ring the buzzer and summon my Nazi nurse. Maybe I'd get someone halfway pleasant for the day shift. The urgent pain won over the need for sleep and I carefully shifted onto my good side to reach the buzzer. I opened my eyes, blinking in disbelief…or horror. Riley sat in the chair next to the bed, close enough I could see the scar just below his right brow from where he fell and hit a rock when we were working on the pond.

"Shit."

Riley grabbed my throat. "You ass! How could you do that to *her,* let alone your own brother."

"Riley!" I coughed. "Damn, ugh, let go." I pried his fingers from my neck, feeling the IV needle in the top of my hand, roll with the muscles. "Hell!" I choked.

He dropped back in the chair, glaring at me. "You had no right, Jaxson! Stealing Kaylee is low, even for you."

"I didn't *steal* her little bro. She came to me of her own free will."

Riley leaned over the bedrail, cheeks puffing hard, teeth clenched. "Girls never come to you of their own *free will.* What did you promise her?"

Unable to stop myself from playing the asshole, I shot back an ugly reply. "A good time. I guess you fell short in that department."

One hell of a bruise would radiate across my shoulder from Riley's punch. Damn, when did he get so strong? Breathing deep against a painful wince, I stared back and found my worst nightmare…Riley, with *tears* in his eyes. Well hell. The Martin males were a bunch of wimps.

"Fine, maybe I sort of led her on. Don't blame her, Riley. Sixteen year old girls are 'in love' with the idea of being wanted by someone older—not their high school boyfriend." I raised my arm to block the fist, but Riley kept it in the air. "Really? I didn't think you cared that much."

"Did you go all the way with her?" he asked, the words forced through a locked jaw.

"Hell no! I'm not going to jail over some 'wannabe-prom-queen'. Besides, I was too drunk to even, you know…"

"But dad said her shirt and bra were in the car."

"Dude, don't hit me because I've got enough internal organs trying to die right now. She came on to me. I mean, I'm not innocent. I teased her into taking off her shirt, but the bra? Totally her idea."

Riley silently considered whether to believe me. I told the truth to that point. What I didn't tell him, was *what* she tried to do while I drove. She may have been drunk on her ass, but knew exactly what she wanted. Made me wonder if my little brother had experienced Kaylee's special talents.

The other secret I'd take to my grave. Kaylee jerked the wheel when I wouldn't let her unzip my pants, crashing us into the oversized headstone, changing the name of our fine city from "Wellsville," to "Ellsville." A stupid spoiled brat, but too young to have a record. Me on the other hand, all they had to do was give these charges new page numbers.

"Riley, I'm telling the truth. I did nothing to her beyond maybe cop a feel. That's all, I swear."

"Who was in the backseat?"

"Dude . . ."

"Who? Dad's worried they're hurt and he's drilling me for your friends' names."

Great, more secrets. In Riley's present state of mind, if I told him Kaylee's friend, Shar, and my friend, Brandon, hooked up in the back, he'd blab it to Dad, if not the whole damn high school. Brandon would be in jail for sure, and Shar's parents would have the power to charge him with sexual assault because of their age difference.

Brandon, surprisingly, had been accepted to an ivy-league college and planned to become a hot shot lawyer. If the truth got out, his career would be over before it started. Nope. Not telling. If discovered later, it would be through someone else. Not by me or Riley.

I semi-faked a reaction to a bad pain. However, the "call of nature" competed with my spleen on the pain scale. "Riley, it was just some couple from the party. To be honest, I can't even remember their names. Let it go. If they're hurt, they've already seen a doctor."

Riley stood, knocking the nurse call button off the side of the bed. "You're a lousy liar, Jaxson." He walked out without looking back, or giving me the controls.

"Hey!" I yelled out with too much force from my gut. "Nature" won, and thanks to Riley, I now needed my bedding changed."

Six

GRANDMA'S HOUSE
Taylor

Sunlight peeked between the eyelet lace curtains on my bedroom window, sending a dotted shaft of light to the braided rug beside my bed. Tiny dust particles danced and twirled in the lemony ray, bringing a fond childhood memory to mind. I'd try to catch the sunbeams in my hand, or whirl around in the midst of them, pretending they were magic dust that could make me fly if I concentrated on happy thoughts, the same as Wendy in *Peter Pan*.

Life seemed simpler in my childhood and easier to keep a happy thought. But that was before my world shifted sideways. A few days ago, my parents gave me a most memorable gift for my eighteenth birthday. They announced their divorce—even showed me the paper signed by the judge when I doubted them. I still felt the anger that surged; toward Dad for leaving and at Mom for letting him go.

When Dad left, suitcase in hand, and Mom drove away in her shiny new Mercedes—her "buy-off" gift from dear old 'daddy', I packed a suitcase, grabbed my laptop and my mother's credit card from the bureau drawer in her office. I booked a flight and came to Grandma's— *my* parting gift. Before leaving, I emailed each of them, knowing they'd get my heartfelt message with their morning coffee.

Thanks for fucking up my life. I'm going to Grammy's and if you're smart, you won't come after me. I'll decide when I'm coming back...if ever. You've made enough decisions for me. This one's mine.

–Taylor, formerly known as "Mommy's gummy bear" and "Daddy's princess."

Grammy's back faced me and she talked in a hushed voice on the telephone. I crept across the hall and hid in the dining room where I could eavesdrop, unnoticed. Once closer, I didn't have to hear the words. Her tone revealed who she spoke with—her own wayward daughter. Mom.

"Grace, give Taylor some time. She'll come around. Let her spend the summer. It will do her some good to be away from all the confusion and clear her head with some country air. Maybe you could use the time to figure out what you're going to do with the mess you call your life right now."

Apparently, Mom hung up on Grandma. "Well, I'll be. She's still a disrespectful brat." She poured a cup of coffee without turning around. "You can come out now, cupcake. The wicked witch is parking her broom in Boston a while longer. You're safe."

"How did you know I listened?"

"Oh, angel baby, Grandmothers know everything. God gives us special gifts, especially where our favorite grandchildren are concerned."

"I'm your *only* grandchild."

"That's why you're my favorite." She kissed my hair and handed me the cup of coffee, something my mother would have thrown a fit over, if she knew. "I believe you like your cream and sugar warmed with a bit of caffeine?"

I laughed, already feeling relief with my troubles thousands of miles away. At least for a little while.

"So, no 'words of wisdom' or questions. But, we'll have to talk about this soon, Taylor."

"Okay, Grammy. Just not today. I'd rather have waffles instead."

"Yum. I haven't eaten those forever. I hope the waffle iron doesn't catch fire." She peered at me through the steam coming off her tea. "Blueberries?" She sized me up, using fruit as an excuse.

"Just plain today. I want things simple for a while."

She smiled. "You always were good at mind games. All right. 'Simple' it is for now."

A basic, non-messy life. I had no idea moving halfway across the country to a little town named Wellsville would turn out to complicate it even more. Once I passed the broken town sign, I'd crossed into another dimension. One having the potential to shatter my already bruised heart.

**

An entire week passed uneventful and what once seemed peaceful, became boring. This afternoon I perused Main Street, finding a quaint boutique actually having cute clothes and fashionable accessories rivaling anything in Boston.

When I walked in, the lady behind the counter appeared frazzled, tossing sheets of plastic bubble wrap in the air while she talked on her cell phone. Hangers screeched across the metal wrack as I sifted through several shirts, but she didn't notice me. I loitered at the jewelry display listening to her talk about preparations for someone going into the military. When she discovered me standing with an armful of clothes, she motioned for me to follow her to the dressing rooms, never missing a word in the conversation.

After I settled on two dresses to buy, one for church (a requirement for living with Grammy) and a cute sundress, I draped them on the counter along with matching sandals and a new navel ring. The woman finally disconnected from her call and wiped the back of her hand across a tear dampened cheek. She feigned a polite smile.

"Sorry about that. Life's kind of crazy at the moment." She pointed to the small ring I placed on top of the dresses. "Aren't those little rings cute? We just got them in. I guess toe rings are the latest beach fashion."

I laughed. "They're navel rings." Her nose wrinkled and I lifted the edge of my T-shirt to show her the one I wore. "See?"

"Oh, my! Doesn't that catch on your clothes? It looks painful."

"I forget it's there."

"Well, I only have boys," she answered, scanning the price tags.

"Boys can have navel rings. And nipple rings, too. In fact, I've heard they also pierce—"

She pressed hands over her ears. "No more! I get the 'willies' thinking about body piercing." Then she pointed a manicured finger at me, delivering a caution. "Make sure you sterilize it good, okay? You have no idea how many hands touched it before packaging."

"I'll do that," I giggled, delighted at her old-fashioned thinking.

"Are you new in town?" she asked, ringing in my total purchase…on my mother's credit card. I presently operated in payback mode.

"I'm spending the summer with my grandmother, Lydia Daniels."

"Lydia? I didn't know she had grandchildren. She doesn't come to town much. I see her at church, mostly."

"I think her garden keeps her busy."

She handed me my things tucked in a green and pink polka-dot bag with shiny pink tissue, ruffling the top. "How old are you dear?"

"I just turned eighteen."

"My son, Riley, will be eighteen in a couple of weeks. If you're interested, most of the high school kids hang out at Barney's on the edge of town on Friday nights. They've got bowling, pool tables, and I guess a bunch of arcade games, you know…stuff like that. Riley swears they have the best burgers."

I backed away politely. The last thing I needed was to "hang out" with a bunch of strange kids who already had their cliques established. Nor did I want anything to do with boy drama. I left that back home, too. Nope. Simple life equaled "single life."

"Thanks. I'll think about it." I pushed the door open and breathed with relief once outside the "chamber of interrogation" known as the *Denim & Ruffles Boutique.*

I fingered the card in my jeans pocket. Time for one last purchase, this one, aimed at *dear old dad.*

My feet carried me effortlessly through the doors of "Andy's Auto Sales." Two hours later, after a credit verification on the card—one sending my salesman's eyebrows into his hairline when he validated the allowable limit, not to mention a possible police report to make sure the card hadn't been stolen, and I drove back to Grammy's in a shiny, new blue and white convertible Mini Cooper.

Before signing the final sale document, I had the unfortunate pleasure of talking with my father to authorize my use of the card. How could he argue when he so freely gifted cars to everyone to ease his guilty conscience?

Grammy disclosed a few details from my mother's last vengeful phone call. Dad's new girlfriend's sixteen year old daughter got a barely used Honda Civic for her birthday, two months *before* my parents divorced. I had no choice but to "one up" the wannabe-stepchild. Blood supposedly ran thicker than water. I wondered if when my mother discovered Dad's frivolous purchase, if she wanted to prove the cliché true by making my father *bleed.*

When I pulled into Grammy's driveway, she let out a whoop and jumped in the passenger seat. I lied. My Mini wasn't the last purchase. Grammy deserved dinner out and a new outfit.

Seven
HELL HATH NO WRATH LIKE THE FURY OF A GIRLFRIEND SCORNED
Jaxson

Finally, a chair without wheels. Gingerly, I lowered into the recliner, remote in hand, ready to watch something besides one of the five channels the hospital's cheap cable feed allowed. Mom left for her shop and Dad had errands to take care of, but said he'd be home in a couple of hours. He tapped my new ankle bracelet and reminded me the computer in his *new* cruiser was programmed so he'd know if I went to the bathroom, let alone tried to leave the house.

Mom made Dirk go visit his friends so he wouldn't bug me. My commissioned babysitter and still "madder-than-hell-and-not-so-little" brother roamed somewhere upstairs. He and I hadn't spoken since the day he visited me in the hospital when I confessed to having *his* girlfriend—correction *half-naked* girlfriend, as my illustrious date the night I turned everyone's lives upside down. The pain in his eyes told me he cared more for that stupid teenage drama queen than even he'd admit.

I really blew it this time. My family barely looked at me and the town probably erected gallows for my public hanging. Friends abandoned me for fear of being subjected to my father's probing interrogation, all their dirty secrets uncovered that could make them a bunkmate in my pending jail cell. Nobody visited me during my week stay in the hospital. No flowers, phone calls, or even a stupid card. A written death threat would have at least been an acknowledgement someone cared I lay in a hospital bed.

The only visitor I dreaded coming, but luckily never showed, was *my* girlfriend, Ally. She'd refused to go to the party with me that infamous night, announcing she was fed up with babysitting my drunken ass and fighting off my less than romantic advances after the fact. Her rejection over the phone proved perfect timing for a certain sixteen year old beauty who flirted so heavily whenever she came to the house with Riley, I decided to see if she'd back up her seductive threats. Just as Ally hung up, Kaylee Baker walked through the doors of the convenience store, into my life…and officially out of Riley's.

**

The second stair squawked, giving me fair warning *company* arrived. The creak didn't warn me however, who that company would be.

"Hello, asshole!"

Ally.

"Hey baby!" A slight quiver of fear edged the hysteria creeping into my voice. I was doomed. My only hope for a reprieve from death would be if Riley ironically turned out to be my savior.

"I'll give you guys some privacy," Riley called out, sealing my fate from the top of the stair when he shut the basement door.

I couldn't tell if Ally's eyes were red from crying or if she might truly be possessed and her head would spin any moment. She stood in front of me, arms crossed over the boobs I loved to fondle, her long legs separated just enough to enhance her anger, but not enough to allow me access between them again. The expensive boots I bought her for Christmas tapped the floor, dangerously close to my bare toes.

I clutched the small pillow from the sofa against me like a shield.

"I. Am. Not. Or. Ever. Will. Be. Again. *Your.* Baby."

My cheek stung and undoubtedly would show a well-defined print of her hand for several hours. I covered my face from another ensuing attack of Ally's hands, letting my arms suffer the scratches from her fingernails, instead.

"Ouch! Knock it off, Ally!"

"Not until your sorry ass is buried six feet under!"

I grabbed her arms, struggling with what little strength my bed ridden body left me, to stop the relentless assault. However, I let go when the heal of her boot planted squarely on top of my foot.

"Aack! Damnit girl!"

The adrenaline rush surging through me propelled us both to the floor, landing me on top of her. If nothing else, all the days of loading up on chocolate pudding and Snicker bars, gave me a weight advantage. I pinned her arms against the floor and peered into chocolate eyes, sparkling with tears.

"Ally, I'm sorry. I know it's not enough, but that's all I've got right now. I acted stupid, I know, but my anger drove me to get back at you for not going to the party with me."

"By taking an innocent little girl instead?"

"Trust me. Kaylee Baker is far from *innocent*." Ally's knee tried to insure I'd never have children, but our bodies had fused, leaving little room for movement. Except for one very surprising, and slightly painful one.

"Are you kidding me?" she shrieked. "You're *horny*! You're sick, Jaxson. Get the hell off me!"

I couldn't. I had to deflect my thoughts and wait it out. Her writhing beneath me didn't help, either.

"Believe me, *that's* the last thing I'm thinking of," I lied. "I just need you to listen and not hit me anymore. Please?" She stopped moving. I wish I could say the same and my words came out breathier than expected.

"Ally, I know I hurt you. Hell, I hurt Riley, too. If I could take it back, I would in a heartbeat." My face remained close to hers, her angry breaths warm against my cheek. "Give me another chance, baby."

Cautiously, I pressed my mouth against her velvet lips, my tongue coaxing them to open and let me in. Her lips parted and I pushed forward, not just with my tongue, but other key body parts intimately touching. Ally shifted her body beneath mine into a familiar position begging for less clothing.

I barely touched her skin, letting my fingertips feather down her arms until my hands found their favorite holding place on her chest. Her fingers braided into my hair and she held my mouth captive over hers. My heady kiss deepened and when I thought I found her spine with my tongue, she moaned, I thought with pleasure, however, a sharp pain shot to the top of my head, and my eyes froze in their sockets.

A warm metallic flavor filled our mouths and she shoved me away, spitting splotches of blood all over my shirt. The pain in my mouth radiated through the bones in my cheek and I started coughing on blood flowing down my throat, repaying Ally with a few bloody spots on *her* shirt.

I tried to talk but I couldn't form words. My tongue filled my mouth, protruding slightly. A look of horror washed over Ally's face.

"Oh shit! Riley!" she screamed, scrambling to her feet. "Riley! Come quick!"

Ally threw up in the wastebasket beside the sofa, leaving another mess for my mother to deal with when she returned home. Riley ran down the stairs to answer Ally's murderous screams, and she nearly knocked him over in her escape.

"I think I bit his tongue off!" she cried out, sending me into a state of panic and quickening Riley's descent.

He shoved the washcloth off the bathroom counter into my mouth, soaking a towel in cold water and throwing it on the rug in the family room to dilute the blood stain. I couldn't talk, couldn't feel my tongue, and felt my heart bounce in my chest.

"Damn, it looks like someone got bludgeoned to death." He rushed back into the bathroom and grabbed a new roll of toilet paper. "Come on jackass. We better get you to the hospital before you bleed to death in the basement and I'm forced to bury your sorry butt in the backyard before Mom gets home. You know how she hates it when we don't clean up our messes."

That's when the laughter started.

**

Dad burst through the Emergency Room doors with the finesse of a wild elephant. The flasher bar still rotated on his car. My designer cuff alerted him I'd escaped the "compound," formerly known as *home*.

Mom's car slid sideways with a loud squeal behind the sheriff cruiser. The echo of her heels clicked against the linoleum floor, arriving a couple of seconds before she did. Her hand flew to her mouth and her eyes pinched.

"God, Jaxson! What the hell?" Dad asked, his face scrunched in reaction to my gruesome state. My mother couldn't say anything around the fist she pressed in her mouth. The anguish on her face was almost as agonizing as the headache pounding my brain.

The only one not repelled by the grisly scene of layers of bloody gauze stuffed in my mouth was my evil guardian in the chair next to me. Riley fought to keep from breaking into hysterical laughter again. I'd listened to his hideous revelry the entire twenty minute drive to the hospital. He pointedly obeyed the speed limit during the agonizing trek. Every time he glanced at me with my mouth full of a wads of toilet paper, he launched into hysterics.

Dad's fists pushed his hips, lips pursed tight. Mom blanched and grasped Dad's arm for support. "Well? Anyone care to tell me what the hell happened?" he demanded.

52

Riley snorted, stifling the giggle clamoring for release. "Ally came to see Jax."

Eight
SEEKING SANITY
Taylor

A second week passed and I went stir crazy. My day began with breakfast, or in my case, just coffee—maybe an apple or banana. If Grammy had her way, I'd eat waffles or pancakes every morning and plump to a size that wouldn't fit inside the Mini.

I begged out of tagging along with her to run errands. Everywhere we went, Grams introduced me and I'd have to repeat the story I'd made up about coming to visit for the summer, and once my age was revealed, I'd be offered up to any boy between seventeen and twenty.

To be honest, I wouldn't mind a "summer love." Someone who didn't want anything beyond hanging-out, but might engage in some steamy make-out sessions to release my penned up hormones. Someone who'd understand when the end of August arrived and I said "goodbye," it was forever. I didn't need some clingy boy expecting me to rush back every school break and rekindle something that would never grow beyond lust.

"Love" wasn't something I needed. I didn't want to get involved in a relationship doomed to fail once the body heat cooled, nor did I want the pressure commitment created. I'd walked out of a relationship where commitment meant *confinement.* Also, being on the receiving end of another heartbreak didn't fit into my summer plans. My parents did a pretty good job of mangling my heart and I feared it to be the beginning of many years of missed birthdays, weekend visitations at the mall or worse, at a strange house with a possible "replacement parent" doting to win my affection.

Before I talked myself into the depths of gloom, I decided to get outside and soak up some serious Vitamin D. I grabbed an apple out of the basket, sinking my teeth into its juicy flesh and noisily slurping the sweet nectar before it ran over my chin.

Standing on the deck, I relished the feel of the warm wooden planks beneath my bare feet. Beyond the garden fence, an expanse of bright yellow sunflowers blanketed the meadow. In the distance, a cluster of cottonwood trees and pines formed at the end of a tree line stretching from some unknown beginning, running along the base of the mountain at the edge of Grammy's property. A dark green spot on the horizon of a sea of yellow—a place to be explored.

I slipped on my sandals and jumped onto the grass. The splintered picket gate beneath a jasmine covered arch, whined when I pushed it open. I toed across the weathered stone path through the vegetable garden and set out on a quest to discover what treasure lay hidden within Nature's wooded guard.

Water gurgled and bubbled over rocks, glittering against the bright rays of the early afternoon sun as I followed along the banks of the creek. Stopping to dip my toes in the cool stream, I leaned back against a rock and turned my face to the orb warming my little piece of heaven. Two squirrels playing tag on the rocks across the creek, paused momentarily to study the *human* invading their world. I flicked my foot, sprinkling their fur to send them scurrying to their hideaway.

The dusty dirt turned to mud between my wet toes and grit ground beneath the balls of my feet. I rinsed my feet in the brook running beside me, but soon my sandals felt heavy again from mud caked on the bottoms.

A well worn foot path trailed over a hill and wove through bushes covered with berries and tiny white daisy-like flowers. Thorny bushes gave way to ferns. Overhead, blue jays sang a light melody as they flew through branches laced into a leafy ceiling. A single shaft of sunlight pierced the foliage and came to rest on the still, indigo waters of a pond. An oasis hidden beneath a jacket of shimmering leaves and the heavy scent of pine.

Large boulders rimmed the edge of the water. Stone *chairs.* I kicked my sandals off, felt the chill of the dirt under my feet before wading into the dark water. Small kernels of gravel mixed with the sandy bottom and ripples kissed my legs when I cautiously inched deeper, having no idea when the bottom might give way and suck me into its murky depths.

I slid on the silt, hissing when water covered my shorts and cold tendrils wrapped my stomach. The edge of my blue T-shirt floated outward. Once the initial shock disappeared, the water actually felt refreshing. The single sunlit beam widened around me and warmed my damp skin. I twirled slowly in the water, barely brushing my fingertips on top. My memory banks tickled with a lullaby from my childhood, and I hummed the melody while dancing in my own private lagoon.

Giving little attention to my footing as I pranced, I failed to notice the sides slowly drop. Suddenly, water circled my chest, covering my arms. My last step sealed my fate, and I went under. A circle of waves distorted the light on the surface above me. I gave a strong kick, propelling upward. A second kick gave me a strong foothold again, and I lifted out of the water, throwing my long blonde locks back with a jerk of my head. My lungs filled with a deep breath of fresh air. Two more steps moved me to waist deep waters and I raised my arms to gather my wet strands of hair, twisting to wring out the excess water.

About to walk out of the water all together, I froze at a rustling sound in the bushes ahead. Trapped in a liquid cage, I waited for whatever creature would break through the thicket and possibly devour my wet body.

Nine
THE POND
Riley

Two o'clock in the afternoon. The sun set high in the sky and the air sizzled with anticipated heat. I'd raced through my chores, doing most of them half-assed just to get them out of the way. Mom finally got off my back and left to meet a girlfriend for lunch. Dirk practically followed the shadow of her car out of the driveway, dropping his sidekick to the pavement and rolling off to a friend's house.

Jaxson, tongue still swollen, mumbled something unintelligible when he walked through the back door after his graveyard shift.

"Hey, *Batman*," I sneered as he passed. He replied by extending the middle appendage on his right hand. Jaxson said he hated living the life of a "bat." When he slept everyone else worked and when he worked, everyone played. My nickname stuck after that, mainly because it pissed the hell out of him.

Jaxson's bedroom door slammed and the click of the lock echoed in the stairwell. Only someone with a death wish dared disturb him once that door locked. He'd taken on extra shifts at the rail yard trying to pay off his court fine before his sentencing hearing tomorrow. His drunken stint and joyride at one o'clock in the morning a few weeks back, earned him a bed in the "county's finest" for five years on its own merit. He hoped if the judge knew he worked a steady job and had paid a chunk toward his restitution, he'd get a lesser sentence. Dad warned him he wouldn't get out of jail time, but I think Jaxson still believed in fairytales.

However, crashing into the city's granite marker welcoming those lost or having nowhere else in the world to be, proved a whole other matter. According to Dad, it could pack another year on Jaxson's jail sentence. Destroying the marquee also earned him the wrath of the city council and the right for every old lady in town to voice their disgust for his behavior.

Even Lydia Daniels gave Jaxson a public tongue lashing at the church picnic. A quiet, private woman who owned the house on the other side of the meadow, had no trouble finding words to cut Jax into a dozen humiliating pieces in front of the last of the congregation lingering to clean up. Mom, who stood stoic through the whole ordeal, broke down after Mrs. Daniels' last word followed her to her car.

None of the things giving notoriety to that night; the newspaper, the local radio's daily recount, the judge's harsh comments after slamming the gavel, hurt like watching Mom fall apart. Mrs. Daniels spoke the truth. Jaxson gave no regard to how his selfish behavior affected the one person who never turned her back on us. Mom.

The phone rang, landing me back in the present and I waited to see if anyone—even a stranger passing by, would answer. On the fifth ring I picked it up, hoping they'd hung up.

"Riley, why the hell can't anyone answer the phone?"

Dad.

"I was in the bathroom," I lied.

"Is Jaxson home?"

"Yeah. He's gone to bed."

"Well, wake him up. Company's coming."

"You can't be serious. Jaxson will mash me between the floorboards if I wake him."

"Hell, you sound like a girl, Riley. Man up, would you?"

I waited, clicked my tongue against my throat and mentally planned my escape once I woke Jax.

"You're not going to do it, are you?"

"Nope."

"Fine. Take the phone to him and *I'll* wake him," Dad snarled.

I dramatized a wisecrack play-by-play the entire walk to Jaxson's bedroom. "We're taking the 'stairs of death', slowly, anticipating the monster's ill mood before we reach the lair. So far, the half-eaten body count is over a hundred, their dismembered limbs flung around like confetti."

"All right, enough, smart-ass," Dad barked around a laugh.

I procured a deep breath once I'd arrived at the door to the monster's den. *Here goes nothing* I thought, but may have said it aloud before pounding on the door. Silence. My feet shuffled nervously and I puffed a sigh, blowing my hair in the air. After another round of knocks, I stepped back to allow a safety zone in case Jax's fist came at me.

"WHAT!" sounded the menacing growl from the other side.

"Dad's on the phone."

"Tell him to go to hell! I'm sleeping."

My father blared in my ear. "You tell him I heard that!"

"Dad said he heard that."

"What the fu–" Jaxson wrenched the door open and I held the phone out, receiver facing forward. Jaxson stood in the doorway, his "tighty-whities" looking insanely good on him. He would need to be *really* careful in jail.

"Give me that *perv,*" he snapped, taking the phone and slamming the door.

Jaxson's loud reaction to whatever news Dad delivered, bellowed before I took my second step and I stopped to listen.

"You've got to be shittin' me! The *Guard*? I'd rather do jail. *Two years!*" The quiet on the other side of the door permeated the house. The eye of the storm. A loud crash preceded Jaxson's shrill.

"FUCK!"

I don't remember touching the stairs. Once I heard the floor creak under the weight of Jaxson's step toward the door, I knew I had to get the out the house, or I'd be dead. Jaxson wholeheartedly believed in "killing the messenger."

Later, I'd found out my dad contacted a sergeant buddy involved with the National Guard, calling in an old favor. My brother would go from the courthouse to the recruiting office in the morning.

**

Weeks passed without any rain and the dirt on the trail billowed like brown baby powder over my bare toes, turning my black flip-flops

61

gray. The pungent smell of wild sunflowers growing for miles in either direction, filled the air as I ran through the field. Over the ridge, the line of trees appeared to be planted. Their symmetrical line formed a natural fence along the creek edging the base of the mountain range that guarded the west side of the valley.

I wound my way through the thicket, stubbing my toes on a couple of rocks. Even with the afternoon sun burning in the sky, its beams barely penetrated the thick, leafy canopy surrounding the pond. Streaks of lemon colored light carried sunbeams from heaven and placed them on the wild ferns. Some stirred into the shimmering stream, spilling into the dark, still waters of the pond.

Our pond. Jaxson and I spent an entire summer rolling large boulders from the hillside into the then "bubbling brook" to dam the water. We dragged picks, hoes and shovels from the garden shed, digging and scooping mucky mud, slowly deepening the pool. Three months of hard work and more fun than I'd had in my then twelve years of life, and the pond was finished.

Jaxson turned fourteen that summer and stood a foot taller than me. He was our measuring stick and when the water hit his chin in the center, we were satisfied. It was great…and our secret. We feared if anyone knew, that "anyone" being Dad, he'd forbid us from swimming in the pond and probably send his county cronies to destroy it.

Two years ago, Jaxson discovered Ally and beer, and we stopped working on the pond. I caught them skinny-dipping and threatened to tell Mom if he ever brought her back. He gave me a black eye, but kept his promise, probably more out of guilt, than some brotherly bond.

My jealousy issues with my big brother began that summer. I begged and pleaded to hit any "bases" with Kaylee, but Jaxson just snapped his fingers and Ally became putty in his hands. In middle school, Jax always had girls hanging on him and calling incessantly on the phone. I wanted to be just like him when I got to high school. Funny how those goals changed when I discovered my golden idol turned out to be made of clay.

Still, Jax landed on his feet like a cat from whatever height he fell from. I, on the other hand, feared *heights.* His lifestyle scared me. He resembled a car speeding down a dark highway, the headlights spanned over the flash of dots down the center. Ahead was a cliff, a bridge washed out, or a deer standing and waiting. No one could reach Jax. It seemed the more Mom and Dad tried to rein him in, the harder he rebelled. We just waited for the car to sail off the cliff.

If Jax had yelled for me, I didn't hear him. I left his drama behind and headed for the one place I could find peace and separate myself from everything happening at home. Over the rise of the small hill in front of me and down through the chokecherry shrubs, I'd find my private sanctuary. The pond.

The waterline varies between my hips and a foot or so above the top of my head, depending on whether we've had a rainy spring. Winter yielded a good snow pack in the mountains and a fair amount of rain fell the past few months, so I knew the depth would be perfect for the rope swing.

About to break through the scrub oak and bushes into the clearing surrounding the pond, I skidded to a halt when I heard the sound, damn near landing on my butt when I slid on the loose gravel. Silence enveloped the wooded surroundings and I suddenly worried my breathing sounded too loud.

The light melody started again, carrying on the breeze from angelic lips to my ears. Cautiously, I moved an inch or two where I could see the pond. A beam of light pierced the opening of branches above the water, illuminating the beautiful creature swirling in the water. Her fingertips pricked the top, sending ripples from where she stood to the edges of the pond…and up my spine. She disappeared under the water and I took another step, but remained hidden.

She emerged from the sapphire pool almost in slow motion. Her head flipped, sending her wet, golden mane arcing through the air, the thousands of water droplets sparkling in the sun like a shower of diamonds.

She turned my direction. Dark lashes glistened against pale pink cheeks and full lips still hummed the bewitching tune that stopped my world from spinning. Her wet baby blue T-shirt clung to curves my hands longed to touch and when her delicate fingers braided into her hair, the small silver ring piercing her navel shimmered in the sunlight.

All the saliva in my mouth evaporated. My name escaped my memory and my swim shorts suddenly felt tight. I'd never seen her before, but knew immediately I didn't want to go without seeing her again. Every teenage boy's fantasy—wet and gorgeous. Swimming in my pond.

What I didn't realize in this defining increment of time? I faced my future. No clues warned me my summer plans were about to be altered. That I could handle. What I didn't know, nor could have prepared for, was that in the three short months of summer my entire life would be redefined. I embarked on an unknown journey having the potential to destroy everything I believed, and possibly everyone I cared about, in its wake.

No, none of this I knew. The only thing I did know...I wanted to jump her bones.

Ten
TROUBLED WATERS
Taylor

Dust clouds billowed and swirled like a mini whirlwind in the ray
of gold before me. A high pitched shrill sliced my once peaceful
existence. I froze, the water stilling around me.

What the hell?

Rocks tumbled behind the crumpled lump rolling to the edge of the
pond. I halfway expected some sort of wild animal to crash through the
chokecherry bushes, which would have been enough to cause me to
faint, but I was taken completely off guard when the dirty bundle of
skin untangled itself and stood upright.

Patches of brown powder clung to the bare chest, trailing over
ripped abs and dusting the hair covering sculptured legs. Damn. When
he scrubbed his fingers through his hair, possibly sandy blonde on any
other occasion, a funny feeling wiggled in my gut.

His eyes focused shamelessly on my chest and I realized my wafer
thin bra did little to hide my body's obvious reaction to the cool air
whipping my wet skin. I crossed my arms and watched his eyes drop to
my stomach.

"Stop staring. Seriously, could you be any more obvious?"

"Well ex*cuuuse* me. Shit, it's not like you're naked. Get over
yourself, already."

Okay so my dream god came with attitude and a mouth my grandmother would love to shove a bar of soap in. I knelt below the water line, feeling tiny pebbles painfully press my kneecaps. With my chest sufficiently covered by dark water, I attempted bravery.

"Who are you anyway?"

"Why should I tell you? Besides, you're the stranger here and swimming in *my* pond."

"Your pond, huh? So you like own this whole forest? I mean, last time I checked this was *public* land. I didn't see any 'no trespassing' or 'private property' signs posted." He took two steps towards the water. "Maybe you're trespassing on *my* property."

"Real funny, tough girl."

His march into the water sent a small wave rippling my way, swamping over my chin and into my mouth. I coughed the unexpected surge of liquid out of my throat. "Gross! You're such an ass!" He clamped my shoulders and yanked me to my feet. "Hey! What are you doing?"

"I don't want your backwash in *my* pond."

I watched his Adams apple slide several times with his hard swallows. His hands still wrapped my arms and I suddenly became aware my breasts skimmed his bare chest. Even through a T-shirt and a bra, the sensation sent a shudder skittering through me. My toes grabbed the pea gravel as if to keep my body locked to the earth. If I inched any closer I knew a similar sensation pulsated through his body…and he was a boy. Maybe the cold water would keep the obvious from becoming *obvious*.

As if reading my mind, he stepped back, but remained in waist deep water. I couldn't stop the smile twitching the corners of my mouth. "Everything okay?" I smirked.

"Can we start again? I'm not really an ass and I'm sure you're not really a bitch."

Well that bit. My smug grin vanished and his appeared. *Strike one* for the hot guy.

"You first," I demanded.

"Riley Martin," he blurted, then crossed his arms. "Your turn."

"Taylor."

"Taylor?" He waved his fingers mockingly. "Just Taylor?"

"Yep. Just Taylor."

Gooseflesh pebbled on *Riley's* pecs where my gaze had locked. I felt the same pimply bumps forming under my own fingers and clenched my arms to cover my over-anxious upper body from selling me out again. "This water's freezing. I need to get out."

Riley didn't budge, guarding the only familiar exit. I looked around the pond, not knowing if I swam to the other side, if I'd find another gentle slope or a steep edge with no foot hold to climb out. Behind me, the cerulean water appeared bottomless and a panicky feeling formed in the pit of my stomach.

I batted my eyelashes in dramatic overkill. "Please…move?"

"Well, if you put it that way." Riley turned and without thinking, I took a step back, losing my footing when the bottom of the pond fell away. I screamed and disappeared beneath the water's surface.

"Taylor!"

In a split second, Riley's arms surrounded me and lifted my body to where I braced myself on his shoulders. His hands gripped under my armpits and my shirt wrenched high enough I felt his warm breaths on my bared abdomen. To make sure his lips didn't touch where they weren't invited, I dug my fingernails into his shoulders.

"Ouch!" He yelled, tossing me back into the water. "Drown, princess, I don't give a shit," he spat over his shoulder as he walked out of the pond.

"I don't need you to save me, Mr. Martin. I'm perfectly capable of taking care of myself."

"You're perfect all right," he muttered into the towel he shuffled over his hair. He let go a big sigh. "Do you have a towel? You're going to be sick if you don't get out and then I'll be blamed when you die of pneumonia."

"Murder. They'll charge you with murder."

"Whatever. Where's your towel, anyway?"

My teeth chattered. "I-I d-didn't b-bring one."

Riley unfolded his towel and held it open at the water's edge. "Here, use mine." I regarded him and his brow cocked. "Trust me, the last thing I'm going to do is touch you. I don't need more scars on my body from your claws. Now get your bony ass out of that water."

69

Hating to surrender but no longer feeling my toes, I reluctantly walked out of the water and let Riley wrap his towel in a warm cocoon around me.

"I don't have a bony ass."

"No you certainly don't. You've got curves in all the right places." The corner of his mouth pulled. I felt trapped and unable to move within my terrycloth cage.

"How deep is that pond, anyway?"

He glanced at a thick branch overhead where a rope dangled with several large knots tied at the bottom. "Deep enough to cannonball off that swing without hitting bottom." Riley fiercely rubbed my arms, still trapped in the cloth cocoon. "Want to try it out?"

"No thanks. I've swallowed enough pond water today. Besides, I should get going."

Again Riley refused to move, keeping the towel tightly wound around my body. His head dropped, his mouth hovering over mine.

"What are you doing? I thought you weren't going to touch me."

"I'm not. I'm thinking about kissing you instead."

"Forget it. I'm not kissing you."

"You sure about that?"

At the moment, I wasn't sure of anything. For a split second I thought about biting his lips when they lightly brushed across my mouth, but the need to taste them seemed more tantalizing. Our mouths pressed again in a firmer kiss. The towel loosened, slid to a puddle around my feet when Riley's hands wrapped the back of my neck and my arms locked around his waist.

His mouth tasted of spearmint gum and Dr. Pepper, the combination deliciously mixing with my Juicy Fruit. His hands felt warm against my damp skin, his fingers snaking under my top and pressing my lower back.

Taylor, what the hell is wrong with you? You don't go around kissing strange boys.

Until now.

I pushed away and grabbed the dirt covered towel from beneath my feet, shoving it against Riley's chest before my eyes could be diverted.

"Stop. I don't even know you."

His shocked response sounded breathy. "I thought that's what we were doing? Getting *acquainted.*"

"I'm not into easy introductions. That's not my style."

"Could have fooled me."

I so wanted to slap him, but chose to step back instead. "Yeah, well…sorry if I gave you the wrong idea. I like things slower. I'd at least want to know what kind of car a guy drives, first," I joked, struggling against the urge to kiss him again.

Riley closed out the space between us, cupping my arms. "Toyota Tacoma truck. Red. Chrome wheels and a killer Kenwood stereo system. If you like, I could show you tomorrow night when I take you out for pizza.

"Why not tonight?" I asked, matching his cocky attitude and curious to know the answer.

"I don't want *you* to get the wrong idea. I'm not a 'one-afternoon-by-the-pond kind' of guy." Riley flung the towel over his shoulder. A lopsided smile slid up his cheek and deepened a dimple. His rubbed his lips. "I've got to see if you're worthy to experience another taste off these babies. I've been told they qualify as lethal weapons."

I slipped my feet into my flip flops and took the hand offered. "You're really full of yourself, aren't you?"

"Just stating the facts listed on the warning label," he laughed, helping me over the rocks and into the sunflower carpeted meadow.

"Warning label?"

"In the small print, right here," he said. My gaze dropped to the full bottom lip he tapped and without warning, his mouth covered mine confidently.

"Oh, you're good," I acknowledged, falling in step beside him.

"Yes, I am."

Eleven
MY NEW RELATIVE—"UNCLE SAM"
Jaxson

Every time I drove to town, I passed the city's tombstone. The chunk out of the side of "Ellsville" served as a constant reminder that hell existed and I lived it. Friday night marked the town's fundraiser barbeque and dance to raise money to buy a new marquee, but I'd been informed my dance card had been shredded and I'd attended my last party.

The recruiting office had to be the most depressing place ever. The cinderblock walls were painted robin egg blue, probably from a can of paint off the clearance shelf at the local hardware store. Posters showing movie star smiles and elated expressions on faces too pretty to be real, all wearing the latest designer camouflage fatigues, dotted the walls. The only picture anywhere near realistic was the mega tank with its gun barrel pointed right at me.

Boom. You're dead

The fake leather couch squeaked against my jeans, and when my dad plopped his armor laden body next to me, it sounded like one of us cut loose an enormous fart. My old man even smiled when the haughty receptionist peered over her reading glasses in disgust.

The door behind her opened and a gentleman clearly used as the model for the *Incredible Hulk,* filled the doorway. My dad stood, slapping my shoulder to do the same.

"Stanley Martin, is that really you?" Big Man asked, reaching us in literally *one* step.

"Adams, you're still as ugly as ever."

Big Man hugged Midsized Man and I stepped out of the way, letting them have their bonding moment.

Big Man briskly rubbed the top of dad's head. "Where's your hair? Bev pull it out after all these years of wild sex? You two had that GTO bouncing so hard, I wondered if there would be any shocks left by the time we graduated high school.

My dad's hair appeared snow white beneath the glowing red orb called his head. His throat had to be raw by the time he'd obnoxiously cleared it a hundred times.

"Uh, Adams. The kid here…is my *son.*"

"Oh shit! Well, he's old enough." He poked my dad with his elbow. "He does know about the 'birds and the bees', doesn't he?"

I officially looked for a hole in the floor to drop through. My mind barely wrapped around the news my parents banged their brains out *before* they married, to deal with this jerk's attempt at bad humor.

"Jaxson, here, could teach *you* a few things." He nudged my arm and I stood at attention, mockingly. "Jaxson, this is Colonel Brandt Adams, or as I knew him growing up, 'pee-pee pants'."

Touché old man.

Somewhere behind us, something crashed to the floor and a pencil rolled to the side of my foot. I contemplated returning my dad's smart-

74

aleck comment by addressing Big Man as "Colonel Pee-Pee Pants" but thought better. "Pee-Pee's" lips disappeared, all humor gone.

"Yes, well it's a good thing we learn to be strong while we're young. Speaking of which, young man, I understand you pride yourself as quite the bad ass in this town."

"Yes, Sir. I mean no, Sir."

"Make up your mind. Which is it?"

"*No*, Sir. I don't consider myself tough. More like stupid. Sir."

"If you're tired of being stupid then I can help you. If not, I'm afraid you're wasting my time. Mr. Martin, this deal I made with your dad isn't something usually done. I owe him. He saved my drunken ass one night when I'd reached the end of my rope. Literally. I had a noose around my neck, about to hang myself in my garage. Your dad talked me out of it and stood by me while I endured months of therapy, becoming my best friend.

"Like he said, I'd earned a reputation as a pup that followed me like a cruel shadow into my teen years. From what your dad has told me, your reputation is doing nothing to help you. If you'll trust me like I trusted your dad and are willing to break your little ass to prove everyone wrong, I can help mold you into a man the community will respect, not despise. A son a mother can be proud of, instead of embarrassed about. Your choice, Jaxson."

"You or jail?"

"I can promise you Jaxson, *jail* would be a hell of a lot easier than what I'm offering, but when you're through serving your tour of duty, the only record following you will be one you'll be proud to show off to your kids. Maybe even some sweet little lady."

Ally hardly qualified as "sweet" after trying to sever my tongue with her teeth, but oddly, I wanted to make her proud. I needed to prove to her I wasn't the jerk she believed me to be. And Mom. I owed her so much. Even the Guard couldn't perform such an impossible miracle.

Dad nodded my direction, cocking a brow. "Well, Jax. What's it going to be? This is *your* decision. I'm only giving you the option. What you choose to do is up to you, as well as the consequence. No blaming anyone else. Not anymore."

A rock of emotion rose in my throat and I forced back unexpected tears. Damn, I loved Dad, even if I couldn't say it. He'd put his neck out on the line for me one more time, only this time, he could get his head chopped off if I fucked up.

I squared my shoulders to Colonel Adams. "Can I drive a tank? If so, I'd like to check out your travel plan."

He extended his hand, the shake as forceful as I expected. "I'll see what I can do. Welcome to the Army, Mr. Martin."

Twelve
BRAWLING AT BARNEYS
Taylor

The red shirt joined the growing pile of clothes on the floor.

"Too low. He'll never see my eyes," I grumbled. I stretched a navy blue T-shirt over my head, turning and appraising my profile in the full length mirror in the corner. *Not bad* I thought, smoothing it over my jeans. I twisted to see if my butt looked fat with the embellished pockets screaming "place hands here."

"Damn!" I cursed, pushing the denim off my legs. My derriere faced the door where unbeknownst to me, Grammy leaned on the doorframe.

"How the hell can you walk around with a ribbon of fabric tucked in your craw like that? Looks damn uncomfortable, if you ask me."

"Grammy!" I shrieked, scrambling to find something to cover up my exposed *cheeks*. The "ribbon of fabric" happened to be my purple thong underwear, barely covering my lower regions.

"I didn't know you were there! Please knock from now on, okay?"

She dipped her teabag, raising a disapproving brow. "My house, missy. Besides an open door doesn't require a knock." Stepping inside, uninvited, Grammy pulled the red sweater off the floor. "This color looks much better on you. The shirt you have on is so drab."

"But this one's cut so low, it shows too much cleavage."

"Honey, when you bend over in those low cut jeans and expose that purple dental floss, no one's going to notice the *crack* between your breasts. They'll be too busy measuring the *smile* on your backside."

I didn't have a response to my grandmother's crass observance. My mouth just hung open in shock.

"Where did you say you were going again?"

"Barneys. At the end of town. That lady at the boutique says that's where the kids my age hang out."

She regarded me. "Wear that cute sundress you bought," she stated matter-of-fact. "And wear your hair down, not in a ponytail. Boys like girls who are feminine. No need to give away your secrets all at once."

Great. My grandmother ranked me as a slut.

"Grammy, I'm not meeting boys."

"Sweet angel, the boys will be meeting *you*." She walked out, still dipping her tea bag.

**

The engraved heart pendant Daddy gave me for my thirteenth birthday, dropped to the perfect spot below the hollow of my throat. The sterling silver had antiqued somewhat, dulling the brilliance but complimenting the simplicity of my chambray sundress. I tugged my lace edged leggings over the purple *dental floss* and slipped my feet into my gray and white Converse sneakers.

"Much better," Grammy noted when I bounced down the stairs. I did an eye roll, hating that she was right. She pulled through the long strands of hair falling over my shoulders. "Is that the necklace your dad gave you?"

"Yeah," I answered plaintively.

"Bastard always did have good taste. Got to give him that much. Now, when will you be home?"

"Grammy, I'm eighteen."

"But I'm not, and these old bones won't rest until your home. Make it midnight."

"*Graaamm . . .*" I whined.

"You going to stamp your feet too? Taylor, nothing good happens after midnight, trust me." She walked away, waving her hand. "I'm just sayin'."

**

I parked three rows behind a certain red truck, second guessing my decision. We never really firmed up pizza plans for tomorrow night, but ever since I arrived home from swimming, I hadn't been able to think about anything but kissing Riley Martin.

When I walked inside, there may as well have been a neon sign over my head flashing "fresh meat" by all the leering stares my entrance attracted. Girls cuddled closer to their guys, placing territorial kisses on their cheeks and necks to mark them, while never removing their eyes from me.

Scanning the room, I looked for the one person who consumed my thoughts, but couldn't see him. Shaking my head full of insecurity, but covered in a mane of fantastic hair, I did the clichéd toss of my golden locks. A hot kid with dark brown hair watching me pass from the end of his pool cue, flinched, sending the cue ball hopping over the side of the table and rolling across the floor.

I put my toe out and stopped it. Reaching down as delicately as a prima ballerina, I picked it up and held it, perched on my fingertips. Purposely, I lifted a brow to match my not-so-subtle grin.

"Looking for this?" I asked in a flirty lilt.

The fastest way to flush out a guy would be calling the scent of another one into the *mating ring*.

His hands covered the ball, holding it and my hand a bit too long to be innocent. The voice came out in a husky tone, the eyes dark as dangerous deep water.

"I love it when a girl holds my ball." Apparently, he considered himself to be the magi of charm and seduction, rolled into a crude naïve sixteen, at tops, year-old boy. One who needed to be knocked down a peg.

Withdrawing my hand, I gave a playful pout. "I'm sorry, but I prefer guys with *two* balls." I dropped the cue ball in his hand and used my finger to push his chin up, closing his surprised mouth. His face turned an odd blend of fire engine red and jade green.

Laughter started at the pool table he'd stepped away from, catching on like wildfire in a field of straw. But one voice rose above the others, the timbre familiar and pushed my heart hard against my ribs. Riley had been flushed out.

He sauntered slowly my direction, clapping his hands. "Bravo my lady!" He took a bow and I returned the gesture doing a curtsy, complete with the stretching out of the hem of my dress. He closed the last few inches between us, his eyes rolling slowly over my body before meeting my gaze.

Riley's lowered voice, brought me closer to listen. Another tactical maneuver outsmarting me when his arm curled around my waist. His lips curled over my ear. "Miss me? I thought I wasn't going to see you until tomorrow night."

Our lips came dangerously close to touching. "You wish. I was told this was the place to hang on Friday nights."

His breath felt hot hovering close to my mouth. "You're lying. You want me, so you came looking for me," he whispered.

The smile on my face hurt it grew so wide. "You're right. I want you—to buy me a cheeseburger." I pushed away watching Riley's deflated ego blow out the corner of his twisted lips.

Accepting my challenge, he disappeared and returned to the booth I'd settled into at the back corner of the eatery section, holding red checkered boxes overflowing with steaming fries and burgers.

The low purr of bowling balls gliding down the polished lanes, a few actually causing loud crashes when pins slammed the back of the alley wall, competed with the music pulsing through speakers.

I touched my lip to catch a drip of ketchup. "These really are good," I said, genuinely surprised.

Riley dipped a fry in some tangy sauce and fed it to me. "Barney used to be a grill cook in San Francisco before opening this joint. Sometimes, he makes garlic burgers. They could possibly be considered better than sex."

"You've been dating some pretty lame chicks, if burgers rate that high on your ecstasy meter."

Riley dipped another fry, shoving it in his mouth. His head turned toward a small gaggle of girls giggling obnoxiously. Except one. A petite little thing who would be pretty if someone removed the tarantula eyelashes from her eyelids. She faced us, her gaze locked on Riley...whose gaze locked on her.

"Yeah," he muttered. "I have."

"Her?" I asked, although it was more than obvious.

"Maybe."

"Am I missing something here? She's all google-eyed at you, and well, you're not exactly being subtle in staring her down."

Riley's attention returned from wherever it had wandered. An unmistakable disdain tainted his tone. "We dated for a while, but it's over."

"She cheated on you?"

"Why do you think that?"

I touched his hand, smoothing the tension from his knuckles. "Because your teeth are clenched, your knuckles white...and you look sad." Those eyes flashed to mine and his hand flattened on the table.

"She's not the one who hurt me."

"Sorry. You don't have to tell me. It's none of my—"

"My brother did," he blurted out.

A couple of lumps rolled down his throat. Cautiously, I slid my hand over his again. His fingers wrapped mine, giving my hand a gentle squeeze. "Do you want to get out of here?"

"Yeah, I would," I replied around a smile. We slipped out of the booth and headed for the exit. I hooked a finger over my shoulder. "I, uh, need to use the restroom first. Meet you out front?" He nodded and his smile reached his eyes, ratcheting my heart rate.

When I came out of the bathroom stall, "spider eyes" leaned against the sink, arms crossed and face burning red, clear to her blitz-dangled earrings.

"Stay away from Riley," she warned around what sounded like a mouth of gravel. "He's *mine*."

"That's not what he says." I muscled around her to wash my hands. Suddenly my head yanked backwards. *Jealous ex-girlfriend* had a fistful of my hair.

"Ouch! Let go!"

"Not until you promise to stay away from Riley!"

I swatted backwards with my purse, trying to hit her arm to loosen her grip, but she held tight.

"Listen you little bitch, Riley can see whoever he wants, got that?" I kicked at her shin and she jumped back, letting go, but keeping a handful of *my* hair.

She lunged at me, teeth bared, and I wondered if she could transform into some paranormal beast. I held her arms, keeping her claws from scratching my face, but the weight of her body threw me back against the counter, banging my hip against the edge. Tears rimmed my eyes following the jab of pain.

The bathroom door opened, our screams summoning an audience. "Chick fight!" some ass yelled out. The sound of feet running our direction mimicked a small stampede.

All I could do was roll side to side to avoid her fake fingernails gouging my face, or her hands grabbing my hair again. She stomped on the top of my foot and I screamed out, losing my grip. Her hands fisted into the sides of my hair again and a feral growl spat through her teeth. One lethal nail cut across my bottom lip and a metallic tasting drop of blood dripped on my tongue.

"Bitch!" I shrilled.

Suddenly, the pressure from her clamped hands released and her body pulled away. My hero swooped in and rescued me from the wild creature. Riley.

"Stop it, Kaylee!" She twisted fitfully in his arms, her legs swinging freely as he held her in the air. "I mean it, Kaylee! Knock this shit off right now!" He dropped her when her nails scratched his arm. We'd both need to be checked for rabies.

Riley recovered quickly, grabbing her before she escaped. This time she turned on him, pounding her fists against him. Her growls turned to tears and soon she gave up, burying her head into Riley's chest, sobbing.

"I love you, Riley. Please don't dump me," she cried. Standing close, I heard Riley's reply, barely above a whisper.

"Sorry Kaylee, it's too late. I don't care anymore."

The crowd at the door parted and a large man, wider than tall, burst into the restroom.

"What the hell is going on in here?" He regarded me, hair sticking out in all directions and blood dipping off my lip. He grabbed a paper towel and handed it to me. "You okay, Miss?"

I think I said *yes*, but felt too stunned to know for certain.

The wicked little witch conveniently held tight to Riley, whose expression showed the conflict he felt. The girl in his arms still meant something to him, I could see that, but nothing strong enough to make me feel threatened. But when he embraced her, a touch of jealousy pricked.

I figured out the man filling all the empty space in the small bathroom was *Barney*. He literally pried Kaylee off Riley, keeping a firm grip on her arm. "All right, Miss Baker, you're coming with me." He stopped, holding the writhing demon. "You want to press charges?"

"I'll think about it," I answered, glaring at my attacker. One of her eyelashes hung lopsided. I knew I wouldn't do anything, but she didn't. Let her squirm.

"No! Riley please!" she pled in desperation. Riley's hands went up, palms out.

"Your mess, Kaylee. *All* of it."

Barney pulled Riley's hysterical ex out and shut the door, verbally banning anyone from coming in. Riley remained a few feet from me, scrubbing the back of his neck.

"So, this is what the girl's restroom looks like?"

I huffed a half laugh, pressing my finger to my lip. Riley wet the corner of another paper towel and pressed it to the cut. I hissed against the sting.

"Hold still you big baby." His lips pressed my forehead. "Sorry about 'psycho bitch'."

"She's just desperate to hold on to you," I tried to say with a paper towel pushing my lips crooked.

Riley removed the towel, placing pressure with his lips instead.

"Ouch." He stepped away, but I caught his belt loops and pulled him back. "Don't. I'm fine." I brushed my lip with my finger, "See? It says so right here in the fine print."

"Let me see," he teased.

This time when he took my mouth I didn't care if it hurt like hell. The sensuous feel of his velvet lips, the taste of sweet onion on his tongue, and the gentle touch of hands sliding up my back to pull me into a deeper kiss erased the pain. A hot tingle trickled through my body from my toes to the tip of my head.

"I think it says 'made in heaven'," he said between heady kisses.

My mind swam deliriously. I was making out with a hot boy…in the girls' restroom.

Riley's Pond

**

Riley's tail lights glowed like rubies when my headlights closed in on them. He leaned against his truck, the sexy outline of his body silhouetted by the full moon hanging lazily above the lake. Behind him, the lake shimmered silver from the glow.

"I almost missed the turn off. Don't you people believe in streetlights on your highways? It's so damn dark out here."

His arms slowly drew me against him. "Welcome to the country 'city girl'."

My cheek pressed his chest and somewhere below the warm muscle, a heart thumped fast. Fingers twirled tortuous circles on the back of my neck, and my arms pulled the massive hulk of pheromone overloaded testosterone tighter. I could die right now and be happy.

"Riley?"

"Yeah?"

"I changed my mind. I want to know about 'psycho bitch'."

His arms fell away, his fingers interlacing with mine. Stopping at the side door of his truck, he hit the key fob, momentarily lighting our world with a flash of white. He handed me a blanket from inside.

"Anticipating something Mr. Martin?" I teased, secretly glad I'd have something soft to lay my sore head on when we started making out. Because we would. His palm felt sweaty in my hand and our voices sounded too breathy to be normal.

"I'm a Boy Scout. Always prepared." Still holding my hand, he bent my arm behind my back pulling me close. Our hips bumped clumsily as we walked a few feet away from the truck to a smooth spot on the beach.

I paced, feeling nervous and excited at the same time. Riley dropped onto the blanket, leaning over his folded knees. He patted the spot next to him, beckoning me to sit beside him. Circling his arm around my shoulders, he leaned into me, his mouth close enough I could feel his warm breath on my lips. His long eyelashes fanned out on his cheeks, when his eyes closed.

"So. Did you and that Kaylee girl have sex?"

Riley licked his lips, and sat up, surprised I'd broke the spell and probably killed the mood based on his loud, frustrated sigh.

"Really? You want to discuss my ex *now?*"

"Considering what happened back at the bowling alley, I think *now* is exactly the right time. Next time the little bitch may stab me with her *Barbie* nail file. Honestly, how old is she?"

"Sixteen."

"Ah, get 'em young and teach 'em right, huh?"

Riley's brows knitted. "No, nothing like that. What's going on Taylor? You were all over me in the bathroom, but here, you're an 'ice queen' in training. I mean, seriously, isn't moonlight and a lake romantic enough? Do you need a toilet and 'quilted squares' covering the floor to be in the mood?"

I couldn't help but notice the night breeze could now blow between us. "I'm curious, that's all. She seemed awfully attached to you and, well, you weren't exactly being a hard ass with her. How close were you two?"

Riley dropped backward on the blanket, pressing his fists into his eye sockets. "Shit. I can't believe I've got the hottest chick in Wellsville alone on a blanket, and all she wants to do is *talk*."

I uncurled a fist and laced my fingers through his. "You seriously did not just call me a 'chick'?"

"Hot chick. There's a distinct difference." He turned on his side to face me. "Fine. About Kaylee. We dated for I guess, about nine months. We met at a Halloween party last fall."

He paused, raising on one elbow to peek at me. "You really want to talk about the *physical* stuff between me and her?" I nodded and he cursed. "No. I've never had sex with Kaylee. Wanted too real bad and managed to 'round the bases' but never hit the 'home run'. She was always too scared."

"What about other girls?"

"*Seriously*?"

I lowered onto my elbow, eye level with his dreamy eyes. "Yeah, Riley. *Seriously.*"

"You know I could tell you anything and you'd never know if I told the truth or not."

I lay beside him, our shoulders touching. "I'd know if you lied, trust me."

This time when his mouth hovered, I wrapped the back of his neck with my hand, keeping him from pulling away. "But you won't."

The kiss was gentle, his lips soft. Mine parted and I welcomed the slow, deep kiss and the feel of Riley's body against the length of mine when he moved on top of me. His finger hooked under the strap of my sundress, slowly pulling it down so he could kiss my bare shoulder.

"No, I haven't with anyone else, either," he whispered against my jaw on his quest to sample the length of my neck. His lips curled over my ear, "But I wouldn't mind trying it out with you." His body shifted and molded into my curves. "Taylor, you scare me."

"Good," I mumbled against his moist lips. "Because you terrify me." His hand tentatively moved to cup my breast, and my breath hitched. We stopped kissing, staring at each other. His hand didn't move and I didn't push it away. Our swallows sounded loud in the sudden silence permeating the air around us.

When his index finger slowly reached up and tugged the top my dress down, exposing a bit more flesh than I was ready to show, not to mention his thumb took a torturous liberty, I covered his hand to stop matters from progressing…and me from burning internally.

"Riley, stop. I'm not going there." *Yet.* He rolled off me and an uncomfortable awkwardness fell between us. I folded my arms tight across my chest to stop a sudden tremble and keep Riley's hands off. "I'm still a virgin."

A declaration of importance and totally necessary, given he hadn't even taken me for pizza, as promised. But that supposedly would be tomorrow night. Tonight, I sought him and everything that encompassed Riley Martin.

He hung his hands over his stomach. "And I'm not. Sorry. I lied."

My neck snapped sideways. "Kaylee? You made it with a kid?"

His face came dangerously close when he turned. "No! And, she's not a kid," he defended a bit too strongly for my liking. "But I was." He gazed at the stars watching over us from the blackness above.

Riley's voice quieted. "It was my fourteenth birthday and my friend, Aimee, who've I known since my diaper days, decided we should try sex. No one ever paid attention to us because, like I said, we pretty much shared binkies. Our parents were friends in college. Anyway, we snuck into the playhouse under the stairs her dad had made when she was little. Nobody saw us go in and with the light off, we could sneak in the back and be hidden from the tiny windows cut out the side."

Riley rolled onto his side, propping his head on his elbow. Even in the moonlight I could see his cheeks redden. He looked so innocent and I became mesmerized by the sweetness of his expression when he let his cocky guard down.

"It was awful," he continued. "We didn't know what we were doing. She still had mosquito bites for boobs, but she let me touch them anyway. My dick went rock hard instantly and it looked stupid. I was so scrawny it looked out of proportion."

He flipped onto his back, pushing the heels of his hands against his eyes. "Ugh! Why the hell am I telling *you* this? I feel like such an idiot!"

I pulled one of his hands away and curled it against my throat, snuggling onto his shoulder. "Because I asked, and you owe me for lying in the first place." I kissed the knuckles on the hand wrapped in mine. "And, in an odd, innocent way, it's sweet. So? Did you?"

"Not really," he laughed. "By the time she got her panties off and we tried to cram quietly into the space between the pint size table and chairs, I was out of my mind horny. The minute I climbed on top of her, I was done. Didn't even get the 'car in the garage.' She squealed saying I was gross and when she grabbed the blanket out of the toy crib to wipe off her stomach, the doll cried out "Mamma." She'd barely managed to pull her clothes on by the time her baby sister opened the door to see why the doll talked. I hid behind the plastic refrigerator, trying to zip my pants, which wasn't working because I still..."

"Had a 'hard on'!" we said together, laughing so hard we both started coughing.

"I'm sorry, Riley. Did you get caught?"

"Nah, she shooed her sister out and followed. I waited until the coast was clear, then climbed out and ran home. We never told anyone."

"Did you ever try it again with her?"

"Oh, hell no. She thought the whole thing was disgusting. I wouldn't be surprised if she never has sex. Poor schmuck who tries."

"You've spoiled her for other guys," I giggled. "And *technically*, you're still a virgin."

Riley's free hand cradled my neck and pulled me to his lips. "Sorry if I was out of line, earlier."

"It's okay," I whispered back.

Our lips were about to lock again when my cell phone chimed. "Crap! What time is it?" I dumped the contents of my purse onto the blanket, frantically trying to find my phone.

"12:30. Why?"

One missed call. Grammy. "I'm so dead!" I scooped everything back into my purse and scrambled to my feet, running for the Mini.

"Wait!" Riley yelled, balling the quilt into his arms and running after me.

"Sorry," I called out my driver's side window. Gravel spewed in a semi-circle behind me when the Mini skidded sideways.

"Taylor!"

No time to stop and explain. I needed to book it home before Grams decided to ship me back to Boston, or lock me in my room the rest of my summer vacation. Either one removed any more chances for steamy nights with Riley.

The tires squealed when the Mini launched from the dirt road onto the asphalt, leaving a perfect calligraphy "S" on the highway before I gained control of the steering. I felt horrible ditching Riley, but I couldn't stop for him. However, I had all the time in the world to stop for the red and blue flashing lights, suddenly filling my rearview mirror.

Damn.

My window purred when it retreated into its hidden compartment. The flashlight aimed at my retinas was overkill and I covered my eyes to avoid permanent blindness.

"License and registration, Miss." The voice sounded hard edged, void any inkling of compassion. I handed my documentation over and stewed while the officer went back to his car to see if I could be wanted for any mass murders or bank heists. Between the colored strobe lights and a spotlight that could light up a space station in another galaxy, I *glowed* inside my car.

A second set of headlights pulled behind the officer's cruiser. *Great. Backup.* Dad probably put some alert out on me. It wouldn't surprise me to be arrested for a stolen vehicle, seeing how I didn't really obtain official permission to charge an insane amount of money on his credit card.

The officer reappeared at my window and I braced myself. "Taylor Wilson?"

"Yes."

"Step out of the vehicle," he commanded.

I complied, leaning against the driver door. The officer's badge said "Sheriff Martin." Wonderful. I couldn't get a rookie I could bat my eyelashes at and flirt my way out of a ticket. No. I had to get *the* Sheriff.

"Miss Wilson, I'm afraid you're under arrest."

"Under arrest? What did I do? I'm eighteen. I can be out after curfew."

"It's not for curfew." I swore I saw the corner of his lip twitch, but I couldn't tell with the damn flashlight burning my eyeballs.

"It's for not giving the Sheriff's son a proper kiss goodbye. You're looking at five to life, girl." The reply came from a different voice, *behind* the Sheriff.

"Riley?"

The flashlight clicked off, and between the spots dancing before my eyes and the disco lights surrounding us, I found the cocky, *sexy* lopsided grin attached to the boy who copped a feel from my chest earlier and stopped my heart from beating.

He hooked a thumb at the cop. "Taylor, this is my dad. Sheriff Martin."

"Oh crap. You're the *Sheriff's* kid?"

"You make that sound like a bad thing. I just saved your ass Miss Taylor and that's the 'thanks' I get? 'Book 'em Danno'. Take her away."

"Riley, you're pushing your luck." The Sheriff handed me my license and registration. "Slow down. You could have rolled your car driving that way…and one more thing."

"Yes Sir?"

"Kiss my boy so I can get back to work. He did save your pretty ass. Return the favor."

Riley pushed me against the Mini, his hands framing my waist.

"You're not seriously going to kiss me with your Dad watching, are you?"

His head bent, his hands braiding into my hair. Riley's lips brushed mine, teasing. "You bet I am."

A second hungrier kiss pressed, more possessive, the tongue full and in search of something deep in my throat. As soon as the light show ended and the cop car pulled away, Riley's knee nudged between my thighs.

"Want to play 'house'?"

Thirteen
FAMILY COUNSELING
Riley

Rummaging through my closet, yanking hangers sideways down the rod then back again, I pulled out T-shirt after T-shirt, disgusted with my wardrobe. I couldn't believe I didn't own a decent shirt, one nice enough for a *real* date. Later, I'd take Taylor for pizza as promised, then try to convince her to run the "bases" with me. Something I didn't promise.

After last night, my mind wouldn't shut off. I barely slept and when I woke, other parts of my body remained alert, as well. I wore my tightest jeans to breakfast for fear my usual morning attire of boxers and a T-shirt would scare the hell out of my mom. My body ached, thanks to last night's events.

"You all right, Riley?" Mom asked.

I dropped onto the first chair and scooted tight against the table fast when Mom alerted the rest of the family I acted strange.

"I'm fine," I squeaked an octave higher than normal.

My dad stopped drinking his coffee and peered over his cup at me, one brow arched in suspicion.

"What? I didn't sleep good. That's all"

Mom went back to scrambling eggs. Dad leaned closer. "*Dreams* keep you awake, son? Miss Wilson seemed to have your attention last night. I must say, she's a pretty little thing."

"Who's pretty?" Dirk chirped in, taking a seat across the table from me. "*Kaylee*?" he crooned, doing annoying smacking sounds.

"That's enough, Dirk," Dad said firmly.

No one *ever* scolded Dirk. Dad's reaction surprised Dirk as well as me. Mom sat the platter of eggs and sausage in the middle of the table, exchanging glances with Dad. I guessed she'd found out about Kaylee and Jaxson.

"Leave Riley alone," my mother added, causing a pout to form on Dirk's face. Two strikes against the baby angel? This was *huge*. I needed to save the little beggar before he started crying.

"Yeah, well thanks to *you*, 'douche bag', Kaylee dumped me."

"*Riley!*" my parents chastised in unison. Dirk's face lit up. He officially moved off the hot seat and back onto his pedestal.

"She finally smarten' up?"

Silence impregnated the kitchen. The voice sounded out of place, like purple carpeting in an orange painted room. It had been so long since the timbre came without a snarl, I hardly recognized the tone.

"Well, this is a pleasant surprise," my mother said, moving in jerky motions because she had no idea what to do next. Jaxson *never* came to breakfast. "Let me get you a plate."

My dad folded his newspaper, sliding a sideways glance to me. "Dirk, do you want to take your breakfast downstairs and eat while you watch television?"

Whoa! Life passed through another dimension! Breakfast in front of the TV was considered sacrilege, not to mention food on a carpeted surface being a definite cardinal sin in our house. Unless Mom and Dad were gone. Then everywhere became up for grabs.

"Oh boy!" Dirk stopped to look at Mom. Apparently Dad wasn't the "boss" as he proclaimed. Again with the weird glances between my parents.

"Sure, if your dad says it's okay, go ahead."

My little brother stopped halfway to the doorway, precariously balancing his plate of food and glass of juice. "At least you guys aren't going to talk about sex. Otherwise I'd have to carry this across the street to the Hendersons."

Dad's coffee spurt through his nose onto the table cloth.

Mom followed Dirk, closing the basement door once he settled and became engrossed in some cartoon action flick. She sat at the other end of the table from Dad, leaving Jaxson and me in a glaring contest across from each other. I shoveled eggs in my mouth as fast as I could to keep from saying the disgusting words clamoring to get out.

"All right you two, listen up," Dad commanded. "We've got six weeks until Jax ships out. I expect you both to suck it up and pretend you give a damn about each other. No more fighting or ugly language. We're going to be a happy family until September, if it kills us."

"What-*ever*," Jax mumbled between bites of sausage—bites he had to take on one side of his mouth, thanks to Ally.

Dad slammed his fists on the table hard enough our silverware changed places. "Damnit Jaxson Charles Martin! I've had a gut full of your attitude and it stops now! You hurt your brother in the worst

99

possible way, humiliated your mother and me, not to mention disgrace our family name. *Dirk* doesn't need to pay the price, understand?"

Dad's fork flung scrambled eggs in every direction as he shook it at Jax. "You and Riley will settle your differences here and now. Your mother and I will serve as mediators. That way we protect the furniture.

My mother's voice actually trembled. "Oh, I don't know Stan."

"Why did you take Kaylee to the party?" I blared over her. "What the hell were you thinking?"

"You don't want to know what I thought, bro." Jax stopped eating. "Mom, Dad, I know what you're trying to do, but this is really between me and Riley." He lifted his coffee mug and rose out of the chair. "Let's take this outside, Riley."

"Bring it on." I grabbed my mug and followed him out the sliding door, ignoring my mother's plea to stay away from her prized rose garden.

Jaxson lugged two lawn chairs out to the farthest corner of the yard. "This should be far enough away they can't hear us. Sit your ass down, Riley. We need to talk."

I stood debating, looking over my shoulder at the house. Dad planted his body on the other side of the patio door inside the house, fists pushed into his sides. Mom's head bobbed like a cork in water in the small window over the sink.

Taking necessary precautions, I pulled the chair away to give me room to bolt if Jaxson lunged at me. Between the gym and the loading docks, his arms had grown massive and any punch would be painful, if not bone crushing.

"Okay, I'm sitting," I said, my tone curt.

Jax eased into the other chair. He took a long sip of his coffee, regarding me. "I've been thinking since the day you came to the hospital. There's something I should tell you, but I need you to swear to keep this to yourself. If you spill it to Dad, you won't hurt me. You'll hurt Kaylee."

"Like I give a damn about that little slut."

"You do. Yeah, maybe what happened can never be fixed, but you're decent, Riley. Despite how much you want to hate her, you can't."

He was right. Except about me being decent.

"Just tell me why you took her that night? Give me something. You owe me that much."

"Kaylee wanted to come with me." Jaxson leaned on his knees, fingering his cup. He faced me directly, not dropping his gaze. "Dude, seriously. Didn't you notice the way she always threw herself at me whenever she came around? Riley, I'm sorry. Really I am. I was drunk and stupid, but I'm not responsible for Kaylee leaving you. She'd left you weeks ago, you just haven't paid attention. Hell, Riley, she's fucking your best friend, Cade."

Anger burned through me. "Take that back!"

"*What*? You didn't know? Why the hell do you think he's been MIA the last couple of weekends? Shit 'Sherlock'. Are you really that blind?"

Cade had avoided me. I always got voicemail when I called his cell and last night was the first time since school ended, he'd hung out at Barney's. But Kaylee still hung out with me. It didn't make sense.

"How do you know? Got proof? Kaylee's been with me almost every day since school ended."

"*Days,* Riley. Not nights."

"She works nights cleaning her uncle's dentist office, trying to earn money for a car."

"*Every* night? How do *you* know? Do *you* have proof?"

No I didn't. Even with Taylor slowly capturing my heart, a bigger part of my cardiac muscle burned with anger, jealousy, and fear all at once.

I swallowed the hard bubble in the back of my throat. "Damn," I muttered almost inaudible, feeling deflated and vulnerable. "Still doesn't change what happened between you and her. Between you and *me.*"

"Like I said, I've got something to tell you, but I need your solemn oath it stays between us."

"Sure. Whatever."

"Riley, I'm serious. This *is* confidential."

"Okay, you have my word. Do I need a secret decoder ring, too?"

"Always the smart-ass. No, just a blood promise. I'm calling for the 'brother code'."

We hadn't used the "brother code" since middle school. Any time we did something that could land us grounded for at least a year, or owned a secret we could never tell Mom or Dad without getting ourselves implicated somehow or blamed, we demanded the "brother code" on the other. It was binding. I'd held a lot of blood oaths for Jaxson over the years.

"All right. I swear. *Brother Code.*"

Jaxson leaned back in the lawn chair. "The night of the accident, I asked Ally to go with me to Brandon's party. She said she was sick of dealing with my drunken ass and looking back, she had good reason. I'm a mean prick when I drink.

"I stopped on my way to the party for ice at the gas station, and Kaylee walked in. Riley, she rubbed herself all up my side in the chip aisle. Because I was pissed at Ally, plus sick of fighting off Kaylee, I told her if she seriously wanted some 'Jackson action' to be at Brandon's at nine. She arrived at 8:30. Good thing she's got a body because the upstairs compartment is empty."

"So true, but I've never cared about her IQ. It's always been about me trying to get in her pants and her keeping me out. I can't believe she and Cade hooked up."

"Don't take it personally. Word is Cade slipped her something Grad night. She felt so cheap after and scared of you finding out, she played it out that *she* seduced Cade. Guess they're made for each other."

"That dumb ass! I'll kill him, I swear."

"Thought you didn't care?" Jax reminded inside a smirk.

"I don't care that she's banging Cade, but I care about him drugging her. *That's* not right. It's one thing if something happens, but to force a girl, even a 'stoned' one who wouldn't know the difference, makes me sick."

"Like I said. You're decent, Riley, and deserve better than Kaylee Baker. Especially after what I'm about to tell you."

Jaxson launched into the ugly details of the night of accident. *All* the details, convincing me he told the truth. After he finished, I had a healthy respect for my brother. He shouldered the blame and would pay the consequences for everyone's actions that night.

True, he did take Dad's cruiser, but he pushed Kaylee away when she went after *Jackson Jr.* In retaliation for being rejected, she yanked the wheel hard to the right, careening the car into the town marker. Seeing Jaxson impaled by the steering wheel, Kaylee apparently took off running, but being so drunk, smacked into a tree, knocking her out cold.

Meanwhile, her self-righteous-whore-of-a-friend Shar, managed to talk an inebriated and apparently *stoned* Brandon into removing all clothing from the waist down and well, let Shar do what Kaylee failed to accomplish. When the car smashed into the marker, they also took off with everything but underwear. I imagine Brandon's boxers are marked "Exhibit A" in a box in the basement at the station. Shar's panties probably hung off some rookie's rearview mirror.

Jax was also right about the information he'd passed to my safeguard. If anyone found out, a lot more lives would be altered than just his.

"So why are you taking the fall? You're going into the *army,* Jax, for two damn years. Don't you want some payback for taking the heat on this?"

"What good would it do? I'd still go to jail. I took the car. No one held a gun to my head. This way, the charges are dropped if I keep my nose clean and complete my tour."

Jax looked at me with an expression showing a hint of maturity. "Someday Riley, you'll meet a girl that you'll do anything to make her proud."

"Ally?" I snorted. "Really. *Ally.*"

"I love her Riley. If she never speaks to me again, I'll be okay with that, as long as I prove to her I'm not really a selfish bastard by doing this army thing. I want her to be proud of me."

"Well good luck with that. Hey, can you say 'sneaky snake' for me?"

Jaxson's lisp became pronounced when he got excited or tried to say a series of "S" words. According to Mom, the condition appeared permanent and we were to be *delicate* with the way we approached Jax about it. *Delicate?* She had to be insane. No one in our family even knew the word *delicate,* let alone had any idea how to behave that way.

"I thould beat the thit out of you!"

I started laughing. "That works!" He cuffed the side of my head. "Okay, okay!"

We folded the lawn chairs and faced the mountain at the end of the meadow. Aspen and cottonwood trees shimmered among the dark pines at the base of the hill with the late morning breeze. Tucked out of sight inside the leafy fortress, sat the pond.

"Ever go there anymore?" Jaxson asked, sounding melancholy.

"Yeah. Went there the other day. Still the same."

But completely different. At least to me. The pond held new personal meaning—my liquid treasure chest where I found my prized jewel, Taylor. I decided not to tell Jax about her. A part of me didn't trust him, even after close to an hour of brotherly bonding and sworn promises. She belonged to me. Or at least I hoped she would. I didn't even want her to *see* Jaxson. I couldn't chance another blow to my heart from him.

Slowly we walked back toward the house, chuckling when we saw Mom and Dad collide trying to move away from the window so they didn't look suspicious.

"Think they watched us the whole time?" Jax asked around a smile.

"Oh yeah," I laughed, my gaze fixed on the grass so I didn't step in any dog crap. I ditched out of clean-up duty yesterday, to meet Taylor. "I figure Dad's coffee kicked in about twenty minutes ago and he's been in pain, glued to the glass door."

Jackson started a menacing chuckle. "Then for hell sakes, slow down. Let's torture the old man as long as we can."

"You better stop smiling. Hate for him to think we're getting along."

"We okay Riley?" Jaxson's tone turned penitent, his steps halting.

"That depends. Do you have an *expensive* shirt I can borrow?"

Fourteen
WATER SPORTS
Taylor

Today's agenda included my debut as a water skier. Riley and I would meet his friends at the lake to spend the afternoon boating, then cook hotdogs once the sun went down. Other contact sports were slated for after dark.

Two weeks of constant companionship with Riley had pinned my lust meter in the danger zone, and his suggestion on how to relieve the physical tension building between us centered on a sole thought. *Sex.* The problem being, *I* started thinking the same thing. However, sex to me included a committed relationship, possibly one with a honking diamond on my left hand and a china pattern picked out. But that scenario remained several hundred pages into my life plan. Not on the page "life" currently wrote.

I paced the kitchen, bouncing an orange against my palm. Grammy pulled a tin of fresh blueberry muffins from the oven and the luscious aroma filled the room. She brushed the tops with melted butter, garnishing each with a sprinkle of brown sugar. I wanted to inhale one of the steamy treats, but my stomach had coiled in a nervous knot.

"Something wrong angel girl?" she asked, putting each steamy little cake into a basket, lined with a blue checkered napkin. "I think you've worn a trail in my floor."

"I'm nervous."

"About water skiing? It can't be that hard. Looks kind of fun."

"Yeah, sliding across the top of water on two slats at a high rate of speed, sounds like a blast," I replied with a sarcastic edge. "Especially if you face plant. I've been told the water turns to concrete over ten miles an hour."

Grammy took my orange and placed a hot muffin in my hand. The heat seared my skin and I juggled it between my palms. "Damn, that's hot! Do you have like asbestos hands, or what?"

"Your dainty hands have never been used for anything that could grow a callous. Toughen up." She took two muffins from the basket, rolled them together in a separate cloth and dropped them into a paper bag.

"Take these with you. Tell Riley you made them. Boys like to know a girl can cook."

"But I *can't.*"

Grams held my chin in her fingers. "That's part of a girl's charm. The ability to lie in a disarming, bewitching manner. All a boy has to do is *think* you can cook. By the time he figures out you can't, it's too late. You've already hooked him."

"Are you trying to play matchmaker? I thought you wanted me to cool it with Riley Martin."

"He's growing on me."

I looked around the part of the house visible to me, noticing several vases of fresh flowers dotting various table tops, the fireplace mantle, and the piano. Riley brought flowers to Grammy every day when he picked me up.

"You like the *flowers,* not Riley."

Her quilted mitt-covered-fist pushed her side. "That's not true. Riley's nice enough. At least he's nothing like his derelict brother. When you said you were dating the Martin boy, I worried the slimy older one had caught you too."

"What do you mean?"

She placed the butter in front of me and I pressed a pat to the hot fluffy center of the muffin, watching it ooze into all the tiny holes, coloring the bread dark gold. Grammy put the muffin tin in the sink to soak, took her cup of tea off the counter and pulled out the chair across from me. Her eyes concentrated on the dark liquid in her cup, rippling with the motion of the tea bag she dipped.

"The older boy is a 'looker'. Seems to never lack for female attention." Her eyes lifted to mine, a crease wiggling through the wrinkles on her forehead. "Talk around town is he's a real heartbreaker, but not the most scrupulous 'playboy'. Rumor has it he's single handedly responsible for all the teen pregnancies in town."

"Grams!" I gasped. "Don't tell me *you* believe that gossip."

Her head bent slightly, her gaze back to her tea. I could see her arched brow through her gray bangs. "I'm just sayin'."

The doorbell rang and I scurried out of the kitchen. Behind the thousands of faceted pieces of glass welded with beads of lead, stood *my* 'playboy'. Riley. He gathered me into his arms, fusing my body to his while his lips stole a hungry kiss.

"Blueberries? Yummy."

I towed him into the living room where Grams stood, anticipating today's floral delivery. Riley pulled a bouquet of white petals wrapped in brown paper and handed them to her.

"Daisies! My favorite."

Again I took inventory of the flora decorating the room. "What, not the yellow roses? Or the purple lilies? What about the orange Gerbera daisies? I thought *those* were your favorite."

"All right missy, you've made your point. Now what time can I expect you to have my granddaughter home, Mr. Martin?"

"By midnight."

"Good because you know . . ."

"Nothing good happens after midnight," I finished in a huff. We know, we know.

She handed me the small paper bag containing our muffins. Two big grease spots had formed on the side.

Grams cocked her head to Riley. "Taylor made these, just so you know."

"Grammy," I growled.

Riley took the bag, slinging his arm around my neck. "No, I did *not* know Taylor was so domestic."

"I'm not," I murmured. "She's lying. She said if a guy knows you can cook, you can snag them easier."

Riley's lopsided grin turned my bones soft. "I must say now I know you *can't* cook, I may have to rethink our relationship. Food is very important to me."

My elbow found his gut and he doubled over with a half cough. "Thanks a lot, Grams."

Grammy giggled deep in her throat. She slipped back into the kitchen for a vase. When she returned, she had her purse slung over her shoulder.

"I'm going with the church auxiliary ladies to play bingo in Hampton for the day. I'll be home before you, so don't think otherwise. I trust you two can behave?"

"Yes, Grams. We'll be responsible *adults*." I kissed her cheek and her eyes sent a signal she hadn't passed on my comment.

"*Age* doesn't automatically give you maturity. And don't think I didn't catch the double meaning behind "responsible" either. I'm trusting you, Taylor." She poked her finger into Riley's chest, "And I'm especially going out on limb with you, Mr. Martin, so don't let me down."

"Gouged *and* speared. You ladies are dangerous. Yes, Mrs. Daniels. I'm aware my brother's reputation precedes me, but, I'm not my brother. I promise."

A horn honked a rapid burst. Grandma smiled and nodded her head. "I'm just sayin'," followed her out the door.

Like smoky tendrils, *sex* loomed around Riley and me, silently curling into our thoughts. After Grammy left with the other dinosaurs

112

in her church group, we stood facing each other, our thoughts intertwining with the same sinfully delectable ideas as if sharing the same brain. Riley's arms knew their way around my waist, drawing me into him while his lips tried to suck mine off my face.

"Slow down big boy. We've got the whole day to ourselves."

"We could just stay here, you know." His hand settled over a favorite curve, his thumb stroking the spot where my brain vaporized, taking all common sense away.

"Riley," I moaned, already getting that hot dreamy feeling all over my body. "Don't do that."

His lips pressed my ear, his breath hot. "Do you really want me to stop?" I braced myself against his purposely placed knee, feeling my body becoming supple as soft wax in his arms.

"No..."

He lifted me in his arms and all the way up the stairs, the voices in my head jumped up and down excitedly. *This is it! Today's the day you let him go all the way!*

Yesterday, I treated myself to a waxing to insure smoothness where it counted, and a pedicure, so my feet would be soft. Yes, this would be a good day to lose my virginity.

Riley closed my bedroom door and flipped the lock. He eased onto the bed, pulling me off the pillows and under him. Each button undone met with a kiss, until my sundress lay open and my red bikini exposed. I waited, holding my breath until his lips touched the swell of my breasts, his tongue drawing a wet line inside the fabric line.

113

"Damnit Riley, " I writhed against him, feeling his *eagerness* pressing into my thigh through his swim trunks.

His smile turned wicked when his lips, hot and swollen, pressed mine. "I love torturing you," he whispered. Riley's hand stroked my stomach, slowly smoothing over the stretchy fabric of my swimsuit bottoms to a place they hadn't touched before. Panic struck.

"No! I can't, I'm not ready," I hissed against his lips.

"That's not what your body's telling me, baby."

My nails dug into his arms when his leg pushed mine apart and he pulled at the fabric.

"No, Riley, I mean it. I *can't.* Please stop!"

His hand moved away and my legs quivered under the weight of his body.

"Okay," he whispered, giving a favorite curve of his a light kiss. "You know I'll never push you."

I rolled on my side, facing him. He slipped a loose strand of hair behind my ear and grinned lazily, his eyes still sensually dark. I slithered closer, placing a light kiss on his mouth.

"Sorry. I guess I'm scared about going all the way. I want to, really, and *with* you, but I just can't."

He pecked my lips back. "It's okay, really."

"Maybe it's being inside Gram's house. It's like she'd *know* the minute she walked through the front door. I swear she's got *sex* radar."

We both laughed, easing the tension slightly. Riley climbed off the bed and pulled his T-shirt over his head. My eyes raked over his ripped body, noticing a certain *part* stretching a flower printed on his shorts as he watched me adjust my bikini top.

"As you can see," he smiled, his cheeks pinking, "water skiing in *cold* water better happen sooner than later." He flipped his cell phone opened, "Hey Cade, we're running late. I'll call when we get to the dock." Riley paused in the conversation. An odd look covered his face. "Shit. Well lay down the ground rules before we get there. Oh and, *friend*, I *know*. Good thing I don't give a fat rat's ass anymore. Good luck to you." Riley shut his phone, staring at the floor. "Kaylee's coming."

"Is that going to be a problem for you?" I asked, deciding whether it would be for me.

One side of his mouth pulled up. "No." He pointed to his shorts, *almost* back to normal fit, "This bad boy only wants you, baby."

I knelt on the bed, tugging the sides of his T-shirt and bringing him close for a kiss. "I noticed."

Without breaking out locked lips, Riley lifted me off the bed and held my legs around his waist. "Girl, you drive me crazy. I'm falling for you fast, so I hope you've got a safety net to catch me."

I kissed him back, hard. "I'll never let you hit the ground, I swear."

Our foreheads pressed, our breaths blowing on each other's face. "Don't make promises you can't keep," he said solemnly. "Life's full of surprises. You never know what's swimming in deep water, babe."

"As long as I have you for a life preserver, I'll never drown. You won't hurt me Riley, I know that. By the way, I'm not *falling*. I fell for you the minute you rescued me from the pond."

**

The water felt icy and I could no longer feel my lips. My teeth chattered, but I refused to give up. I would water ski, if it took my last breath.

"*Number twenty-four…*" resounded the obnoxious chant echoing at the end of a seventy foot rope. The glittery neon blue paint on the boat bobbing on the water, blinded me whenever a ray of sunlight caught it just right.

"Come on babe! You can do it!" Riley's vote of encouragement came through a laugh and sounded loaded with doubt.

I secured a deep breath, wrapping my hands around the spongy handle and pulling my knees close to my chest. *Keep the tips up. Pretend you are sitting on the toilet.* Damn, I tried, but each wave rolling my way pushed the tips to the right or left. I had to wait for that one split second when all the planets in the universe lined up and the tips stayed straight.

"Go!" I yelled, assured *this* time I'd "pop" on top of the water. The rope went taught, and my eyes went wide when I felt the familiar yank of neoprene between my fists. I didn't have time to take a breath, and fought with all the strength I could muster in my legs to keep the tips straight against the wall of frothy water fighting from the other side. I

116

tucked the handle to my chest, *trying* to let the boat pull me up and not force myself to stand.

Suddenly, I landed on top of the water! The skis clacked against the washboard surface speeding beneath them and I thought *yes!* I'm skiing! I let out a whoop and leaned too far back. The water slammed my back and my arms went straight up, allowing my lifejacket to slip off effortlessly, taking my swimsuit top with it! One ski escaped. The other twisted my ankle the wrong way with the current of the wake from the boat when it made the all too familiar cut to the left, circling back.

Water washed over my head and my world became a cloud of fizzy bubbles. I bobbed back to the surface, gasping for more air, before I finally released the other ski from my foot to tread water.

Riley dove over the side of the boat with another life vest hooked over his shoulder and swam towards me. He disappeared under the water for a moment and I panicked. His head popped up in front of me and his arm circled my waist, holding my *bare* chest against his and taking over kicking for both of us. His finger held up the strap of my swimsuit top.

"Missing something?"

I couldn't breathe, but not from fear of drowning, but by the way my breasts felt pressed against Riley's chest. My fingers tugged the fabric, but Riley held tight.

"Not so fast. I kind of like the way things feel right now."

Riley wrapped the life vest around my hips, keeping my half naked body below the water line and pressed to him. "You okay?"

My arms locked behind his neck. "Yeah, I'm fine."

"I'd say you're a hell of a lot better than *fine*. Shit, Taylor. I'm horny."

I smiled back, *feeling* Riley horny. "I know," I giggled.

"Twenty-five, twenty-five…" The chant and clapping started again.

"You want to try again?"

"Technically, I *was* skiing."

"Thirty seconds hardly counts. What do you say? One more try?"

I locked the rubber vest over my chest, leaving the swimsuit top in Riley's fingers. "Twenty-five's my lucky number." Riley looked confused, holding my top up. I pressed a hard *cold* kiss to his lips. "Keep it. The extra weight is throwing off my balance."

"Damn girl, you're evil."

"Send me the skis and rope. If I don't get up this time, you get to take off the vest and warm me up. If I ski more than two minutes, you don't get the peep show and I get my top back."

"Will *show and tell* be a 'hands-on' experience?"

"Maybe. But, if you don't help me get the skis, this cold water will shrivel everything up like prunes. I poked his belly under the water, "Including what's inside your shorts."

Riley helped me strap the death traps back on my feet and grabbed the rope when the boat circled again to bring it closer. He kissed me. "I've never wanted you to fail at something as bad as I do *this*."

118

He tied my swimsuit top around this arm and swam back to the boat. I resumed my "toilet seat" position, determined to make attempt number *twenty-five* work. Drowning would be easier to survive than feeling Riley's warm hands on my cold boobs. After this afternoon, *hands on* would apply to more than "chest compressions."

**

Riley sat on the quilt overlooking the lake.

"You can turn around now." I refastened my bikini top, making sure my *assets* were covered. He glanced over his shoulder at me, pouty lips turned down in dramatic overkill.

"Quit sulking. I told you *twenty-five* would be my lucky number."

I managed to stay on top of the water almost ten minutes, finally letting go of the rope near the shore because my legs were tired. Riley didn't try to hide his disappointment, barely saying two words.

"You don't play fair," he growled a little too seriously. "You're such a tease."

"I beg your pardon? *You're* the tease." When he wouldn't return my banter, I kneeled behind him, looped my arms around his neck and flicked my tongue along the edge of his earlobe.

"Don't be like this Riley. I'm having fun. Don't spoil things." The vein behind his ear visibly throbbed, hinting that other parts of Riley may be as well. I kissed his neck, noticing the slight tilt of his head to allow me access to the full length of tanned skin. I found a spot midway, and started sucking. As soon as I thought fangs might appear in my mouth, Riley flipped me on my back, his body pressed to me.

119

"A *hickey*? You gave me a damn hickey?"

"I marked my territory. You're now bound to me by bloodlust," I giggled.

"Your *territory,* huh?" he mumbled against my lips. "I think I like the sound of that." He pinned my hands over my head in a surprise move. "Prepare yourself. Paybacks are a bitch, baby."

**

The warm shower soothed my sun parched skin. Every muscle in my body ached and my stomach felt queasy from all the junk food I consumed. *Hot dogs* turned out to be a side dish.

I wrapped the towel around my moist skin and wiped the steam off the mirror. Streamlets of water trickled over my shoulders from my wet hair and puddled against the rim of terry cloth across my chest. When I raised my arms to comb through my hair, the bright purple bruise peaked over the edge. The quarter size mark proved more painful than all the muscles in my leg. I peeled the towel down and Riley's *payback* on my breast glowed like a beacon.

Damn you Riley! Yeah . . . *damn.*

"Good Lord Taylor! Is that a hickey on your *boob*?

Apparently, I forgot to shut the door again.

Fifteen
A TRULY "RELIGIOUS" EXPERIENCE
Riley

"I'm serious, Riley, don't come over today."

The clock said 7:15 A.M. *Sunday* morning. Taylor had to be insane calling me this early. I eased against the headboard and slapped my face to wake up so I could understand her because she whispered so close to the phone receiver. The room came into focus after a couple thousand blinks.

"Why are you whispering? And what do mean I can't come over?"

Not seeing Taylor would never be an option in my life anymore. I needed her worse than food and water to survive. She was my oxygen supply.

Her hissing in my ear continued. "Because I'm not supposed to be talking to you. Riley, we're in deep trouble. Grams saw your *brand* on my, um, chest, and she's pissed. She thinks I'm a slut, and well, I can't repeat what she said about you."

"What? How the hell did she see your boob? *I* didn't even get to see your boob."

Jaxson slapped the wall on the other side of my bed. Waking "the dead" could bring on my demise. I tossed my pillow to the foot of the bed and leaned on my stomach.

Taylor started crying, putting me at a loss. "Babe, calm down. You're *eighteen.* She can't *ground* you."

"It's worse. She told me if this is how I behaved with boys, she wanted no part of it. Riley, she wants to send me back to Boston."

Okay, *that* would not happen. Taylor and I didn't do anything worth sending her back home and taking her away from me. We still a month of summer left and I wouldn't let old lady Daniels screw things up.

"Hell no!" I yelled out, surely waking the entire upstairs. Jaxson slammed the wall hard enough I expected to see his fist on my side. I walked into my closet, lowering my voice and searching for something to throw on. "I'm coming over to talk to her. We didn't *do* anything."

"No! I told you I can't see you today. Maybe after church and a good dose of preaching she'll mellow."

Hmm. Taylor home alone. "How long do we have the house to ourselves?"

"*What?*"

"Grandma at church equals Riley and Taylor together. *Alone.*"

"Not unless you're coming *to* church. Today, apparently *I* need the preaching. I'll be thinking of you the whole time 'hellfire and brimstone' is being shoved down my throat."

Taylor grew quiet. "Riley, it will kill me to go a whole day without seeing you, but if I do everything Grammy wants today, maybe I can suck your lips off tomorrow? I've got to do some major groveling to get her to let me stay."

"What am I going to do without you, today?" I sagged against the wall in my closet. "Taylor, I think I'm in love with you."

122

Where the hell did *that* come from? And who tells a girl they love them over the phone, let alone from inside a closet piled with dirty socks and underwear? Someone desperate and scared of losing the first person who really mattered. Me.

"What?" Her voice calmed, her question sounding of childlike innocence.

"I love you." I said it quieter, believing the words for the first time. "Sorry, I didn't mean to—"

"I love you, too," she announced over me. "I wanted to tell you yesterday, but I thought you'd run away."

"I'm not going anywhere, babe. Except maybe to church. Grams can't kick me out of God's house, so save me a seat. If you're going to Hell, you're taking me with you."

**

Mom dropped the spatula when I asked for help knotting my tie. "*You're* going to church? I hope the roof doesn't come crashing in."

"Funny Mom. Can't a guy get a little religion without it being national news?"

Jaxson looked up from his breakfast, visually inspecting my attire. "Well, whoever she is, she's got your nuts in a vise if you're going to church."

"Jaxson!" Mom scowled. "Wouldn't hurt you to get your 'nuts' tweaked if it got you inside a chapel."

"MOM!" Jax and I cried out, shocked. She *never* called body parts by proper names, let alone by slang references. If Mom had her way, we'd never know we had a penis.

She held her hands up and talked to the kitchen ceiling. "Why couldn't you have given me *one* girl?"

Dad and Dirk bounded into the kitchen dressed in their finery, making Jaxson sitting in his boxers, appear severely underdressed. Dad poured a cup of coffee while Dirk gave me a once over.

"Who died?" Dad quipped.

"His manhood," Jaxson retorted. "It appears Riley's got a noose around his neck with a leash attached to someone with boobs. Dad smacked Jax's shoulder, pointing to Dirk.

"Well, I'm going to thank her. Maybe adopt her," Mom said.

"It's Taylor, huh Riley?" Dirk spilled the beans along with half his cereal on the floor. "She's nice. If we adopt her, can we sell Jax?"

We all lost it with that one. Even Jax.

"One for the *oops* child," Jaxson laughed.

"What's an '*oops* child'?" Dirk asked.

I didn't want to even look at Mom or Dad, let alone stick around to hear the explanation. I followed Jax back upstairs to grab my truck keys. He stopped in the hallway, dropping his voice to barely a whisper.

"Did you know Mom and Dad were champion 'humpers' in high school?"

"No way!"

"Yep. Their little secret was revealed by Dad's old chum and my new drill sergeant."

I smirked, raising a brow, "Maybe *you're* the 'oops child'?"

"Maybe."

**

Sweat moistened my palms and my collar felt too tight. I hadn't been near a church since the fiasco with Lydia Daniels after Jaxson's escapade, when Mom insisted and Dad threatened, we go to the church picnic as a family to show a united front. That turned out to be disastrous so why shouldn't I worry that this time with Mrs. Daniels would be different? Before that lovely incident, the last time I'd set a foot in someplace holy was Grandpa's funeral, four years ago.

I purposely waited in my truck until the preacher finished greeting everyone at the door. Before Mom went inside, she scanned the parking lot, undoubtedly looking for me. I purposely parked behind the Henderson's monster van that transported their tribe of six kids.

Her shoulders slumped, probably thinking I'd lied or changed my mind. I could have waved, but then she would have trapped the minister until I got to the door. After an embarrassing explanation as to why I never came to church, Mom would undoubtedly latch on my arm and force me to sit beside her. Nothing would make her happier than to have the congregation see her as the "model mom" with her offspring joining her on the pew for church services. Except if one of us happened to be a girl.

Once I saw the arched wooden door slowly shut, I booked it across the parking lot. I had to get inside before the services started, drawing attention to my late entrance. I didn't want to embarrass my mom…or tick off Lydia Daniels.

However, it wouldn't have mattered if I'd appeared with a host of heavenly angels flanking my sides. When I dropped on the pew beside Taylor, her grandmother's eyes "sliced and diced." She even looked upon my feeble attempt at a polite smile with disdain. After all, she only saw me as the boy who sucked her granddaughter's boob last night. There weren't enough flowers growing in the world to erase the picture she'd formed in her mind.

I took Taylor's hand and held it tight, suddenly needing her strength to supplement my insecurity. Her fingers curved over mine and the gentle squeeze confirmed that whatever happened after today, we were committed to seeing it through together. We were irrevocably in love and there would be no turning back.

The sermon drummed on, but in my head I kept playing yesterday over and over. The feel of her naked breasts against my chest. The sensual sensation her sucking caused on my neck, and the grand finale . . . the delicious taste of her tender skin against my own lips when I indulged in *hickey payback.*

I lied to Taylor. When I searched for her blood supply, her breaths were rough, causing her swimsuit top to gape just enough I got a perfect view of her chest. Every succulent detail. The same *details* I

126

sampled in her bedroom on her bed, when my body went wild as I touched…

Taylor's shoulder shook against mine, whirling my dirty thoughts back to present. I glanced sideways to see her lips pursed in a tight smile. She stifled a giggle. My brows knitted, confused. I felt her finger move ever so slightly. I looked down and realized my church pants were about to rip at the seams!

Grabbing a hymn book as discreetly as possible, I covered my lap. Here I sat in a spiritual setting, listening to the words of God being preached from the pulpit with a hard-on. I was going to Hell for sure.

**

Taylor never pulled her hand from mine, even when we walked into the cultural hall for punch and cookies after the sermon. Her fingers felt like they belonged between mine and when I looked down, I swore I couldn't see where hers ended and mine began.

As we approached the table covered in trays of cookies and brownies, I noticed my mother, followed tightly by Dad and Dirk, practically shoving people out the way to get to me. I couldn't avoid the inevitable and brought Taylor's knuckles to my lips for a quick kiss.

"Prepare yourself to meet the family," I warned.

When our personal space vanished with the invasion of my parents and little brother, I slipped my arm around Taylor's tiny waist and pulled her close. "Taylor Wilson, this is my mom, Beverly Martin, and you already know Dirk and my dad."

"You're the lady who owns that cute boutique downtown," Taylor acknowledged.

My mom studied Taylor, then her eyes widened in recognition. "You're Lydia's granddaughter!"

Damn. I was in deep trouble.

"Riley, why didn't you tell me? And how come your father and Dirk know Taylor, but your own *mother* has been kept in the dark?"

"Mom, don't get hysterical. We're in a church. Dad met Taylor unexpectedly, and she and I took Dirk to the Star Wars marathon at the drive-in last week when you were doing inventory."

"You two had Dirk out all night?"

Taylor squirmed and I stroked her arm to settle her back against me. "Mom, lower your voice," I murmured. "I only kept Dirk out until midnight. I had to have Taylor home by then. That's her curfew."

"And apparently, *that's* too late for some teenagers to be left alone."

Lydia Daniel's snarl from behind me brought my neck hairs to attention. Taylor's body yanked out of my arm and my mother's expression turned guarded, noticing the not so subtle action.

"Come on Taylor. It's time to leave."

My mother touched Mrs. Daniel's sleeve, stopping the retreat. "Lydia? Is something wrong?"

Taylor's fingers reached for mine and I held my hand back until I felt them securely interlaced between. Her free arm wrapped mine and

she clung to me. I wanted nothing more than to wrap her in my arms
and protect her from whatever was about to go down.

"Ask your son."

"*Grandma,* not here," Taylor pled quietly. Several congregational
members ceased munching and obviously eavesdropped at this point.

"Riley?" Mom asked, her eyes begging for it not to be anything
bad or embarrassing. Something I couldn't give her. Luckily, my dad's
intuitive training brought his intervention.

"Ladies, I think we have an audience." He glanced at Dirk.
"Children have big ears. Can we take this somewhere more private?"

The smile Lydia Daniels contrived was this side of evil. "Of
course. Bev, might I invite you and Riley to join me and Taylor for
lunch? I have a small ham cooking which would feed the four of us
nicely."

Shit! *Mom don't agree! Please!* I begged with my eyes, which only
made her more suspicious.

She straightened the lapel on my dad's jacket. "Stan, maybe you
and Dirk could get a burger and spend some time together? I'll have
Riley bring me home. We shouldn't be too long."

My arm went numb from Taylor's fingers clenching so tight. Dad
gave me a look that meant *we* would talk after Lydia Daniels chewed
me up and spat me out.

**

Lunch proved horrible, except for the ham. It tasted delicious, at
least the three bites I got in before Taylor's grandmother filled the glass

bowl in the center of the table with small multi-colored wrapped packages. I saw her make a detour into the drug store on the way home, leaving Taylor in the car. I figured she probably needed denture cream. Never would I have guessed *these* were what she purchased.

"What are those?" my mother asked with sincere innocence.

"Well they're not throat lozenges," Mrs. Daniels smirked.

I intently studied the floral pattern on the table cloth when my mother removed a lime green packet and brought it closer for inspection. Taylor's toe tentatively touched my foot and I stretched out my legs to hold her feet between mine.

"They're sure colorful."

I winced with each crinkle between my *mother's* fingers.

"Oh for crying out loud, Bev. You can' tell me you're *that* naïve."

I, too, struggled with my mother's seemingly innocent attitude, especially given the noteworthy intel Jaxson revealed earlier.

"They're *rubbers,* Beverly!"

"I know perfectly well what they are, Lydia. What concerns me is why *you* have such an assortment."

Way to go Mom.

"Because I want to make sure *your* son has plenty at his disposal if he's going to date Taylor. Did you know Riley helped himself to a sucking frenzy on my granddaughter's breast? She doesn't need to be tending to babies at her age!"

Lydia Daniels stared me down with eyes of cold steel. "Taylor's been accepted to *Harvard*. Did she tell you that when you were stripping her clothes off?"

No she hadn't.

Taylor reeled back when her grandmother's finger pointed dangerously close to her eyes. "And what about Michael, Taylor? Does he know you're hiding in this tiny town, swapping spit with one of the locals?

Nor had she mentioned anyone named *Michael*.

"Are you seriously throwing away a life with a young man who has a promising career in a prestigious law firm, for the son of the local sheriff? Come on, Taylor the sex can't be *that* good."

Something snapped inside me, probably fueled by the gigantic jealous monster rearing its ugly head. My fists slammed the table.

"Enough! For your information *Grammy,* your precious granddaughter is still a virgin so *Michael* has nothing to worry about." I looked at my mother, who no longer had eyebrows. "And so am I. Nobody's been compromised!"

I leaned over Lydia Daniels who cowered in her chair. "The damn blood blister that's got your old lady panties in a wad was payback for this!" I ripped the band aid off my neck, pointing to my own bruised brand. "I doubt Taylor is pregnant from sucking my neck, unless she managed to extract my sperm through the skin!"

"Riley!" Mom shrieked.

Crazed, I reached into the bowl, glaring at Taylor when I grabbed a hand full of *lozenges.* "Mrs. Daniels, thank you for providing these. Next time I'm out with Taylor I'll have her snap one on me to see if you got the right size. I hear country boys' dicks are bigger than city boys'. I tossed the colored packets onto the table, landing a few among the sliced ham and inside the cheesy potato casserole.

"I'm *so* out of here. Coming Mom?" I yelled over my shoulder as I marched out the front door. Taylor chased after me, yelling my name. Mom and Lydia Daniels argued loudly on the porch behind her.

"Riley!" Taylor screamed again, but I ignored her, unable to trust my actions at the moment. I'd never been so enraged. Not even when I found out Kaylee went with Jaxson…or boinked my best friend, Cade. I didn't love Kaylee. She could do whatever the hell she wanted. But not Taylor. She couldn't. Not now. Not after telling me she loved me.

Taylor grabbed my shirt and I spun around, clenching my fists to my side. Her eyes shimmered. My heart sank and I wanted to fold my arms around her.

I would not touch her.

"I-I'm s-so sorry! I didn't purposely keep things from you, honest. W-We've just been having so much f-fun, I didn't w-want to spoil it." When I wouldn't embrace her, she stepped back and wrapped her arms around her body, holding the remaining pieces from falling apart. She spoke softly, plaintively. "I meant what I said this morning. I *do* love you, Riley."

132

"Better check that word out in the dictionary, Taylor. I'm quite sure *love* doesn't include secrets like guys named 'Michael'," I charged in an icy tone.

"Get in the truck, Riley," my mother ordered.

I obeyed without comment, feeling the vein in my jaw pulse. Taylor's beautiful face puckered and tears trickled over her wrinkled, reddened cheeks. I rolled up my window and sped off, leaving a cloud of dust hanging at the end of the driveway. Halfway home my mother finally spoke.

"Lydia had no right saying those things about you, Riley. She doesn't know you."

I stayed silent. Suddenly, my head snapped, a searing pain covered my right cheek.

"What the hell was that for?" I shrieked, placing my hand over my burning cheek. "Why did you slap me?"

"I don't know! I'm so angry at you for putting me in this situation. Jaxson's one thing, but you, Riley? I expect more from you. I certainly didn't deserve to have that woman rub my nose in the fact I didn't know what a *rubber* was. I've never felt so stupid."

She punched my shoulder. "And sucking her granddaughter's breast? Honestly Riley!"

"Mom! We are *not* having this conversation. I'm eighteen. My life is my business."

"Unless it screws with mine. Then son, it becomes *my* business. You boys don't seem to get that."

Neither of us said another word. When we got home, I marched up the stairs, giving my dad a deathly glower as I passed. Mom followed close behind, pretty much giving Dad the same look. I slammed my bedroom door. She slammed hers.

Dad's feet padded heavy on the stairs. "Does someone want to tell me what's going on?

"No!" we both screeched.

**

It felt like I'd stared out the patio doors into the blackness for hours. Each time the lightning flashed, the scene changed as Nature played hide-and-seek. If I'd let my imagination have its way, I could have sworn at some point I saw something running along the ditch bank at the back of the property. Possibly Sasquatch or a werewolf.

When the phone rang at the same time a loud clap of thunder boomed, we searched for the hearts we'd coughed across the room. Mom held her book against her chest, acting out a heart attack.

"I don't which I hate worse—thunderstorms or the phone ringing this late Never good news."

The unspoken rule was that once the sun disappeared and Dad still roamed the house, *he* answered doors and phones.

"It's only 9:15, dear. Not midnight."

No one said anything, but we all shared the same thought wave. Jaxson. His shift at the train yard ended at 8:30. It took twenty minutes to cross our booming metropolis behind a slow school bus. Jax was late.

Dad pulled a long, steady breath and picked up on the third ring. "Sheriff Martin."

A couple seconds later, Jaxson barreled through the garage door into the laundry room, drenched. I swore the drapes hanging next to me rustled from Mom's sigh of relief...or my own.

"Dad, the water was rising fast under the bridge on Highway 40, when I crossed over. If this rain keeps up all night, it might take out that old bridge and the rail yard will be cut off from town. Not that I wouldn't mind a few days off."

My father raised a hand Jax's direction, his gaze settling on me. "Hang on, Lydia. Riley, phone's for you. It's Taylor's grandma." Dad turned to Jax, "What's that again about the bridge?"

The two disappeared upstairs. Mom looked up when she heard who was on the phone. I walked to the farthest corner of the kitchen and leaned against the counter, hoping to be out of earshot. Lightning flashed again and thunder chased almost immediately. Hell of a night for anyone to be out.

"This is Riley."

"I know I'm the last person you want to talk to, but I need your help. Can you come over to the house?" Lightning flashed again and the power flickered.

"Mrs. Daniels, I don't know with the weather—"

"Riley, Taylor's gone. I don't want to bring your father into this, if I don't have to. Please."

"I'll be right there." I grabbed the keys off the hook by the laundry room door.

"Where are you going?" my mother asked, crossing the room in superhuman speed.

"I'll be back. Taylor needs me."

"Riley, I don't—"

"Mom, can you trust me just once? It's not like I'm driving down the interstate. I'm only going a mile away."

"Okay, but don't be long."

"Do me a favor? Don't tell Dad. Let him handle the bridge thing, not micromanage me right now." She nodded and kissed the cheek she'd slapped earlier. She pulled the laundry room door shut so no one would hear me sneaking out the side door.

The rain soaked through my sweatshirt just running from my truck to Mrs. Daniels's front porch, where she waited in the open doorway. Once inside, I took in her swollen red eyes and blotchy face. My inner radar told me more than an argument took place after we left. The wilted yellow roses scattered in a wet puddle on the floor beneath the piano confirmed it.

"Where is she?" I asked trying to keep the hysteria out of my voice.

"I don't know," Mrs. Daniels answered, a slight warble of fear in her voice. "We had a horrible fight after you and your mother left. She stormed out of here and I figured she needed some space. When the wind picked up, I went into the garage to get some plastic to put over

136

my tomato plants, and found her car still there. The hood felt cold to the touch. Wherever she's gone, she's on foot. I've called everywhere I can think of, but with it being a Sunday, not too many places are open."

"Exactly how long has she been gone?"

Her eyes fell away. "Almost four hours."

"Four hours? In this weather? Why the hell didn't you call earlier?"

"In all fairness, Riley, I thought she left in her car. It never occurred to me she'd take off walking." Her fingers trembled when she touched the tip of her chin. She looked past me into some other dimension. "She's only wearing that thin cotton dress from church and sandals."

The color drained from her face and she teetered. I helped her to the sofa in the living room. "Okay, let's not panic."

Let's freak out instead.

I pulled my cell out and dialed Barney's private number. "Barn, its Riley. Taylor didn't happen to show up there this afternoon, did she?"

"No man, I haven't seen her since Friday night when she came in with you."

"Do me a favor? Walk around the building and see if she's tucked out of the weather under the eaves or something."

"You in trouble? She run away from you?"

"Something like that. If you see her, don't say anything. Just call me-K?"

After he agreed, I paced, trying to figure out Taylor's mind set. The lake was too far. Maybe the church? Shit, after four hours, she could be anywhere.

"Can I check her room?"

"Sure, but I didn't see anything missing."

Without answering I raced the stairs, two at a time. I wasn't looking for what might be missing, but more so, what could be left behind giving me some clue. Her room appeared neat and organized. Nothing out of place. The total opposite of my haphazard lair.

Her tiny bathroom even appeared spotless. I picked up her cologne and sprayed it into the air. Hollister's *So Cal*. A knot twisted in the pit of my stomach. I checked my watch. 9:30. Where the heck could she be?

I stared out her window, seeing the lights of my house off in the distance. The lightning flashed again and the same strobe-light scene appeared in its white-hot glow, but no gnarly creatures lurked along the stream.

Settling on the edge of her bed, I grabbed a pillow to hold. Her diary lay open under where the pillow lay. Cardinal rule—*never, ever*, read your girlfriend's diary. Technically though, it appeared Taylor belonged to someone else, so the rule didn't apply. I picked up the black and pink polka-dot notebook and "committed sin."

Dear diary. That always sounds so stupid, but I guess it's tradition. Today, I met the most amazing, pig-headed, gorgeous hunk. His name

138

is Riley Martin. He rolled down this little hill and landed on the banks of the pond I swam in. When he stood up, I was in awe and wanted to wrap my body around his. Gorgeous! When he kissed me, I ached in places I didn't know existed and I wanted him to touch me all those places. I think I'm in love! Coming here is the best thing I've ever done in my life. Well second best. Kissing Riley Martin is the first. I decided my little tree covered hideaway with the pond is magical. It's my gift from my guardian angels. My sanctuary. It's where I found Riley and gave away my heart. 'Nite diary.

My body jerked, connecting to my feet already in transit down the stairs. My voice came out in a rush. "Do you have a flashlight and an umbrella? Oh, and a blanket."

"Why, what's wrong?" Lydia scurried down the entry hall, gathering the items I requested. To me, she moved in slow motion.

Blood thrummed loudly in my ears. "I think I know where Taylor is. I just don't know *why* she's still there. She's got to be freezing."

She piled the quilt on my arms. "What can I do?"

Turn on all the lights on the back of the house so I can follow the trail back. Wait for my signal. I'll wave the flashlight. If you don't see the light in thirty minutes, call my house and tell my mom to send Jax to the pond...and to call my dad."

"*Pond?*" An unmistakable alarm rang in her voice. I fought to keep my thoughts from following hers. I couldn't let myself believe Taylor would do something stupid like purposely hurt herself, but after today, I wondered if I knew Taylor at all.

My feet slid over wet stalks of wild wheat as I ran through the field. The *werewolf* running along the creek earlier must have been Taylor. Panic gripped when I realized over an hour had passed since then, and when the storm was its angriest.

The beam from the flashlight bounced on the ground in front of me. Tiny puffs of steam escaped with my labored breaths. I stopped at the edge of the property before disappearing over the ridge to the streambed below. The back of Lydia Daniels house lit up like a carnival ride. Good. I would use it as a beacon to aim back toward. The creek would serve as my guide in the darkness. I just prayed I didn't stumble onto a hurt, or worse, Taylor. *My* Taylor.

Positive thought, Riley. Taylor's smart. She found a place to wait out the storm, that's all. She's fine. She's fine. Please…be fine.

The mud may as well have been a sheet of ice. I slid down the small embankment, losing my grip on the flashlight that proceeded to roll ahead of me.

"Damn!" I hissed, feeling my ankle to make sure I hadn't twisted it. I'd managed to keep the quilt out of the mud, but broke the umbrella when I landed on it.

When I reached down to pick up the flashlight, my gaze followed the beam fanned out to the banks of the pond. There lay Taylor, curled up against a rock. The branches from the trees overhead, kept most the

140

rain out. Inside the thicket, only a slight drizzle fell instead of the monsoon pouring from heaven outside.

"Taylor!"

Running to her felt like being stuck inside a cartoon slide show, not moving until the next page flipped. She still wore the dress from church, the flimsy cotton drenched and clinging to her body. Her leggings had a hole with a long raked run stretching over her calf, and the heel was broken off her sandal.

I brushed her wet hair away from her cheeks, stained with streaks of mascara. "Taylor? Baby, it's me. Riley."

"Riley?" Her voice sounded feeble, her eyes searching the darkness for my face. When our eyes met, she grabbed my sweatshirt and pulled her trembling body to me. "Riley, I'm so sorry! I don't know why Grammy did that? Why she embarrassed you and your mom? That's not like her."

"Taylor, I don't give a shit about your grandma right now. She's back at the house scared to death something's happened to you." I wrapped the quilt around her and lifted her into my arms. "Why are you down here, anyway?"

Her wet nose nuzzled into my neck and I swaddled her tighter. Even though the quilt was wet, it served as a layer between her and the cold air. I sat on the rock cradling her in my lap.

Her lips tickled my throat when she spoke. "After you left, Grams and I fought and I said some awful things. I threw the vase of roses on the floor and I ran out in a tantrum. When I got down by the river, I lost direction. It started raining, so I headed for the thicket when the lightning started. I didn't want to be in the open, although after today, God is probably looking to barbeque me.

I couldn't help laughing. "If God was looking for someone to roast, he'd have fried up my brother, Jaxson, a long time ago."

The flashlight dimmed. Not a good sign. Taylor sneezed and I suddenly pictured our bodies being found sometime next week, shriveled and turned to stone.

"Come on, I need to get you back."

"No! I won't go back. I refuse to talk to her until she apologizes."

"Taylor, you're going to be sick if I don't get you indoors."

The flashlight flickered again then died, leaving us in pitch blackness. I knew I'd never find my way back to Lydia Daniels, especially carrying Taylor. The terrain was too rocky and the riverbank steep. Even if her house burned like a torch, I wouldn't see the flames for at least a quarter mile, and that's if we didn't slip off one of the drop offs and smash our skulls on the rocks.

I only had one choice—to go the one way I knew. Home. I'd take Taylor there, then call her grandmother.

"I'll take you to my house." She sneezed again. When I tried to set her on her feet, she yelped and I lifted her instantly.

"I twisted my foot on some loose rocks. I'm not sure I can walk very far. Maybe you should go get help. There's no way you can carry me up those steep banks.

"Leaving you here is *not* happening." I bent down, "Climb on my back and hold the quilt over both of us."

Taylor shifted onto my hips and I locked my arms under her thighs. The weight of the wet quilt pulled me off balance and for a second, I panicked we'd tumble into the mud. She fumbled with the blanket, pulled it over both our heads with one hand and wrapped her free arm around my neck.

She kissed my cheek. "Thanks for saving me. I do love you Riley."

Thoughts of this afternoon, reeled in my head. "Don't say that. I'm too confused right now to believe you." She tried to squirm out of my arms, but I held tight. "*No! Stop it!*" I shouted. "I'm getting you someplace warm and dry. We can argue later, if you don't die from pneumonia, first."

She started crying and all my macho posturing vanished.

"Taylor, I'm sorry. Let's just get you somewhere warm, okay? My house all right?"

"Yeah. But promise me something."

"Anything."

"Don't leave me. Not tonight. Not ever. And keep my grandmother away from me."

"Okay." There wasn't time to argue the finer points of our verbal contract. My back ached and large, flat drops of rain pummeled us.

I literally crawled over the rise from the pond, keeping Taylor tucked under the quilt. When I stood again, I adjusted her weight and started across the meadow. Heavy gray curtains of rain blurred the lights to my house in the distance. The waxy leaves of drenched sunflowers turned the ground beneath my feet slippery. We stumbled to the ground once, but I managed to take the hit from the hard ground first.

When we finally stepped onto the back deck, Lucky barked wildly inside. The lights came on one by one, starting upstairs, down the stairwell and through the house, illuminating the kitchen.

Jaxson looked half crazed with his hair matted to one side of his head, his gray T-shirt crinkled over pajama bottoms. He approached the door, baseball bat in hand. We both knew where Dad kept the shotgun, but were instructed bat first. Bullets second.

Jaxson wrestled Lucky by the collar, holding her back while he flipped on the outside lights. He let out a high pitch squeal when the light shined on us. Apparently, I couldn't be recognized as "Riley with a girl on his back." We looked more like a mass of mud with pink rosebuds peeking beneath the filth.

"Jaxson, it's me Riley. Open the door, quick!"

Between wrestling Lucky and fighting the sticky door latch, Jaxson pretty much used every swear word in his vocabulary. Finally the door opened and I pushed through the opening, hissing at Lucky to stop barking. I felt Taylor's legs wrap around my waist away from Lucky's mouth.

"Shut the fuck up!" Jaxson yelled, grabbing her collar and hauling her to the laundry room.

"Well, that woke everyone," I scowled. '

"Dirk's downstairs watching a movie, but more than likely, asleep. Once that kid shuts his eyes, he's in a coma.

"Where's Mom?"

"She went to Lydia Daniels to wait for you. Dad's checking the bridge, so she left me in charge of the 'mini Martin'."

The quilt fell to the floor and Jaxson sized up my *back pack.*

"Well, well. My guess is you're Taylor, Riley's secret and the cause of a chain of events rivaling my last crime spree."

"Taylor, this is Jaxson, the blackest sheep possible belonging to our family. Jax, this is Taylor and she's off limits, understand?"

"Nice with the whole 'trust thing' bro. No worries. I'm sworn off girls." Taylor slithered down my side and I curled my arm around her waist to keep her steady. Jaxson gave her his usual once over, tallying the numbers in his head to rank her on boobs, face, legs, and butt.

"Maybe I'm not. I give her a 'nine'. Nice work. Let me know when you're done with her."

"You're disgusting!" Taylor snapped, launching into a coughing spell with a bark offering stiff competition to Lucky's.

I bent to lift her in my arms again, but hissed against a jab of pain on my right side. "Damn, I must have pulled something when I fell."

When Taylor teetered on her sore ankle, Jaxson swooped in and lifted her effortlessly. "I presume we're going upstairs?" I followed behind them, trying to not focus on Taylor's hands locked around my brother's neck, or his hand poised to the side of her breast, his other arm secured under her thighs.

145

At the top of the stairs, Jaxson carefully placed Taylor on her feet at the bathroom door, letting his hand slide a bit too slow across her rear. She shot him a look that should have vaporized him, but didn't say anything.

"There are towels in the cabinet. Get in a hot shower and I'll put some dry clothes outside the door." I paused, noting Jaxson still lingered and motioned for her to step closer so I could whisper. "What do you want to do about underwear?"

Her cheeks reddened under the mud caked to her face. "I'll go 'commando'," she whispered and shut the door.

"My kind of girl," Jaxson smirked.

"Go to hell."

"Already am. Army in three weeks, remember?"

I had no comeback. He was going "Hell" and as each week brought the time closer, joking about it seemed cruel. Still, I had to give him something.

"Just so you know, Jax, you scream like a girl."

**

After I finished my turn in the shower, I scooped Taylor's dirty clothes off the bathroom floor and put them in the washer with mine. I hopped on top of the rumbling washer and made the daunting call to Lydia Daniels. After she chewed through me when I told her Taylor would stay here tonight, my mother lectured me on "appropriate behavior under *her* roof."

Quietly, I slipped into my room where I told Taylor to stay to avoid Jaxson. The lamp on my computer desk washed the room in a warm glow. Outside, the rain pulsed relentlessly against the window, but in here with Taylor curled on my bed, her damp head on my pillow, everything felt perfect. I didn't want anything to change. I never wanted tomorrow to come.

When I crawled on the bed next to her, she nuzzled into me. "I called your grandma to tell her you were all right."

Taylor's brows wiggled into a serious knot. "I'm not going back."

"You don't have to. I told her you were staying here tonight."

"What about your parents?"

I wrapped my arms around her, smelling the coconut scented shampoo lingering in her hair. Nothing mattered outside this moment. "They'll have to deal with it. Right now, I need to know you're safe and I can only feel that if you're in my arms."

While usually this close proximity would trigger certain body parts to prepare for action, tonight I only wanted to protect Taylor, not ravage her. Maybe because my sweatshirt and sweatpants completely covering her naked body looked anything but sexy, but probably because she felt vulnerable to me. I kissed her forehead, tugged her closer.

"Taylor, who's Michael?"

Her long dark lashes brushed her pale cheeks, now clean and glowing from moisturizer. "He's my *supposed* boyfriend back home, or I should say the boy everyone thinks I should marry." My body stiffened, but her arms held tight. "Relax, Riley. I don't love Michael and have no intention of marrying him, regardless of what everyone wants me to do."

"Sounds like he's going to be rich someday. Your future would be secure."

She settled deeper in the bend of my arm, her eyes still shut. "He'll be rich because his daddy will give him money. Not because he earned it. I know what it's like to have your future *bought*. Grammy's right. I've been accepted to Harvard, but I haven't decided to go. That's why I didn't tell you. My dad wants me to follow in his footsteps and become a lawyer."

"What do you want?"

She yawned wide. "Honestly? To be a school teacher or counselor. Anything but a lawyer. What about you?"

"Anything but the 'son of the local sheriff'. I've thought about becoming a doctor—one for kids."

"You're good with…"

She never finished her sentence. She'd fallen asleep. I stared at her slumbering in my arms, her breaths warm and feather soft against my skin. I found it hard believe someone as special as Taylor could be in to me. I didn't deserve such a gift.

The soft rap at my door sounded in my dreams, until it happened a second time, interrupting my fantasy dirt bike race. I'd rounded the last berm, heading for the finish line when Lydia Daniels's voice blared over the speaker system, instead of the announcer.

"Riley, can I come in?" she asked.

I wanted to sit up, but Taylor snuggled deep into my curves, my legs spooning under her hips. No way would I disturb her. I covered her with a quilt and motioned for her to come in. I pushed my finger to my lips.

"Quiet. She's finally asleep. Don't wake her."

Mrs. Daniels nodded and pulled my desk chair closer to the bed. The lamp still glowed and the room actually had a cozy feel to it. Of course it didn't hurt that I held a gorgeous girl's body in my arms, enhancing the effect.

"Your mom said you found her by some pond?"

"In the thicket, there's a pond Jaxson and I made years ago. That's where I first met Taylor. She found it on a walk and was swimming when I came to do the same."

"Oh. I had no idea one existed."

"No one did until tonight."

"Riley, about what happened earlier. I was out of line. My accusations were harsh. You and Taylor are adults, and as hard as that is for me to face, it's really none of my business if you two are having sex."

Hearing the word "sex" come out of Taylor's grandmother's mouth sounded nasty. From now on, if I needed anything to stop my lustful urges from getting out of control, I'd picture Lydia Daniels's thin, pale lips mouth the word *s-e-x.*

"Well, we're not. The hickeys really were just playful."

At least mine. Taylor's, on the other hand, was a pure unadulterated *turn on.*

"Promise me you'll be responsible, Riley. Use protection."

Okay this reached beyond the boundaries of weird. Taylor sighed, shifting her sweet, round bottom against my stomach. "Riley Jr." awakened. I tucked the quilt between us and draped my arm over her waist, wishing Lydia Daniels would go home. *Now.*

"Riley, there's a reason I lost it. You see, I was only seventeen when I got pregnant with Taylor's mother. The baby's father was a smooth talker who worked on our ranch for the summer. He made me promises of a life together, traveling and seeing exotic places—a fantasy that appealed to a young girl trapped in farm town, facing a future as a rancher's wife.

"My boyfriend was backward when it came to romance, so when 'Mr. Tight Jeans' told me he loved me, I believed the lie. He knew all the right things to do and say, even promised to marry me if I gave him what he wanted. Then one morning I found the bunkhouse empty, his room cleaned out. He'd left me behind with a shattered heart.

"I lied and told my boyfriend the baby belonged to him. We'd had sex a couple of times, so he didn't question me. But then Taylor's mother was born a month early at a healthy eight pounds, her head was crowned with thick blonde hair. We both had dark brown hair. He finally asked the ultimate and I told him the truth. The man had the decency to stay with me another three years, working two jobs to give me enough money to survive on my own. That's when I bought the house down the way. I raised Grace by myself.

"When she went away to college, she met Richard, a law student with a promising career like Michael. I pushed her into marrying him when I found out she was pregnant with Taylor, even though she had her doubts. I didn't find out for ten years, that their marriage had been a sham. He'd dated other women behind Grace's back, and the worst was, she allowed it. All for the sake of appearances. Not even for Taylor. On Taylor's eighteenth birthday, they announced their divorce, spinning her world out of control. She arrived on my doorstep the next day.

"Riley, my point to all of this is that I don't want Taylor to repeat history. She's got a chance to break the bad karma. You're a nice kid, but Michael can give her the life she needs to survive. That's why I got so upset.
If she got pregnant it would ruin everything. Michael's made it very clear he wants Taylor to be a virgin when they marry."

At this point, my head snapped back in the game. I'd tuned out most of the story because I didn't want pictures in my head to match the words describing Lydia Daniels as a barnyard slut.

"They're *engaged*?"

"He's asked her, but with the divorce, she told him she couldn't deal with the pressure. That's the main reason she's here. She needed time to sort through her feelings before starting law school in the fall."

"Taylor doesn't want to go to law school. She doesn't want to be with Michael, either. She says he's who everyone else wants her to be with. Not her."

"Love is overrated, Riley. With the way the world is, she needs security. Not love."

Taylor turned over and nestled onto my chest, mumbling. I folded my arms tightly around her, keeping her safe from the outside world grabbing at her. Safe from her grandmother—safe from *Michael*.

"No offense, Mrs. Daniels, but you're wrong. Taylor deserves to be loved."

"Riley, you're not saying you're *in love* with my granddaughter, are you? You can't be in love this fast. You're too young and naïve to think otherwise. Sorry, boy, but the only thing you're feeling is *lust*...not *love*."

I wanted to wipe the smirk off her face. Every muscle tightened, causing Taylor to stir again. I didn't want her to wake and find her grandmother sitting next to the bed, nor did I want anyone taking her from my arms. Not tonight.

"Mrs. Daniels," I hissed as quietly as possible, "I'm going to ask you to leave."

"I'm taking my granddaughter with me."

Her voice jarred Taylor awake and she looked at me, blurry eyed, then to her grandmother. "Grammy? What are you doing here?"

"I could ask you the same thing, cupcake. Don't you think this behavior is a bit questionable? You're in a boy's bed for crying out loud!"

"Shhh! Grammy, you'll wake everyone in the house. And I'm not going anywhere. I'm staying here tonight."

"Taylor!" she gasped.

"What? Is *my* behavior inappropriate? Would it be better if we were screwing in a stall on pile of hay?" All the oxygen in the room swirled and circumvented into Taylor's grandmother's gaped mouth. "That's right. I heard the last of your sordid story Don't sit in judgment, Grams. I'm spending the night with Riley. You on the other hand, can take your sanctimonious self home and *wonder* what I'm doing in his bed. I'm not planning on having sex, but if I do, that will be *my* business."

The door slammed against its frame and Lydia Daniels's feet clicked loudly on the stairs, the echo following her out the entry door.

I kissed Taylor, welcoming the taste of minty toothpaste on her tongue and the torturous way it stroked the roof of my mouth. I focused on her lips, swollen and covered in a dewy sheen.

"So you're thinking about having sex with me, huh?" I teased.

"Riley Martin, I'm *always* thinking about having sex with you."

Sixteen
MORNING HANGOVER
Taylor

Riley's breath felt warm on the back of my neck, the raspy sounds of a snore rattling deep in his throat. I turned, nuzzled my head under his chin, feeling his arms constrict tighter.

"Morning," I whispered, praying my morning breath wasn't lethal.

His eyes remained shut, but the corners of his lips pulled. "Shhh. Don't remind me. If I don't open my eyes, you won't disappear."

"I'm only going to disappear across the hall to the bathroom. Keep the bed warm for me?"

"Better hurry. You could have company if *Riley Jr.* discovers its morning."

I giggled and lightly kissed the smile on his face, before tiptoeing to the bathroom. There were no signs of life, all the bedroom doors shut. When I'd finished my business, I opened the bathroom door, finding Riley leaning against the door frame. I also noticed other parts of Riley awake. His boxer shorts showed obvious signs of being tighter than normal.

"You ogling, woman?"

"Impressive," I commented before scurrying back across the hall and burrowing beneath the covers. I snuggled into the spot in the sheets still warm from Riley's body heat.

He snuck in beside me, his cold feet brushing mine. When I tried to move away from the icy appendages, he trapped me inside his arms and tucked his toes between my legs.

"Riley!" I gasped, only to have my protest silenced by a deep kiss. Hands slipped under my sweatshirt, his cool fingers feeling alarmingly wonderful on my bare breasts. "Riley," I moaned quietly.

I fisted my hands in the sides of his T-shirt, pushing the fabric up so I could taste his chest. Salty—a musky smell caught in the fine hairs tickling my cheeks. He yanked his shirt off, then mine. I didn't protest, relishing the wonderful feel of skin on skin. Soft, warm, brushing—a silky slide, opening every nerve ending.

Maybe it was Grammy's lecture, her hidden secret, or my mother's weakness toward my father that fueled my need to be reckless. In any event, I didn't censure Riley's advances, until he slid his hands slid inside the waistband of my sweatpants.

"No, Riley—I'm not ready."

"No, not okay. I'm dying here, Taylor. I want to go to the next level. I don't want bits and pieces of you. I want you, baby. *All* of you." He kissed me hard, his fingers tickling the sensitive skin below my navel.

I shoved against his chest. "I said no! Can't you take what I can give right now without pushing for more?"

He flipped onto his back, heaved a loud, frustrated huff. I pillowed my head on his chest, listening to his heart slam against his ribs. His fingers pulled through the strands of my hair, twirling circles on my bare back that sent shivers down my spine.

"Is it that Michael guy? Have you taken some oath of celibacy?"

"While Michael would like to be the one to *pop* my cherry, it isn't happening. I told you, Riley, I don't like Michael that way." I crawled on top of Riley, pressing my lips to his. "If there's any 'cherry picking' to be done, I think I'd like you to be the one doing it."

His smile was so wide it had to hurt. Something crinkled in his fingers and he held up a bright blue foil packet. "So I should keep a couple *lozenges* in my pocket, just in case?"

"Sounds like a good plan. 'Be prepared' like a good Boy Scout." Our next kissing frenzy was interrupted by the sound of a door closing in the hallway.

"Shit! 'Parent alert'." He threw me the sweatshirt I'd been wearing, and quickly pulled on his jeans and a T-shirt.

"Turn over and pretend you're asleep," he whispered.

Riley grabbed the bedspread off the bed and wrapped into a cocoon on the bean bag chair in the corner. The door creaked and Sheriff Martin poked his head inside. Without looking, I could feel the burn of his eyes in the back of my head.

"Riley?" he whispered. Riley faked a raspy half-snore. "Riley!" he hissed.

"Huh?" Riley grumped. "What?"

"Can I see you downstairs?"

I could sense the tension snaking into the room. The bean bag chair squished under Riley's weight and the door creaked shut. I waited to make sure no one remained in the room watching me, before rolling over. The sound of muffled voices carried up the stairwell and under the crack at the bottom of the door. I slipped from bed and peeked into the hall. No one lurked, so I stepped out and perched on the top stair to listen.

"Riley, I'm not sure what to make of this situation. Lydia Daniels is worried sick about her granddaughter and the fact she spent the night in your *bed* isn't helping."

"Dad, we weren't *sleeping* together."

"Riley, you're old enough to be responsible for your actions. Be safe, or be ready to change your name from 'Riley the stud' to 'Riley the dad'."

His dad launched into some lecture about safe sex and casual relationships, all the mundane stuff drilled into teenagers from every angle about abstinence. Except one. The Trojan commercials.

A hand tugged the back of my sweatshirt, startling me. Jaxson took a seat beside me on the step. "I believe the last time I saw you, that tag was on the *inside*." My cheeks warmed. "Way to go, Riley."

"You're wrong, so dial down the 'man parade'. Nothing happened last night. Sorry to disappoint." When I stood, Jaxson's hand wrapped my ankle.

"Too bad. Just so you know, my door doesn't have a lock. Riley sleeps pretty sound. You can come play with me then crawl back next to him and he'd never be the wiser. But *you* would."

"You're a pig. No wonder Riley keeps you hidden. Now let go of my ankle and crawl back under your bridge, before I scream."

Jaxson's hands went up in defense. "Someone's not a 'morning person'."

No longer interested in the discussion downstairs and more concerned with ditching his leering brother, I retreated back into Riley's room. My underwear and dress were washed and folded on the dresser. I must have slept at some point and Riley took care of things, or his mother knows I slept without my underwear. I chose to believe Riley handled matters.

I fastened my bra, slid on my lacy white thong and had my hands trapped inside my dress, suspended over my head, when the door opened. I froze, picturing Jaxson drooling, his Dad clenching his heart, Dirk never looking at my face again, or his mother barring me from coming within a mile of her son.

"Wow. A butterfly tat on your ass! Hot stuff, babe."

Riley.

I yanked my dress over my shoulders and turned to face him, fumbling with the buttons. His hands covered mine, finishing the top two. He kissed me tenderly, pensively, keeping a slight distance. I desperately wanted to drop my eyes to see if there was a big reason he couldn't come closer, but I met his eyes instead.

158

"I should go."

"Let me drive you."

I didn't argue. Walking a mile this early in the morning didn't appeal to me, nor did sitting at Riley's kitchen table and facing his father, or worse, *Jaxson.*

**

We pulled to the side of Grammy's house after nearly disappearing in a couple of deep puddles in the driveway. She would be awake, but I didn't want to go in. I also knew after last night, she wouldn't call me inside either.

Riley looked contemplative, his chin pressed to his fist, gaze somewhere beyond the windshield.

"Penny for your thoughts, handsome."

"Careful, don't bankrupt your trust fund," he grinned, angling to face me.

I giggled. "Seriously, what are you thinking about?"

"Don't make fun of me."

"I won't, I promise."

"See the rocking chairs? It's weird, but I can see you and me sitting in a couple of rockers on a big porch, holding hands and watching the sunset."

"Are we old and gray?"

"Ancient. But you still have a killer bod. My dick will be skinny and poking you while you cook my dinner."

"Gross! Riley Martin, is that all you ever think about?"

"No! I'm offended you find me so shallow," he replied inside a smile and leaned closer. "Sometimes, I picture you naked on a Harley Davidson."

I playfully slapped his chest and he caught my hand, bringing my wrist to his mouth. My bones softened and heat squiggled through my veins.

"Taylor, I've never had a 'picture' before. No one has ever mattered enough for me to see them in my future. Only my present. Taylor Wilson, I love you. Pure and simple. Every time I picture the future, you're inside the frame."

"Riley, you're a hopeless romantic." I stole the soft kiss waiting on his lips. He laid my seat back and plucked a couple of buttons open on my dress. I covered his hand. "Not *here*. Honestly! Besides, Riley Martin, my fantasy 'first time' will not be a memory held in the backseat of a vehicle."

"Nor will it be a fantasy," he teased, his lips open and inviting another deep kiss. "It will be the real deal. Is it okay to tell you a thousand times a day how much I love you?"

"Only a thousand?" I laughed.

"Do you think Grams is watching?" he asked, his eyes dancing with dangerous mischief.

"Undoubtedly."

"Well don't freak out and slap me, but I want to do something for Grammy. Okay, and maybe for me, too."

160

Riley's hand cautiously slid up my thigh and under my dress, the calluses on his palms feeling rough against my skin. Tentative fingers smoothed over my hip and I realized thong underwear was really useless, or maybe in this case, *perfect.*

"I'm not freaking out," I spoke breathy against lips already attacking. Riley's finger slid around the lace edge and for a moment I longed for him touch me. *Really* touch me. But he didn't. His hand traveled slowly back along the track it had taken. However, I decided if he got a "free feel," so did I.

"God! Taylor!" he gasped, his breath hitching and lips trembling over mine when my hand rubbed over the front of his jeans. The moan easing from the back of his throat, vibrated across his tongue, telling me I did something very right. My conscience, however, told me the opposite. I pulled my hand away and Riley fell on top of me like dead weight.

"Sorry. I've never touched a guy before. Did I do it wrong?"

"Oh, hell no. Two more seconds and I could sing the' Hallelujah Chorus'." His breaths were short and fast against my cheek. "Damn girl. Stay still and give me a minute, okay? One wrong move and its going to be a repeat of my 'birthday nightmare'. Sure you don't want your first time to be in a truck? I mean technically, we're in the *front* seat."

I laughed. "Somehow doing it in my grandma's driveway in broad daylight doesn't work for me. I want darkness, candles, and to happen outside."

"Outside?"

161

"Yeah. Doesn't the thought of your naked body exposed to the wind sound sexy? Making love for the first time under the stars sounds so romantic."

"Okay, can we talk about something else? *Anything* else? Please."

I kissed him, wishing for darkness with the Milky Way brighter than ever…and me, naked in his arms. However, I didn't imagine the truck horn blaring.

"Shit!"

"Aack! What happened?" I cried out, pushing my frightened heart back in my chest.

"Your hand must have tripped the car alarm."

In my lust crazed fantasy, I'd reached again to a newly found favorite spot, but apparently pushed the lump in his *pocket*, first. Riley flipped into his seat with lightning speed, reaching for the key fob.

The honking stopped, but the silence proved equally frightening. Grammy stood at the driver's side window, dipping her tea bag…for heaven knows how long.

Seventeen
REALITY BITES
Riley

I tugged the dog shit brown polo over my head and tried to decide
if one button or two buttons undone made it look any better. *BARNEY'S*
embroidered in a complimentary mustard color across my left breast
didn't help, either. I was scared to death to turn around and see the
embarrassing life-size bowling ball poised under the huge gold letters
BARNEY'S FAMILY FUN CENTER plastered across my whole
backside. If wearing the awful shirt wasn't enough, Barney required
that I wore it *tucked* in the waistband of khaki pants. *Pleated* pants.
Hell, I looked like my old man in my "fluffed" front, minus the beer
gut.

When Barney called to tell me I could have the job I'd begged for
before summer started, I almost turned him down. The timing sucked.
But, he promised to work around my soccer schedule and give me
every other Saturday off. Luckily, the place closed Sundays. I just had
to suffer the humiliation of *serving* my friends on Friday nights, instead
of hanging out.

Damn. I needed the money, especially with my goal to accomplish
a miracle and graduate early. I'd have to help with expenses if I wanted
to go to a decent college. Maybe someplace close to Harvard? Close to
Taylor, whose company I needed on a daily basis in order to breathe.
Whose lips and tongue playing inside my mouth I would miss tonight

because I had to *work*. My first Friday night without Taylor. I hated the job already.

Only a couple of weeks remained before school started and I wanted to spend every second with her. Spending my nights and weekends spraying the insides of stinky bowling rental shoes or busing tables didn't fit into my current plan. However, my bank account had nearly dried up with no sign of being replenished any time soon.

I wanted to get Taylor something awesome to remember me by when she went back to Boston. My mom's business partner and best friend from high school, Pam, who lived in New York and did most of the buying for Mom's boutique, told me about these cool sterling silver charm bracelets the girls were into. The damn thing took my last hundred dollars and I hadn't even bought the heart charm to go on it. That was another hundred dollars because it had a real diamond in the center.

Pam kept the bracelet for me so Mom wouldn't find out and lecture me about expensive gifts, diamonds for girls, or whatever other guilt tactics she could use to keep me from giving Taylor the bracelet. Too bad. Taylor held my heart and I wanted her symbolically to take it with her. Besides, Michael would see it.

Michael. I fought to beat down the jealousy that flew to the surface every time I thought about him asking Taylor to marry him. And more frightening, her actually thinking about saying *yes* to the "King of Virtue." I wondered if he had a small penis and that's why he acted like some pompous idiot. Taylor confessed that day in her grandma's

164

driveway that she'd never touched a guy, so she wouldn't know until it was too late.

If he demanded Taylor be a virgin, no one probably handled his precious *jewels* either. Or did they? Did Michael, who I'd chosen to call "needle-dick" if for no other reason than to boost my own self-confidence, believe himself above the rules of chastity? Maybe he spent his time sampling the "buffet table" before settling down with the "main course." The thought made my stomach roll, and not because Taylor existed as the main dish, but because she deserved someone who thought she was everything from hors d'oeuvres through dessert.

My cell phone chimed, swirling my thoughts to present, but not far from where they'd traveled. Taylor. I pushed my murderous thoughts aside. Taylor loved me, not Michael and I had to start believing that.

"Hey baby? Missing me?"

"You only left here thirty minutes ago," she laughed, the sound of her voice musical. "But, yeah, actually I am. What time's your dinner break? I have this unbelievable craving for French fries. Maybe I'll even stick around until you get off...*work* that is."

"Vicious and beautiful. I have to work until midnight, so you *getting me off* tonight isn't happening unless you sneak out."

"Not an impossible task. You could text me when you're leaving and I'll meet you."

"After what happened the other night? You and I may be put in cages."

Last Friday night when I took Taylor home at promptly 11:59, I'd barely climbed into bed with all my steamy thoughts and the taste of her lips still on mine, when I received *the* text.

Can you sneak out? I'm thinking there's a full moon, a sky full of stars qualifying as heavenly candles, and well, maybe tonight...

I certainly didn't need a second invite. My jeans were on, a fresh splash of cologne and my teeth brushed in record time. I tiptoed down the stairs, avoiding all the floor boards Jax showed me squeaked, sneaking out the back patio door to avoid Lucky, sequestered in the laundry room.

By the time I drove the mile stretch between our houses with my headlights off, I'd developed perfect night vision. Parking my truck around the bend in the street in case her grandmother looked out the front window, I walked back and kept close to the hedge edging the property, out of view of the outside lights. Once around back and verifying no lights burned on the main floor, but Taylor's bedroom still glowing, I sent her the text.

I'm here.

She looked out her bedroom window and I waved my open cell phone so she'd see the light. Maybe a minute passed before she crept out the back sliding door and tiptoed across the wooden deck until her bare feet hit the grass. She took off on a run and jumped into my open arms, wrapping her legs around my waist, and proceeded to devour my face off.

We tumbled to the ground, behind the two pine trees framing the back corner of the yard. My hands made a once over her chest to verify nothing other than the knit camisole came between my fingers and her boobs. Meanwhile, her hand made sure *Riley Jr.* was awake and responding to her gentle squeeze.

Dear God, let it be tonight before my balls explode.

My T-shirt disappeared fast, or maybe ripped apart by Taylor's fingers, clawing at the fabric. Her mouth bathed my chest with wet kisses and she purposely lingered a few seconds over a couple of spots, sending my eyeballs rolling in their sockets.

I kissed her hot lips with a savage demand, relishing the feel of our tongues darting in and out of each other's mouths, twisting, sliding from tonsils to teeth. My skin prickled with so many nerves splayed open and raw. I pushed her camisole over her head. Her hair spread across the grass in a sexy halo around her head. Her skin smelled fruity, tasted both salty and sugary, and felt like expensive silk in my hands. *Delicate...*wonderful.

Taylor's fingers raked through my hair as I ravished her mouth, kissed the pulsing spots on her neck, nibbled earlobes, licked the salt from her skin every inch I tasted and touched with hands and lips, sometimes soft—teasing, other moments losing control and selfishly taking.

I pulled back, needing to fill my lungs with air, stop my heart from exploding, but the sight of her body shimmering in a damp sheen under the moon light from where my mouth sampled, drove me near insanity. She was beautiful and about to be mine completely.

Trying to be suave while out-of-my-mind horny, I clumsily tugged down the cotton pajama bottoms covered in tiny green frogs, and swallowed my tongue when she lay there wearing only pink lacy panties. It took everything I had to slow down at that point and not rush the moment—the moment I'd prepared my entire teenage hormone crazed life for. A single fragment of time that would change both our lives.

Taylor popped the snap open on my jeans and tugged my zipper down. When her hand slipped over *Riley Jr.* through the knit fabric of my boxers, there was no more slowing down. I could feel my heartbeat pound in every cell of my body. I tore the corner off my *lozenge* with my teeth when she pushed my boxers off, so I'd be ready—*responsible.* Her hands locked behind my neck and she pulled me back to her.

I slid my hand over her panties, the rough edges of my fingertips snagging the fabric. She moaned in my mouth and arched to fit my touch.

Shit.

Shaking, I peeled the last layer away. Her body shuddered beneath me when I eased on top of her and I stilled, committing the moment to memory—the feel of her warm satiny skin running the length of mine, her eyes dark and mesmerizing, lips full, damp and open, with breath smelling of minty toothpaste and panting hot against my cheek.

Time stood still, locked until we turned the key. I trembled with anticipation—*fear.*

"Are you sure?" I whispered over her ear, barely able to speak the words.

Taylor drew a short breath, "Yes, I'm sure. I want this. You."

Her lips pressed mine, the kiss tearing down all the cautionary walls, erasing the boundaries, and giving permission. Her leg wrapped my hip and I fumbled through the blades of grass and clenched the foil packet.

"God, I love you, Taylor, " I declared, taking her mouth, her body rising to meet me.

My mind swirled deliriously as we explored each other with tentative fingers, bruising our lips in hungry, demanding kisses and at times breathing so hard I felt dizzy and then…not breathing at all.

A sudden flood of light washed through the pine needles, reeling both of us back into bodies that felt alien. Taylor quickly pulled up her pants and I flipped on my back, tugged my jeans on and carefully zipped over a very painful throbbing. Damn! My fourteenth birthday all over again. At least Taylor didn't know.

She walked into the light to face the enraged woman stomping across the back deck, deflecting attention from me. I could barely stand, let alone run, but I had no choice. I grabbed my sneakers, shoved my boxers in my back pocket, and balled my T-shirt in my fists, then slipped behind the hedge.

Several burrs punctured through my socks and pricked the bottom of my feet by the time I'd walked the property line back to my truck. I waited in the black silence, watching out the back window for a "shotgun wielding" Lydia Daniels. Suddenly, my body convulsed from the adrenalin rush, and I threw up in my T-shirt.

After twenty minutes passed, I saw the upstairs bedroom lights shut off. Whatever happened was over. I took the back road and circled back home on the highway, a six mile diversion, but with headlights. When I pulled back into the driveway I debated whether to text Taylor, but decided against it, in case her grandmother took her cell phone. Lydia Daniels was too old to spend life behind bars for a double murder.

**

Taylor's voice in my ear evaporated the sultry memory, pulling me back into the conversation, but not without consequence. I adjusted in the driver's seat to find a more comfortable position without much luck. I'd just have to wait it out and hope I could drive with crossed eyes.

"Grammy still doesn't know you were with me. She thinks I went out to stargaze because I couldn't sleep, which isn't a total lie."

"She had to know, Taylor. I must have trampled a dozen tomato plants making my getaway. Plus, she gave me the stink eye in church. Did you ever check out there to make sure we didn't leave anything behind?"

"Why? You missing a body part? I know I yanked pretty hard when I jumped."

170

Taylor laughed, but I didn't. That *yank* deflated my macho image of holding off until *I* decided to let go. Taylor controlled *everything* in my life.

"Very funny. *Riley Jr.* is not detachable."

"Too bad."

I paused a beat in shock.

"Where has my shy, but insanely sexy girlfriend gone?"

"Girlfriend? Really?"

I started my truck and backed out of the driveway, hoping no one patrolled this part of town right now. Driving the speed limit *and* getting to work on time wouldn't happen.

"Yeah. *Girlfriend*…at the very least. I get a thirty minute break at 6:30. Wear something low cut so I can chuck fries into your bra for a late night snack. Love ya, babe."

I yawned wide.

"Well, about time you woke up 'Sleeping Beauty'. Spend the night texting that Martin kid instead of sleeping? I thought once he started working, you'd settle down."

"What do you mean by that? I'm *settled* fine, thank you."

"Like hell you are, cupcake. Want waffles?"

Grammy started pouring batter into the waffle iron so it would be useless arguing.

"Sure."

I'd meet Riley for lunch later. It sucked he had to work on a Saturday, but at least with the day shift, we could do something later tonight. Our half hour dinner date last night and a steamy kiss goodbye left my body restless all night.

"At least you haven't snuck out to meet him anymore."

My inner alarm pinged. "What are you talking about?"

"The other night? When you came out from behind the pine trees with some story about watching the moon? I got suspicious when I noticed your top on backwards, but when I didn't see Mr. Martin's truck I dismissed my paranoia to you getting dressed in the dark and not paying attention. Until the next morning when I found this."

Grams reached into her robe pocket—the only robe she owned—the robe she wore when she dang near caught Riley and me in our compromising position. She slapped a ripped red *lozenge* package on the table next to my plate. A vague memory of Riley fumbling with the package with one hand while torturing me to the brink of insanity with the other, slipped into my head, flushing my cheeks hot.

"Doesn't look like he got a chance to try it on for 'size'. Please tell me that's because I stopped you and not because things got out of control too fast."

I felt her burning gaze, but I didn't turn around. I just stared at the crumpled package on my napkin.

"Nothing happened," I confessed in a small voice.

We ate breakfast in silence. When she took my plate to the sink to rinse off, I slipped the embarrassing proof in my pocket and walked up to my room. I'd almost hit the last stair when the phone rang.

I wanted to race back down the stairs to grab it in case it was Riley, to spare him the humiliation of another one of Grammy's self-righteous lectures. She answered cheerfully, so I trudged up to my room, partially upset it wasn't Riley, but relieved at the same time. However, that momentary rush of relief ended with her next statement.

"Taylor? Phone's for you. It's *Michael*."

Damn!

I grabbed the phone from her and stomped upstairs to my room, slamming the door. Grammy undoubtedly stood in the hall with a glass to the wall. I opened the window and sat on the floor below, facing the wall to deflect the conversation from her curious ears.

"Hey, Michael. How's Boston?" I asked, trying to sound like I cared.

"Lonely. When are you coming back? I thought you were just going for a couple of weeks, not the whole summer. I miss you, Taylor."

"That was my original plan, but I'm just not ready to come home."
Face my parents...see you.

"I heard about the divorce. Sorry, kid."

"Don't call me *kid.* You know I hate it."

"What's with the attitude? I've always called you 'kid'. You are three years younger than me, which I like, by the way. Keeps you *teachable.*"

I knew what he meant and cringed at the memory, instinctively curling into myself. "Don't go there."

A dark chuckle sounded. "Oh come on. You can't be serious. That's ancient history and was nothing, you know that."

If it's so "ancient" how come you knew immediately what I was talking about, Ass.

The whispered rumors about Michael's fetish for girls who "put out" were dismissed as frat party antics worthy a college boy. Deep down, I knew otherwise. The silver-spoon-fed-trust-fund-baby thought rules didn't apply to him. However, his ultimate bragging right, the one he announced to the world whenever he had the chance, was that he'd only marry a *virgin.* I represented his "prize."

I, on the other hand, decided after my last "lesson" from Michael, when my moment of surrender came it would be with the body of the boy *I* loved....not my family's choice. Michael didn't fit that mold. Riley did.

But just as I felt free of my dark past, the harsh reminder of a promise I'd made in a moment of fear, spoke through the receiver.

"Taylor? Babe, you still there?"

"Yeah, I'm here. Michael, I think we should cool things. I'm not ready for marriage. I'm only eighteen. I want to wait a couple of years."

"*What?* But I've planned a fall wedding, right before the holidays press in. We can honeymoon in Los Cabos for a few weeks and be back by Christmas. I've found an apartment close to campus and when you come back next week, we'll go shopping for furniture."

"*Next week*? I'm not coming home next week. In fact, I might stay with Grammy until I start Harvard in January."

"If I didn't know better, Taylor, I'd think you were breaking our engagement. Is there someone else? What about your sworn 'promise' to me?"

A promise made in fear...an oath pledged for sanctuary.

On the eve of my eighteenth birthday, I saw the dark side of Michael—one the elite society of Boston didn't know. His mother threw me a "pre-birthday" dinner party, but only invited *her* friends. A couple of Michael's fraternity brothers stopped by and Mr. Barnes invited them to stay. After dinner, I joined them and Michael for a game of pool, during which, the glasses increased on the bar counter, the stares my direction becoming long and awkward.

Michael watched me intently as I chalked the end of my pool cue. I placed the cue over the knuckle of my first finger, crinkled one eye to target a green striped ball for the corner pocket, and gave him a flirty wink in hopes his steely glare would soften.

His friends made a couple of crude comments about how I rubbed the cue between my fingers and the way my butt looked bent over the pool table. I scraped the tip of the cue stick across the felt when Michael slammed his glass on the bar. Shards of glass rained across the deep maroon fabric, sparkling like diamonds under the overhead lamp. I jumped back, clamped my hand over my mouth to silence the shrill.

Michael leveled a deadly glare at this comrades. "Get out. Game's over," he ordered. He glanced at me, frozen in the doorway. Behind me, the party ensued unaware of events playing out a few feet away. "Taylor, get my keys and wallet off my dresser. I'm taking you home."

I mentally counted the empty glasses behind Michael. *Driving* didn't seem the best idea.

"Michael, it's okay, I can call my dad—"

"Didn't I tell you to do something, girl? Don't argue."

The room seemed to tilt when I stepped backward, clumsily knocking the doorjamb. As I climbed the main staircase, Michael took the one off the kitchen. When I walked in his room, something felt off—the air warm, perfumed, the inky blackness too thick. The hairs on my neck rose. I flipped the switch, but no lights came on. From the faint light in the hall, I could see the glint of his keys and the black leather wallet folded to the side.

When I lifted wallet, the light from the hall disappeared and the door clicked shut. My heart bounced and I fumbled for the toggle to the lamp. A hand covered mine, the scent of expensive cologne choking the air I fought to breath, the weight of a body pressed behind me.

Michael.

"Don't. I like feeling my way through the dark and listening to your reaction to my touch," he whispered in a husky timbre. His lips pressed my neck. "Tonight, I want show you something new."

Warning bells clanged in my brain. I didn't need to learn something *new*. "Old" still felt like a learning curve. When I stiffened against the touch of his fingers gliding down my arms, Michael's lips curled over my ear, his breath hot.

"Relax, baby. I'm not going to do anything you won't like, trust me." The fingers on one hand tangled with mine, his other hand sliding around my stomach. He wrenched my arm behind my back.

"Ouch! Michael, that hurts." I made the mistake of reaching back with my free arm, and he grasped both hands in a grip behind my back.

I tried to wiggle free when his hand deliberately explored my chest over my silky blouse before slipping underneath, and he wrenched my arm tighter until I folded to the floor. His body crushed mine into the carpet.

"What the hell was that about tonight? Flirting with my friends to make me jealous?"

"No I wasn't," I argued.

"Are you calling me a liar?"

"No, but—"

In the blackness I didn't see it coming, but the painful sting tingled over the top of my head and along the side of my left cheek. The coppery taste of blood seeped from the corner of my mouth. I pressed a hand to my face, feeling the throbbing against my palm from where he'd slapped me. I started to cry.

"See what you made me do!" He stroked my cheek and pressed a kiss to my bruised lip. "I'm sorry baby, really, but you've got to understand, no one can ever love you as much as me. I won't let them."

Champagne slobbered in my mouth and his tongue hit the back of my throat, making me gag. He tugged at the zipper on my jeans and when I fought against his hands, he pinned my arms with his knees.

"Stop fighting me! You'll *never* win."

"D-Don't force me to do this," I choked, struggling to stay calm.

"*Force* you? Baby, when I'm ready to take you, and I *will,* you won't fight me." His hand moved over the front of my jeans and cupped hard between my legs—a place no boy had ever touched. "No, I'm not taking your precious virginity tonight, but you've got to realize you're mine, Taylor." His fingernails scraped my skin as pushed his hand inside my pants, his fingers probing deep. I gasped against the pain.

"Swear you'll never let another guy touch you." When I didn't answer, he pushed hard.

"Okay, I swear!"

Michael pulled his hand away, slapped my thigh. "That's my good little girl."

I curled into a ball, shoved the wallet that had fallen to the floor between my teeth to keep from screaming. Michael bent around me, pushing my hair away so he could kiss my neck.

"Marry me, Taylor. I'll give you a good life." I flinched when his hand rounded my hip. "Say you'll marry me. Tell me you love me."

I whimpered the words he wanted to hear, knowing he'd keep attacking if I didn't. When I begged him to let me go home, Michael brushed the hot side of my face.

"Give me your word you won't say anything about our rough play? I'd hate for your daddy to get the wrong idea. After all, he's up for partnership."

I rolled back, pushed against Michael's chest. "Leave my dad out of this. He's earned that partnership. Playing this against him isn't fair." He held his hand flat, inches away from my cheek. "If you hit me again, he'll figure it out." His fingers curled into a fist and my stomach dipped. "I promise I won't say anything."

No one would believe me, anyway. You're "Michael Barnes."

Luckily, my parents never waited up for me so I snuck upstairs without anyone knowing. I scrubbed my body in the shower until my skin felt raw and the water turned cold.

By morning, the red mark faded, leaving only the corner of my lip swollen. I pushed what had happened into the deep recesses of my brain, stupidly dismissing Michael's behavior to too much champagne, even convincing myself I shared the blame—until I rounded the corner to the kitchen. The ugly events of the night before suddenly became the tip of a larger iceberg about to slam into my lifeboat.

Mom and Dad sat formidably across from each other at the table. Neither even held a cup of coffee. Dad's suitcase sat waiting in the corner by the back door. Mom stared out the window, avoiding any eye contact when I walked in. Dad shifted in his chair, his eyes darted from me to my mother.

"Taylor, honey, sit. We need to talk to you," he said, his tone flat.

They announced their divorce in such a casual, cavalier declaration you would have thought they discussed paint colors. I decided the "happy news" about my forced nuptials could wait. In fact, I decided a lot of things in the twenty minutes I sat numbly listening to them advise me of the visitation schedule they'd so thoughtfully planned.

Happy Birthday to me. A sentiment, by the way, I never heard from either of them. Mom's steely glare at Dad and his sheepish expression clued me to the finer details without them being disclosed.

No way did I want this lifestyle. *Ever.* No marriage—no Michael and his controlling, abusive behavior, and definitely *no* splitting weekends between Mom and Dad's new family. I decided that moment to leave Boston and go live with Grammy.

**

The nightmarish flashback gave me renewed resolve. I deserved better and had found what I needed in Riley. Kind, loving, and accepting. The opposite of Michael Barnes…of my parents.

I sucked a brave breath. "Michael, I'm not the same frightened girl who left Boston a few months ago. Yes, I guess I am ending our engagement, if you want to call your physical threat such a term of endearment." For once, I hoped Grammy *did* eavesdrop.

"Taylor, I did *not* threaten you."

"Are you joking? You know what you did to me! I told you I'd marry you only to stop you from hurting me." Tears pushed forward and I dropped to the edge of my bed to keep from fainting.

Michael calmed, but his tone scolded. "Taylor, I was drunk. I felt awful the next morning when I realized what a jackass I'd been. But by the time I got off work, you were gone. I never got a chance to say goodbye, let alone apologize."

I didn't give him an inch, sent back a snarky response. "So why now? I've only received a handful of texts or emails since I left, none mentioning an 'I'm sorry'. This is the first time you've even called. I figured you found someone else to ease your guilty conscience."

"I get it. You're hurt and mad. But don't direct your anger at your parents' breakup at me."

"You're a piece of work, Michael. My parents have nothing to do with this."

I bit my bottom lip hard to push down the rage. I inhaled another deep breath, fearless with Michael thousands of miles away.

"You know what, Michael Barnes? You disgust me. I'm not forgiving you and I never want you call me again. We're so done!"

I tossed the phone onto the bed and screamed into the quilt lying to my side. Brushing frustrated tears from my cheeks, I marched to the closet and proceeded to get ready to meet Riley. Midnight curfew tonight would be violated. I needed to erase Michael and all the bad memories, and the best way to do that would be to make new ones. Before leaving my bedroom, I dropped *two* "lozenges" into my purse.

Nineteen
A GLIMPSE INTO THE FUTURE
Riley

Taylor's silhouette framed against the shaft of afternoon light when the door opened, started my heart racing. I'd already ordered our cheeseburgers and fries, waiting until she sat her perky bottom on the chair before punching the time clock. I wanted every single second of my thirty minute break spent with her.

She wore my favorite light blue sweater with a neckline low enough if she bent forward, I got a view of what bra she wore, not to mention catch a whole lot of fries.

"Hey, baby. How's my favorite girl?" She leaned across the table and pecked my lips. Blue and pink stripes covered my two favorite "hand holds."

"Are you checking out my bra?"

"Guilty as charged. I don't think I've seen this particular one. Is it part of a matching set?"

She laughed, "Yes, not that you're going to see, however."

I clutched my heart. "I'm wounded! Why would you deprive me from the simplest joy?"

Taylor pushed a torn, crinkled foil packet across the table with her finger. "Grammy found this."

"Shit. Busted. Too bad. If I remember, it smelled like strawberries."

"Riley you're impossible!"

"And you're beautiful. So I'm thinking I get off at seven. Why don't we order a pizza and hang at my place and make-out until your carriage turns into a pumpkin?"

"You have to tend Dirk, don't you?"

"Am I that transparent? Afraid so. Jaxson starts graveyards again and Dad finally has a night off so he's taking Mom on a date."

"Sounds wonderful, actually. I could use someplace to hide tonight."

"Oh? Care to indulge me?" I waved a fry in front of her nose, watching her eyes cross. "I'll trade you a greasy potato stick for information."

"Michael called."

The fry dropped from my fingers and I pulverized it against the table with my thumb. "So what did 'Mr. Wonderful' want?"

"He wants to know when I'm coming home."

Hating the whirlwind of emotions building, jealousy gaining fast, I leveled my gaze to hers and let a fake smirk pull one corner of my mouth. "You told him *never,* didn't you? That you are madly in love with a guy who looks insanely hot in a polo shirt and pleated khakis?"

Taylor's eyes dropped and her smile disappeared. My world wobbled. Something felt wrong, scaring me.

"Lie to me, Taylor. Tell me I don't have to worry about this Michael dude. Please."

184

She looked away, but I still caught the shimmer of tears in her eyes. A lump rolled down her slender throat and a deep sigh pushed her boobs upward. Another hard swallow slid before she faced me.

"Riley, can we not talk about this right now? You have to get back to work in a few minutes and I don't want to spend it talking about stupid shit like Michael Barnes." She reached across the table and took my hands. "I love *you*, Riley. Not Michael."

The wicked smile on her lips barely eased my anxiety.

"Can you come out to my car for a few minutes and play 'tongue tag'? Maybe you could check out my new *stripes*, and later, if we drug Dirk and get him to bed early, you can check to see if my tattoo shows through?"

We left our half eaten burgers on the table and headed for the Mini.

**

I think Dirk had as big a crush on Taylor as me. He managed to plant himself between the two of us during the movie, laughing at everything Taylor said. When I tried to stretch my arm behind him to touch the angel driving my hormones insane, Dirk pretended to scratch the back of his head, knocking my arm away. I allowed that for about five minutes.

"Hey, dufus, move my arm again and I'm going to tell Taylor you're in love with her and want to kiss her.

"I do not! You're such a loser!"

"Riley," Taylor scowled, pushing the most adorable sexy pout on her lips. "Stop teasing. I already know Dirk is madly in love with me, and because he put more popcorn in my bowl than you did, I'm thinking of dumping you and dating him."

Dirk turned three shades of red and giggled. Taylor twirled a lock of his hair making it worse. "Tell you what, Dirk. If you'll go upstairs and leave me alone with Riley so I can break up with him in private, I'll give you a kiss goodnight."

He didn't have time to react. Taylor cupped his face in her hands and planted a big kiss on his lips. Dirk's eyes went wide. He quickly rubbed her kiss off his mouth.

"Gross!" He handed me the bucket of popcorn. "She's all yours."

We couldn't help laughing. Taylor instantly filled the space between us, curling under my waiting arm. "Night, Dirk." She blew him a kiss and he took off up the stairs, shutting the door.

"You're wicked, Taylor."

"I think he tried to slip me the tongue. Want to check and see if you can taste his breath in my mouth?"

I recoiled into the corner of the couch. "Okay, now you're grossing *me* out." I'd also strategically stretched my legs out, making a nice "body bed" for Taylor to lie on. She played into my tangled web of deceit, slowly crawling on top of me until her lips fit perfectly against mine.

"You're so obvious, Riley Martin."

"I know, and you fall for it every time."

"I fall for *you* every time."

My arms folded around her and I braided my fingers through her silky hair. "Taylor, I know we're young, but I'm serious when I say I can't see my future without you. My heart hurts thinking about you leaving me in a couple of weeks."

"What if I told you I was thinking of waiting until after Christmas to leave?"

"I'd say I'm the happiest guy in the world. But then what?"

"Well, you said you were going to graduate early, and I don't start Harvard until January, so maybe we could go to college *together*."

"I hate that my birthday missed the cut off and I'm a year behind you in school. It makes *you* seem so old."

"What? Are you saying I'm *old*?" Taylor shrieked, tickling my sides.

"Okay! Stop!" I fingered a loose golden curl. "So why Harvard? Does this have to do with Michael? You never did tell me about your phone call."

Taylor sat up. "Thanks for the major buzz kill, Riley."

I remained reclined in the corner of the couch, but raised my knee for Taylor to lean against. I watched as she fiddled with her fingers, picking at them like they were covered in lint.

"Babe. Talk to me."

She pulled her knees to her chest. "My dad is up for partnership with his law firm—the firm Michael's father owns. Because of my grades and more so, Michael's interest in me, I received a scholarship to Harvard from the firm. Most of the lawyers who work there, including

Dad, are Harvard alumni. If I turn it down, I might put his partnership in jeopardy."

"Wait. I thought you wanted to be a teacher."

"I do, but with my dad's law office backing me, I have a good chance of becoming an associate attorney there and working my way up the ranks. Then I could move to any law firm I wanted. The pay is a damn straight more than being a teacher."

But Michael works there. He'll be working his way up the ranks, too. Taylor's.

I had to choose my words carefully. I brushed her hair over her shoulder so I could watch her face.

"But would you be happy as a lawyer?"

What about me? Where did I fit in? Did I fit in? Shit.

I mentally tore down the caution tape. "What about Michael? Me?"

She snuggled back onto my chest. "You'd be with me in Boston, remember? Michael and I would run into each other at the office, but my heart and mind would be constantly lusting you. Besides, the only attorney job that appeals to me would be one that helps people who can't afford an attorney. Unfortunately, doing work for "free" isn't something Michael's firm believes in, so my time there would be short."

A minute near Michael is too long.

What was I thinking? I couldn't afford Harvard, even if I got accepted. But, I also couldn't lose Taylor. This fantasy bubble was about to burst if I didn't come up with a new one *fast.*

"What if you could go to any college, where would you go?"

"Well, Cornell University is probably ranked the highest, but I like the idea of University of Colorado in Denver. Far away from Boston."

"And Michael."

"Yes, and Michael. What about you?" She slid her lips across mine. "What college do you want to go to when you *grow up*?"

"Ouch! Hit me with the age thing. I told you. I want to be a pediatrician. Cornell would be great, but too expensive and too close to the ghosts from your past. California has earthquakes. Colorado sounds perfect."

Taylor raised her little finger. "Pinky swear that one year from now if we're still madly in love with each other, we'll meet under the school marquee at University of Colorado on the first day of school."

A whole year?

I pushed the panic down and linked my baby finger around hers. "I 'pinky swear' that in one year I'll still be insanely in love with you and will go wherever makes you happy." I tugged her closer, teasing her lips open with my tongue and tasting deep. "I just want you to be happy, Taylor."

And with me.

Her eyes sparkled with unshed tears. "No one's ever asked me what would make me happy."

"Well, I am. Your happiness is vital to mine, got that?" She nodded and I kissed the tear trickling over her cheek, hating to see her sad.

God, I loved her so much. I desperately wanted to know about her phone call with Michael, but I didn't want to cause her anymore pain.

Instead, I hooked my finger in the neckline of her shirt and pulled it out. "Hey, didn't you promise me some private time with those stripes? And what about the panties under these tight jeans? Are they like your "Sunday School" ones?"

"Why don't you find out?" she challenged.

I slipped her shirt off without a fight. Pink and blue stripes never looked so sexy. I ran my finger along the inside of the waistband of her jeans until I felt the elastic lace. I hooked my finger through and tugged, testing my *thong* theory.

"Ouch!"

"Church worthy," I laughed.

Her hand smoothed over the aching lump in the front of my jeans. "Boxers or briefs?"

Suddenly, the second stair creaked.

Twenty
LIES AND BROKEN PROMISES
Taylor

Only two weeks remained before I returned home as demanded by
my mother. Riley hated my change of heart, but ever since Grammy
discovered the ripped package with the rubber we intended using,
things had grown horribly uncomfortable between us. She interrogated
me every time I left the house and waited up until I got home to repeat
the same. Riley could only come over when she was there to
chaperone. I didn't dare ask if I could stay longer, nor was I sure I could
handle her constant monitoring.

I started working afternoons at the *Denim and Ruffles Boutique*,
not for the money, but because it got away from the "grandmother
watchdog" and gave me something to do while Riley worked. I also
snagged some killer deals on the new stuff that shipped in on
Thursdays.

At first I worried Mrs. Martin wouldn't speak to me after finding
me tangled with Riley on the basement sofa. How Riley managed to
cover me so fast with the afghan off the back of the couch, shocked me.
I refused to acknowledge he might have performed the same maneuver
on Kaylee enough times to perfect the skill. Still, it bought me enough
time to hide my sweater and bundle the knotted yarn around me. I
almost burst out laughing when she offered hot cocoa to warm me.

Leaving the boutique at four o'clock gave me enough time to get home and change before Riley picked me up at six. I'd barely pulled the Mini into the driveway when my cell phone rang. Expecting Riley, I answered before checking the caller ID.

"Taylor?"

"Dad?" I hadn't talked to my father since the day I indulged myself with a new car and had to actually ask permission to put it on the credit card. Someday, I'd like to know the limit on that card, if it allowed me to purchase a car.

"Hi, sweetheart. Sorry I haven't called, but to be honest, I wasn't sure you'd talk to me."

"Probably not. You left us, Dad. You picked someone else's family and walked out on ours." My world bubbled under a veil of unexpected water and the kernel in my throat threatened to strangle me.

"Taylor, it's more complicated than that. Your mother and I have struggled with our relationship for years."

"Because you've had a hard time being faithful to your marriage vows."

"All right, stop. I didn't call to argue my moral standing. But keep in mind, Taylor, there are two sides to every story. Someday when you're done hating me, ask your mother about her therapist, Dr. Shephard."

His revelation brought me up short. Mom wasn't the best parental example, but not because of immoral behavior. Just self indulgence. I guess taking the literal meaning of lying on a counselor's couch to

192

accept personal *therapy* could be considered "self-indulgent." Given the story Grammy so freely shared with Riley, however, Dad's news shouldn't have surprised me. But it did.

"Are you saying *Mom* had an affair?"

"She's the one who'll have to color in those pictures for you. Jealousy has a way of turning to vengeance if fed, not that that justifies my actions by any means. Speaking of which, I had a strange conversation with Michael yesterday. Is it true you two are no longer an item?"

After my surprise phone call, I wrote Michael an official "Dear John" letter, telling him *in writing* I never wanted to see him again.

My breath hitched. Why did Dad suddenly care about my personal life? I hesitated on wanting to share intimate details but decided if I told him, the message would get back to Michael, reinforcing the fact our relationship had ended.

"Yes. I don't want to marry Michael. I never did. I only pretended to make everyone happy and well, make sure it didn't screw up your chances for partnership. Since I've been at Gram's, I've had time to think about what I want. Dad, I'm not going to Harvard either. I'm sorry if that messes everything up, but I don't want to be a lawyer. I want to be a teacher."

"A *teacher?* Where the hell did this come from? Who's talking such nonsense into your head? Is Michael right? Are you involved with some 'hick' in that godforsaken farm town?"

"I beg your pardon! Not that it's any of your business, but *yes,* I'm dating someone who treats me far better than Michael Barnes ever did. And if you'd paid attention to *my* life the past few years instead of your buffet of vaginas, you'd know I've wanted to be a teacher for a long time. *Never* a lawyer."

Dad's tone edged of steel. I'd crossed a line. "Young lady that's enough ugly talk. You can sling all the mud you want in my face, I don't give a damn. But I've *always* paid attention to your life, as much as your mother allowed. You're right, I didn't know you were serious about being a teacher, but if that's what you want, I'll talk to the board members and get the scholarship withdrawn. But I think you're making a mistake."

"By choosing my own destiny?"

"No Taylor. By throwing away the opportunity of a lifetime. Become a lawyer or not, Harvard University, even if only for the one year, would boost the credentials in your portfolio for whatever career field you choose, not to mention open the doors to any university you want to attend. We can talk more about it when you come home."

"What if I don't come home?"

"Taylor, stop acting like a petulant teenager. Neither your mother nor I will allow you to stay at Lydia's past summer. You need to go to college, *somewhere.*"

"Why do you care, anyway? Shouldn't you be worrying about your *other* so-called 'daughter'?" I jumped in the seat when he yelled back.

"Enough damnit! Life's complicated and messy, Taylor. No one gets the storybook ending. All you can hope for is that the good times outweigh the bad. And another thing, *don't* dismiss a future with Mr. Barnes just yet. Have your fun, but remember Michael can keep you in this lifestyle you've become comfortable living. By the way, what color is the Mini?"

"Blue and white," I answered feeling a ping of guilt in my stomach. "Dad, I'm not changing my mind about Michael. You don't know him. You only know the Michael that comes into the office, not the one who….." I stopped, realizing I almost said things I promised to keep secret to protect my father.

"Everyone has two faces, Taylor. Even you and the 'country bumpkin' jumping your bones."

"Nice one *father*. Again, none of your business, but I'm still a virgin. My 'country bumpkin' respects me, which is more than I can say for the other men in my life. Tell Michael to go to hell. My advice to you, *Daddy,* is find another firm to work for. I've got to go. I have to get ready for a date with my 'hick'."

I flipped my phone shut without saying "goodbye" and wiped my wet cheeks with the back of my hand. The phone rang again, only this time I checked. I wasn't having another bantering contest with "daddy dearest."

"Riley?" A sob heaved in my chest unexpectedly.

"Taylor, what's the matter?"

I felt guilty for finding pleasure in the worrisome sound in Riley's voice. Someone cared about me.

"I just got off the phone with my dad. Not a pleasant conversation, but then, they usually aren't with him."

"Are you okay?"

"Yeah, now that you've called. We still on for tonight?"

The hesitation lasted too long. "About that, babe. Barney called. Andy is sick and Barney said he'll pay me double if I stay and cover his shift. I'll be done by ten and can come by then to hang out if you want."

"Damn! Not tonight," I whined. "I need to see you. You've worked three nights straight! I miss you." Tears rimmed my eyes again.

"I know, I'm sorry. I'll call Barney and tell him 'no'."

Apparently the "self-indulgent" gene ran prominent through me too, but my conscience kept it in check. "No, don't do that. I'm being selfish. Promise to come by later?"

"I promise, and for the record, I'm so damn horny I can't see straight. If I don't see you soon, I may go blind."

"Nice to know you care."

"You know I'm teasing. About going blind. That's a myth."

I laughed. "Thanks, Riley. I needed that. Tell me you love me."

"I love you and for a hell of a lot more reasons than just lusting after you. You rock my world, girl. I'll be there as soon as I can. Maybe I can knock off early for good behavior."

He smacked a loud kiss in my ear and hung up. I sat in my car a while longer, listening to my iPod and allowing myself a good old-fashioned cry fest. Maybe the tears would wash out all the pain inside and make more room for me to love Riley without feeling guilty about hurting him.

Reality bit hard. Dad was right. Harvard University's credentials were golden and my year had been paid for. Riley still had his senior year of high school with lots of dances, football games, and cheerleaders to make out with under the bleachers. I'd be nothing more than a fond memory to him a month after I left here. Riley, however, would hold a piece of my heart long after I went back to Boston. Probably forever.

**

Grammy sat out on the back deck, enjoying the afternoon sun, and of course, her cup of tea.

"You're an habitual dipper. You should seek help," I joked.

"I'll keep that in mind. Care to join me? You look a little forlorn. Want to talk?"

"Dad called."

"Oh."

"Riley cancelled our date. He's coming by later, if that's okay."

A sigh heavy enough to sway the house blew out her nose. "Don't you think it's time you slowed things down with Riley, Taylor? After all, you'll be going home soon and your life will be going a different direction with Michael."

"Actually, Grandma, I broke things off with Michael."

197

Grammy's tea bag stilled, as did the air around us. She shifted in her chair, her eyes narrowed. I watched the brows above her eyes curl tight. "Are you crazy, Taylor? Michael is perfect for you. He spoils you rotten—has a promising future at his father's law office and can give you everything you'll ever want or need. Don't fill your head with silly romantic thoughts about the Martin boy. Your little summer romance is nothing but a teenage fling. Be realistic, Taylor. There's no way it's going to last past the summer."

She turned her focus on the meadow, letting the sting of her words bite silently. A part of me hated that she, like Dad, could possibly be right. Especially about me and Riley. As much as he claimed to love me, being separated such a long distance could cause his heart to wander…not "grow fonder" as the cliché suggested. I watched the feline predators study him when he worked at Barney's and heard their feral growls whenever he publicly kissed me—which he did a lot.

But whether I went to Harvard or not, I couldn't stay in Wellsville forever, or with Grams. We'd murder each other sooner or later. But even if I lost Riley, I wouldn't go running back to Michael. The thought of being with him made my skin want to crawl off my bones.

I leaned against the railing. "Regardless of where this *fling,* as you so callously refer to my relationship with Riley, goes, I know I don't want to spend my life with Michael. Riley's brother, Jaxson, would be a better choice than him, believe me."

Grammy's lips flattened. "You don't mean that, Taylor. You've just been away from Michael too long. The two of you need to rekindle

198

your relationship—spend some time getting to know each other again. Time alone with Michael is precisely what you need to get your priorities back into focus. That's why I invited him here for the weekend."

Air exited my lungs so fast I felt them stick to my ribs. A flicker of rage ignited. Now *Grams* controlled my life! When the hell did *I* get a say in my destiny? My eyes flashed in horror.

"*What*? No! Grammy, say you didn't! You don't understand. I *can't* be with Michael—"

Grandma lifted from her chair, her angry posture matching mine. She closed out the space between us in two incensed steps. "Nonsense!" she interrupted. "Now go upstairs and make yourself presentable. He should be here in an hour or so."

My eyes swam with tears and I felt dizzy. Why the hell did I tell Riley it was okay to work an extra shift? He'd have been here within the hour and we'd be gone. In fact, knowing Michael was coming would have had me convincing Riley to run across the state line and never come back. Hell, I'd even have sex in the truck with him!

In my letter to Michael, I made special mention of his last attempt to "brand me" as his property—a reminder of the monster he kept well hidden. I knew Michael would consider Grammy's invitation as a challenge to reclaim what he felt rightfully *belonged* to him. Me.

The thought made me livid. I moved the extra inch, practically touching Gram's nose. She could feel the spit of every cantankerous word. "I can't believe you did something so underhanded without asking me. This is *my* life. You're no different from my parents."

Grammy blenched at my brashness. "Taylor Wilson! Michael is your fiancé. The way you gallivant around with Riley Martin, it's only a matter of time before you two become intimate and ruin your chances with Michael. You know how he feels about your chastity."

A blustery half-laugh burst from my mouth. "For your information, *Michael* is far from *chaste*. Riley has been nothing but respectable to me that way. If you're still freaking out over the damn hickey, you should know Mr. Barnes's hands haven't exactly been idle on my body."

Her brow arched. "But you're engaged to Michael. It's different. You're his—"

"What? *Property*? I don't think so. And, we are *not* engaged! I'm barely eighteen and not marrying anybody, *chaste* or *unchaste*. For the record, I'm not you or my mother."

Grammy's hand covered her mouth and her eyes widened.

"I wasn't asleep like everyone thought that night at Riley's. I have no intention of repeating history, which is why I broke it off with Michael. I don't want to end up with another control freak in my life, in particular as a *husband.*"

I paced the deck, arms wrapped tight around my stomach. Panic pricked at the idea of confronting Michael, especially after telling him to take a hike. No one *dismissed* Michael Barnes. *Ever.*

"God, Grammy! Why did you invite him here?"

"Because regardless, Taylor, he's still a better choice for your future. You need to spend some time with him before you do something stupid with the Martin kid. In fact, it might be a good idea if you went back home with Michael. I understand he's already found you a place to live. And, I agree with him. A fall wedding would be wonderful. You need to unleash those raging hormones with a man who's right for you. Not some high school jock."

My tennis shoes squeaked against a wood plank when I stopped abruptly. "You know nothing about Riley! He's ten times more of a man than Michael will ever be!" Tears streamed steadily over my cheeks. "Grams, you have no idea what you've done by bringing Michael here. You've sealed my fate."

"Let's hope so." She brushed past me, talking over her shoulder. "Go put on something flirty for your fiancé. Let him appreciate what he's about to lose if he doesn't take charge of this situation."

She slammed the back door and I stood frozen, baking under the August sun. Michael would soon be here. God help me.

**

Grammy sent me back into my room three times until I came out dressed in something she deemed appropriate. Unfortunately, a short floral skirt and lacy camisole. She tousled my hair over my shoulders and pushed my slouching shoulders straight. At this moment, I hated my grandmother. How could she barter my soul without a second thought?

"There. You look feminine and pretty." The doorbell rang and my heart climbed into my throat. "Smile. Your parents spent a fortune on those teeth. Show them off."

She walked down the stairs and I remained hidden around the corner. I tried calling Riley again, but no answer. I wanted him to come as soon as possible and save me from whatever unknown knotted my stomach. I had this sick feeling that by the time Riley arrived, it would be too late.

Michael's voice sounded like a premonition of something horrible sliding out of his mouth. I sent Riley an S.O.S. text praying he got it fast.

Leave work a.s.a.p.! I'm in trouble. xoxo -T.

I felt Michael's evil presence the moment he crossed the threshold and entered the house. His overpowering, expensive cologne wafted up the stairwell, seeking me.

"Mrs. Daniels, have you gotten younger since I've last seen you?" His fake flattery sickened me and Grammy's school girl snigger made me want to vomit.

"Oh, Michael, you're still the charmer, aren't you?"

"The only girl I apparently need to charm is Taylor. Where is she? I can't thank you enough for inviting me here. My heart shattered when I got her letter. I couldn't bear the thought of not having her in my life. I think you're right. We're just missing each other."

"Taylor?" Grammy trilled. "Michael's here."

I pushed against the wall, wishing to melt into the wood. Grammy's feet padded heavily on the stairs. Her fists pushed hard on her hips when she found me hiding around the corner.

"Get your little fanny downstairs!" she demanded quietly, yanking my cell phone from my fingers. I stepped to the top of the stairwell, her whispered warning hot on my ear. "Behave yourself, young lady. He's come a long way to mend things. Give him a chance, for your sake."

For everyone else's sake.

Standing in the doorway to the living room, I faced Michael, strategically poised against the piano, holding a bouquet of red roses. He always knew what gallant gestures to pull off to sway people his way.

I faked a smile and stepped forward…a sacrificial lamb heading to the altar.

Grams morphed instantly into the false "sweet old lady" she used to impress. I went rigid when I saw her grab her purse and car keys.

"Well, I'm just going to leave you two lovebirds alone for a few hours. I've got some errands to run. There's fresh lemonade and ice tea in the refrigerator, and some blueberry muffins Taylor made this morning," she lied. One more on top of the many others.

I grabbed her elbow, a trembled whisper rushing from my mouth. "Don't leave me alone with him, Grammy. Please, I beg you. Stay."

She patted my arm. "You'll be fine. Taylor. He's not going to bite, for heaven's sake."

Biting would be the least of what Michael could do to me. The front door shut, taking all the oxygen from the house in its wake. The snap signified finality. I watched Grammy's shadow shrink away and my body shivered with an unexpected chill.

Michael's feet shifted behind me. I couldn't avoid the inevitable and turned. A malevolent smile twitched on his lips. I imagined the same smile must have graced Lucifer's face when he fell from Heaven.

"Taylor, honey? I hope my visit isn't a total shock. You had to know I wouldn't just give up and walk away." Each word brought him a step closer. His finger lifted my chin so our eyes met. "You're too important to me." He leaned in for a gentle kiss. "Here, these are for you," he said, handing me the roses.

"Thanks. I'll go put them in some water."

He caught my arm, halting my retreat to safety in the kitchen. The timbre of his voice changed. Sinister and threatening.

"No." He took the roses out of my hand and set them on the entry bureau. "We only have a couple hours and I don't want to waste time putting flowers in a stupid vase." His arms wound around my waist, drawing me into him. His lips pressed my neck, nipping their way to my earlobe, where he did place a gentle *bite*.

"Where's your bedroom?"

Fear clamped my heart turning my body rigid. "No, Michael. Grammy will freak out."

"*Grammy's* not here." He threw me over his shoulder like a sack of potatoes and headed up the stairs. "We've got unfinished business, baby."

I pounded and scratched at his back. "Put me down, Michael!" I screamed.

"Go ahead, yell it out, Taylor. No one's going to hear you. The nearest house is a mile away and you know it." He dropped me onto the bed, kicked the door shut and flipped the lock.

"Take your clothes off." He unzipped his pants and the bulge in his probably dry cleaned white briefs alerted me I wouldn't get "fingers" this time. My voice disappeared in my throat. Only a whisper escaped.

"No, please." I jumped to my feet, but he was faster, clamping my arms. "Michael, this is wrong. You can't force me to—"

Michael's mouth took mine, stopping my protest. His mouth tasted of a cheap breath mint, the sugary residue clinging to his tongue. His hand unzipped my skirt, pushing it to the floor, the other hand held my head tight against his lips. Both hands cupped my butt, grinding me against him.

Terror reached out and gripped every limb, every muscle, and ricocheted in my heart. Every time I tried to break Michael's ravaging kisses, he bit my lip, forcing my mouth open so his tongue could probe deeper.

I tried to move sideways, but became trapped in my skirt, wrapped at my ankles like a vice. Michael shoved me toward the bed, but my feet remained imprisoned in the fabric cuff and I fell into the nightstand, smacking my elbow on the corner. Tears burned instantly against the smarting pain, but I forgot my elbow when Michael yanked me upright, pushing me with the weight of his body deep into the mattress.

He grabbed the bedspread, ripping it from beneath me. "Don't want to mess Grandma's quilt."

My body turned to stone, my limbs refusing to bend against his demands. I slapped, pushed, and twisted, but nothing worked. He was stronger. And meaner. His breaths were short, ragged, and hot on my neck. His legs pinned mine and I sensed time running out, my body growing weary.

Calm...stay calm. Cry. Michael hates it when you cry. Reminds him how young you are. Do it! Act like a little girl.

I gasped for air, pleading through sobs, "Michael, stop, please. Don't hurt me."

Again.

It worked, for a second. He rose, studied my face. His knees on my thighs cut off the circulation and my toes tingled. Cautiously, I moved my right leg slightly, managing to free it from beneath his. He bent, his thumb brushed over my quivering lips and I stared back, quickly setting my foot against his shoulder in an attempt to shove him off balance and release my other leg.

Someone screamed. Possibly me.

A balled fist thrust into my gut, knocking the air out of my lungs and bile licked the back of my throat. Michael had gotten smarter. Hit me where no would see the marks.

"Okay. Don't hit," I begged, barely able to cough the words out.

Michael placed a soft kiss on my forehead, his hand smoothing over my hair. I lay still, fighting for breath. His fingers gently caressed my cheek, outlining the edges of my face. My entire body trembled. Even my teeth rattled. When he spoke, it was quiet, falsely comforting.

"That's more like it. You know I hate hurting you, baby." His lips pressed mine gently before he stood, pulling me onto my feet. A menacing smile snaked on his mouth.

"Take your top off, babe. Slowly."

Moving robotically, I eased my camisole over my head while Michael watched with a dark, sick leer. I felt the tremors start at my knees and climb over my arms to the top of my head while I waited, exposed for Michael's examination in just my bra and panties.

He pulled his Ralph Lauren polo off, tossing it to the floor. Sweat shimmered over his chest. A slight breeze ruffled the curtains, beading the moisture against the gooseflesh. I shuddered as if it were an Arctic wind.

Michael trailed a finger slowly down my left arm. Eyes sharp and glistening with excitement showed how much he relished the power he held over me. His puppet.

"Now the bra."

I reached behind me, pretending to struggle with the single hook and stall for time, which didn't work to my advantage. His fingers formed a vice over my jaw.

"Stop messing with me, Taylor." He reached behind me and flipped the clasp like he'd practiced a hundred times. On someone else.

Instinctively, I crossed my arms over my chest. Michael had never seen my bare breasts. He pulled my arms apart, locking my wrists. "No!" The word sounded feeble, lost in the holes of the eyelet drapes. A tear dropped onto my lip before escaping to the floor.

Eyes of black onyx took inventory of his newly acquired possession. "God, you're gorgeous. And mine."

Slowly, he lowered me onto the bed, his hands moving aggressively and his rough tongue abrading my skin. I cried. My youth taken from me and I couldn't stop it from happening.

Inside my head, I schemed to find one last possible chance at freedom—to escape to Riley's house for sanctuary, even if only wearing thong panties. The hopeful thought gave me the strength to try one last time. My knee made contact with Michael's groin and he recoiled in agony, rolling just enough to the side for me to move from underneath him.

I got two steps towards the door before Michael had my hair, wrenching me to the floor. He wrapped the locks tight around his fist and I flailed my arms, trying to reach his hands. I felt my scalp stretch. His foot kicked me hard in my back. He still wore his boots.

A sharp pain stabbed under my arm when he yanked me off the floor and shoved me against the wall. He raised his hand and I pinched my eyes shut, anticipating the blow. Nothing happened.

"A black eye will make Granny suspicious. Wouldn't want that, now would we?" I only nodded, still trying to breathe against the searing burn in my lower back. Without loosening the grip on my forearms, he literally *threw* me onto the bed and followed, his underwear dangling off one leg like it had to nowhere to escape either.

I turned myself off. No more emotion. No more pain. Nothing. I stared at the ceiling, barely aware he'd removed my panties and thrust his ugly self inside me. Another piercing jolt of pain that blended into the others.

Michael grunted and moaned in his own fantasy world. Desperate to disappear, I found a mental sanctuary—something simple to focus on, taking me outside my body. A display of delicate white petals with bright orange centers edged the ceiling, looking all happy and bright as if growing on a warm summer day. I counted each cheerful flower until Michael collapsed on me, sweaty and lifeless.

Three hundred and sixteen daisies.

Twenty-One
CONFUSION
Riley

The truck's engine screamed when the tachometer tipped the red scale. An hour had passed since Taylor's *S.O.S.* text. Barney doubted I had an emergency until I threatened to quit if he didn't let me go. I promised if it wasn't serious I'd be back, lying through my teeth. He thought Dirk sent the message and I let him believe Dirk was home alone.

I took the back way to Taylor's grandmother's, avoiding the route by my house in case someone saw me. I hated explanations, or worse, *lies*. Mrs. Daniel's house came into view on the rise and a sense of urgency filled me unexpectedly. When I pulled up, I spied a strange car parked in the driveway with Massachusetts license plates. My stomach whirled in a dizzying spin.

Dear God, please be her parents.

Taylor answered the door, the look in her eyes distant, scaring the hell out of me. She looked *through* me. A faint smile curled on lips swollen and bruised. Her eyes watered, but she swallowed the tears down.

Shit.

"Hi," she said in a small voice, standing guard in the doorway. She looked like she'd been sleeping. Her hair lay matted and her silky camisole, my favorite pink one that billowed when my hands slid underneath, appeared wrinkled. She stood pigeon toed, her bubble gum pink painted toes fidgeting like her fingers did when she was nervous.

"I got your message. Are you okay?" I reached up to touch her face and she flinched against my touch. Warning sirens wailed in my brain. "Taylor?"

A hand appeared above her head, pushing the door wider. Chiseled jaw, fairly toned arms, not as big as my own, but sizeable. A ripped chest made the little embroidered horsey on his shirt noticeable, and long legs placing his body a head taller than Taylor, appeared behind her. Not a hair out of place. My guess was he had his chest and arms waxed, and probably had his nose hairs coiffed and styled. Handsome and smelling of money by the scent of his certain expensive cologne.

The bastard from Boston.

His hand eased over Taylor's shoulder and an unmistakable shudder rippled through her body. "Taylor, *love*, aren't you going to introduce me to your friend?" He kissed the top of her hair and my blood boiled to a rage in less than a second. She didn't need to tell me who the asshole was touching *my* Taylor.

"Riley, this is Michael."

That's when I noticed it. She raised her left hand to brush hair away from her face, or maybe to shove Michael's hand off her shoulder. Whatever the reason didn't matter. The huge diamond caging her ring finger blinded me. A diamond that had never been there before.

I swallowed a hundred times, maybe two hundred, pushing down emotions suddenly rising. Taylor was *engaged.* Officially, "diamond clad" engaged…to *Michael.*

"Prince Charming" extended one hand to me, keeping a proprietary hold on Taylor's waist, where *my* hand should be. I stepped back as if by touching him, my skin would disintegrate.

"Nope. Sorry." I glared at Taylor. "Congratulations. Hope you're happy." I never felt the cobblestones rubbing beneath my feet. In fact, I never felt my feet rapidly propelling me toward my truck.

"Riley!" Taylor called out but stopped, abruptly. The front door slammed shut and I thought I heard her cry out.

I studied the front porch where two rockers moved ghostly in the late afternoon breeze. The rockers I pictured Taylor and me sitting in while watching our grandchildren play tag on the front lawn. The edges of my picture frayed when the memory flipped to the sparkling rock on Taylor's finger. She belonged in someone else's picture now.

Still, I waited, listening. The lace drapes on the door window moved slightly—someone watched me. No noise, just an eerie silence that made my skin swim against my bones. Something seemed off, but my mind couldn't move past the jealous rage building to figure it out. When the curtains shifted again, I held up my middle finger, saluting the happy couple.

By the time I'd taken the last few steps to my truck, I couldn't see for the tears blurring my vision. Why the emergency text? To rub my nose in the fact that she was engaged? All the endearing words spoken over the past weeks, twisted into meaningless lies?

Then it hit. A brick to my head. The crumpled skirt. Bare feet and legs. The wrinkled camisole. Her matted hair and swollen lips. Her *scent.* Not her flowery sweet signature fragrance. No, a pungent odor like vinegar, but not as sour. Natural, almost primal. She smelled of *sex.* Michael had popped Taylor's cherry. *My* cherry!

I hated being decent. For once I wish I could be more like Jaxson, taking what I wanted and begging forgiveness later. Why wasn't I programmed like that? Why did I care? Why did I fall in love with Taylor Wilson? And how bad would it hurt falling *out* of love with her?

Excruciating.

Twenty-Two
NOW WHAT?
Jaxson

Life closed in on me fast. Three weeks and I shipped out of this hellhole town. I didn't know what I looked forward to the most—being able to breathe air outside the confines of everyone's stares and my family's strangulating sham of happiness, or losing my ankle shackle. I couldn't go anywhere without calling one of my babysitters for approval. I hadn't seen a movie, eaten out in a decent restaurant, or socialized with anyone. Hell, I hadn't even had a damn beer.

Done with being the model prisoner, I leaned on the refrigerator door and stared at the amber bottles meticulously lined up on the second shelf, each containing the smooth ale my body craved. One. Just one.

The back door slammed and instinctively, I shut the fridge. Riley stomped into the kitchen puffing like a mad dragon, dropping the "f-bomb" every other word.

"Whoa, slow down. What the hell has your tighty-whities bunched up?"

When Riley turned, his expression shocked me. Not even in the hospital when he discovered I coerced Kaylee into going to the party with me, had Riley appeared so torn up. He dropped onto a kitchen chair and buried his head in his hands.

"God, it's all a lie," he cried. Literally *cried*. "How could she do this to me? To *her?* She despises the guy for hell's sake! How can she marry him?"

"What? Who's getting married?" Dots connected. "*Taylor?* She's just a kid. Is she knocked up?"

"No! She's still a virgin. Or *was.* I'm guessing *virtue* went the wayside this afternoon."

"Dude, you're not making any sense." I took two beers from the fridge and popped the tops, handing one to Riley. "Here, you need this."

"Jax."

"Shut up and drink."

Riley guzzled like a pro, his bottle plunking loudly against the wooden tabletop. He wiped his mouth with his arm and brushed away the tears washing his cheeks.

"Taylor dated this guy in Boston before she came here. A 'Michael' somebody. Anyway, she's had nothing nice to say about the guy. In fact, she didn't even tell me about him. 'Gremlin Grandma' announced his existence the day she freaked out over the hickey I sucked on Taylor's boob."

"Is *that* what the 'international incident' was about? A damn 'monkey bite'?" I laughed. "Dude! On her *boob?* You make me proud, bro!"

"Shut up, Jax. That's not even an issue anymore. Grams took up morality patrol and has enforced a stupid midnight curfew on Taylor ever since. Between my dumb ass job and the 'granny police', I'm lucky to cop a feel, let alone get *Riley Jr.* out of the corral. Maybe this Michael guy's the real reason Taylor's been so skittish about messing around. I mean I'm allowed free reign on the 'top floor', but if I come close to touching the 'basement', she freaks. Now, I know why. Her 'basement' apparently has a guest room reserved for Michael."

"That's messed up, Riley. I've seen how she acts around you. Bro, she's seriously into you. Something's whacked here. Did you do something to piss her off?"

He looked at me, stunned. "*No.* We've been fine. Better than *fine.* When I'm working, Taylor comes to Barney's and eats lunch or dinner with me, and she's been helping Mom at the store. She's even taken Dirk to the movies, which, by the way, we need to watch the munchkin. He's going to surpass both of us with the ladies before he's twelve."

Riley stared past me, lost somewhere beyond the patio doors. "I don't get it. I'm telling you, Jax, the ring on her finger? I've never seen one that big. The dude has bucks. No way can I compete with that."

I snapped my fingers, regaining his focus. "I can't believe Taylor's all about the money, but if she is, take it from me—you're better off without her. I know that's not what you want to hear, but a high maintenance chick is a recipe for disaster."

Riley chugged back the last of his beer. "Are there more? I'm thinking a 'bender' is what I need. Numb the pain and forget the bitch."

I knew I'd pay royally, but I couldn't stand seeing him hurt. No girl was worth this misery. Whatever bad karma came to Taylor, she deserved it. I popped another beer and handed it to Riley.

"Thanks, I'll owe you. I'm going for a walk. Oh, and *if* 'princess' calls? Tell her I'm fucking Kaylee and can't be disturbed.

Twenty-Three
LOST AND FOUND
Taylor

Grammy fixed a pot roast, complete with potatoes, gravy, and apple pie, which when she opened her mouth to give me credit for, I pinned an angry glower her direction.

"Don't even try. Michael's not stupid. He knows I don't cook."

He reached over and patted my hand. My fingers recoiled into a fist. "You'll learn, baby. I'll teach you."

I shoved away from the table. "I'm going to bed."

"But it's barely eight o'clock, cupcake. What's wrong?"

The list echoed in my brain but Michael's cold stare kept me silent. I forced a small smile. "My stomach's queasy, that's all. Thanks for dinner." Michael rose from his chair and I pressed my hand to my stomach…where the bruise from his fist grew larger every minute. "Michael will help you with the dishes, won't you *babe.*"

Climbing the stairs hurt like hell. A burning ache radiated from the bruise on my lower back, and the tenderness between my legs stole my breath with each step. Alone in my room with the door locked, I faced the nauseating drama of the hell I'd been through…would spend my life inside of now.

"Michael, stop, please. Don't hurt me…don't hit….don't…

Michael's trophy…

You had to know I wouldn't just give up and walk away…

His puppet…

Take your clothes off…slowly…

His property…

You officially belong to me …

His slave…

Marry me…it's your only choice now…

His fiancé.

Michael slid an enormous diamond ring on my finger after he'd *finished.* Like all the men in my life, a large payoff seemed to be the quickest way to forgiveness. I didn't even look at it. I just stared at the ceiling.

"You raped me," I had stated in a voice I didn't recognize.

"I did not!" He held my diamond decorated hand in front of my face. "Who the hell is going to believe that bullshit story? Baby, we've been together so long, people automatically assume we did the *deed* months ago. *Rape?* You're nuts. You enjoyed every minute of it. Hell, you didn't even fight me off. Deal, baby, and get over it."

I did fight. Didn't I? I cried…he ignored me. I pushed him away…he punched me. I ran…he kicked me. I gave up…he raped me. I called Riley…he left me.

"Your little boyfriend will never want you now. You're used merchandise. But I'll still marry you," Michael had said, watching me dress with the same sick sneer on his face he had when he demanded the strip tease earlier.

Not true.

Then I remember Riley's words. *Hope you're happy...* I was anything but.

Anger consumed me. I ripped the blood stained sheets off the bed. The stain of sin. The witness of my non-consensual descent into adulthood. I couldn't bring myself to even touch the mattress or the pillow *his* head had lain upon...his cold eyes taunting, *you're mine...you'll always be mine.*

I dragged the quilt, the only thing in the room not touched by skin or bodily fluids, wrapped it around me and settled into the rocker to sleep, or tried, anyway. All I could see when I closed my eyes was the hurt on Riley's face. I had no way to prepare him. Hell, *I* wasn't prepared for today's horror show. I rubbed the bruise on my arm under my sweater—the one Michael gave me when he squeezed my arm after I called out Riley's name.

I had to find a way to talk to Riley. In my heart of hearts, I knew forgiveness was out of the question. I took him beyond breakable. I shattered him. It wasn't fair. He didn't deserve this. That's why the ring still circled my finger and not flushed down the toilet like I thought about doing when I finally realized what happened. In the space of an hour, I'd become damaged goods...no longer deserving of someone as good as Riley. I'd been branded "property of Michael Barnes."

Riley wouldn't answer my calls and his voicemail was full. When I texted, I received notification my number had been blocked. I felt like a hostage in Grammy's house with no way to escape. I peered out the window, pondering how many bones I'd break if I jumped. Riley was less than a mile away—within walking distance, but he may as well have been on another planet.

The *expected* knock came at my door around one in the morning. I stopped breathing.

"Taylor, open up, baby."

Michael.

Part of me wanted to hurl myself out the window to my death rather than face what awaited me if I opened the door. The other part just wanted to pretend to be asleep, hoping he'd give up and go away. Who the hell was I kidding? *Michael* stood on the other side of that door. He'd never give up. A second, louder knock, confirmed that.

I uncurled from my safety blanket and walked to the door, my heart slamming my spine with each step. If I didn't answer the door, I faced more bruising, more punches or kicks. My life turned to a waking nightmare.

I obeyed and opened the door, letting the bastard inside my last sanctuary. His lips covered mine, his hands covered everything else.

This time, I counted the daisies going the other way.

**

Michael's heavy breath on my neck and limp arm draped across my stomach clued me he'd fallen into a deep slumber. Carefully lifting his arm, I waited, but he rolled away and started snoring. Gingerly, I eased off the bed, grabbing my clothes from the floor. I couldn't chance opening a drawer or a closet and waking the monster who took his sick pleasures out on me over the past few hours. I lost count. Lost my soul.

Something possessed me to bundle the soiled sheets in my arms and take them with me.

Dressing as I tiptoed through the house, ducking into shadows to listen for footsteps, I made it to the kitchen, grabbed my purse off the counter and the keys to Michael's car. I planned to exit through the laundry room and go around the back of the house to where I left the Mini parked.

Bless you Grammy! My clean laundry lay folded and stacked on the dryer. I opened a clean pillowcase and dumped the sheet, some clean underwear, socks, a pair of jeans and T-shirt inside. My tennis shoes sat in the basket by the door. I picked my sweatshirt off the hook and gently pushed my way through the back door, cushioning the screen with my fingers.

I ran around the side of the house and skidded to a halt. Michael had parked behind the Mini! Damn! I couldn't chance the alarm going off on his car, so I threw his keys in the bushes and hid on the other side of the hedge where I changed my clothes, shoving my dirty ones in the pillowcase with the sheets.

I took off on foot for Riley's, the pillowcase slung over my shoulder. Dawn barely edged the sky and I knew I might wake somebody, but I had to talk to him. He needed to know *everything*. I couldn't let Riley believe our relationship had been a lie…that my feelings for him weren't real. He had to hold on to the truth—that I loved him, *only* him, because if he didn't… I couldn't go there in my head. Our love for each other was my lifeline. Without it, life meant nothing.

An empty garbage can leaned against the side of his house—a fitting receptacle for my disgusting satchel. I scribbled a note on the back of the dairy order telling Riley to meet me at the pond, and slipped it through the mail slot of the entry door. The smell of coffee drifted back to me from the tiny opening. Someone was or soon would be awake.

I headed down the trail off the back of the house. As I dropped over the ridge, I heard Lucky bark and prayed Riley found my note. If I waited too long, the excuse I went for a walk wouldn't fly and I'd pay the consequences. My life had turned into a series of choices and consequences and the pit I fell into, seemed bottomless.

My third attempt at skipping stones across the still pond resulted in five taps before the stone sank and Riley spoke.

"Looks like your time with me wasn't a total waste."

"Riley!" I gasped, pressing my heart back into my chest.

He walked slowly around the opposite side of the pond, easing a hip onto a rock. I wanted to run to him, throw my arms around him and feel his heart beat against my cheek. His arms were a sanctuary, my most favorite place on earth, but now forbidden territory. By his guarded posture and the hard angles etching his face, his feelings were steeled away along with any warmth or compassion I might have expected.

"So what could you possibly have to say to me that I would give a damn about, now?"

My throat tightened. The words stuck and felt painful coming out. "Riley, I'm so sorry about yesterday. I had no idea Michael was coming. Grammy invited him without me knowing. When he showed up at the door, I texted you. I hoped you'd get there in time to save me."

"*Save* you? From what? Did you need me to hold your hand to support the diamond because it's too heavy? You could have warned me he was there, Taylor. Not let me find him with you. Alone." He threw his hands in the air and paced in angry dusty strides. "I'm such a damn fool! I honestly believed you loved me….that I had a chance with you…..a future. What a fucking idiot I am!"

"Stop, Riley! You're not an idiot and I *do* love you. But our future…." The tears came too fast and choked my words out.

Riley walked toward me and I actually thought he would embrace me and tell me he'd fix everything and life would be okay. But instead, he grabbed my left wrist and forced my hand in front of my face.

"You don't love one person and promise to marry another! It doesn't work that way. Not for me. And by the way you looked yesterday, you *sealed* the deal." He dropped my hand and stepped away. "Go away, Taylor. Take your lies and get the hell out of my life, and don't look back. Hope you find everything you're chasing after in Michael Barnes." He turned and walked toward the trail.

"He raped me!" I shouted, surprising myself at the blunt declaration. Riley stopped, his fists opening and closing several times.

224

"Michael raped me," I breathed quieter through a sob, "and beat me. When he was through with me, he put the ring on my finger."

Riley turned slowly. Confusion clouded his expression. I watched his eyes go through several emotions; bewilderment, anger, hurt, then settle again on anger.

"Well, that's one for the record books. *Rape*. A bit of a stretch, don't you think? I mean come on, Taylor. You and I haven't exactly been *virtuous*, and we've only known each other a couple of months. You've been with Michael, how long? Almost a year? If you've let me put my hands all over you, I can hardly believe you'd stop 'loverboy' from doing the same....or *more,* given your 'promised relationship' long before you came to our sleepy little town."

"Are you calling me a *slut,* Riley? You know me better than that!"

"Do I, Taylor? After yesterday, I'm not sure I know you at all. Maybe I never have. Good luck with the 'rape story', sweetheart. Wonder if Grams or Mommy thought to use that excuse."

I lunged at Riley, clawing his face. He grabbed my wrists and held them tight. "Don't even go there, Taylor. I don't need the drama."

He started for the trail again and I called after him. "Wait! I have a favor to ask. I know this is huge, given what's happened, but I need you to trust me one last time. Please." He regarded me, undoubtedly struggling. A drop of blood squiggled down his cheek from my scratch and inside I died.

"Riley, you have to admit I never actually *lied* to you. I didn't tell you about Michael at first, because I didn't want to ruin what was going on between us. Michael is also the reason why I left Boston."

Riley sat on the rock in front of me. He smeared the blood across his cheek with the back of his hand. "Shit." I opened my mouth to apologize, but his eyes locked on mine. His arms crossed his chest, his demeanor less than forgiving. "Go on."

I gave Riley a condensed version of the night Michael first manhandled me, explaining that was why I pulled away whenever he tried to touch me.

"Okay, I believe that really happened, but I can't swallow the rest. Sorry. Don't you remember that night in the backyard? We were almost *there,* Taylor. Naked. No boundaries left."

I swallowed the tears threatening. "I'll never, *ever* forget that night. Michael can't erase my memories of you—especially not that one."

Riley heaved a resigned sigh, his voice soft, the way I'd always remember it. "So what's the huge favor I'm supposed to trust you on?"

"I need to borrow your truck. Just for an hour, tops. I have to take care of something in town and I don't want to go back to the house. Michael has the Mini trapped with his car. He can't find out what I'm doing."

"What about me? Can I ask what you're doing?"

"I'd rather not tell you. I swear, it's nothing illegal. Just personal. Please?"

Riley's feet scuffed the dirt, creating puffs of dust to circle his legs. He reached into his pocket and handed me his keys, holding my fingers a couple of seconds before letting go. A jolt of electricity zigzagged through me at the slight touch.

"What if Michael comes looking for you?"

"Tell him you haven't seen me. That you have no intention of ever speaking to me again."

"Not exactly a lie, is it?"

"No. I'm pretty sure I'm lucky you even came out here to talk to me."

"Leave my keys in the driver door when you get back. I don't want to see you again, Taylor. Sorry, but it's the only way I can deal with the pain."

"I understand. Thanks again for the truck."

He started up the trail. I followed close behind, longing to reach for his hand. When he stopped at the top of the ridge, we nearly collided. For a split second, the familiar glint of what he once felt for me flashed in his eyes, but faded just as fast, as if I imagined it.

"One hour. If you're not back, I'll tell my dad you stole the truck." He sprinted across the field for his house. I walked further downstream and took a different trail, keeping hidden in the trees.

One hour to erase the past twenty-four. One hour inside Riley's truck, smelling his cologne, running through memories pressed into the tweed fabric where I'd laid many times. One last hour in his life before I disappeared…before *I* became a memory.

227

**

Tissue crinkled under my butt and I tried to wrap the paper gown under me, but it was no use. The doctor came in, scrubbed her hands then told me to put my feet in the stirrups, which must be kept in the freezer, they felt so cold.

"I can't believe I need an exam to get a 'morning after' pill."

Marrying Michael may be out of my hands, but getting pregnant, remained mine to control. No way would I give birth to the "spawn of Satan." Michael was an only child. I'd end the Barnes's abusive blood line.

"It's procedure, Miss Wilson." Her mouth twisted funny when she touched my legs. "There's some serious bruising here. Did Riley do this to you?

"God, this is a small town! No! Riley would *never* hurt a girl. He's not like that."

"Do you want to tell me what happened?"

"Nothing happened. Besides, I'm eighteen. Now, do I get my pill or not?"

"Yes, of course you do." She scribbled something on a pad and gave it to me. "See the girl at the front desk." She turned back before closing the door. "Taylor, tell *someone.*"

I slipped behind the screen to dress without answering.

**

Riley's driveway appeared empty when I returned and I wondered if everyone in his family knew what happened, or at least Riley's version. A line of pines shielded Riley's house from view and Gram's house sat far enough away, unless someone had high-powered binoculars, I wouldn't be discovered.

I stole a pencil and some paper from the clinic to write Riley a note, or more like a set of instructions. I placed it under my cell phone on the floorboard by the gas pedal. I retrieved the pillowcase full of soiled laundry from the garbage can and shoved it under the passenger seat. Per Riley's instructions, I tucked the keys in the side pocket of the door.

I debated whether to knock on the door and beg to see him one last time, but changed my mind. I'd already been gone too long. Michael would be out looking for me, or waiting impatiently for my return. Hopefully, I'd soften the blow, literally, by agreeing to follow him back to Boston. Maybe even move the wedding date up. No sense putting off the inevitable.

By the time I reached Grammy's front door, I folded from sharp cramps. I doubted the pill worked that fast and when I did the math in my head, I realized I could have passed on the pill and embarrassing exam.

Michael sat fuming on the sofa. "Where the hell have you been?" he demanded. Grams wandered in from the dining room, surprise in her expression. She'd never had the privilege of seeing Michael's evil side. Only his phony, charming personality.

"I went for a walk."

"For two damn hours?"

"Yeah. For two damn hours! I needed to sort through stuff. Yesterday, was overwhelming, to say the least."

Another wave of cramping hit. Stronger, catching my breath. "Shit. I've got to get to the bathroom."

"Why?" Michael yelled after me.

"Because my period started!"

I heard his curse before the bathroom door shut.

Twenty-Four
REVELATIONS
Jaxson

I pulled the bill of my hat tight over my eyes and stared into the mirror above the bathroom sink. I was head-to-toe camouflage in my government issued gear. "Picture day." Soon I'd be off to boot camp and my ankle shackle a thing of the past. The doorbell sounded in time with my foot hitting the last stair.

"I'll get it," I hollered to no one.

A tall, fairly good looking guy stood across from me. Crisp, pressed gray slacks, not jeans, and a black on black striped shirt. Not anyone from around these parts.

"Can I help you?"

"I'm looking for Riley Martin. Is he around?"

Something about his guy set my teeth on edge. He wasn't a salesman. Door-to-door salesmen didn't drive convertible Mercedes.

"Who are you?"

He extended his hand. The skin felt too soft and the handshake, limp. "Oh, forgive me. I'm Michael Barnes. Taylor Wilson's fiancé. I know she's friends with Riley, and well, she's been gone a while and I thought perhaps she'd stopped by, or maybe he knows where I might find her?"

So this is Michael. The demon seed.

"Actually, Riley's gone to work. I haven't seen Taylor.

"Oh, well. Okay then. If she stops by, tell her Michael is looking for her."

"Sure. Hey? You got a card or something? You know, in case she stops by I can call you, or if I hear from Riley?" Being a cop's son paid off sometimes. *Contact information* would prove crucial in case Taylor or Riley ended up disappearing. We'd know how to contact the "main suspect." Being a pompous idiot and not having a clue, he handed one over without questioning my motives.

"Thanks again, and, uh, thanks for what you guys are doing for our country. I appreciate you."

Took me a minute to figure out it was my uniform that had him making assumptions, and probably why he handed over his card. His little sports car left an indelible black arc on the asphalt when he spun around and headed back from wherever he came from. Riley's truck was gone, so technically, I hadn't lied. I just knew I didn't wanted this psycho finding my little brother or the so-called *fiancé*.

Riley walked through the patio slider, startling me. "I thought you were gone. Your truck is, so why aren't you?"

"I borrowed the truck to Taylor. She supposed to have it back within the hour or I'm having her crazy ass arrested for stealing it."

"*Taylor*? When did you see Taylor?"

"A while ago. Down by the pond. She left me a note to meet her on the milk order." Riley poured the last of the coffee into a mug. "Is Mom or Dad here?"

"Nah, just me. Even the 'squirt' left. Why?"

232

"Got a minute? I could use your advice."

"Now, I'm beyond curious. *My* advice? Must be something illegal."

"No, but you're more experienced with girls."

I tried to not smile, but I couldn't help it. My ego took a bow. "Fairly certain you're right on that one." I wet a paper towel and handed it him. "You've got blood all over your cheek."

Riley wiped his face, then flipped a kitchen chair backwards and straddled the seat, hanging his hands off the top rung. He rolled his mug between his palms, staring out the sliding doors at the back yard.

"Let me guess. This is about Taylor?

He kept his gaze trained elsewhere. "Yeah. She, uh, claims Michael *raped* her. Said she had no idea he was coming and when he was *done,* he put the ring on her finger and told her they were engaged."

I set my coffee on the table and drew a contemplative breath. "Do you believe her? I mean, *rape* is a pretty hefty accusation."

Riley swallowed the last of his drink and put his cup next to mine. He scrubbed his fingers though his hair and scratched the back of his neck.

"I don't know what I believe. She's told me barely anything about Michael until today. I know they've been together for a long time, and well, she and I have kind of messed around, so I know she's no 'preacher's daughter'. But on the other hand, she's never lied to me. Not telling me isn't the same as lying.

233

His arms hung from the hands clasped behind his neck. "I'm so confused, Jax. I do know that when I met the guy, I didn't like him. He gave me the creeps."

"Well, speaking of 'creeps', you had a visitor." I laid Michael's card on the table. "He's looking for Taylor and when I told him I hadn't seen her or you, he wasn't happy. Left his signature mark on the street when he smoked the rubber off his expensive tires. Your truck was gone, so I assumed you were at work. Maybe you should tell Dad."

Riley picked up the card and studied it. "I don't know. I'll think about it." He put it inside his wallet. "I've got to get to Barney's. Taylor better have my truck back by the time I change or shit will hit the fan if I'm late. I already took off early yesterday when she...."

Riley stopped, pushing his fist against his mouth. "Shit! She must have known something was up, because whatever *did* happen, took place barely an hour from when she sent the text and I got to her house. He jumped up, tossing the chair sideways. Damn! What if she *is* telling the truth and I could have stopped it?"

I picked up the chair and leveled my eyes to his. "Don't go down that road, Riley. *You* are not responsible for any mess Taylor's gotten herself into. Don't start feeling guilty because some chick had sex with the wrong guy. Not your choice *or* your consequence. Like you said. She's known this jerk a long time. If he was capable of doing something like that, she would have known long before yesterday."

Riley's fingers nervously tapped the table. "Actually, she did have a clue." He didn't elaborate, just shoved his wallet in his back pocket and raced up the stairs.

When I opened the garage door, Riley's truck sat parked in the usual place, but no sign of Taylor. The engine ticked, cooling off, so she'd brought it back within the last few minutes. I walked back inside.

"Riley, your truck's back." A faint *thanks* echoed back, but nothing more. "Not my problem," I muttered before leaving to get my new "mug shot" taken.

Moving from one warzone to another.

Twenty-Five
EVIDENCES OF TRUTH
Riley

Dirk rolled into the driveway on his bike, skidding sideways just as I climbed into my truck. "Hey bring me home some fries, would ya?"

"I'll see. You going to be all right for a bit? Jaxson had to go to town and I've got to get to work. Mom should be home anytime."

"I'm not a baby."

"Sure you are. I saw your secret stash of Pull-Ups in the bathroom."

"You're such a lying piece of crap, Riley!"

"Better 'a lying piece of crap' than a 'baby'. Hey, I see you got the training wheels taken off your bike? Does that mean you don't have to drink from a sippy cup any more either?"

"I hate you! You're scum!"

"Whoa, easy with the names. I might get my 'big boy feelers' hurt."

I ignored the raspberry he spit my direction and shut the door. The cab of my truck smelled sterile, a definite antiseptic odor tingeing my *Mango & Coconut* air freshener. The seat still held the hint of an indent from where Taylor sat, and my knees smashed the dash, reminding me of how petite…how perfectly she fit under my chin.

Damn.

My foot kicked something under the seat when I started the truck, and my heel slipped on some paper. It had been a while since I cleaned out my truck. I tossed the paper into the trash bag hanging off my cigarette lighter knob and rolled down my window to continue teasing Dirk.

"Get in the house and climb in your playpen until Mommy gets home."

"You're such a loser, Riley."

"Later, *baby.*"

"Loser!" he yelled after me. I checked the rearview mirror and swore I saw a special single finger salute waving my direction. He was fast becoming one of "Martin's finest."

When I pulled into Barney's parking lot, some punk in a low-rider truck that actually *pulsed* with heavy bass sounds, cut me off. I slammed on my brakes and leaned out my window.

"Watch where you're going ass-wipe!" Another finger waved my direction. *I'd like to break that finger off* I thought, zipping into my parking space with barely two minutes to spare before I'd be late. When I climbed out, my foot kicked whatever had slid out from under my seat.

A cell phone. *Taylor's.*

I flipped the face up and the wallpaper picture caused my throat to tighten. The two of us at the county fair, sharing cotton candy. Damn. I didn't need that image in my head starting work. It was Friday and I offered to work a double for Andy, who, it turned out, had mono. It would be a long day and letting my feelings about Taylor tear me up, wouldn't help.

I tossed the phone into the glove box. I'd return it to her grandmother tomorrow. Taylor and Michael would be on their way back to Boston by now, and Lydia could mail it to her. Like Jax said. I couldn't feel responsible for Taylor's messy life. The diamond on her finger changed everything.

Work proved a living hell. I swear everyone from high school came in. School started next week, so those who'd come home from summer vacation, camp, or just woke up since Spring, crowded the place. Barney and I worked side-by-side, with Cook and his daughter, Jenny, doing double time with the burgers and fries.

Two bowling lanes jammed with the pins suspended and I spent a lot of the night running behind and jiggling wires. Walking up one lane, I had the displeasure of running into Kaylee, who dropped her ball, narrowly missing my toe.

"Oops! Sorry." She pressed her hand against my chest, letting it stay there a bit longer than comfortable. "Hi, Riley."

"Be careful, Kaylee. Those things will break a foot."

"Better than a heart."

"Don't start. I've got to get back to work."

"Mind if I stick around until you get off?" She giggled, thinking I'd missed her innuendo. I hadn't, and a vengeful thought flared in my mind. If I couldn't have Taylor, why not have Kaylee? Maybe I'd feel better about Taylor screwing some other guy, if I was doing some myself."

"Suit yourself. I work until ten. Just stay out of my way and don't bug me."

I walked off, ignoring her loud girlie squeal, which surely matched some stupid jumping fit. Maybe she'd get bored and go home with someone else. Maybe Taylor would walk through the door and tell me she dumped the asshole and beg my forgiveness.

Maybe I was just fucked up.

Ten o'clock came way too fast and I found Kaylee perched on the hood of my truck when I walked out.

"Damnit, Kaylee! Get off the hood. You'll scratch the paint."

She sat by the passenger door waiting. Sometimes I hated that my mother taught us manners. I opened the door for her.

"Thanks, babe," she offered in voice dripping with sugar.

What the hell was I thinking taking Kaylee home? I thought I needed sex, that's what. Hell, eighteen and still, technically, a virgin. I should be in a wax museum as the oldest teenage boy to have never experienced "the real deal."

Kaylee's hand found my knee, slowly working her way up my thigh. I kept my eyes on the road and made no effort to stop her. I took the turn off to the lake, to the same spot I'd spent many nights exploring Taylor's curves.

Damn. Taylor. Just *thinking* her name hurt like hell. She had to be hundreds of miles closer to Boston by now, and hundreds of miles further from me. From *us*.

I rolled down the windows to let the night breeze blow through the cab. Kaylee didn't wait for me to come around and open her door when I reached into the back seat and grabbed the quilt. I tossed her the blanket and checked the glove box, retrieving a couple of *lozenges*.

Kaylee lay back on the blanket, her hair fanned out behind her, the same way Taylor's did. A halo of sexy silk around an angel's face. I blinked to erase the image of Taylor and concentrated on the little vixen waiting, her chest heaving deep, sultry breaths. *Riley Jr.* twitched and already I hated myself. But the self-loathing soon dissipated when we started kissing.

Shit, she tasted good. Just what I needed. The lust burned through me like fire chasing gasoline. Every nerve ending in my body pulsated and I felt the familiar aching sensation pulling me to the edge of sanity.

Kaylee's hands knew what to do. We were going down a well-traveled highway. I hissed when she squeezed too tight. "Shit Kaylee! Too hard!"

"Sorry! It's just been….a while," she murmured against my lips.

My hands went under her shirt and snapped her bra loose. Her jeans folded neatly at her knees, and my pants were pushed away seductively by Kaylee's manicured toes.

Suddenly, I flew outside my body, watching this animal grab, taste, and take whatever he wanted from the innocent victim beneath him. I became a *Michael.*

"Damn!" I shrieked, flipping onto my back. When Kaylee moved to climb on top of me, misreading my loud declaration, I held her back.

"No! I can't do this Kaylee. Not even to you."

"Why? I want you to, please!" She lay her head on my chest and started crying. It wasn't fair that girls could instantly turn on the water works and make a guy feel like crap. "What do you mean 'not even to me'?"

"Kaylee…" I pulled her jeans up and patted her rear end. "Baby, we both know this isn't going anywhere."

She lifted her face, her mascara streaked cheeks shiny with tears. "You still hate me, don't you?"

"No, I don't. What you did with Jaxson is in the past. We can't go back and change things."

Fixing Kaylee's and Jax's mess didn't even register on my priority list. If I could wave a magic wand to change anything, it would be me telling Barney to shove it when he wanted me to take Andy's shift. Taylor and I would have gone on the picnic I planned to surprise her with down by the pond. We would have been gone when Prince Charming arrived in his sporty *steed,* and if life had gone according to plan, Taylor and I would have spent the night counting stars and making love until dawn. *Our* relationship would have been consummated, not *theirs.*

"Riley, I love you. I want you back."

"I know, but I don't want you back. I don't love you, Kaylee and despite everything, you deserve better than this."

I folded upright, zipping my pants and yanking my shirt over my head. Being part of the male species, I couldn't help another slow look at the naked boobs staring at me.

"Get dressed, Kaylee. I'm going to 'water a bush', then take you home."

Kaylee sobbed most of the way back to her house. I hated being the asshole hurting her, and I really didn't mean it as payback, but she couldn't see it any other way. The truck barely rolled to a stop in her driveway before she wrenched the door open and took off running for the house. First day of school should prove interesting. Shar would probably have my tires slashed by lunch.

My heart thumped wildly when I crested the hill where Lydia Daniels house sat. The big two-story Victorian appeared dark, which I expected considering it was past midnight. What I didn't expect? The rush of feelings that attacked when I passed the driveway. Empty. Michael's car was gone…along with the Mini.

I could hardly see by the time I pulled in front of my house from the haze of water clouding my vision. I doubled over, keeping the pain in my gut at bay. Taylor was gone! She really *left*. My nose ran in a steady stream from bawling my eyes out, and I reached into the glove box hoping for a napkin, but found nothing. Wiping snot across my registration didn't seem wise.

My fingers wound around Taylor's cell phone and I clutched it to my chest, letting another wave of emotion rock my body. I couldn't even call to beg forgiveness for being such an ass and not believing in her, because I held the only link I had to her in my slimy fingers.

I rummaged through the garbage bag, searching for a used napkin, tossing trash onto the floorboard. The faint smell of a cheese burger drifted up my nostrils when I wiped the end of my nose with a crumpled napkin.

I turned on the overhead light and proceeded to clean up the mess. Picking up scrunched receipts, paper cups, and stray straws took all my strength. A large bundle appeared wedged under the passenger seat. I tugged, but it wouldn't come out.

What the hell?

I had no recollection of shoving something under there. It would have to wait until tomorrow. I only wanted to dump this garbage and go to my room to indulge in a private pity party. Two sheets of folded paper lay on each side of the overflowing bag. I picked up the one closest and pushed it deep inside, but when I reached for the second, it unfolded.

Dear Riley seized a heartbeat.

Headlights filtered through the pines, slowly crawling closer. I didn't want anyone to see me in my emotional state, let alone try and explain. I grabbed the bag of garbage, and slipped around the side of the house to the back, praying the slider was unlocked. Lucky met me halfway with a menacing growl.

"Hush. It's me." Her tail wagged frantically and I breathed, knowing the door would be unlocked if she hadn't been put in for the night.

The garage door moaned and whined behind the laundry room and I took the stairs two at a time, barely making it into my bedroom before footsteps slapped across the kitchen floor. I locked my door, and grabbed the flashlight I kept in the nightstand drawer, not wanting to turn on my bedroom light. I had to appear *asleep* to avoid company.

The bag of garbage toppled over, spilling its contents once again when I dropped it on the floor. Quickly, I dragged my beanbag into my tiny walk-in closet, pushing the folding doors together as close as possible. The chair hissed under my weight and I commanded my heart to slow. The shadow of feet blocked the gold strip of light spreading beneath my floor, and the door handle jiggled.

"Riley?" Mom whispered through the doorframe. I remained silent, hoping my breathy pants weren't too loud. She waited a couple of seconds, repeated my name, and finally gave up. The ribbon of light disappeared and I waited until I heard the creak of my parents' bedroom door, followed by the clack, signaling closure. I flipped on the flashlight.

Dear Riley,

I don't know how I can make things right. Maybe I can't, but I have to tell you I love you so much. With all my heart, which I'm leaving with you, so please take care of it. Being with you, feeling your hands on my

244

body, your lips on mine, your laughter in my ear—Riley, those are the only things that seem real to me, and they're only memories. Ones I'll cherish.

Believe me when I tell you that when Michael touches me, I <u>don't</u> pretend it's you. That would make me "feel" and ruin what shred of happiness I have left with your memory. I feel nothing. I don't even hear his voice. I'm dead. He's with a corpse, because I'm no longer there.

That's what scares me, Riley. Each time it happens, I move further into some black space where I feel nothing. I don't even feel my heart beating. Thoughts of death are more welcoming than being with Michael. I don't believe he'd ever kill me, but I wish for death every time his eyes go black. Maybe that's why I stole Grammy's bottle of sleeping pills. Maybe next time when he touches me, I'll just disappear and never come back.

Riley, I have to leave today. I know when I go home he'll be waiting and he'll be mad that I snuck out. I'm hoping I can ward off or lessen my punishment by agreeing to go back to Boston with him. I'll be gone and out of your life by the time you read this, if you ever do.

Be happy, Riley. I can't bear to think of you sad. You deserve the best, and I'm damaged. Find someone who makes you laugh, because your laugh is magical. It makes all the bad go away. Just promise me you won't go back to that slut, Kaylee. She doesn't deserve you, especially after what she did.

Fill your picture frame with somebody who'll worship you and treasure every minute with you. If she's a teacher, all the better. Teachers rock!

Yes, I'm going to marry Michael. Not because I want to, but because I have to. He's made it clear my dad's job is at risk, plus he'll make my life hell forever, if I don't. So, I guess I am like Mom and Grams after all. I'll live a loveless marriage to keep up appearances, only I swear I'll never give the bastard what he wants. An heir to his throne. You were the only one I ever dreamed about having kids with. Michael won't get that dream. Not from me.

Love you, baby. Thanks for teaching me what true love is. Try not to hate me forever. Knowing how you've been raised, you probably need proof to "support the truth." If so, follow the instructions on page 2, but I warn you. You may never look at me the same, but it won't matter, because I'll never see you again. Only in my dreams. The ones that aren't nightmares.

Here's me kissing you goodbye. Forever yours, Taylor.

Page two? A second page existed? I kicked the closet doors apart and crawled to the pile of garbage spread across my floor. The other folded piece of paper glowed against the dark carpet. I held it in my fist and scrambled crablike back to my hideaway.

The lump in my throat made breathing nearly impossible and my chest hurt where my heart tried to break through my ribs.

"I warn you. You may never look at me the same..."

246

The words played in my mind like a ticker-tape warning of impending disaster. But Taylor was right. I needed proof. I just didn't know that proof would spin my world backwards. I unfolded the page, unsealing the catalyst to my personal apocalypse.

Riley, if you're reading this, then you must still not believe me. Not sure how I feel about that. Okay, here goes. Today when I went to the clinic to get one of those pills to make sure I didn't get pregnant after Michael raped me (that's why I borrowed your truck), I decided to document what I could, in case I disappear you'll know who to look for, or how to identify my body.

I took pictures with my cell phone before changing back into my clothes. Maybe it was what the doctor said about telling somebody. Maybe it was because I need you to believe me.

So, I've left you my cell phone, partly for the pictures, partly so you can never contact me again. Scroll to My Pictures and under the envelope labeled "Death" you'll find what you need. Each picture is dated so you'll have the proof I didn't lie. I'd never lie to you Riley. You are too important to me to disrespect you with untruths.

Sorry, baby. I wish I could take it all back and rewind the clock. But I can't. It's over. If you still need more proof, which I'll probably hate you for, under your seat are DNA samples. But I warn you, Riley, if you have to go that far, we're done forever. You'll have taken the last shred of decency I leave this world. Whatever. At this point, it doesn't matter. –T.

My stomach swirled with nausea, but I'd come this far. I couldn't turn back. I flipped open the phone. An angel smiled back, a puff of pink spun sugar sticking to the end of her nose. God I missed her and loved her with every shredded piece of my broken heart. How could she say I'd never see her the same? I'd sell my soul if I could have Taylor in my arms again. If I could be her "super-hero."

The phone stuck to my sweaty palms. I swallowed a baseball size lump. My breathing stopped a long time ago and my head buzzed with the panic filling every cell in my body. I clicked on "Death" and set the demons free.

Picture one: Her round boobs that fit my hands like they were meant to be there. At first I felt confused. Why *this* picture? But my brain and eyes finally connected. Red spots dotted her porcelain skin. *Hickeys? The asshole is a fucking vampire!* But they looked wrong. I enlarged the photo on one of the strange marks, waiting for the pixels to catch up.

I could have sucked my dresser across the room when the picture cleared. *Bite marks!* I felt the shudder roll down my spine and a slow burn ignited. Having no choice, I pressed the next frame.

Picture two: Taylor's toned tummy. The one I loved to smother with kisses, listening to her musical giggles from the tickling of my stubbly chin. I could barely make out the tiny silver ring piercing her navel, except that the metal shined against the large green and purple bruise surrounding it. The bastard had to have punched her hard to

248

make that size of a bruise! Fingers of rage clamped my jaw, holding the scream inside.

My thumb rolled over the next image. Picture three: I recognized the lazy seductive curve of her back, the way it scooped slightly before rounding into her tight ass. There was the butterfly, fluttering high on her hip, marking the boundary between lusting and losing control. It's pretty pink and yellow wings edged a dark burgundy, purple, and ghastly green mark. I flashed the light to my raised foot. The mark had to be at least a size ten—a *boot* size ten.

One picture remained, but I couldn't bear to see more. I knew where more bruises or bite marks would be and my stomach couldn't take it. I don't remember crashing out of my closet, or the slam of my bedroom door against the wall, knocking my soccer team picture to the floor. All I knew was the feel of cold porcelain against my palms and the burning, uncontrollable heaves of acid bile my gut wrenched into the toilet.

"Riley!" Mom gasped from the doorway, wrapping her terry cloth robe tight around her waist. She went on *autopilot,* grabbed a washcloth from the cabinet next to the sink and doused it in cold water. The cool wetness wrapped my neck, tempering the spasms in my throat. Her fingernails lightly massaged my scalp, her hushed whispers calming me slightly.

"Sweetheart? Are you okay?"

I flushed my horrid reaction away and leaned back against the wall, drawing slow deep breaths. Mom lowered beside me, staring with a deep crease between her teary hazel eyes.

My voice rasped when I finally spoke. "Where's Dad?"

"He should be home any minute. He got called to the station on some new case during the movie, so I came home alone. Why? Is something wrong?"

"I need to talk to him. Something's *really* wrong, but it's not me." I slipped my arm around her shrugged shoulders and feigned a weak smile. "It isn't Jax either."

I stretched onto my feet, reaching a hand out to help Mom onto hers. "I need some air. I'll be out on the deck." My thumb eased the slice in her brow. "Stop worrying, okay?"

"Not until I'm six feet under and then I'll just haunt you."

"Promise to make that scary 'oooh' sound?"

She smacked my chest really hard.

**

August would soon end, hopefully taking the sultry nights with its departure. I sat in a patio chair, staring into the glittery spatter against a black velvet backdrop overhead. My T-shirt clung to me with the humidity and I closed my eyes, picturing Taylor pushing it over my head while her lips sampled my salty skin.

This night would have been a perfect night to lie beneath the stars on a blanket together, naked, basking in the afterglow surrounded by colorful ripped packages. A night we talked about, teased about, and

250

planned. Our first *real* time together, crossing over the threshold in each other's arms, leaving our childhood behind. A dream that never came true. A threshold she was forced to cross without me there to save her.

I pinched my eyes against the painful image in my head. Jaxson went back on the graveyard shift at work, but he was the only one I could release my secret to at the moment. The only person I'd confided to, which proved our brotherly bond had been reinforced. I flipped my phone open.

She didn't lie. I have proof. Telling Dad.

I shut my phone off and rested my head against the chair's metal frame. My neck felt moist from unacknowledged tears and my sobs were silent to my ears until my father's voice penetrated the deep silence.

"What the hell is wrong? I haven't seen you cry like this since you were little."

Mom's body fit into the space of the open sliding door, her nails nervously rapping against the metal frame.

"Dad, tell Mom to go inside. I need to talk to you alone."

"Riley, what's this about?" he asked.

"Please Dad."

He considered me a minute longer, then without removing his gaze from me, he called out to my mom. "Honey, go inside. This is between Riley and me."

"But—"

"Bev." A sharper, but kind demand. A tone we all recognized as the "end of discussion."

The slider rolled shut and I watched her walk away, defeated.

A lingering sob shuddered over me. "Thanks. I hate doing that to her, but I can't deal with her reaction right now." I faced my father, his eyes still studying me. "I'm not sure I can handle yours, either, but I have no choice."

Dad pulled another patio chair in front of me, placing us knee-to-knee; eye-to-eye. Even with the black surrounding us, I knew he'd watch my eye inflections to see if I told the truth. It took me and Jax until age fourteen before we learned to hold his gaze without shifting eyeballs. Jax could pass any retina test. Poor Dirk. We'd be long gone by the time he'd need to learn our cagey skills.

I pulled all the air I could into my lungs. "Dad, Taylor's been hurt. Real bad, and I don't know what to do about it."

My dad's head dropped, his question mouthed to the rotting wood slats beneath us. "Did you have anything to do with her being hurt?" Something in the way he said it made the question sound as if he directed it at a *suspect*, not his son.

"What? Are you thinking *I* hurt Taylor and this is some warped confession?"

"You tell me, Riley. You were pretty torn up when I came out here, and you didn't want your mother to hear what you had to say. You set the stage for suspicion, not me. You and Taylor have been joined at

252

the hip for the past two months, which would make you the number one suspect."

I jumped to my feet, screaming into the darkness. "NO!" Suddenly, the word "suspect" silenced my rant. My dad's eyes steeled his emotions when our gazes locked. He had on his "cop face" and I figured out fast, I was being *interrogated.*

"Wait a minute. What did you mean *I* would be the most likely 'suspect'? Has something happened to Taylor?" His eyes dropped and my heart slammed to my toes. Salty tears burned the edges of my eyelids. I prepared myself for the worse.

"Dad, I've never asked you about any case you were investigating, but this is different. This is Taylor we're talking about. I'm asking you to cross the line this once, for me. Please? What's happened to her?"

A few uncomfortable minutes passed, feeling more like hours as I waited, the fear inside me threatening to unleash the beast within.

"Dad?"

The sigh sounded heavy and resigned. "Sit, Riley."

"No."

"Fine, suit yourself. I received a call tonight from Dr. Scott at the Planned Parenthood Clinic about a patient who came to see her this morning. The patient was eighteen years old and didn't want to give any information, but Dr. Scott said her conscience wouldn't let it go. Especially when she thought *I* might become personally involved and she wanted to forewarn me. I didn't know she was talking about Taylor, until you said something. I put two-and-two together based on your emotional instability, and just realized Dr. Scott thinks *you're* responsible for Taylor's injuries."

"*Injuries*?" Besides the ones I knew about? The thought terrified me.

"Keep in mind, Riley, I'm sticking my neck out here. Your mouth has to remain shut, regardless of your personal feelings. This is an ongoing investigation and I can't risk your jealous heart getting in the way and fucking it up so the asshole who *is* responsible, walks free and hurts someone else. Swear Riley you won't utter a word of what I'm about to tell you."

The pebble in the back of my throat didn't go away when I swallowed. "I swear."

"First, I'm going to ask you a very personal question and I need you to tell me the truth. The extent of your involvement with Taylor Wilson is pertinent to how we'll proceed in levying charges. Have you and Taylor *ever* had sex?"

"No." The answer came quick without so much as a breath to slow it down.

The sound of relief huffed through my father's lips. "Thank God." He drew another breath and I waited. "Dr. Scott said Taylor had significant bruising on her thighs, and well, other injuries associated with a violent assault. A rape. Son, Taylor was pretty battered up. Dr. Scott was alarmed at the extent of damage."

Picture *four*.

"You and Taylor have been quite the item around town and unfortunately, Dr. Scott had her suspicions that *you* were the perpetrator."

"*Me*? You honestly think I'm capable of doing something so brutal? To *Taylor*?"

I felt as if perched on the roof, watching the transformation take place when my "man-beast" erupted. My chair flew over the railing. My voice shrilled to the highest volume I could manage, feeling the strain on my vocal chords. There would be premature balding where wisps of hair pulled through my fists; my cries, heart wrenching and beyond consolation. I dropped to my knees and buried my head in my hands.

When my sanity returned and the beast retreated, my father held me in his arms, my mother crying over both of us. She yelled at Dirk to shut his window and go back to sleep—that everything was okay.

Two new guests closed the circle surrounding my emotional breakdown. Pete and Jaxson.

"*Jax?* What the hell are you doing here?" Dad barked, probably irritated the lid could be blown off his investigation. "And Pete? I didn't call for any back-up"

"Jaxson's *jewelry* set off the alarm when he left work before the scheduled time."

"Don't worry 'robo-cop'. I had permission to leave. You can call my boss to check, which you will."

"Damn straight," Pete retorted. He stepped back and dialed a number on his cell.

Jaxson's fists pushed his waist. "Why the hell didn't you answer my texts, Riley? What do you mean you have *proof*?"

My dad's caring arms disappeared, his brow arched my direction. "What *proof* Riley?"

"Does someone want to tell me what's going on?" Mom asked.

"Bev, as much as I want to tell you, especially because I see how worried you are for Riley, babe, I *can't*. Although this involves him, he's not responsible."

"This has to do with Taylor, doesn't it?" the question directed at me, not Dad. "She called this morning to thank me for letting her help out at the shop. She said she was going home a week early, but didn't have time to come by and say goodbye."

"She's *gone*?" both Dad and Jax asked on the same breath.

I eased onto my feet. "Yeah. She went back to Boston…with Michael."

"Shit!" they both responded on an outgoing breath.

My mother dropped into Dad's patio chair and folded her arms. "Sorry dear. Now *I'm* involved. This is a family matter as much as a police matter."

Pete closed out any remaining space in our group. "Uh, Chief? Jax is cleared, but sounds like maybe I should stick around?"

"Well, we're not doing this out here. Everybody inside and downstairs. *Dirk* is not invited to this 'three ring circus'. Pete, get the recorder out of the cruiser. Bev, make coffee."

Over the next two hours, I answered repeated questions about my relationship with Taylor. My mother tried to remain unaffected when I described unsavory, intimate details. But everyone squirmed uncomfortably when I showed the pictures on Taylor's cell phone to Dad, listening to him describe the gruesome details of her injuries into the recorder. Tears streamed over both mine and my mother's cheeks.

"That's what made you sick?" Mom asked in a small voice when the recorder turned off.

"Yeah. I'd just finished reading her letter telling me the pictures were on the phone. When I got to the huge bruise on her back, I lost it. Who could do something like that to someone as sweet as Taylor? To *any* girl?" Tears reappeared from some unknown water reserve in my body, because I didn't think it was possible I could still cry. "I don't know what I'd do if I'd seen the last picture, or the DNA…"

Shit!

I ran up the stairs with Jaxson chasing me. "Riley, what the hell?" I pressed my finger to my lips and gestured for him to follow. When I got out to the truck I tugged the bundle under the seat, ripping the cloth cover on the metal frame.

"What's *that?*"

"I'm not sure I want to know. Taylor said this had the DNA proof, but we were through forever if I found it."

"You're through forever anyway, now that the monster has her."

"You know what Jaxson? I do *not* need to hear that ever again! Got it?"

"Fine. Give that to Dad and walk away. Then you can honestly say you don't know what it is." He regarded me. "But that's not going to work, is it?"

"No, damnit. I have to know it *all*."

Three sets of eyes watched us descend the stairs, the second step groaning loudly against our heavy steps. I handed what I came to the conclusion was a pillowcase, to Dad.

"Here. Taylor's letter said this would give you DNA proof."

I stepped back as if the contents when dumped, would release some rabid creature to attack me. Dad reached into the case and the first item he pulled out sent me running upstairs to my bedroom behind my locked door. Taylor's *church worthy,* white lace thong panties.

I swear I never touched a single stair on my retreat. I couldn't face whatever else had been packed inside that pillowcase and whether I ever saw Taylor again or not, I couldn't betray her. Even if she never knew, those secrets remained hers.

**

Sleep never happened and when dawn's pink rays slid through the slats of the blinds, I forced myself upright. The dry air etched my red eyeballs and the soreness of my stomach muscles mimicked hours of lifting weights. I couldn't muster a drop of spit from crying all night.

The coffee maker gurgled the last drops of black gold and I knew it would take more than one pot to get this family through today. Lucky bounced up and down until I pushed the slider open, setting her free.

I stepped into the morning air, feeling the ripple in the seasons starting. The mornings were cooler with September knocking on August's door. In the distance, a light fog followed the river bed from the cooling rain showers early this morning.

The patio door hissed on its track when my dad appeared, already in uniform and a steaming mug of coffee in his hand.

"You better this morning, son?" His tone resonated apprehension and the air around us crackled with suspense.

"No," my answer mournful. "I may never be okay again." A long burning gulp seared my throat. "Dad, I've got to save her from that bastard. I don't know how, but I can't sit here and do nothing. Every day she's with him, she's in danger."

"Riley, these things take time. I can't have you going off half-cocked and doing something stupid. I promised you last night I'd keep you apprised of events, but you are going to have to trust me to handle matters."

"I can't promise anyone anything, right now. Not even you." A couple of blue jays played tag overhead filing the uncomfortable silence. I knew better, but I had to ask. "Did you find anything useful in the pillowcase?"

"Do you really want to know?"

"Part of me does. The other part of me feels like I've betrayed Taylor by giving it to you."

"Son, you helped Taylor. Not betrayed her. I won't get the lab tests back on the sheets for a couple of days, but hopefully, it will give us enough to contact the authorities in Massachusetts and start the paperwork to put that son-of-a-bitch in jail."

I swallowed hard. *Sheets.*

"Riley, I'm going over to Lydia Daniels this morning. If you're up to it, I'd like you to tag along. Pete will meet us there in thirty minutes."

He didn't have to ask twice. Lydia Daniels had to answer for her part in this hell.

**

I climbed out of Dad's car and froze on the front lawn. My "picture" stared back through shattered glass, as if my frame had been thrown against a brick wall. Two rockers; their paint chipped and faded, moved ghostly side-by-side as if Taylor and I were sitting in them, holding hands. Old and gray, but happy and still holding hands.

Lydia Daniels answered the door, clad in her robe and holding her cup of tea. Her furry slippers were dirty around the edges and she looked like she hadn't slept either.

"Morning, Sheriff." She wrapped her robe tighter. "Come in. I've got fresh coffee brewing."

Dad patted her shoulder. "Sorry for coming by so early, but the sooner we move on this, the better for Taylor's sake."

"Taylor? What's happened to Taylor?" she asked, hysteria capturing into her voice.

"She was *raped* by your asshole Michael, that's what happened to Taylor!" I stated with so much anger in my tone, it even surprised me. The glower from my father clued me I stepped out of line. I didn't give a damn. No polite way existed to "tiptoe" around this and I wanted to make sure Lydia Daniels knew the truth about her saintly "city boy."

"*Raped*?" she gasped.

We followed her into the dining room, all of us settling into a chair. Mrs. Daniels dipped her tea bag with enough force to cause the tea to slosh over the cup, forming a dark green circle on the crocheted tablecloth. She looked at the ring slowly spreading as if something foreign, and fell into a state of shock.

"I'll get a rag," I offered, trying to earn some points in my favor.

"Why are you here, Riley, if this is a police matter?" Lydia Daniels asked.

"Right now, Lydia, I'm just gathering information," Dad explained before I could say anything. "Taylor left her cell phone in Riley's truck. There were some disturbing pictures suggesting she…the bruising would corroborate sexual assault."

"So that's where my cell phone went. I thought about reporting it stolen, but Taylor must have taken it."

She talked like this was any other day and nothing out of the ordinary had happened. Suddenly, her bright denim blue eyes flashed with recognition of what Dad told her. I expected her to be enraged and validate the anger I felt, but she reacted the opposite. She *defended* Michael.

"*Bruising?* I can't believe Michael would do something so vile to Taylor. He loves her. They're engaged for heaven's sake! How do you know *Riley* didn't hurt Taylor."

I jumped from my chair. Rage boiled over and nothing stopped the words from exiting my mouth. "*Me?* You've got to be fucking kidding! *Michael* punched Taylor and kicked her. And you freaked out over my *hickey*? That jerk put *bite marks* all over her. Don't defend him!"

I reeled around drawing a deep, dizzying breath. Tears welled in my eyes so fast I couldn't see the room beyond the sheets of water. "You did this," I accused, my jaw clenched so tight I worried my teeth would crack. "You brought Michael here to take Taylor away from me." I swore by the guttural growl in my throat, I'd shape-shift into some creature any moment.

"I believed it was for the best. Taylor needed to reconnect with Michael before—"

"*Reconnect?* Well, they reconnected all right. And who is Michael the best for? Taylor or *you?*"

"That's enough, Riley!" Dad shouted.

"Is it? I don't think so. Good old Grams here thought *I* wasn't good enough for Taylor. Me. The 'son of the local sheriff' couldn't give Taylor the life she deserved!"

My face remained so close to Lydia Daniels she could smell my coffee breath and feel the contemptuous spit of my every word. "So tell me, Grammy? Does Taylor deserve the life *Michael's* giving her now?"

I stepped back when Dad and Pete closed in on me, raising my hands in surrender. "I'd *never* hurt Taylor like that. I love her. *Love* can't be *forced* and it sure as hell can't be *beaten* into someone. You disgust me, Mrs. Daniels. You have to take responsibility for the mess you've created, instead of sitting on your sanctimonious high horse!"

Pete grabbed my collar and dragged me away while my father apologized for my outburst."

"No, Stan. Don't chastise Riley for speaking the truth," she confessed quietly. "I did believe Taylor deserved better than your son, and forgive me, but I just can't wrap my head around this. Michael's always been such a dear boy."

Dad's finger went up and pointed my direction. My cue to remain silent. I planted myself on the bottom stair and Pete stood guard.

"Lydia, unfortunately, these types of people can be very deceiving."

Mrs. Daniels absentmindedly dipped her teabag, staring across the room with a pained expression. "Why wouldn't Taylor say anything to me? We've always been close."

"To save her dad's job," I interjected.

My father's head snapped my direction.

I held my palms up. "What? It's the truth. She told me in the letter. Michael threatened to have her dad fired if she said anything."

"Unfortunately, I can see Taylor doing that. Despite her parents' rocky relationship, Taylor loves her father." She folded her arms and inhaled a deep breath. "Show me these pictures."

"Lydia...."

"Stan! Show me the pictures!" she demanded. My father handed her the cell phone. Her eyes pinched in anguish at each picture. "Dear God. I was so wrong. So very, very wrong."

"Lydia, do you mind if we check out Taylor's room?"

"No, of course not."

I waited until my dad was out of earshot, though I doubted that was ever possible. The guy had "super-human" radar, why not hearing, too? But I still held one last secret.

"Mrs. Daniels, the night Taylor ran away you made it sound like maybe she'd purposely hurt herself. In her letter, she said she took your sleeping pills. Do you think she's capable of..."

"Riley, I don't know what she's capable of. None of us do because we're not walking in her shoes. If it was me, *yes,* I'd absolutely be capable of ending the nightmare."

I took the stairs two at a time, bursting into Taylor's bedroom. My legs ceased moving and hundred pound weights seemed attached to my feet. The room still had pale yellow walls with a daisy flower border running along the top. The lace curtains blew gently with the breeze from the open window. But my eyes couldn't focus on anything but the bed filling the room, appearing to grow in size as I stared at the diamond quilted satin fabric.

I ignored Pete and his fancy flashlight contraption. I knew what he was searching for, but I didn't want to acknowledge the findings. That way, everything remained in a fake world—one I could erase from my memory, pretend didn't exist. But it did.

The patchwork lap quilt usually folded over the back of the rocker, lay in a lumpy pile at my feet. I stared at the patches of fabric sewn together, none matching the other, but complete as a whole. Like me and Taylor. We were total opposites but together, a perfect fit.

I had to find her. I wanted a second chance at saving her from the monster who robbed her of the one thing she could never get back. I hated him. Wished him dead. A *violent* death for retribution. Searing him in hot oil would be too kind.

Dust curled around me as I ran the lane home. I vaguely remember Dad calling out to me and Lydia Daniels standing in the entryway, handing my dad a business card to contact Taylor's father. Pete might have tried to chase me, but lost interest when a possible heart attack threatened after five feet of physical exertion. The man *was* a doughnut.

I crashed through the front door, leaving it open for any person, critter, or mass murderer to enter. I crammed jeans, socks, underwear, T-shirts and Taylor's letter into my backpack, with my toothbrush, deodorant, and what I hoped to be a sharp razor, stuffed into the front pocket.

And my bottle of BLVGARI. Taylor bought it for me after sniffing the sample stick for hours. I never thought I'd be jealous of a piece of cardboard, but that cologne sample received more attention than I felt comfortable with. I bathed in it the night I snuck out and almost made the "homerun" before Grammy shed light on our sensuous moment. A moment meant to be our

first.

Hell, I never even got a *last.*

Dad and I collided at the bottom of the stairs. "Where do you think you're going?" he charged.

"Boston. Where else."

"How did you expect to get there? Your truck has over a hundred thousand miles on the odometer and the tires 'shine' they're so bald."

Either exhaustion took over or I slowly morphed into a girl. The flood gates opened again. I couldn't speak. I just stood there with a scrunched quivering lip while my shaking shoulders sold me out.

Dad's arms were a fortress around my body, shielding me from all the monsters pulling my world apart. I dropped my backpack and clenched his body to mine so tight I swore his badge would be forever imprinted on my chest. The clock on the mantle loudly ticked each second as I cried in my father's embrace. If I wasn't mistaken, I swore his shoulders shook with mine.

My mother's soft touch settled both our souls. "Hey, what's wrong with my guys, huh?" She rose on her tiptoes and stole a kiss of my father's cheek. "Stan, remember what it was like to be eighteen and in love. Riley's head and heart aren't communicating right now, so show some compassion."

Then she turned to me, holding out her hand. "Your keys, young man."

"I'm eighteen, you can't—"

"You're still in high school and living under our roof," she clarified, talking over me. "Age is not a factor in this case and you're in no frame of mind to make any decisions." She snapped her fingers impatiently and I handed her my keys. "School starts next week and Jaxson ships out. Life goes on, Riley. You can't stop the world and get off when something bad happens. I'm sorry for Taylor, really I am, but you are *my* priority. For now, you're going to have to trust your father to handle things."

I opened my mouth to argue, but realized it proved useless. My mother seldom interfered, leaving Dad to play the "heavy," so her playing the part now, plus knowing everything she'd been through this past year with Jaxson, I owed her.

For the first time in my life, I felt miles past helpless...I felt *hopeless*.

Twenty-Six
ATONEMENT
Jaxson

My palms felt sticky. I checked my breath against my hand, grateful I'd given up my nasty smoking habit, but craving a whole pack at the moment. My feet shuffled again over the doormat and I finally mustered enough courage to ring the doorbell.

I was shocked Ally agreed to see me, but I couldn't leave without at least saying goodbye…beg forgiveness…profess my undying love.

A breath lodged somewhere in my chest when the door opened.

"Hey, Jax."

"Ally. You, uh, look great. No, *beautiful.* Um, could I come in? I'm dying here. Please?"

Her body moved with the door, pressing against the wall and allowing me passage. I followed her into her father's study. The room never ceased to amaze me with built-in shelves on every wall and books lined up tightly, alphabetically categorized just like the city library. A set of open architect plans stretched over the top of the massive oak desk—the new strip mall slated for construction next spring.

I traced the angular lines of the proposed entrance with my finger. "Impressive. Your dad's done a good job."

"He'd like to think so. I just hope they bring some good stores in. Your mom's place is the only decent shop in town."

"Her friend, Pam, buys the stuff. She lives in New York and keeps up on the popular trends."

An uncomfortable silence took over. I moved from behind the desk, closing out the space between us, but when I tried to touch her, she stepped out of my reach.

"Ally?"

She walked to the floor length windows on the other side of the room. Something in her body language told me I wasn't allowed to follow. Keeping her back to me, she offered an explanation for her standoffish behavior. One that blindsided me.

"Jax, I'm with Brandon, now. We're even talking about maybe getting married in June."

I dropped my eyes when she turned to face me, not wanting her to see the tears forming. "Oh," I responded, almost inaudible. When her shadow threatened to cover me, I assumed my stalwart stance, minus the salute. However, the whine in my voice didn't match my posture.

"Brandon? *Why*? He's a player, Ally. He'll end up cheating on you."

"Like someone else we both know?"

"I *never* cheated on you that way."

"So there's *degrees* of infidelity? Some more acceptable than others? You let a teenage girl give you a blow job, Jax!"

"*No,* I didn't! She tried, but I wouldn't let her. You've got to believe me, Ally."

"Believe you." Stated, not questioned. Her arms crossed over her chest. "I don't think so, Jax. Been there done that, remember? Like I said. We're done."

"Yeah, I heard you. Tell me, sweetheart, is it different going down on Brandon?"

"Get out!" she screeched, throwing a book from the corner of the desk at me.

I paused in the doorway, moving slightly to avoid the second literary projectile aimed my direction. "Don't worry, I'm out of here. You can have your miserable life, Ally. You and Brandon deserve each other."

My reflexes were right on. I whirled around and clenched her wrists, stopping her fake nails from raking across my face. Lost in my seething jealousy, I dropped one last bombshell.

"Oh, and by the way, let me give you an engagement present. Your 'truly beloved'? He was in the backseat the night of the accident letting Shar Richards get him off while I fought the demon child in the front seat. I'm surprised she didn't bite his dick off when Kaylee jerked the wheel and slammed the marquee."

Her arms went limp. I regretted my immature and hurtful revelation when I saw the pain in her eyes. "Sorry. That was cruel. I shouldn't have said anything."

"Is it true?"

"Yeah. But, no one knows. I didn't want Brandon, or even the girls to get in trouble, so I took the blame. Please don't say anything. It's over now."

I released my grip and she stepped back.

"Brandon owes you. I could care less what happens to the 'baby bitches'. Sorry, Jax, I just assumed…"

"It's okay. I've heard the rumors." I opened the front door and stepped onto the porch. "I ship out in three days. I only wanted to stop and say goodbye. I also wanted to say I love you and apologize for being an asshole the whole time we've been going out."

"You weren't an asshole the whole time," she smiled.

Her kiss was soft, but quick, and not followed by an invitation for another. "Take care, Jax. Come home safe. You're family needs you."

"What about you, baby? Will you ever need me again?" I already knew the answer and the tear rolling over her cheek and dropping off the frown on her lips, confirmed it. "Guess not. All the same, I want you happy, Ally. With Brandon, or whoever. Be happy." I hugged her tight and kissed her cheek. "Take care."

**

I pulled into the driveway, buried my head in the gym T-shirt I'd left on the back seat, my tears reviving a sweaty stench. Riley dropped into the passenger seat, surprising me.

"Your dick fall off, 'Nancy'?" he jibed, poking fun at emotional state.

I looked over at Riley whose eyes were also rimmed red. "What's your bra cup size up to 'Alice'?" I retorted.

"Size C. I'm growing big ones."

"God, we're pathetic." I regarded Riley when he didn't have a flippant comeback. "You okay little bro?" He shook his head and looked away. "Riley, Dad's got this you know that, don't you? He won't let you down."

"He won't let you down either, Jax."

"I know. We're damn lucky. Hell, I'm even going to miss the old man." Riley remained too somber. I elbowed his shoulder. "But I won't miss you."

"Sure you will. The minute you say 'Sir, yes Sir, Sergeant' and spit on an officer, you'll think of me," he laughed.

My new lisp had become Riley's favorite attack spot. I reached out to playfully punch him, but gathered him into my arms instead. We didn't say anything, just clung to each other, shouldering each other's burdens for a few seconds.

We parted, both of us flicking away wayward tears. I grabbed my crotch. "Just checking," I teased.

"Hey," Riley sighed. "Act surprised when you go around back. We're celebrating your birthday, too, because you'll be gone when it rolls around."

"Ugh no! *Really*?"

"Yep. You're getting the pony you always wanted."

"Forever the smart-ass, aren't you?"

272

"No, just smart. You do 'ass' much better." He was out of the car before I could reach him.

Mom's gaze over my shoulder when we rounded the side of the house looked confused. I couldn't tell if she felt sad or relieved I hadn't brought Ally back. However, my eyes left hers and met Brandon's immediately. By the grimace on his face, he knew where I'd come from and the fact he didn't have the balls to tell me, brought a rush of anger close to the surface.

Riley stepped beside me. I'd given him an overview of what happened at Ally's as we walked to the back yard. "Well, this should get interesting. I'm not big on the whole advice thing, but remember Brandon's been around a lot longer than Ally. Plus Mom will be majorly pissed if you spoil this for her. Keep your cool, Jax. You can duke it out with Brandon later."

After some uncomfortable and not deserved praise for my so called *choice* to join the Army, we were allowed to eat. Somewhere between the baked beans and the grill steaming with steaks, Brandon cornered me.

"Jax, can we talk?"

"Nothing to talk about. Ally told me. Wish your gonads were bigger and you'd told me yourself. Shit, Brandon, we've been friends since third grade. I've covered your ass more than once. The least you could have done was tell me you were banging my girlfriend."

"*Ex*-girlfriend."

"Whatever, dude. We never made it official. By the way, I told her about the accident. Everything. Including Shar."

Brandon paled and he yanked me away from any eavesdropping ears, although our private conversation in the corner of the deck met with more suspicion than if we'd kept arguing and spooning salads.

"Why the fuck did you do that?" he snarled.

"Relax. Believe it or not, Ally wasn't that upset. Maybe she really does love you. But take my advice, keep your tongue in your mouth until you're sure," I laughed.

Suddenly, Ally being with Brandon didn't hurt so much. I did love her with all my heart, but if she was happier with Brandon, then that's what I really wanted for her. He would probably end up making a lot of money, winning her dad's approval. Something I never achieved in the two years we dated.

"We okay, Jax?" he asked pensively.

"Just don't hurt her, dude. I want her to be happy, so if you're really my best friend, make it happen. Otherwise, I'll kick your ass when I get back."

**

The sun started its decent in the western sky, and any food not consumed had been stacked in the refrigerator. Brandon left to spend the evening with Ally, sending a jolt of jealousy straight to my broken heart. I dumped the trash and returned to the backyard, where Mom gave the Hendersons a tour of her rose garden while Dad paced, cell phone plastered to his ear.

274

In the distance, Riley slowly walked toward the thicket where the pond lay hidden. I reached into the tin tub of ice and pulled out a beer. Dad's brows knitted.

"Don't worry. I'm sure I've got a surprise pee test waiting in the morning. I don't want anything but Mom's lemonade on the dipstick." I gestured toward the disappearing figure and my dad shook his head, his glower darkening. "Okay, then this *is* for me." I pulled a long sip and stepped off the deck to follow Riley.

Waiting until he cleared the rise, I followed, undetected. I watched from atop the small hill as Riley skipped stones across the pond, sending sparkling ripples over water that resembled gold glitter with the setting sun peeking through the treetops.

"So what's the record," I asked, startling him.

He walked over to the tree where our pocket knives had carved the scores. "Hard to tell with the sap oozing out of the cuts. Looks like eleven, maybe? Has your initials by it, so it must be a lie."

"Nothing here was ever a lie," I stated.

We both stood in quiet reverence. Leaves rustled overhead and birds chattered in the pines at the far end of the pond.

A heavy breath escaped my lips. "I still can't believe we made this. I remember how excited I'd get when school ended, knowing we'd spend the summer working on it. Damn those were the best summers."

"Seems like a lifetime ago. When did life get so complicated, Jax?"

"When our dicks reacted to boobs. I swear girls are descendents of the Devil. They're a fucking amusement ride—one you're scared to

275

death of, but when it's over, you're addicted." I handed him the beer. "Here. Thought maybe you could use one."

"Dad know?"

"Do you honestly care?"

"Not really."

Riley took a couple of long pulls, then poured the amber ale into the dark green pond water.

"Hey, that's my good stuff!" Dad brushed his pants off after he slid a few feet in the dirt. "Why are you pouring it out?"

"Christening the pond," Riley replied.

"It's going to a far more deserving place than the sewers of our fine city," I joked.

Dad let out a long noisy breath, his neck craning to take in the surroundings. "Can't believe I let you boys keep this death trap. Tried the rope swing once and damn near tweaked the 'family jewels' off."

"You were *naked*?" We both shrieked. "EEWWEE!"

"Just because I'm over forty doesn't mean I can't relive some of my youthful memories."

"I'm draining the pond," Riley declared.

"Burn the rope swing while you're at it," I added. Both of us looked at each other, thinking the same thought. *Not touching it.*

"All right, I'm joking. I didn't swim naked in the pond for the same reasons you're thinking. I figured you two had already done disgusting things in that water," Dad laughed.

"Only Jax," Riley proffered.

The joviality died as fast as it rose and Dad scratched the back of his neck, nervously shifting his feet. "Jax? I need to talk to Riley, privately."

"No problem. See you back at the house."

I'd loved to have been a beetle tucked under a rock to listen to their conversation. Judging by my father's demeanor, Riley was in for some bad news. He should have finished the beer.

Twenty-Seven
WHEN "WORSE" GETS "WORSE"
Riley

Jaxson left a little too fast and gooseflesh skittered over my arms. Dad perched on one of the boulders we'd dragged and rolled for "seating." It was a wonder Jax and I didn't suffer hernias or permanently damage important body parts moving the large rocks.

I stared at the dirt, milk chocolate in color with different sizes and colors of pebbles jutting through the powdery imprints left from the soles of my shoes.

"What." The statement echoed, splitting the air.

"The preliminary DNA tests proved positive on the sheets and panties. Based on what Taylor told you, the pictures, and the estimated time, uh, the alleged attack occurred, there's enough evidence to support a rape charge against Michael Barnes. Lydia Daniels admitted to not being home, so Taylor was alone with him. The degree of color changes in the bruising also collaborate Taylor's story, along with your eyewitness account of her physical and emotional state when you first saw her. I would guess you arrived within thirty minutes of when…"

"The animal killed his prey. Taylor's eyes were 'dead' when I saw her, Dad. Vacant. I should have known right then. If I'd been paying attention to something besides my stupid jealousy and that damn diamond, I would have…*should have* known something was wrong."

I lifted my eyes to Dad's. "I heard her scream. Did I tell you that? When she called out my name after I said the cruelest things I could to her—just before I reached my truck. I didn't even turn around. The door slammed and she screamed. The bastard punched, kicked, bit…hell I don't know! But he hurt her while I stood a few feet away, self-absorbed and going ape-shit. I could have ran back, busted the damn door down and killed the asshole! I had a second chance to save her and I blew it. I. Let. Him. Hurt. Her!"

Dusty tendrils curled into my mouth, covering my tongue with a gritty paste. I choked when the dirty mist strangled my breath, and rolled onto my side, coughing up Dad's precious *ale* into a puddle next to my cheek. I never remembered falling to the ground.

Dad's arms scooped in my armpits, wrenching me upright and landing his foot ankle deep in the water when my body weight shifted in his arms.

"Damnit Riley! Snap out of this!" He pushed me back onto the rock and slapped my cheek."

"Ouch!"

"Look at me." His fingers gripped my chin, forcing me to stare at him. "This is *not* your fault. None of it. Nor is it Taylor's. She's an innocent victim of a deviant jerk who gets his 'rocks off' abusing girls. Just like you said. A monster. But one you're no match for, Riley. Thank God you *didn't* go back into that house. By being selfish, you may very well have saved Taylor's life! Got that? If that asshole was okay with doing what he did to her in that short of time, who knows what he would have done if you'd pushed his anger over the edge."

"But what kind of a life did I save her for, Dad? How long before something worse happens?"

Dad dropped to his haunches clamping my shoulders. "Riley, I'm fairly certain Taylor isn't the only girl this Michael guy has hurt. This sick behavior didn't just manifest itself one afternoon. My guess is, she's not his first victim—just the one he wants to marry, or I should say *own*. If we can keep that from happening, we might buy some time to find the others. The more who come forward and accuse Michael, the longer he'll stay locked up."

"But what does stalling their wedding do for Taylor? He'll just keep beating her."

"Maybe. But based on what Lydia Daniels has told me about Michael, he'll want Taylor to have a virtuous appearance and be *unmarked* for their wedding. Personally, I believe this 'nut job' fantasizes, Riley. He'll want things to be perfect…including Taylor."

"And if you're wrong?"

My dad took the handkerchief out of his pocket and wiped my face. "Let's pray I'm not." He hoisted me onto my feet, handing me the cloth. "Wet that and clean your face. You'll scare the hell out of your mother."

I looked at his wet pant leg and a half laugh burst through my caked lips. "And she'll think you missed the bush or didn't get your zipper down in time."

He looked down at his feet. "Damn. These are my good shoes, too."

Twenty-Eight
PRETENSES
Taylor

We waited almost two hours before being seated for dinner. The law firm rented out *The Landing*, Marblehead's popular waterfront restaurant for the celebratory dinner. Dad got his promotion and Michael got me. A merger benefiting everyone. Except 'yours truly'.

I wore a strapless cranberry dress, cut low enough in the front for Michael to leer at my chest, but high enough in back to cover the yellow-green bruise on my back. Luckily, the one on my arm shrunk and I covered it with make-up. I had no idea how I'd manage eating a full meal. I barely kept anything down because my stomach still hurt from where Michael's fist made contact a couple weeks ago. Weight fell off me every day.

The one thing I was grateful for? The bleeding. Constant bleeding. Turns out my period came right on schedule. Coupled with the side effects of either the morning-after pill or internal injuries, I'd been blessed with a two-week reprieve from Michael even attempting to get close to me. Apparently, he's grossed out by the whole monthly "female issue." Little did he know, this would be the longest menstrual cycle I could possibly contrive.

Michael's car had two seats with a long console that kept my body separated from his. He opened the top for the ride home and I leaned back, letting the cool air blow through my hair. A sliver of peace filled me.

I made it through dinner, smiling and nodding when appropriate, pleasing Michael. He'd been attentive, handling me carefully so no one would notice me wince if he held too tight. The kisses he lavished on me frequently during the evening, were his "public showcase" kisses, keeping his tongue in check and pressing only lightly so he appeared the perfect gentleman.

The façade worked. We appeared happy and excited about our pending nuptials slated for two weeks from tonight, thanks to Michael's formal announcement, which trumped the congratulations intended for Dad. I held out hope for an October wedding, wondering if I could follow a Halloween theme and walk down the aisle as a ghost, because I felt like one.

I blamed myself for the twisted change in dates. When we returned from Wellsville, I made the mistake of suggesting we hold off having sex until married so our wedding night would be "special." I made the offer more enticing by explaining that by then, the bruises would be gone and my naked body would appear unscathed.

Michael actually considered the idea, until he stopped by my house the other night to pick me up for another one of his family's dinner extravaganzas. He walked in my bedroom catching me wearing only my panties. He demanded sex right that second…in my bedroom…with my mother across the hall, getting ready to join us for dinner.

"No! Mom will hear us," I argued. I knew damn well she didn't care. She'd let Michael come into my bedroom unannounced. Everyone believed his chaste charade, never thinking he'd "deflower" me before our wedding.

Michael also entranced my mother. His presence in my bedroom reassured her the wedding would happen and her daughter would marry Boston's most eligible bachelor. What a feather for her socialite hat.

I remembered how Michael's eyes roved my body, his nose wrinkling momentarily with disgust at the bruise covering my stomach. We'd only been home a week and the visual mark of his abuse had actually turned a darker purple.

The eyes I hated darkened with sick pleasure when they rested on my bare chest. Two steps brought him across the room and his hands on me before I could reach for something to cover myself or move out of the way. He pinned me against the wall with his body, the bruise on my back smarting against the pressure.

"Ouch! What are you doing?"

His mouth moved over my chest, "I think it's obvious." Fingers stroked the inside of my thighs, his pulse quickening in the hot lips pushing hard on mine.

I closed my mouth and pushed him back. "My period is still going."

"Shit." He stepped away. "How long does that go for anyway? I'm dying babe. I've got to have you."

"Honestly, given what happened in Wellsville, it'll probably be awhile." He hated when I reminded him of that day. I punctuated the moment. "If you want, I can go to a doctor to make sure nothing's wrong?" Just the ice needed to put out the fire.

"No. Nothing's wrong, anyway. You're perfect." He kissed me lightly and left me to finish getting ready.

Thinking I bought myself some time, I semi-relaxed later at his family dinner. Until dessert. Michael tapped his fork against his glass.

"Everyone? Taylor and I have a surprise." He turned to his mother, his face shifting into a boyish pout. "I hope this won't cause you too much stress, Mommy, but Taylor's kind of anxious...*you know*. So I agreed to let her move the date up." He raised his glass and my stomach lurched. "We're getting married in two weeks!"

The room transformed into jubilation and chaos. Two weeks. Not six. Not even four. Two weeks until imprisonment in matrimonial hell. My mother squealed in elation.

Later, alone with my dark thoughts, I finally allowed the floodgates to open. I gave permission for my heart to ache for Riley...to miss him. On the drive home to Boston from Wellsville, I forbade a single tear to drop. I knew if one fell, I'd be admitting to my heart I'd made a horrific mistake by leaving. The recognition of such a grave error in judgment would also acknowledge *I* existed. And I didn't. I'd turned into a shell of some girl who once knew true love, but now, knew only anger, hatred, and unbearable loneliness.

**

Michael's hand sliding under the edge of my skirt, his fingers stroking my thigh, reminded me my present nightmare still played on. Cautiously, I brushed his hand away. He moved it to my bare shoulder, caressing my neck.

"Your dad acted strange tonight." His fingers purposely pinched my skin. "You didn't say anything, did you?"

"Ouch! No way. I've kept my promise. Why do you think he acted strange?"

"After dinner, he got a call on his cell and left the dining room. When he returned, I swear his eyes shot lasers through me. He kept giving me these evil stare-downs. I tell you, baby, the guy weirds me out."

"You're imagining things. My parents are thrilled we're getting married." A match made in Hell.

Michaels' hand wrapped my hair, tugging my head toward him.

"What are you doing?" I protested. He kept pulling.

"Babe, you've got to give me something. Two weeks is a long time."

His knee propped the steering wheel and he unzipped his pants. Suddenly, I knew what Michael wanted.

"No! Don't make me, Michael. Please! Save it for when we, uh…have more room. Besides, the console's in the way."

All the times Riley and I spent together he never even hinted about me going down on him. Never. Sometimes he tortured me by kissing my stomach, but that was as far as he took his mouth.

Tears welled in my eyes. I wanted nothing more than to be with Riley. With him, I felt safe. He respected me and never pushed. When I said "stop," he did, without whining. I knew I got him worked up all the time, but if I said "no," he didn't question. *Begged,* but only being playful. If Grammy hadn't turned on the flood lights that night, *stop* would have been the last thing I'd have said.

Michael kissed my hair, whispering over my ear. "If you want, I can pull over. There's a blanket in the trunk." He arched his pelvis and his knee lost grip of the wheel, swerving the car across the highway.

"Michael!" I screeched. My heart stopped beating as I watch white dotted lines dance sideways.

He stomped on the brakes, sending clouds of billowing smoke in the air. The car launched off the side of the road, into a crevasse. The airbags remained intact, but the engine killed and wouldn't restart.

"Fuck!" he shrilled, the nasty word chasing its echo into the darkness. No cars had passed us either way in the past half hour, probably because it was past midnight.

Nothing good happens after midnight.

Michael flipped on the car GPS and sent the satellite signal to his phone. He confirmed his coordinates with the towing service and snapped his phone shut. "Thirty fucking minutes!" he snarled.

His head snapped my direction and his hand clamped the back of my neck. "This is your fault! If you weren't being such a prude, we wouldn't be sitting in the middle of nowhere waiting to be murdered!"

Murder. A welcome alternative to what lie ahead for me.

"You're such a whiny bitch, Taylor!" He yanked a fistful of my hair. "You've got thirty minutes to convince me forgive you. Make it count baby!"

Bile licked the back of my throat. I prayed my dinner stayed down. Or maybe I prayed it didn't.

Twenty-Nine
PARTY CRASHERS
Riley

Wednesdays were worse than Mondays. I pulled late shifts on Tuesdays, which cut into my already sleepless nights. My three AP classes were on Wednesdays. I became mentally drained by the time the last bell rang, which then signaled soccer practice.

This Saturday marked the big match with our rivals, Edgemont High. I had to be on my game. I would lead out. However, since Taylor left, my head refused to get into any game except the one I planned.

Taylor would be getting married in five weeks. I volunteered for every shift I could trade for at Barneys, socking money away. My bus pass lay tucked between my mattresses. I would go to Boston and persuade Taylor not to go through with the wedding. If I had to kill Michael to help her make that decision, then I would—with pleasure.

Nobody knew about my plan. Not even Jaxson, whose departure date got postponed for two weeks. Next Monday he'd ship out. I guessed Dad and his sarge buddy cut some deal so Jax could stay longer and watch over me. Talk about the world rotating the opposite direction. *Jax* guarding *me*.

I tossed my backpack onto the kitchen table and went straight for the coffeemaker.

"Riley, that thing will scratch the wood tabletop. Please put it on a chair," my mother scolded, shepherding Dirk towards the garage. "And don't be late again. Your father said if he gets another call from that Sylvia woman in the attendance office, your job at Barney's is over."

"*Mom...*"

Dirk wrangled out from under Mom's arm, nearly spilling her coffee. "Dirk!"

"Sorry, Mom!" followed after his clonking footsteps running up the stairs. "I forgot my homework," he shouted before slamming his bedroom door.

"Honestly," my mother mumbled. Her eyes lifted to the ceiling. I decided God lived in our attic, right over the kitchen. "One daughter? Would that have been too much to ask?"

I bent and kissed the top of her head, desperately fighting the urge to tease her about the gray starting to form a silver stripe against her fake blonde hair. "Someday we'll all marry sex starved girls and you'll have three daughter-in-laws. Hell, you've probably already got at least one granddaughter from Jaxson somewhere in the world."

She slapped my arm. "That's not funny, Riley." Her expression softened and her thumb brushed over the permanent crease between my brows. "Riley, you'll find someone special again, I promise."

I stepped out of her reach and Dirk reappeared, breathless, holding a fistful of paper. Mom's attention turned to him, lecturing him all the way through the laundry room about how wrinkled his homework would be. "Don't be late, Riley!" were her parting words before the garage door slammed.

I poured a cup of coffee and stepped out onto the deck to drink it. The morning fog hovered, dampening the railing of the deck and hiding the thicket behind in a misty gray curtain. Unable to stop my thoughts from wandering, I let them trail off to an imaginary place where Taylor and I were still together…holding hands or touching body parts, depending on how long I had to daydream.

Jaxson's voice destroyed the fantasy of Taylor's lips about to press mine, reeling me back to my hellish existence. "Bro, someone's here to see you." I spun around, puzzled. "Lydia Daniels," he whispered.

I spied her through the glass door.

"What's *she* doing here?"

"Said she needs to talk to you. Do you want me to send her out so you have some privacy?"

"No. Anything she has to say needs a witness present. Or a bodyguard. I still blame her for Taylor leaving."

"Bro, don't go there again. Please. Let go."

"*Never.*"

I muscled past him, making no attempt to hide my disgust toward Mrs. Daniels. I set my mug on the counter. "What do you want?" I asked, mustering as much contempt as possible.

In her trembling fingers dangled an ivory envelope with mangled corners. She held the envelope out to me. "Here. This came in the mail yesterday. Apparently, I'm an afterthought, or a threat."

"What is it?"

"Open it, Riley." She paced the length of the dining room, muttering. "Saturday. I can't believe she'd do such a thing." She stopped and faced me, just as I pulled the engraved invitation from the gold lined envelope. "You were right. Michael's a monster."

I read the gold embossed words, one phrase in particular, over and over.

...pleased to announce the marriage of Taylor Grace Wilson and Michael Bradford Barnes. Celebrate their joyous union by attending a reception held in their honor...

"They're married?" I choked, feeling the warm wet trail of a single tear crawl over my cheek.

"*This* Saturday. Michael moved the wedding up, according to Grace."

"Taylor?" I rasped, tasting snot mixed tears dripping off my top lip. "Is she okay?"

Lydia shrugged, her own eyes shimmering. "No one will let me talk to her. I believe her mother would say something if she wasn't. My invitation is just a courtesy. Grace said Michael only wants immediate family present for the ceremony."

"He's keeping her isolated," Jaxson chimed in. "Easier to keep her under his control if there's not a lot of outside influence."

"Trapped is more like it," Mrs. Daniels sneered. "I can't believe I didn't see the signs before. The way Michael shadowed her wherever she went, never giving us a moment alone. When I think back to those last couple of days...how quiet Taylor was after I returned—"

"Shut up already! I don't want to hear *Michael's* name again. Ever!"

I rushed up the stairs, leaving Lydia Daniels alone with Jax. I couldn't handle another word out of the woman's mouth. *She* brought Michael to Wellsville. *She* ruined everything. *She* not only destroyed Taylor's life, but mine as well.

My fist clenched the wedding invitation. I looked at the clock. First period was well under way. Dad would be getting "the call" any minute and I'd be grounded. That meant I barely had an hour to act on the thoughts rambling in my head. Dad would come here if I didn't show up at school by next period. Wonder how he'd handle finding me absent from *home*?

I grabbed my duffel bag, dumping in a change of clothes, shoes, and a pillow for sleeping on the bus. Fumbling between the bedding and mattress, I located my ticket to Boston. I shoved my iPod and earphones in my pocket and grabbed the wad of cash I'd been saving from under the old aquarium in the top of my closet. Almost four hundred dollars.

As soon as I heard the front door shut, I made my way down the stairs, rounding the corner to the kitchen and smacking into Jax. He tugged the strap slung over my shoulder.

"What's up with the duffel bag?"

"Nothing."

"You lie like a rug, Riley. What's going on?"

I scuffed my toe against the tile. "I'm going to Boston. I've got to stop Taylor from marrying that freak."

"Then what?"

"I don't know, Jax. But I can't sit on my ass waiting for 'justice to be served'. I didn't protect her before, but I can sure as hell give it one last shot."

"How are you getting there?"

"What are you? My surrogate parent?" I held up the bus ticket. "Satisfied?"

"So what do I tell Mom? She'll be furious. And Dad? Shit Riley. You could blow the case wide open. That ass could walk free!"

"He won't be walking anywhere when I'm through with him. At least not standing up straight."

"Jail's not worth it, Riley."

"No, but Taylor is."

Jax didn't argue my statement. He scrubbed the dark stubble covering his head. "Don't move. Give me fifteen minutes and don't answer the phone." He took the stairs two at a time.

"Huh?"

Jax stuck his head out of his bedroom. "I'm going with you. We'll take Bessie."

Bessie was Jaxson's restored Boss 302 Mustang. Candy apple red, the engine bored out to peak performance, fat tires and chrome mags that shone brighter than the sun when polished. The scent of the black leather interior, mingled with just the right combination of air fresheners hanging from the cigarette lighter, could be bottled and labeled "SEX."

I dropped my bag in the entry, placing my bus ticket on the credenza. I hurried back to the kitchen and wrote a note, propping it against the fire hydrant jar full of dog treats. I grabbed a box of Cheese Nibs from the pantry.

"Dude, you're not eating in my car."

"Jax, we'll to have to drive twenty-four-seven to get there in time. We're eating in the car."

"You will vacuum every speck of imitation cheese dust when you bring her back, understand?"

I slung my bag over my shoulder and shoved a baseball cap on my head. "Bessie or Taylor?"

"Both. I hope. Now let's get the hell out of here before Dad pulls up. We're both in deep enough shit as it is."

I locked the front door, leaving my common sense beside my bus ticket on the entry table. The rules of the game just changed. Jax became my partner-in-crime, supporting me in a plan I hadn't created yet. Hopefully by the time we reached Boston, I'd receive a revelation telling me exactly what to do.

Until then, I'd enjoy my box of cheese crackers and daydream.

When I pulled up to a sleazy motel off the interstate in
Connecticut, Riley went ram-rod straight in the passenger seat. "Why
are we stopping here? We're almost there!"

"I'm exhausted and so are you, not to mention we have no plan
once we arrive in Boston. Do you even know where this 'blessed event'
is taking place? Boston isn't Wellsville, Riley."

"Ellsville," he corrected under his breath.

"Shut the fu—"

"Fine! I get it. Four hours, Jax. That's it. I can't risk being late. Shit,
that asshole has probably talked her into eloping. This could all be for
nothing."

"Riley, for the love of God!" I shouted, exasperated with his
attitude.

I threw open the driver's door and reached behind the seat to grab
my own duffel bag. Everything I needed for training camp was packed
inside. As soon as Riley stopped Taylor from saying "I do" and I
helped him hide Michael's body, I'd be on a plane for Virginia to catch
my unit. I just had one more loose end to tie up. Call Dad.

Disturbing described the room when we opened the door. Two
beds with mattresses sagged close to the ground, framed a small night
table missing part of a leg. So that's why the huge yellow page

directories were still in print. Dive motels across the nation used them to hold up broken furniture. I held the coffee carafe up for inspection. A milky residue swarmed the glass.

"We'll get coffee on the way in the morning."

"Morning! I didn't agree to a fucking *overnight* stay!"

"Calm down Riley. These walls are almost transparent they're so thin. You going off half crazed will summon the police, if not an entire S.W.A.T. team and chopper crew. We'll both be in jail instead of Boston. Dad will leave our carcasses behind bars to rot and Taylor will be the bride of Frankenstein, so drop the 'drama queen' routine."

I tossed my duffel bag onto the bed near the door, trying not to imagine how many millions of bedbugs I sent scurrying. I'd need to sleep with one eye open not only to keep Riley from escaping, but to make sure my body didn't get carried off by an oversized arachnid during the night.

"I'll take this...*bed.* God, I can't wait to see the bathroom."

Riley dropped into the vinyl chair in the corner next to what I surmised to be a television. His long legs stretched out and his head lulled to the side against the back of the chair.

"I'll sleep here." His eyes slowly closed.

"I'm going to check on the car. You sleep. I promise we're out of here before the sun comes up and we see this room in daylight.

"Whatever." Riley's words already slurred. His arm fell limp to the side of the chair and I slipped quietly out of the room to make the dreaded call.

I used the disposable cell phone I bought at one of the gas stations we stopped at early this morning. The last thing I needed was Dad tracing the call until I was certain he'd be on board.

"Sheriff Martin." The voice sounded clipped, edgy. His stone heart failed to beat by the sound of his frigid tone.

"Dad. It's Jax."

I should have had a note pad to write down all the new combinations of swear words he used, some I'd never heard of and thought quite creative. In the background, Mom shrieked, then started using her own "gosh darn" church approved cuss words. When my dad realized I didn't respond, he stopped to acknowledge the silence.

"Son? You still there?"

"Are you through? I don't want to interrupt."

"Cut the cocky attitude. Where the hell are you? Please tell me Riley's with you."

"Yes, he is, and don't insult your profession by pretending you don't know where we are."

"Your mother found the bus ticket when she got home from work. Why now?"

"Didn't you see Riley's note?"

"What note?"

"The one next to Lucky's treat jar. Lydia Daniels stopped by yesterday morning. Taylor's getting married tomorrow afternoon. Riley's hell-bent on stopping the wedding and I came along to make sure he didn't do something stupid."

"*You*? Sorry, that's not exactly comforting. The treat jar? Wait."

Dad grunted. His pastries surrounded his "waisty."

"Here's the note. It must have slid to the floor when Dirk put the mail on the counter." He mumbled the words Riley wrote. "So what diabolical plan has Riley cooked up? How many felonies will be committed?"

"Aside from murdering Michael, there really isn't a plan. That's why I called. Dad, you've got to do something."

"Jax, it isn't that simple."

"Don't give me your bullshit about following procedures! I didn't get a 'join the army and stay out of jail' pass through any ethical channels. Rub that damn magic lamp you have stuffed in your desk drawer and tell your fucking genie to grant Riley's wish! You can't let him down! I won't let you. Don't you get it? He *loves* Taylor. He will do *anything* to save her from that asshole!"

"And what if I can't Jax?"

"Then make sure we share the same jail cell. *One* of us is going to help Riley. If you won't, I will."

"What about Sargent Adams? Does he know you're A.W.O.L.? I'm no magician, Jax. I can only save one of your sorry asses."

"Then make it Riley's. I'll cover my own. And I'm not A.W.O.L. until midnight tomorrow. As long as I'm on that airstrip in Virginia before the clock strikes midnight, I get to keep my glass slippers."

"I'll see what I can do. What time's the wedding?"

I filled my dad in on the details while I walked back towards the room. I could see Riley through the crack in the cowboy print drapes, slumped sideways in the chair, snoring. I sat inside Bessie, watching Riley and writing down coordinates to the small chapel on the outskirts of Boston where the ceremony would take place.

In exchange for Dad calling his buddy and concocting some believable lie to buy me an extra day in case things went from disastrous to catastrophic, I divulged our whereabouts. Together, we spent the next hour brainstorming a half-assed plan.

My job would be to keep Riley hidden and level headed until my dad and the local authorities arrived at the church with the arrest warrant for Michael. But my task paled in comparison to the one Dad had to pull off—make Mom stay home.

**

Riley damn near broke the window with his class ring when he rapped the glass to the side of my head. I didn't remember falling asleep in my car, but the painful crook in my neck was a far cry more comforting than if I'd woke up with my face planted in that disgusting motel bed.

"Let's get moving. After all the death threats Dad left on my cell phone, there was a message from Lydia Daniels. The wedding's been moved up two hours so the 'happy couple' can make a flight to Paris."

Still moving in a sleepy stupor, I loaded the trunk with our stuff and dropped the room key in the overnight slot before Riley's news update kicked in. Two hours had just been shaved off "the plan." I had to notify Dad immediately without letting Riley know. I needed coffee first.

Riley didn't argue when I chose the first open diner. We settled into a booth in the back and ordered the first of many cups of steaming hot java.

"I've got to go the 'can'. Order whatever you want. My treat. It's probably our last decent meal. Trust me, rations behind bars suck, and that's the local jail. I can't imagine how tasty the government menu could be someplace the size of Boston."

Once out of Riley's line of sight, I called Dad. I had to hand it to the old man for always pulling through when the stakes were high. He anticipated the possibility of complications and already boarded a flight, warrant in hand.

"Jaxson, I can't stress this enough, but neither you nor Riley can be discovered. I know Riley's going to want to bulldoze in and save the day, but he can't. The local authorities are meeting me at the airport. We'll take care of Michael Barnes. You take care of Riley."

"Speaking of impossible tasks, how's Mom?"

"I'm checking into cruises as we speak. I've never been in so much trouble. She locked herself in the bedroom and I slept on the sofa downstairs."

"When you end up being the hero, she'll forgive you."

"And if I don't?"

"Dad, Mom will always be there. Riley's the one you'll lose."

"Jax, I know we've had our differences, but you know I've always loved you, son, don't you? While I'm not the warm fuzzy guy your mother wants me to be, I've hugged you in my heart constantly. I'm proud of you, Jaxson, for turning things around. By the way, I also know you took the blame for what really happened."

My stomach flipped. "How?"

"Brandon came and talked to me. Don't worry, we've worked it out with the town council. Brandon will take care of the marquee and you'll pay for half of the damages to the car. *I* get to pay the rest. Good thing no one else wants my job."

"The girls?"

"Will do three months community service, and in turn, I won't file charges. Everybody wins."

"Dad, I'm really sorry about the car…and everything else I fucked up."

"You're righting the wrong now. Unfortunately, life's lessons aren't easy. By the way, I was only able to get you a reprieve until noon tomorrow. My last magic trick."

I heard the flight steward tell my dad to shut off his phone. He would be here in four hours. By my rough calculations, that allowed barely thirty minutes for the cavalry to ride in and save the day.

Thirty-One
MASQUERADE
Riley

"A minivan? Are you joking?" My chin slammed the pavement when Jax pulled up in a gray Honda Odyssey. When he told me we were renting a car so we wouldn't be recognized, I went along with the scheme, but this seemed overkill.

"This is all they had left."

"We look ridiculous."

"That's why we have to get some different clothes. We won't be able to get within a mile of the church dressed in the jeans and T-shirts we've slept in for two days."

"I can hardly wait to see what fashion statement you have in mind to match the 'family wagon'."

Forty-five minutes later we pulled behind the church. Jaxson convinced the kid guarding the parking lot we were with the wedding coordinator. Dressed in matching white shirts, black pants and skinny ties, driving a van that would allegedly transport items from the church to the reception—even I believed the lie.

"You scare me sometimes, Jax. How the hell did you come up this idea?"

Jaxson shut off the van and angled to face me. The door locks slammed down.

"Riley, I have something to tell you and I need you to stay calm."

My shoulders stiffened, my hands coiled into tight fists. "O-*kay*."

"This wasn't entirely my idea. I called Dad last night after you fell asleep."

"You did what? Why!" I fumbled with the handle but couldn't open the door.

"Child locks. Now shut up and listen—and stop rocking the van."

I inhaled a deep breath, let it slide out slowly. Jaxson told me about his conversations with Dad last night and also this morning. Part of me felt relief, knowing Dad would soon be here with a warrant to put Michael's ass in jail. But the bigger part of me feared he wouldn't make it in time, or that someone would catch on and ruin the surprise attack. I understood the importance of remaining hidden. If Taylor saw me and freaked out, all hell would break loose.

Leaning against the wall of the church, I hid to the side of a tall juniper tree while Jaxson did covert surveillance out front and called Dad. The Mini sat parked beside Michael's Mercedes and a half dozen other expensive vehicles. The wedding party had arrived before us and I closed my eyes, picturing Taylor inside, getting dressed.

The one day a girl rocks it in the gorgeous department and the guy looks cheesy in a penguin suit. The most important day in Taylor's life and all the effort she'd put into becoming a vision of beauty would be wasted on a guy who'd never appreciate her.

Anger flared again and I kicked the ground with my foot, scattering rocks everywhere. I bent and retrieved one close to my foot. Shaped like an egg, but flat on one side and marbled with brown and green. The color of the pond on a stormy day. I palmed the stone, feeling the cold smoothness against my skin, the way the water felt in the hot summer heat. A day like the one when I met Taylor.

A watery ripple flowed in my vision and my heart burned deep in my chest for Taylor. God I loved her! Why couldn't I be the cheesy guy standing at the end of the aisle watching an angel come to me? Why Michael?

"Dude? You *crying*?" Jaxson asked in a hushed voice.

I pocketed the stone and wiped my cheeks with sleeve of my shirt. "No," I lied. I checked my watch. If on schedule, the wedding would start in twenty minutes. "Tell me Dad's here."

"He's landed and on his way."

"Shit! We're running out of time!"

"Relax, bro. You've got to trust the old man on this one." Jax squeezed my shoulder. "Riley, he'll be here."

Jax left me and returned to the front of the church to watch for Dad. We had our cell phones on vibrate with each other's number programmed on speed dial. One buzz signaled the rescue posse's arrival. If there were two buzzes, we were to meet at the van and get the hell away fast. But that was Jax's plan. Not mine. I wouldn't leave without Taylor. Not this time. I was also tired of standing behind a damn tree. I opened the first door I came to and snuck inside.

Thirty-Two
WEDDING JITTERS
Taylor

I clenched Dad's arm. My stomach rocked back and forth. I hadn't been able to keep anything down the past two days and my nerves were beyond frazzled. This should be the most important day of my life—the day I'd dreamed about since I was a little girl. Today, I'd walk down an aisle and start my life with the man of my nightmares instead of the one of my dreams. Once our farce of a wedding ended, Michael's good behavior would also come to a wretched end and I'd pay the price. At least my punishment would come with a view of the Eiffel Tower.

Dad pried my fingers off his arm and kissed the side of my veil covered head. "Taylor, you don't have to do this," he whispered.

The bones in my neck cracked I whipped my head so fast to meet his eyes. "What?"

"If you don't love Michael, you shouldn't marry him. Life is too short to spend it with someone you don't love."

"It's too late!" I hissed, fighting back the wave of water searing the edges of my eyes.

A ribbon of sunlight crossed the carpet, turning the crystal beads along the bottom of my dress into dotted rainbows. I turned to face the light, spying the parking lot and the Mini. For a split second I wanted to believe it was a "sign." A glimpse of my possible escape, but then the door shut silently, barring any hope and jerking me back to reality.

"It's never too late, Taylor. I'll take you away myself."

Before I could catch the breath I lost, the chapel doors opened. Definitely too late. The path to Hell spread before me, covered in rose petals. The sun shining through the stained glass window sent a shaft of light illuminating my prison shackles, tied to the satin pillow held by Satan himself. Michael.

The wedding march started, sounding more like a funeral dirge. Dad sensed my hesitation in stepping forward and his hand covered mine, which wrapped his arm in a trembling iron grip.

Are you sure? His eyes questioned. I nodded slightly and took the first step toward the end of my life. A slow step, followed by another. The organist actually slowed the melody to match my tentative approach and I caught Michael's dark glower.

Too damn bad. These last few moments of my life I controlled, and I savored every crush of carpet tuft beneath my feet.

I scanned the room, hoping beyond hope Grammy's face would appear, but no. My heart sank. Michael refused to let me talk to her and forbade me to invite her to the wedding. He wanted all ties to Wellsville severed—all memories extinguished. Grammy's presence would serve as a reminder my heart remained with someone else. Michael could have my body, but he would never have my heart and he knew it. My heart and soul belonged to Riley.

Nevertheless, without Michael's knowledge or permission, I mailed Grammy an invitation. When I found out my soon-to-be prison warden moved the time up on the ceremony, I made Mom call her.

She argued at first, taking Michael's side, but I threatened to elope if she didn't, and she knew Michael wouldn't hesitate if I suggested the option. After all the preparations she'd made to make ensure the reception met with the approval of Michael's mother, eloping and abandoning her in her shining moment would be her social death.

Mom called Grammy and yesterday morning on the way to my required pedicure, manicure, and *waxing,* I secretly had a plane ticket couriered to her with a personal note, begging her to come.

I held my last step for as long as possible before placing my foot on the floor and squaring my body to face the demon I'd pledge my life to. Dad squeezed both my shoulders hard, allowing his fears to mingle with mine before stepping away. I placed my hands in Michael's and stared into his flat, soulless eyes.

Thirty-Three
DISOBEYING ORDERS
Riley

Opening the first door I came to on the backside of the church, I half expected to land in a kitchen. Instead, I found myself on the opposite end of the main foyer. Taylor stood in the middle of the long hallway with some old guy I assumed to be her father. I froze. She looked breathtaking. Beyond gorgeous. *Angelic*.

Their hushed conversation ended and luckily a part of my brain communicated with my feet. When Taylor turned toward the light, I ducked into a dark alcove and held my breath. My fingers wound around another door knob and being more careful this time, I eased the second door open.

A long, narrow corridor, covered by heavy drapes along one side, extended before me. I stepped into the shadowy hall, peeking through a slit in the drapes. I ended up inside the chapel, near to the last rows of pews. This must be where someone disappeared to escape a boring sermon, or like me, hid to spy on their girlfriend's wedding. One he wasn't invited to.

The organ started the *tum-tum-de-tum* and my stomach dropped to my nerdy shiny shoes. My worst nightmare started to play out and I stood helpless to stop it. The back doors opened and the small crowd inside the chapel gasped in awe. Taylor, clenching the man standing with her, stepped inside, taking everyone's breath with her beauty.

White lace with patches of sparkle sashayed slowly up the aisle. Taylor's face hid behind a thin layer of fabric, but even from my limited vision I could see the terror in her eyes. She didn't want this. Taylor looked like a dead girl walking to her grave. She barely moved. Even the music slowed to an awkward tempo.

Before the doors closed, I spied a couple of people tuck into the back pew on the opposite side of the chapel. Among the late stragglers, sat a woman—one whose profile I'd recognize anywhere. All she needed was a cup and a tea bag to dip. Lydia Daniels. Damn! I wished I stood behind the draped hallway on the opposite side of the room. I could have reached out and strangled her.

I moved to the next parting in the drapes and stopped. People filled the pews the rest of the way forward. If I went further, someone would catch the stench of a person who hadn't showered in two days and presently sweat profusely behind the fabric wall. Plus, all the legs to wrangle around would stop my surprise attack.

In my mind, I would throw myself on the altar, dragging Michael with me and locking him in a chokehold, holding him until either the cops arrived…or he died from lack of air.

I moved back to the side of an empty pew because so far, my imaginary plan appeared to be the only one I had. My fingers fumbled inside my pocket, wrapping my cell phone. I checked to make sure it was on. Where was Dad? Jax? The ceremony had started! I cringed when Taylor took Michael's hands. I watched her creamy shoulders

310

pull slightly, the bony blades rigid like stone wings wanting to burst through and carry her away.

The music stopped and the preacher dude said a couple of memorized sentences before Taylor spoke. My lungs seized as I listened to the words she said, soft, heartfelt…and not intended for Michael. The vow she muttered on a trembling voice was meant for *me*.

Thirty-Four
PLEDGES OF ALLEGIANCE
Taylor

Michael insisted we write our own vows. How does one come up with words of love and devotion for someone they hate?

I wish you dead. Rot in hell. I hate you!

Those were the only words I could write for Michael. But a vow of undying love, of a broken heart safely tucked away for someone else, I could write. My wedding vow would be a pledge to Riley. Maybe by saying the words aloud, they would magically carry a thousand miles on the wind, until they settled inside his heart, into piece carved away for me.

In time, I prayed his memories of me would wane warm and soft. Riley's heart would mend and if my words were safely tucked inside, they would be forever sealed and a part of his soul.

As the preacher pronounced the standard marriage mantra, I studied Michael's face, trying to remember what made me believe I loved him, *ever*. The first time we met, I was fifteen. We'd just moved to Boston and my father had started working for the law firm. In an effort to impress his new boss, Dad dragged me to some high school basketball playoff game. His boss's son supposedly played the starring jock. We sat a row above Michael's parents and before the game started, Michael rushed over to talk to his dad, all the while watching me. I remembered his eyes—the color of blue hidden in the deepest part of an iceberg.

I worked the summer between my junior and senior year of high school at the law firm as a filing clerk. Michael had spent the summer in France and when he returned, he worked with me until he started Harvard. He came home for the holidays and our family had been invited to the company Christmas party at their house. By the end of the evening, I'd agreed to go to a New Year's Eve party with him, and after that, we dated exclusively.

Michael took advantage of my naïve view of life. Handsome and charming, not to mention filthy rich, he was a teenage girl's dream god. Thinking back, there were so many clues I chose to ignore, whispered rumors I dismissed, even when one of those twisted tales came from my best friend, Delany. She'd secretly gone to a party with Michael when I was sick with strep throat and couldn't go.

Delany shied away from me after that and whenever I wanted to gush about Michael, she changed the subject. After my high school graduation, Michael started talking marriage and Delany confessed, warning me Michael had a dark side. When she accused him of being a pervert I cut off our friendship. A month later, Michael assaulted me in his bedroom. I had no one to tell. Michael had destroyed all my friendships, being especially pleased to discover Delany had been the last casualty.

A moment of reckoning slapped. Delany *knew* about Michael because *she'd* been one of his victims!

Michael's hands squeezed mine and I realized the preacher whispered my name. "Taylor? Your vows to Michael?" the preacher asked.

Heat flushed my cheeks. "Sorry." *So very sorry for so many wrongs I'd never get to fix.*

My eyes locked on Michael's. His lips curved into a half smile and I took a deep breath, letting my imagination change his face to Riley's. Time for the performance of my lifetime.

"Finding true love," I began, "is like rising from the cold depths of a dark pond. When your face breaks through the water's surface, the sun warms your skin. Your eyes open and discover the love of your life standing there watching over you with eyes full of compassion and arms waiting to enfold you. A strong protective embrace, but soft enough to hold your fragile heart without breaking it. Someone who'll never hurt you or force you to become anything other than who you are."

Tears filled my eyes and anger filled Michael's. He knew not one blessed word I poetically professed, belonged to him. I didn't give a damn and to prove my point, I gave him the warmest loving smile I could manage. Even batted my eyelashes.

His brow cocked sharply. Payback would come, but I didn't think it would be now.

"You know," Michael announced to the room with an alluring lilt, "I have no words that can match the beauty of those my darling bride

314

has confessed to me. Nothing as magical or thought provoking. No prose can come close."

He faced a confused preacher. "Let's skip all the traditional bullshit and go straight to the part where you declare Taylor is mine—just don't forget that little part about her promising to always *obey*."

Thirty-Five
ROCK JUSTICE
Riley

Fuck! No! I reached into my pocket for my phone and grabbed the rock instead. I rolled the stone inside my hand until I formed a tight fist over it.

Damn you Michael! Damn you Dad!

I surveyed the scene from my limited portal. Taylor begged Michael to say his vows as if she knew help was on the way and needed to stall just a few more minutes. The expression on Michael's face revealed absolute power and he savored the taste of control. Taylor's proclamation of love for me pushed him over the edge. Her words took him beyond angry and me, over the top with elation, but put Taylor in real danger. Rage colored Michael's face bright red.

I pulled my phone from my other pocket. Still nothing! I'd ran out of options.

Or had I?

Cupping the stone like a small baseball, I flexed my wrist to judge the weight. I'd played a lot of baseball and usually from the position of "pitcher." From where I stood, Michael would be an easy target. With just the right spin and precision release, the stone would hone in on the target—Michael's head. But if I missed? If the arc didn't curve high enough or the velocity too slow, I'd miss the demon and hit Taylor. I couldn't chance that happening. Nevertheless, I had to do something to stop the wedding…halt the words from sealing Taylor's fate.

Michael pulled Taylor roughly against him, facing the officiator who uttered a few standard phrases. I juggled the rock between my hands, waiting for the vibration in my pocket or the doors to burst open, feeling only silent abandonment. The preacher peered out into the crowd. Desperation carved sharp angles in his face. He no more wanted them married than I did.

"Is there anyone with us today who can find just cause why these two people should not be joined in holy matrimony?"

My gaze turned to Lydia Daniels. Why didn't she jump up and protest? She knew everything I did, even more. She saw *all* the pictures. Surely she said something to Taylor's parents. Why didn't *they* stop this sham of a ceremony? Did Michael really wield that much power? Or did Taylor? Did she view a marriage to Michael as a security blanket for everyone in her family, not just for her father?

The thought brought my constant simmering anger to a raging boil. She was only eighteen years old! How could her family *use* her like this? Why should Taylor be the one sacrificed? Damnit!

The preacher's voice cracked. "If so, let him speak now, or forever hold his piece."

My cue. The cell phone buzzed in my pocket, but a second too late. The rock had left my hand.

Thirty-Six
HELL BREAKS LOOSE
Taylor

A sticky bead of sweat trickled between my breasts. My breaths turned short, ragged, and forced. The preacher's face dissolved into a million twinkling stars and I felt my legs turn to liquid. My God! This was really happening! Only a few words remained before I would officially become Mrs. Michael Barnes—my freedom finally taken, my life caged, and my body someone else's to use or *abuse* as he deemed fit.

A torrent of nausea coiled in my stomach, climbing into the back of my throat. If I didn't pass out soon, I'd project something vile all over the preacher. I dropped my head, hoping his shoes would take the brunt of my reaction to being pronounced "Man and Wife." *Master and Slave.*

The preacher's next question announced my ending neared.

"Is there anyone with us today who can find just cause why these two people should not be joined in holy matrimony?"

Michael fused my body to his, purposely placing his hand at the side of my breast. A declaration of ownership by publicly feeling me up in front of the altar of a church! What an ass! Surely my mom saw? My dad? The preacher? Why didn't someone race up the aisle and punch Michael for demeaning me like this? Rescue me? Save me? *Kill Michael?*

Did I have no hero? Please, *please…*

I fisted the skirt of my beautiful dress—the one I exchanged for the monstrosity Michael chose, just to prove I had some say in my wedding. I stared at the lace edge, kissing the burgundy carpet, the crystal beads shimmering like tiny diamonds. I felt beautiful and deserving of much better than this. Whether or not I'd ever be worthy of someone like Riley again I wasn't sure, but my self-worth meant more to me than wasting what little I still owned on an jerk like Michael.

I pushed Michael's hand down with my elbow, feeling a retaliatory pinch to my side. I didn't care. We were in a public setting—one full of the elite of Boston's society. Turning me into a punching bag in front of his parents would never happen.

Neither would this marriage. Dad was right. I did *not* have to do this. My mother might die of embarrassment, but she'd recover. My father's finances would suffer a blow, although his ability to pay if he loses his job may prove a problem. But not *my* problem. This was my life and if I didn't take charge now, I'd never be able to look at myself in a mirror again.

The last plea stuck in the preacher's throat. "If so, let him speak now, or forever hold his piece."

I lifted my head high, ready to declare my freedom and damn anyone who stood in my way. My mouth opened to shout *"No!"* but a scream raced across my tongue when a loud bang permeated the silent tension.

Life happened in slow motion, the moments shifted in still increments. Glistening shards of brightly colored glass twisted and curled on their way to the ground. Everyone cowered, shielding their faces from being sliced by the beautiful, razor sharp pieces spreading over the crowd.

Michael's mother stumbled over his father, holding tightly to the peacock feathered hat adorning her head. She fell and rolled across the aisle, exposing her lavender panties when her skirt ripped up the back. How pretentious could she be? Her underwear *coordinated* with her silk suit. The heel broke off her shoe, becoming airborne and hitting an unsuspecting "social butterfly" in the nose, spattering blood droplets on those nearby. I watched in horror as the tiny ruby dots appeared suspended in air.

Michael's voice, a low warble, stretched my name in a distorted pitch. I spun away from the claws reaching from the sleeves of his tuxedo. Bundling my cloud of lace and chiffon under my arms, my legs lifted me over the crumpled, shrieking Mrs. Barnes, past her bleeding victim, and somehow, I twirled between my parents' outstretched arms.

My heels smacked the floor hard jarring me out of slow motion and into present panic mode. Luckily, my brain connected with the fact I'd escaped the mayhem behind me and didn't even pause long enough to turn around. I just ran.

Something came from the side with such force it knocked me to the ground, pushing the air from my lungs in a painful swoosh. When I inhaled, tears burned the back of my eyes and my heart pinched. The

320

heady scent of cologne swamped me, bringing a sense of peace and wonderment. BLVGARI.

Riley!

Somewhere inside the pillow of sparkling chiffon encapsulating us, his arms held me firmly against his chest, my cheek vibrating against the heavy pounding of his heart. I was about to raise my head to make sure the lips adorning my hair with thousands of tiny kisses truly belonged to my imagined savior, when one voice shattered the spell and turned my body to stone.

Michael.

"*You!* I am going to break every bone in your fucking body!"

Riley covered me—my super-hero shield. Another loud commotion; something broke, smashed in the background, which brought a flurry of new screams. The floor vibrated from the thud of bodies dropping or running.

"Freeze!" Echoed with the force of a cannon shot inside the chapel, followed by what sounded like a million clicks. Silence…thick and deafening. The world eddied into blackness.

Thirty-Seven
AFTERSHOCKS
Riley

I sat. I stood. I paced then sat again. A spider busied itself spinning an intricate silken web in the corner of the tiny window high above my head. Dust particles churned in the patch of sunlight I passed through.

What the hell was going on? I'd been sequestered in this room for over an hour and no one had come. Not Dad, Jax, or any other member of the militia firing squad who broke down the doors of the chapel. Between the splintered wood and shattered glass, the holy sanctuary looked like a bomb had exploded.

The curtains keeping me hidden were shredded and pulled from the heavy bars holding them when Michael tried to escape, summoning the S.W.A.T. officers to follow him into the narrow passage way. Padded and heavily armed, wearing boots large enough to crush small children, I watched in amazement as they moved with the ease of ballerinas, leaping, jumping, and twisting over benches, through ribbon wrapped floral arrangements, and totally freaked out wedding guests, before cornering the cowering bastard dressed in the designer tux. Next to hearing Taylor whisper my name when she realized I held her, the snapping sound of the cuffs locking around Michael's wrists was music to my ears.

When the idiot purposely spit on Taylor's dress as he walked by, Dad's hands clamped my shoulders. But his weren't as fast as Mr.

Barnes's, who leveled a fast, powerful blow to the side of his son's jaw. "Terms of endearment" were shouted between father and son. Michael's father ended up in cuffs, too, when he tried to pull out Michael's gelled, coifed hair.

I just bent tighter over Taylor, shielding her with my body. She went limp in my arms and I knew she probably fainted, but until that asshole had been officially removed, I wasn't letting anyone near her. Even then, my dad and Jax pried my arms from her waist and restrained me from running after the gurney carrying her away. Her eyes locked open, holding mine in a watery gaze, but she remained silent, dazed. Dad said she was in shock, but would be all right.

I couldn't be as sure.

**

The door opened and a large man filled the space. The one I recognized as Taylor's father.

"Son, do you want to tell me what the hell you were thinking when you decided to take on the world this afternoon? Have you any idea the damage you've caused, not to mention the repercussions something of this magnitude will generate? The grounds are swarming with news crews, the chapel is in a shambles, and the stained glass window that earmarked this church is shattered."

He bounced the weapon in this hand. The rock I threw without giving a second thought when I aimed it at the window above Michael's head. The felonies piled up, but I didn't give a damn. The sand disappeared in the hourglass and something had to be done to stop the wedding. Something epic. Like a rock hurling through a window and sending glass exploding everywhere, giving Taylor the opportunity to choose Michael or freedom.

Unbridled joy and excitement filled me when she took off running away from everyone, even her parents. The communication system inside my brain malfunctioned and no longer received common sense signals, when I bolted from my hiding place for Taylor. I vaguely remember Lydia Daniels screaming, but Michael ran for Taylor and I was hell-bent on not letting him ever put his hands on her again.

However, I misjudged my speed and strength when I reached the runaway bride, sending us both crashing to the floor. I'd barely got my arms around her body, buried in the layers of lace and fluffy fabric, crushing her face protectively to my chest when Michael's fist aimed for her. The bruise on my shoulder would eventually heal and the bones in Taylor's face were saved.

Michael grabbed my jacket and when Taylor's father reached for him, he let go of me to swing a punch his direction. The double doors in the back of the chapel burst open, one actually dropping from its hinges into a mangled pile of wooden slats. A small army of dark clothed officers pointing guns appeared. I'd never been so glad to hear my father bellow the command "*freeze!*"

My thoughts swirled back with the smacking sound of the stone slapping the skin of Mr. Wilson's hand. I watched the rock go up then down, almost falling into a hypnotic trance. When Taylor's father finished listing the evidences of destruction, he paused.

"So you fancy yourself a 'Sampson going up against a Goliath'?"

"Maybe. I just needed to save Taylor."

"And so you did. My daughter is safe because of you." He held his hand out. "Richard Wilson. It's an honor to meet a young man of your caliber, Mr. Martin. My daughter is a lucky girl to have someone like you in her life."

Not really, I thought. *Lucky* would mean I believed Taylor in the first place and had pulled my biblical stunt the minute I met Michael Barnes.

"Is she okay? She wouldn't talk to me."

"Taylor's in shock and emotionally spent. Her mother took her home to rest."

"Can I see her?"

"I'm sorry, but that's not possible. The trauma of what's happened coupled with the embarrassment she feels, may be too much for her. As her father, I'm not willing to risk it. Surely, you understand."

"No, as a matter of fact I don't. We love each other."

"Well," his tongue clicked the back of his throat, "that may be true, but I still forbid it. If at some future time Taylor wants to contact you, she will."

Mr. Wilson took my hand and dropped the stone into my palm. "I recommend you hide that."

"How did you know it was *this* rock?"

"Until you just told me, it was an educated guess. Baseball was my chosen sport in high school. There aren't any other rocks in the garden below the broken window that could have carried that much force." He handed me a business card. "I've got a feeling you may need a lawyer. I'd like to help, but call the cell phone number. I suspect my job has been terminated with my current law firm."

The door creaked open and I nonchalantly dropped the rock into my pocket. Dad and the preacher entered. Introductions between the men commenced and I moved back to the chair in the far corner, feeling light headed. I was in deep shit. Taylor's dad wouldn't let me see her and we were leaving for home first thing in the morning.

After Richard Wilson excused himself, Dad and the man who could immediately hurl my soul to Hell, stepped toward me. I stood, respectful and silent.

"Riley, this is Pastor Smyth. I gave him a condensed version of events leading to your irrational decision to chuck something through his *expensive* window. He's graciously conceded not to press charges against you in exchange for monthly payments of a hundred dollars for one year. He's also asked that you never enter this church again, but attend ours at home on a regular basis. Perhaps he believes there's still a chance to save your sorry ass...I mean *soul.*"

I wicked my sweaty palm across my pants and shook his hand vigorously. "Thanks. I mean it. Sorry about the window." I kept *how* I broke the window a secret. Confession would come later under my father's relentless questioning.

The gentle smile on the preacher's face made his soft gray eyes twinkle. "Son, I figure the good Lord heard Miss Wilson's prayers and

used you as His instrument to keep the Devil from intervening further."
His eyes turned to the ceiling, just like Mom. Maybe God just preferred
attics. "I only wish when He chooses to move in mysterious ways, he'd
give some advance warning."

The tension eased with our irreverent laughter. The preacher left
the room and Dad's fingers clamped the back of my neck. "If I didn't
have to face your mother, I'd throw your delinquent butt in a jail cell
for a couple of days so you could reflect on your choices."

I wrapped my arms around him and pulled him to me. "Dad,
thanks for believing me and saving Taylor."

"I didn't save her, Riley. *You* did that all by yourself. Today, you
were her hero."

**

I twirled the empty coffee mug back and forth. The sun blazed
sideways through the shutters on the diner window, giving me a
headache. None of us slept much last night. Dad undoubtedly saved my
interrogation for the ride home. Last night we had a quiet dinner and
spent the last hours we had with Jaxson. We presently sat at the airport
café waiting for his flight to Virginia.

Jax kicked my leg under the table. "Bro? What's with the long
face? You saved the day! You should be happy, not all pouty. Geesh,
Riley, reach down and check your 'boys'."

Dad's coffee exited his nose and I burst out laughing. Jax knew
exactly what to say to cause a reaction from Dad and lighten my mood.

"Damn, I hope the army teaches you a few things, Jaxson," Dad snarled, blotting the coffee bubbles on the plastic placemat.

"Don't count on it old man," Jax replied.

"Yeah, you'll probably still *hiss* your 'S' words. Say 'Sir, yes Sir' for me, please?" I teased. Jax swatted me with his cap and Dad ran interference, as usual.

Simultaneously, we glanced at the neon clock over the counter. Fifteen more minutes and my brother would become property of the U.S. government and not the Martin family. Deep down I already missed him and knew when he came home for Christmas, he'd be different—changed, probably for the better.

Jax gave a heavy sigh and pulled his duffle bag from the corner of the booth, lugging it over his shoulder. "Little bro, it's been fun breaking the law with you one last time."

I pressed my fist hard against my mouth and stared out the window. Fighting back tears proved useless as one chased another over my cheeks. The big brother I'd spent a good portion of my life plotting his death, embarked today on a new life. I, on the other hand, would return to my old one lone…without Taylor.

"Riley?" Dad asked pensively.

A sudden sob stole my breath. Jax dropped his duffle bag and leaned over the table. "Dude, what's wrong? You can't be missing me already."

I half laughed, blowing snot out my nose.

"Now that's gross," Jax said.

I grabbed a napkin. "I have to see Taylor. I can't go home without seeing her."

"I'm hurt," my brother teased. He tapped his finger on the table top. "So go see her."

"Her father asked that we leave her alone," Dad explained. "Riley can call her in a couple of weeks, or she can call him sooner, if she wants."

Jax checked his watch and lifted his bag. "Dad, if Mom had gone through all the bullshit Taylor has and you busted your balls to save her, would you go home without seeing her?"

"Hell no."

"Exactly. Take Riley to Taylor, or check your 'stones'. She needs to see him as much as he needs to see her.

"You two can't be mine with those mouths. And for the record, my *stones* are just fine, but you better get going or you'll miss your flight."

I'd become a babbling bawl-baby by this point. Jaxson whistled for our waitress, much to my dad's dismay.

"Hey sweetheart, can we get some napkins? Got a whole mess of cry babies over here."

Laughter erupted around us and the waitress brought Jax a stack of napkins. He pulled her into him, laying a big kiss on her lips, which she seemed to thoroughly enjoy.

"I might die tomorrow and kissing a waitress is on my 'bucket list'."

The one thing the world could always count on would be Jax making a spectacle of himself…in our father's presence.

**

We leaned against Bessie watching Jaxson walk across the parking lot for the airport terminal. He didn't want either of us at the gate to say goodbye, but we managed a couple of burly hugs and shed a few more tears, before letting him go. Dad made him talk to Mom on the phone, which consisted of the two of them crying and saying "I love you" a thousand times. I swear the ground around our feet looked like a monsoon had washed through.

The long walk to the terminal building I suspect would be used to pull the pieces together and arrange them back into "bad-ass Jaxson," who would forever be my guardian angel—with black wings and a halo made of stainless steel instead of gold. He'd probably want an electric guitar instead of a harp, too.

**

The coin toss put Dad in the driver's seat first. We sat at the edge of the driveway waiting to pull into traffic. Going left took us to the interstate. Turning right sent us the direction of Taylor's house. Bessie's blinker ticked loudly, the little green arrow pointing left. My eyes gazed the other way.

"*Shit.* I'm going to regret this."

Leaving a few fingers wagging our direction and horns honking on our behalf, Dad punched the gas and turned Bessie right. Joy bubbled in my chest. I'd see Taylor after all.

Thirty-Eight
CLOSE ENCOUNTERS OF THE WEIRD KIND
Taylor

Our usually empty house buzzed with people hovering and watching my every move. I couldn't even go to the bathroom without Mom standing outside the door, making it next to impossible to pee. The clock radio on the counter hadn't been used so much since last fall when I'd blast it every morning while I got ready for school. Anyone else might welcome the attention, but I found it strange. Irritating, actually. Where did this sudden concern come from? Maybe if my well-meaning family members had shown an ounce of this concern earlier, I wouldn't be in this damn mess.

The smell of something seasoned with garlic wafted up the stairwell and the gurgle in my stomach urged me to investigate. When Mom brought me home from the hospital, *Dr. Shephard* sat a bit too comfortably at the kitchen table, indulging in a cup of coffee. Even stranger, though, Dad sat across from him, the two engrossed in conversation.

I rounded the doorway to the kitchen finding much the same scene, except a new, unexpected and not wanted visitor had joined the peculiar gathering, busily making lasagna. My "screwing-my-dad-hoping-to-be-my-new-stepmother," Olivia.

"What's *she* doing here," I snarled not hiding my disdain.

"*Taylor*," my mother chided under her breath as she passed by. The fake smile on her face clued me she was every bit as happy about "company" as me.

Mom eased next to Olivia, putting together a green salad. I couldn't help but notice the heavy chop to the lettuce head, and wondered if Olivia's face appeared to Mom right before she wielded her culinary weapon.

"Olivia kindly offered to help out with dinner. We didn't know how long…you would be…at the hospital." My dad's carefully calculated words tripped over themselves.

My teeth chomped into an apple instead of Olivia's arm when she reached around me for more seasoning. Her strong perfume overpowered the aroma of the bubbling lasagna in the pan next to her.

"Don't you mean to say you weren't sure if they'd let me come home or just lock me in the psych ward?" I responded, pushing limits as usual.

The good Dr. Shephard felt compelled to interject words of wisdom at this point. "Taylor, what your father meant, was—"

"Hey, Doc. I know what my dad meant. All of you are watching me like I'm going to self combust any moment. The tension is so thick it's suffocating. I'm not a porcelain doll. I'm not going to break."

"Taylor Wilson, show some respect, please," Mom scolded, protective of the good doctor. It appeared Dad's comment that day on the phone held some merit. Respect? She wanted respect from me?

How ironic. I decided to check the cautious moods surrounding the room full of plastic people.

"Mom, when you tested Dr. Shephard's couch, was he on top or bottom?"

The glass bowl holding the garden fresh work of art, shattered when it smacked the tile floor. Olivia's dainty scream summoned my father to her side, and Dr. Shephard's coffee complimented his sage colored shirt.

I left my half- gnawed apple to the side of the lasagna, leaning precariously on the edge of the counter. The last ghost finally slithered out of the closet. My rape had stiff competition for priority on the "Wilson family drama scale."

The quarter I tossed into the air, glittered in the overhead lights as it turned end-over-end onto the dark purple carpet. "Heads," Dad would be the first one to burst through my bedroom door. "Tails," Mom, accompanied by her outed side-kick.

George Washington's face leered at me through the woolen threads.

"What the hell was that about!" Dad demanded. "How could you disrespect your mother in such a vile manner, young lady?"

I didn't bother to remove my gaze from the sun, slowly dipping on the western horizon. Why turn away from one fiery ball of heat to face another?

"Who gave you the right, Taylor, to—"

I lost it.

"I. Have. No. Rights! Remember? *My* right to make choices was stolen from me, first by you and Mom when you decided to break our family apart, and then by Michael!"

My dad's voice softened and the fury in his eyes changed. It remained, but not directed at me any longer. "Taylor, the thing Michael did to you was uncalled for."

"He *r a p e d* me. The 'thing' has a name and 'uncalled for' is hardly the correct description. Not only did he take my virginity, the *last* personal thing I owned, but he took my self-respect. He did more than fuck my body. He fucked up my life!"

Mayhem exploded in the ten-by-twelve foot space. I cursed the almighty "F" word, forbidden, even under the most justifiable circumstances. Like now.

Mom shrieked so loud, my ears rang. Dad shrilled at her in response, defending my sudden right to speak anyway I wanted. The cupie doll sharing my father's bed and the upstanding gentleman apparently acquainted with my mother's, cowered in the doorway, witnessing the Wilson family at their finest. I closed my eyes, waiting to be struck by lightning or torn limb-by-limb by one of my crazed parents, when a third voice resounded loudly, silencing the room.

Riley.

Thirty-Nine
MEET THE WILSONS
Riley

"SHUT UP!"

I couldn't believe the drama scene playing out in front of me.
Taylor sat in the window seat across the room, watching her father and
mother act out some primal control dance, probably derived from
insane apes. A guy in a cardboard pinstriped suit, wearing a shirt with a
huge brown stain covering his stomach and crotch, consoled a platinum
blonde Barbie doll.

Dad wheezed loudly beside me, winded from running up the long
cobblestone drive leading to the mansion, then taking on the hundred or
so stairs leading to the sound of domestic violence. I ditched him as
soon as the car slowed enough to insure I wouldn't be ran over, and
bolted through entry doors, ready to take on anybody who tried to stop
me from seeing Taylor.

Knowing his lungs were too deflated to speak. His only recourse
would be to discharge his weapon and fire a shot through the ceiling. I
spared him the possible lawsuit and shouted again, *enhancing* my
earlier command.

"SHUT THE FUCK UP!"

I didn't know humans could cease making noise so fast. Taylor
jumped to her feet, frozen, her body a perfect shaped silhouette against
the golden halo radiating through the window behind her.

The man closest to me straightened to a defensive stance. "I beg your pardon? Who do you think you are—"

"Riley." Taylor spoke my name softy, sending it back to me on angel wings.

Her dark image and most of the sunlight were suddenly blocked by her father when he stepped protectively in front of her. My father mirrored him, stepping in front of me as well. All they needed were swords or six-shooters to start dueling.

"There's a restraining order in place against your son, Sheriff Martin. His presence here could land him in jail and the charges so carefully omitted from this afternoon's horrendous happenings, imposed to keep him behind bars for a very long time."

"I'm fully aware of the restraining order."

He was? Why didn't he warn me? If I'd known I'd go to jail for seeing Taylor, I would have at least given it a respectable ten seconds of thought, before barging ahead. Dad knew a court order wouldn't stop me. Nothing could.

"I'm calling the police," Taylor's mother informed in her icy, high-society voice.

Before she reached me with her purple painted claws, the "coffee tester" clamped her arms, halting her attack.

"Wait, Grace." Keeping hold of his prisoner, his eyes glanced to each occupant in the small bedroom. "I think we should leave Taylor alone with her guest…*if* she wishes."

"Are you insane?" Taylor's father accused.

336

"Perhaps. But for your daughter's sake, we need to respect *her* choice in the matter."

Taylor's father turned. "Taylor? You don't have to do this. Not until you're ready."

"Ready for what, Dad? Until *you're* comfortable leaving me alone with a boy? Riley's not Michael."

"I'm not saying he is. You're vulnerable and I don't want anyone taking advantage, that's all."

I bit my tongue hard enough to draw blood before speaking. "With all due respect Mr. Wilson, I've *never* taken advantage of your daughter and I don't like being lumped into some generic category of guys who think girls are only good for one thing."

"Riley!" My dad's breath was hot on my ear. "Apologize." I glared at him for publicly chastising me. "A-p-o-l-o-g-i-z-e…out of respect for Taylor."

I hated when he made sense.

"I'm sorry, Sir." I moved my body in line with Taylor's feeling the magnetic bond instantly reappear. "Taylor. Can we talk privately? We can leave the door open, if you want."

She shuffled her feet on the carpet and bright white flashes of static current flashed.

"I think I'd like that." She lightly touched her father's arm. "Dad, it will be all right. Please."

Her mother started to object, but Taylor raised her hand in defense.

"Mom, I'm sorry about what I said earlier. I was out of line and disrespectful to you and Dr. Shephard, but right now, I need you to respect *my* wishes, okay? Go downstairs. We'll be down in a while."

One by one, they passed by me, their eyes evaluating. *Barbie* gave me a creepy once over. Even *Riley Jr.* became fearful.

My dad's body filled the doorway.

"Son—"

"Sheriff Martin," Taylor interrupted. "Trust me. Riley is the one person I need right now."

Dad huffed in surrender, his lip twisting into an unsure corkscrew. He leaned close to my ear. "Keep your hands off her. She's not ready."

As soon as I heard his footsteps retreat down the stairs, I faced Taylor, unsure of how to act. I wanted to rush to her, pull her in my arms and tell her nothing bad would ever happen to her again. That I would protect her. Believe and trust her...like I didn't before. But I remained a statue, several feet away from the one person still possessing my heart.

"Taylor?" I released her name delicately on a whisper.

Before me stood a beautiful dream, suspended in a fragile bubble I feared reality's needle would burst any moment.

"Riley, lock the door."

I did.

Miles seemed to separate us. I shoved my hands deep into my pockets. It felt like hours instead of seconds passed before she spoke.

"Thank you for saving me today. I prayed for a miracle and there you were."

"You're not mad I ruined the wedding?" She shook her head, dropping her eyes. In the corner, the lace wedding dress she wore, hung from a tall mirror.

"For what it's worth, you looked gorgeous, but I'm glad you didn't marry Michael."

"Me, too." She followed my gaze to the dress. "I picked it out. I pretended I bought it for *our* wedding."

Those were the words I needed to hear. I closed out the space between us, ignoring my dad's threats of death and wrapped Taylor in my arms. Her body eased from rigid to liquid in my embrace and when the tears came, the weight of her grief dragged us both to the floor.

I leaned against the foot of her bed, cradling her while she purged the pain and soaked my shirt with tears. Her hair smelled of fruity shampoo, the texture silky against my cheek. A hot tear trailed across the bridge of my nose, followed by another…then another, until I couldn't tell whose body shook worse, hers or mine.

"I'm so sorry, baby," I muttered over and over. "I should have believed you."

Her warm fingers held my cheek and I kissed her palm.

"You're right. You should have loved me enough to believe me. I can't forgive you for that, yet. You hurt me."

"I know," I cried. "I hate myself. It's my fault."

Taylor moved out of my arms and perched on her knees. "No, Riley. What happened to me is *not* your fault, any more than mine. Michael shoulders that blame alone, understand? He's sick and demented. If not me, someone else would have been his victim, or maybe there already are others. But you couldn't have done anything to change his twisted mind. Got that?"

I pulled my knees to my chest. "I should have come earlier. Told Barney 'no'…"

"Changed the direction the world spun that moment?" she responded. "Trust me, I know. I've played it over in my head thousands of times trying to figure out what I did or said to bring on Michael's wrath, but never have I said 'if only Riley had done this or that'."

Taylor lifted my chin. "Riley, Michael's actions had already been decided. I'd become the possession he obsessed about owning. 'Taking me' proved the only way he could own me, and he knew that."

"Don't hate me, Taylor. Please don't hate me."

She pressed her lips to my forehead. "I can't hate something I love so much. Regardless of what's happened, I love you Riley Martin. I only wish I wasn't 'damaged goods'."

Damaged goods? How could she think that?

I moved onto the edge of her bed. Oddly, she stepped further away, leaning against her desk. I felt a brow lift in my confusion. Suddenly, *clarity* hit…rather hard. The *bed…me* on the bed. I sprang to my feet.

"Taylor, you don't think I'm trying to make a move on you, do you? I mean, not that I wouldn't because *all* of me misses you, babe,

340

but…not here…not now." My words tangled into each other and I watched Taylor shrink away.

Without thinking, I gathered her into my arms, feeling her body stiffen and air rush into her lungs when I touched her. Instead of leaning her curves into me, her body changed to hard angles and sharp edges. She pushed me away.

"Don't, Riley."

Common sense stumbled far away from me because I didn't listen. If she'd only let me hold her, absorb her pain, the "elephant" between us would disappear. I pulled her back to me.

"Stop! No!" she shouted.

"Taylor, I'm not Michael! I won't hurt you," I argued. The thunder of feet on the stairs signaled my executioners attacked, imagining the worst.

Releasing her so fast, she teetered, I begged in a small voice I didn't recognize. "Baby, please don't send me away."

Fists pounded the door. "Taylor! Open this door!" Her father. My warden had to be one of the several other voices screaming for entrance as well.

A hot tear betrayed me, tumbling over my cheek. "Please," I mouthed silently.

"I'm fine! Go away!" she commanded the small army behind the door. The pounding stopped, but the hall light coming under the door disappeared by the number of feet pressed together. My dad's voice boomed.

"Riley!"

"Hey, we're having a fight, okay? I'm not touching her. We're just yelling. Nothing else."

Taylor stepped toward the door and I held my breath, but she stopped before turning the handle. Her voice softened.

"I said I'm okay. Give us some privacy."

"I don't want this door locked," her father snarled.

"It's not about what *you* want right now. I locked the door to keep you out…and Riley in."

Feet shuffled against the wood plank floor, slowly retreating, although I knew not far.

"Thanks. I'm sorry I scared you."

Taylor leaned against the wall, keeping her distance. "Riley, you reacted normal…did what you always do. But *I'm* not normal. I'm broken."

"You're not broken, Taylor. You're hurt. Afraid. *Normal* for what's happened. But I don't ever want you calling yourself 'damaged', again."

"I'm not perfect."

I flipped my arms out sideways. "Hell, Taylor, you never were! Shit, you're impossible, bull-headed, bitchy, and sexy as hell, but not *perfect.*" We laughed—a sound I doubted this room ever heard.

"Thanks. I needed that. I needed you to be 'Riley'. Not some cautious version." Taylor stepped closer, reaching for my hands. Our fingers reacquainted, loosely intertwining.

"Riley, things will never be like before."

"I know, but we can start over."

"You know too much. Things might be too awkward." Our fingers wrapped, unwrapped, and wrapped again.

"What do you mean?"

"The stuff I left in your truck—"

"Is locked in the evidence room at the station," I said over her. "Taylor, I only saw the first three pictures. I couldn't take seeing what he did to you. I gave your phone to my dad along the pillowcase. I never looked inside. You said we'd be through if I did, and I needed you to trust me one last time."

Taylor's delicate fingers wrapped my rough, calloused hands and drew them against her lips. Her eyes pinched, brows wrinkled, and red blotches dotted her cheeks. Tears rained from beneath lashes already glistening.

I couldn't move, my own world blurred behind a veil of water. The stream of tears from her eyes mingled with the water from her nose, both covering my hands, but I didn't pull away. What someone else might think gross, to me, felt wonderful. She held tight to me, not worrying about stupid stuff like snotty noses or mascara streaks— exposed and trusting me enough to let her guard fall away.

"I love you," she mumbled between sobs. "I didn't mean to hurt you, I swear. Don't leave me, Riley, don't hate me."

My arms cradled her against me, her cries muffled in my chest. I kissed the strands of hair knotted in my fingers, laying my cheek on her head, sighing when her arms finally locked around my waist and pulled me into her. We swayed back and forth, crying, kissing, hugging…loving.

"I hate to break it you, baby, but I'm not going anywhere. I don't scare that easy. You're stuck with this 'country hick' forever."

Forty
FACING DOWN THE DEMONS
Taylor

Everything looked the same. Everything looked different. The blue rockers on the porch ghostly rocked with the cold wind swirling and biting my nose. Icy shards of frozen grass crunched as we approached the front steps. My feet fused to the cement walkway and stopped moving.

"Taylor? Honey, come on. It's going to be all right."

"You don't know that."

Dr. Shephard or *Marshall*, now that my mother's finger sparkled with a diamond crusted band, gaudy enough to work in her society circle, stepped beside me. I couldn't help but like the guy, and hated that I felt more at ease with him than my real father.

Marshall served as a shield between my fragile emotional state and my mother's *"stop wallowing and get on with life"* attitude. Her level of compassion dropped drastically after my allotted four week self-pity party expired.

"True, we don't, but as you and I have talked, until you face down the demons here, Michael still retains a hold on you." He carefully patted my back, not quite comfortable with showing affection, even though in three weeks, I'd be his stepdaughter.

"Remember, you're not alone in this. We're here to help, aren't we Grace?"

Mom's eyes rolled, having heard this speech countless times. "Yes. Of course we are. Now can we go inside before my skin is permanently chaffed?"

Stepping over the threshold into Grammy's house brought a flood of emotions attacking. Memories swamped me, fast forwarding in my brain, each one making my heart race so fast I became dizzy...*Riley* holding fresh flowers for Grammy and bedroom eyes for me...*Michael* clamping my arms, forbidding me to move away until he said so or slapped me.

Mom and Marshall walked into the kitchen, chatting nonchalantly about the smell of the turkey cooking, whether apple or pumpkin pie tasted best, and how long they'd be required to stay before returning to the hotel.

I couldn't breathe or find a place to sit. The sofa held the vision of Michael leering at me when Grammy closed the door and left me alone with him that fateful afternoon. The wingback chair next to the piano was where Riley always waited for me so he could see me the minute I came down the stairs.

My stomach lurched and I grabbed the baluster, dropping to the first step.

"Taylor? Are you okay?"

I turned toward the voice—the first demon to deal with. Grammy.

She descended the stairs slowly, considering me when I rose and scrunched into myself under her stare. She remained a stair above, her hand reaching but stopping before touching my hair like she used to. *Changes.*

"I-I'm fine."

"Grace and her new beau in the kitchen?" I nodded. "I hope he knows what he's getting into." We both half laughed and a piece of tension fell away. She stepped in front of me, her voice quieting. "Cupcake, I'm so sorry for what's happened. I didn't know."

"No one did," I replied, staring at the floor. "I take responsibility for that. I never said anything until it was too late."

"Still," I heard the hard swallow, "I should have believed you when you *did* tell me."

"Yes, that one is yours."

She moved a few inches closer, her lavender lotion and green tea breath mixing into the familiar scent I smelled every morning when she woke me and at night when she kissed me goodnight. Tears came without warning and she wrapped me in her arms, stroking the length of my hair to calm me.

"Shhh, little one. It's over. You're safe now." She held my damp cheeks in her palms, a twinkle in her eye suggesting mischief. "I have a surprise for you."

"Oh, Grammy, I don't know…"

"Hey, baby."

Riley.

Grams kissed my forehead and walked away, squeezing Riley's arm as she passed.

"Hi," I said, feigning a smile. I felt confused. I loved that he was here and hated the reason why. Riley closed out the awkward space between us, drawing me close, but not tight. The kiss on my lips was soft and quick. Careful.

"I'm invited to dinner, if you're okay with me being here."

I swiped a wayward tear with the back of my hand. "Of course I'm okay with you here. I wanted to see you."

"Good, because you can smell Grammy's rolls cooking a mile down the road…or did *you* bake them?" We both laughed, reliving the memory of blueberry muffins being passed off as my handiwork.

"Is your mom okay with you spending Thanksgiving with me?"

"As long as we go there for pie later. Mom's kind of bummed out with Jax gone, so Dad's taking her and Dirk out for dinner at some swanky restaurant in Hamilton. She did make pumpkin and pecan pie because she said she couldn't take too many changes at once."

"Yeah, I know how she feels."

**

Mom and Grammy sparred over whether Grammy should come to Boston in the spring, but the "garden" won out. I knew Grams hated flying and the fact she came to my farce of a wedding proved difficult for her, in a lot of ways.

When the chaos erupted at the wedding, I vaguely remember her calling out to me just before Riley tackled me to the ground. Afterward, I became such an emotional disaster that Dad forbade visitors. Mom brought her to the hospital to see me, but at that time, I hated everyone, especially her. She went home and never came to the house.

Riley and I volunteered to do dishes in the kitchen, leaving the "Bermuda Triangle" in the dining room. We kept things light, laughing and painting each other's noses with soapsuds, but an invisible wall separated us.

"Taylor, have you been up to your room yet?" Riley caught the goblet I dropped before it hit the floor.

"No. I can't. I'm not ready."

"Babe, you have to sooner or later. Why don't we sneak up the backstairs without an audience watching?" I just kept shaking my head, feeling the panic bubble in my chest. He looped the dishtowel around my waist, tugging me close.

"I'll be there with you. We'll face the 'boogey-man' together."

"That's not funny, Riley. What's you're asking is hard. The memories are too fresh."

Riley lifted my fallen face and held my gaze. "Sorry, I wasn't thinking. I can't begin to understand how hard this is for you, but seriously, Taylor, until you face *all* the memories, you'll remain frightened. Please, let me help you with this one?" He placed a tender kiss on my mouth. "Please?"

He echoed the good Dr. Shephard's sentiment. If I didn't deal with the demons locked inside my old bedroom, Michael still owned me. I didn't want to be connected to the evil asshole anymore, and in Boston,

I managed to handle the news reports, the preliminary hearing at the courthouse, and the stares, both real and imaginary.

My throat closed off. I did want to handle this without my mother judging or my step-daddy-to-be, analyzing. Grammy would shadow me and force me to take in every inch of the room, where Riley wouldn't. If I opened the door and couldn't handle it, he'd step away and let me run. Trust. I needed to trust in people again. In Riley.

"Okay," I whispered, "but I'm only opening the door. I'm not going inside, so don't try to make me."

"I won't."

We tiptoed up the back stairs, remembering to avoid the center of the steps that creaked from age. My body trembled when I faced the wooden barrier, chipped and in desperate need of a fresh coat of paint. Riley hesitated, watching me reach two or three times for the doorknob, only to pull my hand back. When he offered to open the door, I agreed, shutting my eyes tight when the latch released, not wanting to see the faded yellow walls…the daisy wallpaper border…the *bed*, before I felt ready.

Riley took my hand and gently tugged me. "No," I hissed, my eyes still pressed so tight, tiny stars twinkled behind my eyelids. His arm circled my waist, pulling me against his body.

"Trust me, this once, Taylor. It will be all right. I promise." The floor creaked when my foot touched the planked floor and I jumped, startled by the noise. My eyes opened in a reflex reaction. The breath I drew hurt it filled my lungs so fast.

The yellow walls had been painted sage green. The white eyelet curtains were replaced by sheer purple gauze panels, puddling on the floor to the side of each window. Wooden roman shades folded halfway up, framed a view of the meadow. A wide, palm-blade ceiling fan circled lazily overhead, replacing the antique glass fixture with faded painted rosebuds.

My feet disappeared in the curly plush purple and green rug at the foot of the bed...*Riley's* bed. Gone were the remnants of my nightmare. Earthy tones and warm woods replaced the pastels and white provincial accents. Various sizes of pillows in gold, maroon and rust complimented the deep purple velvet bedspread, turned back just enough to reveal grass colored sheets matching the walls.

Suddenly, the peculiar questions asked in telephone conversations over the past few weeks made sense. What were my favorite colors? The last place I felt safe. The night I spent in Riley's bed had been the first good night's sleep I'd had in months, and in his arms, he kept me safe from all the bad attacking. That night I discovered the meaning of unconditional love, of sacrifice...of true meaning of love.

The salty taste of unacknowledged tears dripping onto my lips brought my world into focus.

"Did I get the colors right? Is velvet okay? If not, I can take it all back. We'll find something else you like better..."

"It's perfect. All of it. You." I was about to rush into the arms gesturing to everything in the room and end his obvious worry, when our private world became invaded by my mother's sneer.

351

"My, this is beautiful. You never did anything like this for me Mother."

"I didn't do a thing. This is all Riley's doing. All I did was well…have the room cleaned out." All eyes centered on the bed and their thoughts screamed loudly in the sudden silence.

"This is *my* bed," Riley quickly offered. "My brother's moved out and his bed is bigger, so I'm giving this one to Taylor, *er,* Mrs. Daniels to use."

Marshall's mouth opened to ask what I knew would be a slew of questions, destroying the picture.

"Don't!" I warned. "Don't ask, don't judge…just don't *speak.* Please. Don't ruin this for me by tainting this with anything remotely associated with Michael. He's dead to me. Dead! I don't even want to hear his ugly name again. Got that? *Never* again."

Forty-One

MIXED BLESSINGS
Riley

Taylor's laugh sounded natural like before. She and Dirk played some racecar video game, knocking shoulders and shouting when they crossed the pretend finish line. I sat mesmerized, watching from the sofa. Taylor sat on my floor, in my world again. Safe. With me.

Dad received a call in the middle of pie and ice cream, so our being here helped keep Mom's mood light and Taylor away from her overbearing family. Mom curled into the opposite corner of the couch with a paperback. After a few minutes, she motioned for me to move closer.

"Is she doing all right?" Mom whispered. Taylor and Dirk were too engrossed in their game to notice our private discussion, let alone hear anything.

"I'm not sure. She's guarded."

"Did she like your surprise?"

"I think so. She walked around the room touching everything and she looked okay. She loved the palm tree rugs and shower curtain. Thanks for the idea."

"Is your savings drained?"

I gave her a disapproving scowl. "Have I asked for any money?"

"No. I'm sorry. I worry that you'll skip a year before going to college to work, that's all. Once you do that, it's hard to change courses."

"I have every intention of going to college. 'Barney's' is not my dream career choice. Don't worry. I'm keeping *all* my options open."

Taylor turned toward us, her brows puckering. "You two talking about me?"

"We're discussing that sweet little butt crack showing with you sitting that way. Mom's jealous of your pink thong." Taylor gasped and slapped her hand to her backside. Everything was covered, but when she joined Mom in a pillow attack against me, her shirt gaped enough to let me know my educated guess was right on. Pink bra meant pink panties, and a familiar longing to touch her again awakened all key body parts. Headache tomorrow for sure. No way could I even think about getting remotely intimate with Taylor right now. The thought that maybe I'd never be brave enough, or that she'd never let me try, scared me. She was right. Things were different.

**

Mom threw a fit when she caught me filling a backpack with a change of clothes.

"You are *not* spending the night with Taylor young man. It's inappropriate."

"Mom, I'm eighteen, you can't stop me. I'm staying with Taylor tonight so she can face her fears with someone, not alone. I have no intention of taking things beyond 'appropriate' so relax."

Taylor filled the doorway. "You don't have to, Riley. I think I've faced enough ghosts for one day."

My mother's face flushed bright red. Served her right. "Sweetheart, I just meant—"

"It's okay Mrs. Martin. You're not the first person to worry about my sexual issues."

My fists rolled tight. "Ugh! Would you two stop already?" I turned to Taylor. "I'm sleeping beside you tonight. Case closed."

I turned to my mother, nervously fidgeting with her hands. "Stop worrying. I'm not Jax."

Forty-Two
THE TEST
Taylor

"Breathe, Taylor," Riley reminded inside the dark shadows.

"I'm trying. Why can't we leave the light on?"

"Babe, you've got to do this the normal way. Lights off and *sleep.*"

"I'm scared to close my eyes."

"I know, but I'm right here if you need me, okay?"

"Okay."

I faced him, the outline of his body barely visible. He lay on his back, his hands folded over his stomach. His legs crossed and his stocking clad feet rubbed against each other. We were fully dressed, except for shoes. I lay beneath layers of bedding while Riley slept on top.

Sometime in the night, Riley got cold and slipped beneath the blankets. Without realizing, I'd wandered next to him, asleep in the crook of his arm. Outside, the wind kicked up and something clanked against the window pane, startling me. I didn't know where I was for a moment, but I felt a body against mine. When an arm snugged my shoulders and tried to pull me closer, I bolted upright and screamed.

"No! Get away from me! Don't touch me!"

Arms reached around me and an overwhelming panic took over. I slapped and scratched at the dark shadow grabbing at me.

"Ouch! Shit! Taylor, stop!"

The bedroom door slammed against the wall and the room lit up brilliant white. Bodies raced for the bed, first to end Riley's life, assuming he'd done the "unthinkable," then smothered me when they realized we both still wore the clothes we had on at dinner. I'd suffered a *flashback.*

Riley's hand bled from my scratches and I pulled it to my mouth, kissing off the blood. His eyes darkened and my breasts tingled, scaring me. I dropped his hand and turned away, facing a *real* visual nightmare. Apparently, my straight-laced mother wears lacy, sheer nighties to bed. The image would take years to erase, but not as long as the picture of *Dr. Shephard* in a pair of form-fitting briefs.

The focus switched from me, to Mom and Marshall. Grammy left the room loudly "tsk-tsking" her tongue, and Mom ripped the bedspread off the end of the bed to wrap around her and the man whose face I may never look upon again.

Mom smoothed the hair away from my face. "Just a nightmare, sweetie. That's all."

"I think it was more than a *nightmare,* Grace."

"Oh for heaven's sake, Marshall! Can I be right just this once? What Taylor imagined wasn't real."

"I'm right here," I tried interjecting.

"If it wasn't real, then it had to be more of a *dream*...a bad dream," she continued, ignoring me.

"Grace, when someone has suffered something as traumatic as Taylor has—"

357

"Guys! Shut up!" I shouted, silencing their argument. "I'm fine, okay? I had a flashback, I know. Marshall told me it could happen, but yeah, they're kind of like a nightmare, so you're both right. Now leave."

"But—"

Riley leaned forward, locking his gaze on my mother. "Leave. Please." When no one moved, Riley moved to the door, gesturing to the hallway. "Good night. We'll see you both at breakfast."

They shuffled together, nearly tripping over each other trying to stay wrapped in the bedspread. Once around the corner, the spread was tossed to a lump in doorway. Riley couldn't help himself, and blew a cat whistle, resulting in a slammed door at the end of the hall.

"You're terrible," I giggled.

"That's not what I've been told," he teased and I stopped laughing. He sighed heavily. "You want the door left open?"

"No."

"Locked?" I shook my head frantically. "Unlocked it is."

Riley gathered the decorative pillows off the floor and lined them down the center of the bed.

"What are you doing?"

"Forming a barrier. I need to protection from your lethal fingernails."

"Sorry. I didn't know it was you. I thought—"

"Babe, I know. Stop worrying." He turned on the lamp next to the bed before turning off the overhead light, then settled on the other side of the puffy fabric wall.

"Aren't you going to turn off the light?" I asked, curious.

"Nope. This way if you attack me, I'll know you're doing it on purpose. Now go to sleep. I've got a feeling we'll be awakened early."

"God, I just hope they're dressed. Can you believe my mother? And Dr. Shephard?"

Riley kissed his finger and pressed my nose. "Go to sleep." His eyes closed but a grin pulled one corner of his mouth. "Your mom actually looks pretty good." His arm went up and blocked my hand. "It's a compliment, babe. You're going to age really well."

**

The next day, Riley worked and I met up with him for garlic burgers and fries at quitting time. We cuddled and kissed, more like old times, with tongues playing hide-and-seek, but Riley's lips barely grazed my neck and his hands groped my hair, nothing else. Later, when I climbed into bed with him wearing pajamas, he insisted I put my *clothes* back on. Everything turned sideways.

Tonight would be our last night together before I returned to Boston. Riley's mom invited me to dinner, a welcome change from the constant counseling session at Grammy's. After we ate, his dad insisted on helping with the dishes, so I talked Riley into walking down to the pond before the sun disappeared.

A thin layer of ice covered the dark gray water, dusted with ice crystals on the corners constantly shaded. The thicket's dirt floor had a carpet of fresh snow from this morning's surprise storm. Riley walked around the far side of the pond, poking the ice with a stick. I rubbed my arms, wishing he'd fold me inside his and warm me.

"Do you want me to make a fire?"

"No, I want you to hold me. Like old times."

"I hold you," he retorted, wounded. "You're the one holding back."

The truthful words bit as hard as the cold air. "I do not," I lied in a small voice.

Riley unzipped his parka and wrapped me inside. His heart thumped against my cheek and my body ached for him. I desperately wanted to explore his body with my hands, but he stiffened in my arms, when I slid my hands inside his back pockets.

I stepped out of his embrace and removed my coat, then my shirt, standing vulnerable and freezing in the pink and blue striped bra he favored. My nipples pushed hard against the fabric and a bubble rolled down Riley's throat.

"Touch me," I demanded.

"*What*?"

"Put your hands on my boobs."

"Taylor…"

I reached behind me and undid the clasp, feeling the straps slowly slide down my arms and fall from my fingertips. "Why won't you *touch* me?"

"Babe, put your shirt on."

"Not until you put your hands on my boobs."

Riley took two steps, whisking my coat off the ground and wrapping it around me. He held it closed in his fists. "Taylor, I want nothing more than to hold my favorite body parts and feel you give *Riley Jr.* a squeeze, but it's not happening. You're not ready."

"Is there someone else?"

"Shit! No, there's not another girl! What the hell is going on?"

I shrugged out of his grip and put my coat on, zipping it to my chin and leaving my shirt and bra on the frozen ground. Angry tears burned, but I pushed them down.

"Well, if *you* don't want me, no one ever will. It proves my point. I'm damaged."

"Is that what this is? A fucking test!" he shouted. He fisted his hair and angry puffs formed little clouds around his face.

"Damnit Taylor! Of course I *want* you. I love you, but I'll be damned if I'm going to be an experiment to measure your broken heart against. If you don't have any more faith in me than that, then find yourself a Harvard frat boy to test your theories on. Not me."

He started for the trail, "Grab your clothes and come one. It's freezing out here. I'll take you back to Lydia's."

"I can get myself back to Grams." I marched off in the opposite direction, along the creek bank, leaving my embarrassing remnants behind. Riley rushed after me, slipping on the icy rocks. He grabbed my elbow, but I yanked out of his grasp.

"Go to hell, Riley."

"Taylor, you don't mean that."

"You know what, Martin? I'm tired of everyone telling me how *I* feel. None of you were raped. I was. You're right. I should throw myself at someone else, because I desperately need to feel something besides, anger and hate. I also deserve to feel something besides *protected.* I want to be loved…and I want to see that lustful *need* in a boy's eyes again. Not disappointment."

**

After a hot shower, I climbed into bed, naked, wrapped inside a green and purple cocoon. I didn't call Riley to apologize and he didn't call me. Tonight, I'd face my nightmares alone. Tomorrow, I'd return to Boston having killed all the demons and any future with Riley.

Forty-Three
MERRY F'N CHRISTMAS
Riley

"Hey, bro, get your lazy ass out of bed. The munchkin's driving the old man nuts wanting to open presents. Mom says he can't touch one until we're all together."

I refused to open my eyes, let alone acknowledge Jax's presence. "Start without me."

"No can do. You're coming with me. Fuck up Christmas, Riley, and Mom will kill you."

Jaxson came home on a furlough before he shipped overseas for six months. The roles in our house had changed dramatically. He was now revered the "golden boy," fussed over and bowed to every time he entered the room. Me? I'd become the "bad seed."

Since Taylor cut me out of her life on Thanksgiving, I'd taken to staying out all hours of the night, sometimes sneaking in the basement window and pretending to be asleep on the couch with the television going. Luckily, I'd accomplished my goal of completing all my credits to graduate early, so when I didn't show up to school, no one called Dad.

I dated a minimum of three girls at a time, sometimes on one given night, letting my hands wander at will. However, my pants stayed on and my heart remained caged. Sex, as bad as I wanted it, I realized now, played a huge part in a relationship. I wouldn't take anyone's innocence away on a selfish whim. Besides, my bruised heart still belonged to Taylor, even if time passing without hearing from her, fed my jealous fears that someone replaced me. I held onto a glimmer of hope that someday she'd come back and my world would spin right again.

Jax flipped Taylor's striped bra against my head, the snap sending a burning pain across my forehead. I kept it dangling off the bedpost mostly to freak out Mom. It also served as a constant reminder of how I screwed things up.

She'd begged for my touch…pled for me to want her like before, but I couldn't. Yeah, Taylor standing there topless made me bat-shit horny in less than two seconds, but I refused to be a band-aid for a wound that hadn't healed…in either of us.

Taylor's rape stripped the passion from our relationship, turning us from "girlfriend and boyfriend" to "victim and I-don't-know-what." Some days I served as counselor, changing to cheerleader, and without warning, emotional "punching bag." But not boyfriend, definitely not lover. I didn't know how "to be" with Taylor. We became afraid instead of in love, neither trusting we wouldn't hurt the other. Guilt seemed to be the only feeling we shared, but now we suffered that alone. Or at least I did.

**

I stumbled downstairs, holding my hand up to summon silence until I poured myself a cup of coffee. The hot, bitter liquid burned a trail down my dry throat to my empty stomach. Jax was right. I couldn't screw up Christmas. It wasn't my family's fault Taylor and I split. I wasn't sure exactly who should be blamed. All I knew was I felt miserable and lonely.

The day followed the same schedule pretty much as any other day except for the imitation angel choirs blaring through every speaker in the house, and the scent of wassail and burning cinnamon candles filling the air. Thanks to a constantly full punch bowl of Mom's homemade eggnog, Dad stayed in a constant state of euphoria. Jax snuck Dirk a taste when "parental supervision" became occupied entertaining the endless flow of visitors who attended our annual Christmas afternoon open house.

After completing my required shower and pulling on one of the three name-brand T-shirts I'd been given by my current "ladies in waiting," I eased through the bodies filling the entry and kitchen. A bottle of Dad's private stash of ale hidden the garage and I were going for my daily walk past Lydia Daniels. I knew Taylor was on a Caribbean cruise celebrating her mother's wedding, but not because she told me. Mrs. Daniels slipped the information to me last night at Christmas Eve services.

Maybe that could be the reason for my lack of holiday spirit. Secretly, my Christmas wish came wrapped in a prayer for a phone call at least…another one of many wishes lately, not coming true.

Thinking I passed outside Mom's radar detection, I stepped into the laundry room to grab my coat. She caught me before I exited the garage.

"Would you take this pumpkin bread to Lydia for me?" Her brow rose before I could create a lie. "You'll never fool your mother, mister. And you better sneak a bottle out of the box behind the tool chest. He's counted your usual stockpile. I'll replace the bottle when I go to the grocery store this weekend."

God, I loved my Mom. Of all the melodic voices crooning inside the house, none sounded as angelic as hers or matched her face, flushed from a tad too much rum while making her eggnog. She placed the warm bread in my hands and pulled the collar on my coat around my ears.

"Not that I condone you drinking *anything* alcoholic at your age, but its Christmas…and my heart aches for yours." She rose on her tiptoes and kissed my cheek. "Don't stay away long. Everyone will be gone in a couple of hours and I'd like to snuggle with all my Martin men by the fire to see the day out. Okay?"

"Okay. Love you, Mom." I kissed her hair, smelling of everything from this morning's waffles to roasted turkey. "Thanks for the new truck tires, by the way."

"*Santa* thought they may come in handy…you know, just in case."

I bounced the bread, feeling tears burn behind my eyes. "You better get inside before you're missed and I can't break the law." We both smiled, eyes shimmering. When the garage door closed, I grabbed my illegal bottle of beer and walked out into the icy air.

When I took the last crusty sounding steps over the rise to Lydia Daniels's house, my heart pounded with imagined anticipation of finding the Mini parked in the driveway, like it did every day when I passed by. But as I stood at the edge of the snow blanketed lawn watching Mrs. Daniels tiny tree in the living room window blink red and green, overwhelming sadness swamped me. Taylor wouldn't be back anytime soon, if ever.

Mrs. Daniels waved to me from the window and met me at the door.

"Come in here, quick. It's freezing out there." She took the warm bread from my hands and held it to her nose. "Yum. Nothing says "home" like a warm loaf of homemade bread. I'll get some butter and we can share a piece."

I agreed to a cup of warmed over coffee and a slice of bread, not wanting to hurry home and pretend at being "merry." I also sensed Lydia Daniels, like me, felt lonely…abandoned.

After several minutes of small talk, avoiding anything remotely related to Taylor, Lydia offered to return my bed, cementing my fears. I refused. The memory of sleeping next to Taylor, smelling *Herbal Essence* on her silken strands of hair and the bubble gum scent of her favorite chapstick spread over lips, parted and breathing sleepily, would remain with the bed. My heart couldn't take the nightly torture.

After swallowing the last of my coffee, I made my way to the door.

"Wait, Riley. I almost forgot." Mrs. Daniels handed me a small, padded brown envelope, decorated in a ring of postage stamps. "Taylor said if you stopped by, to give this to you. I don't know what's inside and she wouldn't say. In fact, she says very little to me anymore."

"She at least talks to you. I've given up hope."

She pressed her lilac scented hand to my cheek. "Never give up hope, dear boy. Love is a peculiar thing. Just as you think the ashes have cooled, something sparks and the fire is rekindled. Give it time."

"Yeah, well—"

"I'm just sayin', Riley. Just sayin'."

I followed the fence line along her property, filling my boots with wet snow as I forged the trail to the pond. The "rock of torture" stood covered in snow next to the charcoal colored pond, now frozen with crackled ice. The boulder earned its name because Taylor straddled me on it after many a swim, devouring me with heady kisses while her wet bikini bottoms hugged my tight swim trunks. Nine times out of ten, her swimsuit top would *accidentally* fall off so her bare chest and mine could warm each other.

I brushed the snow off and perched myself in a familiar position, feeling only icy cold instead of sensual heat pressing my thighs. My teeth tore at the thick envelope until I could stick a frozen finger into the hole to rip it wider. I shook out the contents. A small antique looking silver key, a little over an inch in length, fell into my palm. Reaching inside the envelope and pushing the bubble wrap edges apart, I found nothing more. No note explaining the strange token, or sentiment warning me of a black magic curse. Nothing. The back of the envelope held a postmark for *Hell's Kitchen.* How appropriate, given my current life status.

368

Dropping the key back into the paper pouch, I folded it in half and tucked it in my back pocket. Trudging through the snow covered meadow toward my house, I tried to figure out some hidden meaning, but the burn of frostbite threatening to claim my legs and possibly *Riley Jr.* by the time I reached the patio doors, trumped my thoughts.

**

The odd, tarnished skeleton key rolled over my knuckles effortlessly, after practicing the move thousands of times. The feeling returned to my toes by the time I mastered my knuckle trick. A heavy R&B beat loudly in my earphones, drowning out the voices downstairs. Some of Jax's friends arrived about an hour ago, and Dirk commandeered the basement with his buddies to play his cache of new video games.

My phone buzzed and chirped several times, finally falling silent when I never answered. Bailey, Cherish, and Ashley undoubtedly filled my voicemail with messages professing undying love, turning to death threats by now. I played "jackass" without a conscience. I'd learned from the master—Jax, not to mention I'd added a few personal touches to the role, according to Taylor.

Taylor.

I chucked the key across the room, hearing the metallic ping when it bounced off the mirror and fell to the dresser top. My bedroom door opened, inviting the unwanted holiday chaos into my dark sanctuary.

"Riley?" Dad stood in the ribbon of light, appearing ten feet tall. He wasn't going anywhere, so ignoring him wouldn't work. I pulled my earphones out of my ears.

"What?" I answered tersely.

"You have a call." I glanced at my cell phone, lying on the floor next to the beanbag chair serving as my bed during Jaxson's stay. The light blinked, alerting me of a waiting message, but I wouldn't break my holiday wallowing to explain myself to any of the drama princesses.

"Tell 'em I'll call later."

Dad stepped closer, handing me the cordless phone from their bedroom. "It's a 'ship-to-shore', son. And expensive, so take the call."

He closed the door, returning my room to its darkened state, with the exception of the small screen illuminating my shocked, frightened face. I barely choked out "Hello."

"Merry Christmas, Riley." Taylor's sweet tone summoned a lump in my throat.

"Hi. I mean, Merry Christmas. How's the cruise going? Wedding done?"

"Yes, Mom is officially the wife of a 'doctor'." An awkward silence passed.

"I miss you, Taylor."

"How's school?" she replied, purposely ignoring my personal sentiment.

370

"I'm graduated, but that's not why you called. What's this really about?"

Her heavy sigh mixed with the on-line static. "Riley, I've met someone. His name is Kai Engal. He's in my support group. His friend was also raped, but never moved past it and committed suicide a few months back. Kai's trying to learn how to cope with what happened and how to deal with his guilt. We've sort of *connected.*"

I did not want to hear about some other guy's 'issues', in particular after Taylor introduced him as her new "boyfriend." *Connected.* What the hell did *that* mean? My lungs collapsed and I fought to remain in control. My heart pounded in my chest, wanting freedom to shatter and bleed.

"Is it serious?"

"Me and Kai?"

"No, you and Donald Duck! Yeah, who the hell did you think I meant?"

"Riley…" Taylor's tone turned hard. I'd crossed another line.

"Is that why you called? To rub me nose in the fact you've moved on with someone who *understands* you better than me?

"Kai is a friend. I don't expect you to understand Riley, but I need Kai right now. He's helping me figure out my next steps, and y*ou.* We're not really 'dating', but I'm going with him to Cornell in January. Michael's dad changed the scholarship to whatever university I wanted. A 'peace offering', I guess. I wanted to be the one to tell you before you heard from someone else."

Michael, Michael, Michael! I'd had a gutful of *Michael*. I tried to check my anger, hold my tongue, but it proved useless. It all hurt too much.

"Cornell. With another guy. Well, I'm glad your life is turning out, because mine just took a major dump. Shit, Taylor. Hell of a Christmas present!" I couldn't steel away my emotions any longer. My voice held a needy whine in between the heavy gasps for air. I grabbed another new T-shirt from its tissue encasement and held it over my tear-snot stained face.

"Riley? I'm sorry. I'm not saying we're *over*..."

"Sounds a hell of a lot like 'goodbye' to me. Tell me, Taylor. If I called you and said 'I've met this really wonderful girl who *gets me* and I'm going away with her to some remote island, how would you see it? I could wrap 'friend' into it a hundred ways and it wouldn't sound 'friendly', just like you telling me this shit about some guy named *Kai*. Honestly, I'm not an idiot."

"I never said you were. And Cornell is not a remote island."

"It is to *me*. Cornell is your dream college, and now, you're going to share that dream with someone else. Not me."

"*Colorado* with you, was my...*our* dream, Riley."

"Not any more, is it? I don't want to argue about this. It's your life, babe. Live it how you want and with whoever you *need*. I'm tired of the drama."

"So that's it? You're done with me?"

I opened my mouth to spit out some sarcastic response and thought better. If I wanted to keep any shred of hope of keeping Taylor in my life, I had to shut my fucking mouth.

"No. I'll never by 'done' with you. I love you, Taylor. This hurts, that's all. I never had a chance to be the 'one you needed', but if this Kai dude can help you get happy again, then I want that for you, too."

"Riley…I love you, too. All this crap with Michael didn't change my feelings for you. It changed my feelings about *me*. Until I can get *me* figured out, I'm not getting involved with anyone. Not even Kai. Okay?"

I mumbled "okay" through a snot bubble.

"Did Grammy give you my present?"

"Yeah. What's up the key?"

A smile eased into her tone, turning her voice warm and tender. "Keys open and lock things. Right now, my heart's locked inside yours, but I can't promise that's where it will stay. I'm letting you decide what to do now. No strings, Riley. You chose when to unlock the cage and set us free. Take care, babe. Bye."

Forty-Four
CAGED CONFESSION
Taylor

I fumbled with the lock, dropping my apartment keys a second time. The phone rang again and again. Where was Kai? Why didn't he answer the blasted thing? Finally, I pushed the door open and grabbed the receiver just before the answering machine clicked on.

"Hello?" I answered breathless, struggling to get my coat off and not get tangled in the phone cord. I swear our apartment was retro sixties with a dinosaur phone secured to the wall and a curly cord that hit the floor.

"Taylor? It's Michael."

I stretched the cord across the kitchen and fell onto a chair. "Michael?"

"Don't hang up. I have some news I need to share with you before anyone else."

I picked up my cell phone, quickly scrolling my apps for the voice recorder. If Michael threatened me, I'd have evidence to keep him locked away.

"Are you still in jail?" My question held some hysteria. If Michael was free, I'd be anything but.

"No. I'm at my attorney's office with half of Boston's police force and Dad. I asked if I could make a personal call, if I didn't leave the room."

I flipped my phone shut. "So you're being monitored?"

"Yes unfortunately, because what I want to say to you is private."

"Michael, I can't do *private* with you ever again."

"I know, but please listen. I don't have much time. Taylor, first off, I'm sorry…for everything. Not just for physically hurting you, but abusing your mind and heart, too. You didn't deserve to be treated like that."

"You're right. I didn't. I hate you for what you've done to me, Michael. You've destroyed my life. How can I trust another guy? God, how do you expect me to *ever* have sex with someone and not think of you, or was that your plan all along? *The unforgettable Michael Barnes.*"

Something possessed me and I spewed every vile thought I'd suppressed, calling him despicable horrid names, some of which flowed off my tongue sounding almost poetic. By the time I finished raging, my head hurt and my voice rasped from a sore throat. It suddenly dawned on me, Michael may have hung up at some point and I continued screaming into dead air space.

But he hadn't.

"Anything else?" he asked, quietly.

"No. So what's your news?"

"The jury trial is cancelled. I'm pleading guilty to all charges, and a couple new ones. I make a mean drunk and a worse drug addict. Turns out I crave pain killers. I'd popped a bunch of pills before I came to see you, making me brave and stupid."

"I didn't know about the drugs, Michael. Why? You had everything going for you. What made you throw it all away? Why hurt *me*?"

"No one ever held me accountable. Not even you, Taylor. You should have told your parents the first time I hurt you. By keeping quiet, you fed my greed for power."

"Don't you dare blame me for you sick choices, Michael!"

"I'm not, Taylor, believe me. But, I know if I'm ever going to straighten out my life, I've got to get some help. I'm signing a document admitting to everything and insuring myself a long future with the Massachusetts Correctional System, but also some intense counseling. You don't have to look over your shoulder any more. You're free of me, Taylor. For what's it worth, you're the only one I ever loved and for once, I'm telling you the truth."

"I-I don't know what to say."

"There's nothing to say. Promise me one thing, Taylor. Don't let what I did to you mess up your life. None of what happened is your fault. You deserve to be happy, and out there, probably in the house next to your grandmother, is a boy who'll love you regardless of my attempt to ruin you. Trust in love again, Taylor. Take care of yourself and find your 'happy-ever-after'. Live your fairytale."

The phone went dead. No goodbyes spoken. I didn't shed one tear.

Later on the evening news, Michael's story broke. I sat on the sofa, tucked inside Kai's arms in a state of shock. Two other girls came forward claiming Michael assaulted them. The pictures posted on the screen showed a girl I didn't know, holding a toddler on her hip I swore was the spitting image of Michael. The second victim's blue eyes pursed through cyber space and locked on mine. Delany.

The flood gates opened and I cried for the first time since Christmas, after I hung up from calling Riley and confessing to my relationship with Kai.

"She tried to warn me. I thought she wanted to break me and Michael up so she could have him. I dumped her instead of Michael."

Kai stroked my hair and I buried into his already damp chest. I curled tighter into his embrace, wrapping my bare legs through his.

"Let it out baby. Open your heart and set the evil free."

**

Pots clanged together, pulling me from my slumber. My nightshirt had worked its way up my waist, but a blanket kept me covered. Always the gentleman. Kai, showered and changed, busied himself making coffee. I stretched my arms over my head and yawned wide, popping my jaw.

"Ouch."

"Morning, pretty girl. Breakfast's ready. Better get a move on or you'll miss your first class."

Refusing to open my eyes past half-mast, I sauntered to the table, clumsily dropping onto a chair. A huge chocolate chip muffin poised perfectly center on a plate.

"What's this?"

Kai mussed my bedhead and kissed my cheek before pouring me a cup of fresh, steaming coffee.

377

"Comfort food. After last night, I figured you'd earned it. How'd you sleep?"

"Okay, I guess. You left me on the couch."

"I laid with you until you started snoring. I've got a test this morning, so I left your beautiful snorting body out here so I could get some decent sleep."

I scrunched my face and stuck my tongue out at him.

"Don't stick that thing out if you're not sharing."

"Funny."

"Serious."

I smashed the final chocolate crumb to my index finger and stuck it in my mouth. "You spoil me."

"Too much, I'm afraid."

Kai replaced the plate with my cell phone. "Taylor, don't you think enough time has passed?"

"I'm scared. What if he's found someone else?"

"That's a chance you took when you started this charade."

"This is not a charade. I told Riley the truth."

"He knows I'm *gay*?" My eyes fell away. "Didn't think so."

"If he knew there was no chance of us hooking up, he would just wait me out and I'd never know the truth."

Kai's leveled a disapproving scowl. "So this little test is to prove he really loves you? Come on, Taylor. The guy didn't run away. What more do you want?"

"I need him to *want* me again. The last time we were together, I stood there, naked from the waist up, begging him to touch me. He couldn't. When he looked at me, I saw pity, not *lust* like before. He's careful with how he talks and even kisses me. I don't want to be with Riley because he feels sorry for me. I'd rather be alone the rest of my life."

Kai lowered on his heels, bringing his face even with mine. He tucked a wiry curl behind my ear. "Sweetie, he just didn't want to do anything that would bring back an awful memory. Cut the kid some slack. He's walking through new territory, too, only you pushed him away. He's been handling this alone, while you've had me to help you."

He pecked my lips then tapped the phone. "You don't play fair Taylor. Call him."

"What if he's moved on? I'll die."

"You won't *die,* but you'll have to convince him you're worth another risk." Kai pushed the phone closer. "Taylor, if you don't do this, you'll always wonder 'what if'? Don't spend your life living with *regret.* It's your turn to take a chance."

**

After Kai left for school, I showered, gave myself a manicure, and proceeded to clean the apartment, completely sacking school. When I couldn't find another speck of dust or an excuse, I checked the clock. Noon. Four o'clock in Wellsville. If Riley worked today, he'd be leaving in an hour.

Call him...take a chance. Kai's words nagged incessantly. I coiled into the corner of the couch holding a decorative pillow to my chest. I punched the cell number in. Deleted it. Tapped it again, my finger suspended over the call button. *Call him.*

"I hate you, Kai!" I shouted and pushed the button.

Four rings. Voicemail would pick up on the sixth. Maybe he'd already gone to work. Maybe because the caller ID said "unknown" he purposely ignored the ring. I gnawed my thumbnail, contemplating what message I'd leave.

"Hello?"

I threw the phone across the couch as if a bomb about to explode.

"Anybody there? Who is this?"

"Do you hate me?" I shouted from across the sofa.

"*Taylor?* Is that you? I can barely hear you."

"Answer me. Do you hate me?"

Silence. The green light flashed, but Riley said nothing. I picked up the phone.

"Riley—"

"No. I love you."

Tears poured from my eyes and snorts rattled my nostrils when I gasped against the sudden sobs.

"I-I need you."

**

The metal cage masqueraded as an elevator. The cables groaned and squealed, the stench of heated rubber lingering once it stopped. I

380

pushed the scissor-action gate to the side and stepped into the hall. Riley clung to the back wall of iron rungs.

"Come on. You don't want it to drop, do you?"

He flew out of the iron box, nearly tripping over his shoes. I laughed so hard I had to brace myself against the wall.

"I don't think I've ever seen you afraid before." I unlocked the apartment door and walked inside. Riley remained in the hall. "Are you coming inside or staying in the hallway all weekend."

"Being scared of your rickety elevator is nothing compared to what I feel right now. Taylor, maybe this is a mistake."

"What do you mean?"

"Staying with you. In your—yours and Kai's place. It feels wrong."

I grabbed his sleeve and yanked him inside, then bolted the door. "You're being ridiculous. We need to talk, Riley, and me coming to Wellsville wouldn't give us the privacy we need to sort through things. That's why I flew you here, so we could be *alone*."

Riley wandered the room, touched the sofa pillows, flipped the top of the magazine on the coffee table. He shoved his hands in his pockets, sauntered to the mantle and picked up a framed picture. "Where is your roommate?"

"He drove to Manhattan to stay with friends. He thought we could use some space."

Riley put the picture back and scrubbed his neck, but still refused to sit. I rubbed my hands down the sides of my jeans, anxious at how

381

nervous he seemed. I still held secrets, but vowed to reveal them all…just not in the first ten minutes.

I walked into the kitchen area, feeling Riley's eyes follow. "Want something to drink? There's beer."

"No thanks. I seem to like it too much." Riley stared at the ceiling. I handed him a bottle of spring water.

"Stick to bottled water then. Don't drink the tap water. The pipes in this building have to be a thousand years old. Oh, and let the water in the shower run a couple of minutes, too. Cleans out the rust." I popped the top of my diet soda and eased onto the arm of the sofa. "What is it, Riley? You're pacing like a caged cat."

"I told you, I'm nervous." He waved his hands aimlessly in the air. "This bothers me. You living with a guy."

"Like I've said a hundred times, it's not like that with me and Kai, okay?"

Riley's water bottle crinkled he drank so hard. "Taylor, a *male* can't be around you and not think about...being *with* you. It's not normal. You're too damn hot."

I smiled. "Thanks, I think. Does that mean you're *affected* by my presence."

"Hell, Taylor, the sound of your voice makes me bat-shit horny. Being here, alone with you is driving me crazy and I'm about ready to jump out of my skin because I don't know how the fuck to act! I'm scared shitless to get close to you. Babe, my heart can't take another goodbye, if that's what this is."

"Seriously? You think I brought you all the way to New York to rub your nose in the fact I'm in a relationship with another guy, which I'm *not*."

Riley picked up the picture off the mantel again. "Damn the guy's sure full of himself, isn't he? I mean he has his picture in a fancy frame for the world to gawk at. Where's yours? Next to the bed? Damn, I can't do this."

He tossed the picture onto the easy chair and picked up his duffel bag. I rushed to the door and stood in front of it, spilling my pop down my shirt.

"Wait. Don't leave. There's something I have to tell you."

Riley's arm pressed the door to the side of my head. I could see the anger starting to build in his eyes. "*More* secrets? God, don't tell me you're married."

"No, far from it. And that picture isn't Kai. It's his old partner. The one who killed himself after he was beaten and raped."

Riley's brows touched. A glint of recognition ignited. "You mean—"

"Kai's gay."

Riley rolled to the side of me, thumping against the door. He heaved a sigh that fluffed his bangs. "Gay. All this time I've been going out of my mind imagining you and this Kai dude hooking up every night. Shit. I don't know whether to be relieved or mad as hell."

He slid to the floor and propped his elbows on his knees, holding his head. Slowly, I eased down beside him, cautious of what came next.

383

Riley shook his head. "Gay," he repeated quietly. His shoulders started to shake and my stomach dipped. I'd pushed too far and upset him.

Suddenly, he lunged at me, pushed me to the floor. My soda flew across the carpet when Riley pinned my wrists and hovered over me.

"You are so going to pay for this, girl."

"*Riley*…don't you dare…" I'd seen this look only one other time and the revenge inflicted turned my world upside down in a most wonderful way.

**

"How long you planning on sleeping?" Riley asked from the doorway. "It's almost noon. Day's half over and you're still in bed…without me."

I rolled over and twisted the clock. "Ugh, why did you let me sleep so long?" I stretched and rubbed my eyes. "Hey? Where's my coffee? And the real question is why *am* I in bed without you? I halfway hoped to wake with you next to me." I pushed up against the headboard. "What happened?"

Riley lowered onto the side of the bed and handed me the mug. "I figured the couch was safer for both of us. I don't want to risk messing this up. Right now, I think we should take things slow, although *Riley Jr.* may argue. Hope you've got aspirin." He looked over at the twin bed across the room. "You guys really share a room?"

I nodded, allowing a warm swirl to slip down my throat.

"Kai ever seen you naked? If so, I may have a problem with that." Riley took the cup and swigged back the last of the coffee.

384

"Saw me in my bra once. Trust me, even my "church worthy" lacies do nothing for him."

Riley moved me back into the pillows, pressing his body to mine. "Trust *me,* he's lying. I'm laying on top of you with a blanket between us and just knowing you *own* thong underwear is causing me serious physical issues." He reached under the blanket and pinched my side.

"Ouch! What's that for?"

"You're not wearing *green.* It's St. Patty's Day. Wear green or scream."

A tickle-pinch fest ensued and soon we were tangled on the floor in the bedding pulled from the bed. I fisted his T-shirt and pressed it to my nose.

"I've missed your smell...the way it filled my hair and clothes after being with you." I curled onto his chest, his heartbeat fast against my cheek. "I love you, Riley," I whispered. "Say you'll take me back?"

"I never did let you go."

"Does this mean I'm still in your picture?"

"No one else could ever fit beside me in that frame, you know that, don't you?"

His expression held an innocence that made him appear vulnerable. I traced the outline of his mouth, moist...warm. Gently, I fit mine against it, testing. Our lips locked and the world disappeared, taking all the bad memories. Riley kissed me like old times, his hand snaking over my body and bringing the dead girl inside me back to life. I melted into the angles of his body, swept up in scent of his cologne, the familiar taste of the cinnamon he sprinkled in his coffee still on his tongue.

All things "Riley."

I struggled against an unexpected wave of emotion and pulled back. "I thought I'd lost you." He flipped the waistband on my panties and I slapped his chest. "I'm serious, Riley. I really believed I'd screwed things up for good."

Riley twirled tiny circles on the back of my neck. "I think we lost each other. I listened to everyone tell me to be careful, not push you…not touch you, but I didn't listen to my heart. I'm sorry." He nuzzled my neck, breathed against my skin and turned quiet.

"Everyone treated me different after the rape, like I'd break or something. My parents bugged me, but when you acted weird, it really hurt. I needed you to stay the same, Riley. When you wouldn't touch me and even kissed me differently, I saw it as your feelings had changed—that you didn't really love me as much as I thought. Your coolness made me believe *I'd* done something wrong."

Riley kissed away a surprise tear dripping from the corner of my eye. "You know that's not true. You did nothing to deserve what happened. You're right, after I saw how fragile you were, I didn't know what to do. I didn't want to freak you out and make you hate me, too."

"Kai said it was something like that." I stroked the side of Riley's sudden pained face. "Tell me you're still not blaming yourself."

"Of course I am. I failed you and to be honest, I'm scared as hell I could do it again—not be there to save you when you need me."

"Babe, you've always been my super-hero. You didn't fail me. You just got caught in your cape."

Forty-Five
ENDINGS AND BEGINNINGS
Riley

The sun bore a hole through my head. The hottest day of the year and I was trapped inside a heavy gown. Why did I decide to go through with this graduation crap, anyway?

"Smile!" Mom clicked her gazillionth picture of me in the silly red satin getup.

Dad scratched the back of his neck. "Enough, Bev. Let Riley say his goodbyes. I'm starving."

"Well, let's just interrupt one of the most important days in your son's life to satisfy your constant hunger, shall we?" she snipped.

I laughed "Mom, ease up already. You guys go on ahead to the restaurant. By the time Dad's had a couple beers, I'll be there."

She shook her finger. "Thirty minutes, mister."

Dirk pointed to an imaginary watch on his wrist, miming Mom. Dad cuffed his head.

"You had a sister once who made fun of your mother. She disappeared the next day."

"Stan!"

Dad delighted in making up a new "long lost sister" story every time we got caught teasing Mom. By the time Jax and I were Dirk's age, we actually believed we had a sister walking aimlessly around the world.

I watched my family wander toward the parking lot, stopping every few feet to acknowledge someone. Thirty minutes would pass before they ever reached the car.

"I'm going to miss your family when I move to California."

"But not me? I'm hurt. Wounded deeply. I may never recover."

Warm, soft lips pressed mine quickly. "You're pure drama." I pulled her close for another kiss. "I'll miss you, too."

A freshly manicured hand tugged the zipper down on my gown. Her fingers ran under the silver chain lying at the base of my throat, and caressed the tiny key. Not moving from my arms, her head tilted the direction of my truck, parked under the trees. A willowy silhouette moved our direction.

"Is this the key to her heart?"

"Sure is."

"She's a lucky girl."

I couldn't help myself. "Yes, she is."

Taylor linked her arm through my other elbow. "I'm what?"

"Damn lucky to have me."

"It appears I'm *sharing* at the moment."

My arm dropped from Leila's waist. "Taylor, this is Leila Brown. The girl I told you about who's *engaged* to Barney's stepson. I've been sort of—"

Leila offered her hand to Taylor. "*Babysitting*. My fiancé left two weeks ago for Southern Cal, but I stayed behind for graduation. Barney assigned Riley as my guardian to keep other boys away, and me out of trouble."

"He assigned *Riley* to keep you out of trouble? Is there another Riley that works for Barney?"

I kissed Taylor's full lips, feeling her smile. "You're the only girl who gets me in trouble, and I can't wait to create some mischief."

As if on cue, Leila's boyfriend appeared. Introductions were made and he whisked her away, leaving me alone with Taylor.

"Should I be jealous?" Taylor asked. "You didn't tell me how pretty she was."

"Nor did you tell me how *pretty* Kai was either. I think you were due some payback." Taylor's lips slowly brushed mine. "Damn girl, stop that." She shook her head and slid her arms around my waist inside my robe.

"When will you be done with dinner?" she asked.

"I'm thinking of skipping dinner and going straight for dessert. Wonder what your lips would taste like covered in whipped cream?" Her tongue tapped my bottom lip and I opened my mouth to taste her long and deep. Her fingers curled into the belt loops of my jeans and her leg eased around my thigh.

"Damn, Taylor, this gown's going to look like a pup tent if you don't stop torturing me." She threw her head back with a deep laugh and I lavished the silken length of her neck with my mouth. Her laugh changed to a soft moan.

"I wish we were leaving tonight. I can't wait to get away with you."

"Come to dinner with me, please?" I begged, not wanting to let go of her, even if we were starting to turn heads.

"I can't. I promised Grammy I'd go with her to a movie at the old Electric Theatre. They're showing that old western, 'Paint Your Wagon', she's always loved. Arriving so late last night, didn't give me any time to spend with her and today's been busy getting things ready."

She stepped back, checking to see if my "tent" assumption manifested. I followed her not-so-subtle glance to my lower region. "Speaking of, are you ready to go?"

"You'll have to be more specific." She slapped my chest. "Ouch! Yes, I've been packed since the day I got my acceptance letter. *Colorado* here we come."

I tried reeling her close, but she resisted, her arms slowly pulling through my hands.

"Go eat with your parents. I'll catch up with you in a couple hours."

I watched my dream slowly disappear into the sea of people scrambling for cars. My cell phone buzzed in my pocket, scaring me near death. Dirk's simple text read *"Save me."*

When I climbed in the front seat of my truck, my foot kicked a package wrapped in plain brown paper, tied with a bright red ribbon. I pulled the bow apart and ripped the paper, wondering how and who got into my truck. Enveloped in black satin, I found flip-flops and a silver picture frame with a hand written "invitation" appearing from the other side of the glass.

Meet me at the pond. Nine o'clock sharp. Wear these.

I held the black fabric up to the sunlight, quickly rolling it into a ball when I discovered the silky cloth to be a pair of boxers! The five course dinner planned would consist of appetizers only. I checked my watch. Six o'clock. Three torturous hours until my official "graduation," I hoped.

**

Eating dinner with my family took forever. We discussed my departure for Denver in the morning. I'd follow Taylor in my truck, loaded with her furniture from her grandmother's. We told no one we were only taking my bed. Supposedly, the two bedroom apartment we rented already had a bed in the spare room, but after spending St. Patrick's Day in New York with Taylor, I hoped we never cracked the door to the other bedroom.

Halfway through dessert, Jax called my cell and offered congratulations. He'd signed up for another six month tour of duty, much to my mother's disappointment. My dad expressed his "pride" for Jaxson finally turning his life in the right direction. Mom and I knew his decision had more to do with a certain invitation to Ally's wedding than patriotism.

By the time I broke free of my strangling family ties and suffered through a dozen more pictures, the sun had dipped behind the western hills, leaving long golden fingers stretching to a darkening sky. A few brave stars twinkled in the deep lavender overhead.

I managed to make my trek along the creek bank without breaking an ankle as I hurried over the uneven terrain to reach the pond. To avoid suspicion or unwanted guests, I parked my truck back at the house and walked along the far side of the property. I was about to break through the thick shrubbery when a voice called out from somewhere in the trees.

"Take your clothes off. This is a 'black boxer' only affair."

"Can I keep my flip-flops on or are dirty feet part of my attire?" I called out to the hidden voice.

A small giggle turned my insides mushy. "Yes, but no shoes. You'll spoil the image."

Wouldn't want to do that!

My imagination went into overdrive creating *images* of its own. I stood at the bushy entrance, feeling the evening breeze bluster up my new flimsy shorts and a frightening thought entered my mind.

Could this be some twisted joke…an embarrassing payback? Heaven knows I've played more than my share of horrible practical jokes and the victims…well, the list was long. For all I knew, me standing in the clearing wearing only billowy silk boxers could be the lead-in story on the local news. With the breeze blowing up my hind side, the cover picture would leave little to the imagination.

"Okay, I'm not walking into some trap, am I? Mom and Dad aren't waiting with a video camera, are they?"

Laughter gurgled across the way. "Trap? Maybe. Guess you'll just have to trust me."

Shit.

Cautiously, I pushed away the last branches concealing my half naked body. Candles in every color of the rainbow flickered from perches on various rocks. Small glass jars holding white candles rimmed the pond from where I stood, to where the stream flowed into the far corner. A fiery fairyland surrounded me, setting the densely covered clearing in a colorful glow.

Across from me, a lithesome figure emerged from behind a pine tree, wearing only black lace panties. Her *church worthy* underwear guaranteed I may be in for a truly religious experience, taking "worship" of the goddess coming closer, to a much higher plane.

Long blonde curls covered my favorite "hand holds" and lips stained the color of blood parted, flashing a brilliant set of perfect teeth.

I couldn't summon a drop of saliva to ease my sudden dry throat or push down the lump closing my airway. My reaction to the glorious creature inching toward me mirrored the same one I had the first day I spied her swimming in the dark waters shimmering at my feet. Multiplied by ten. Silky boxers held no secrets.

Taylor's red painted fingers, barely touched my skin as they trailed up each arm and slowly over my chest, sending a flurry of gooseflesh pebbling from my toes to my chin. I attempted a swallow, the gulp loud enough to echo three states away.

Her eyes dropped to where *Riley Jr.* saluted proudly, a wicked smile of satisfaction drawing up the corners of her mouth. I gasped when her index finger playfully poked my navel and slowly twirled the line of curls coming from further *south,* dragging a sensual line to the dangling key bobbing against my chest. My heart threatened to break free of any second.

An antiqued heart-shaped locket lay against dewy skin begging for my lips to touch. I parted the curtain of golden strands and tossed them over her shoulder, delighted in the delicate gasp when I reached for the locket.

"Tell me, baby, whose heart is locked inside?"

"I don't know yet," she answered breathy. "You'll have to use that key to find out."

"But if I do," I presented against lips barely touching mine, "I will set yours free. I'm not sure I want to do that."

Our lips slid together and pulled back, our eyes locked in each other's darkening gaze.

"You could catch it before it escapes."

Taylor's dark lashes brushed her cheeks and her body pressed into my every curve. I braided my fingers into her hair and held her mouth hard against mine.

"How do you propose I do that?" I whispered between breaths.

"By never letting go of me again."

"I think I can manage that."

Her arms wrapped my waist, her fingers sliding inside the waistband of boxers serving no purpose any longer. My hands left their favorite playground and cautiously rounded the cool skin of her hips. I hooked my thumbs in the black lace.

"I love you Taylor Wilson. More than life itself."

She stepped away, leaving me breathless, I suddenly understood why girls were all into the romantic picture of beds covered in rose petals. Tucked under the boughs of a large pine tree, the quilt from my truck lay spread out over a cushion of pine needles, covered in several assorted foil wrapped *lozenges.*

****

The house suddenly erupted in mass confusion. Who knew a wedding could be so disruptive. My mother spun different directions, depending on who or what demanded her attention. My father fraternized with the guests arriving for the ceremony, deliberately staying out of her way.

I stood on the deck, taking in a backyard transformed into a fairylike setting with thousands of tiny white lights twinkling between the leaves on the trees against the twilight sky. Walking the grassy aisles, I straightened a couple of white linen covered chairs, adjusting the navy satin bows on back as if I knew what to do. I didn't have a clue, but what else was new?

I stole up the stairs to my bedroom. My favorite siren answered my soft knock, pulling me inside and melting her lips to mine in a kiss that brought all body parts standing at attention. She laughed against my lips when I snuggled her hips against me.

"You're the horniest guy I know," she giggled.

"I can't help it when you're in my arms."

Our next kiss sent my tongue searching for internal organs. I loved how Taylor's body molded intimately to my curves, in particular to the curve her hand paid special attention to.

"Girl you're driving me crazy," I whispered and adjusted appropriately, letting her fingers work their magic while I stroked the velvet skin of her bare back. I ran a finger under the lace edge at the small of her back. "I didn't know they made sexy lace corsets for *big* girls," I teased.

She bit my lip.

"Ouch!" Her hand gave me hard squeeze and I doubled over. "Shit! Knock it off! You know I'm joking."

"Don't mess with me, Riley Martin. I'm sensitive about my weight and you know it. Now help me zip my dress. We're running late."

"They can't start the wedding without us."

I trailed my fingers along the arch of her spine, relishing the soft moan my touch could create. I zipped the satin gown and my hands framed her small hips, pulling her back against me. Her head fit just below my chin and she tipped it into my shoulder when my hands slid around the front of her, resting on her rounded middle.

"You didn't sleep much last night, babe," I whispered into her hair.

"Your son kept me awake with his constant kicking."

Lifting a bunch of gold curls, I kissed the back of her neck and pecked my way to her bare shoulder. "Have you thought anymore about names?"

Taylor giggled. "I guess *Riley Jr.* is out, thanks to your twisted humor."

"Pretty much all the men's names in my house are out then."

She slapped my hands, then jerked. "Ouch!" She moved my hand to the side where a foot or an arm pushed against my palm. "See? He never stops. I hope this isn't a preview of what's in store for us."

I pressed my lips below her ear. "He's just anxious to get out, so his old man can get back in." Her elbow gouged my gut.

"You're disgusting."

I caught her before she could move out of my arms. "And you're beautiful."

"I'm a large navy blue satin blob."

"You're pregnant Taylor. That hardly qualifies you as a 'blob'." I watched her eyes shimmer with tears and wrapped her protectively to me, wanting to absorb all the sadness from her. "No tears, baby. Angels don't cry, remember?"

The bedroom door burst open, slamming against the wall. Who knew a four year old could be so strong?

"Speaking of," I gathered the bundle of pink ruffles into my arms.

"Who's an angel, Daddy?"

"Mommy is." I kissed her chubby cheek and nuzzled my nose into the folds of her neck until she laughed. "And you, Miss Lydia, are an 'angel in training'."

Her little arms barely fit around my neck and I nestled my cheek against her silky caramel colored ringlets, squeezing her pint sized body. Who knew I'd turn out to be such a sucker for pretty girls? Taylor eased into my free arm and I held her close, sensing her fragile emotions still hovered close to the surface.

"Patience, baby. You've only got one more month before your hot little body will be back to torturing me." Her shoulders shook with a light laugh.

I kissed her puckered mouth. "Besides, I kind of like you pregnant, babe. Your boobs are a major 'turn on'."

"*Boobs,*" spat on a puff of air against my face. "Mommy has boobs."

"Now look what you've done, Riley! Your mother is going to throw a fit if she blurts that out during the ceremony." Taylor moved out of my arms and picked up her bouquet. "We better get downstairs. Where are the bride and groom, anyway?"

"Gina is in the downstairs bathroom and Dirk is outside pacing somewhere. I can't believe my baby brother is getting married. He's barely twenty-three."

In a few short minutes, Dirk would marry Ally's youngest sister, ironically mixing family matters once again. After a short six month marriage to Jax's best friend Brandon, Ally and he divorced and she married a forgiven Jaxson when he returned from his second tour of duty overseas.

Tomorrow, they would leave for another two year stint on some military base in Germany. My mother had turned into a walking human fountain with her precious baby, Dirk, getting married, and her oldest son moving across the ocean, taking away her only grandson. Taylor and I hoped to keep the sex of baby number three a secret until his birth, but we may have to spring the surprise to cheer up Mom.

"Dirk's only three years older than you were when we got married. You didn't seem to think *we* were too young."

"We were hot for each other. I had to marry you before I died of exhaustion from constantly jumping your bones. Someone had to cook for me before I withered away to nothing."

I deserved the punch to my shoulder for that one.

"Hey, 'man holding child' here. Easy with the brutality."

"We got married because I was pregnant."

"This is the first I've heard such a scandalous rumor!" I teased, ducking. "Still can't believe my parents swallowed the 'honeymoon baby' story."

"Well, Grammy didn't. Good thing she liked you, or she'd have spilled the beans to your mother the first chance she got."

A melancholy memory flickered in my lover's eyes. I caught the single tear sliding down her cheek with my thumb.

"You okay, sweetheart?"

"I miss her, that's all. I wish she'd waited a while longer to give up on life."

"Cancer doesn't give many choices, babe. I believe that's why she sent this little bundle our way." I bounced my armful of ruffles and Grammy's namesake. "She's even got her bright blue eyes."

Taylor tugged Lydia close for a smooch on the cheek. "She's definitely the calmer of our girls. I just hope her little brother follows suit." Taylor gave me a look that made my pants suddenly feel tight. "I can't believe I let you talk me into a third 'Martin munchkin'."

"You took advantage of me in a weakened moment. I had no choice. Besides, I wanted to enjoy 'preggo boobs' one last time."

"Riley Martin," Taylor hissed, covering Lydia's ears, but grinning too wide to be innocent. She kissed me quick for penance.

"Boobs!" Lydia squealed around a laugh.

I turned my cherubic beauty to face me, poking her tummy to get a big toothy grin, "Enough, missy. Where's is your big sister, anyway?"

"Chasing Uncle Jax."

"Well, we better go save him."

I leaned back and stole another taste off my gorgeous wife's mouth. My heart still did funky summersaults when I was near her. I couldn't believe after twelve years, she could rock my world with a mere smile, let alone take me to the brink of insanity at warp speed when she sucked my lips off.

"Let's see if we can get Uncle Jax to say 'sneaky snake'."

Jax still talked with a slight lisp after Ally damn near bit his tongue in half when she found out he cheated on her with *my* old girlfriend. No one noticed unless he says a series of "S" words, which became a favorite game of mine."

"You're pure evil, Riley," Taylor chastised, following me and Lydia into the hall. "But I believe I read a warning in *the fine print* on your lips."

"Fine print?"

Taylor's finger seductively slid across my bottom lip. "Yeah, right here, baby."

Her mouth fit perfectly against mine and I kissed her slow and deep, ignoring the wiggling bundle in my arms. I licked my lips, "Tasty. Can't wait for dessert, later."

She gave my butt cheek an affectionate squeeze. "I'll get the bride. You rally the troops, Dr. Martin."

I playfully jostled my beautiful little girl in my arms as we bounced down the stairs. "Sneaky snake," I hissed, waiting for her to repeat my words.

"Boobs!" she giggled. "Boobs!"

I was in serious trouble, but I knew that the day I found her mother swimming in my pond.

****

Riley's Pond

I hope you enjoyed reading Riley's and Taylor's story as much as I enjoyed writing it. They could be quite boisterous in my head at times trying to get my attention. In the end, I felt like I'd been invited into their intimate lives like an old family friend and had my own seat at the Martin's dining room table.

Thank you my readers.

You can jump onto my website to discover the other stories rambling in my thoughts, in the throes of editing, or ready to soon be unveiled. I love hearing from my fans, so please stop by.

www.harleybrooks.com

ABOUT THE AUTHOR

HARLEY BROOKS grew up with the majestic Rocky Mountains literally climbing out of her backyard. Her childhood dreams were to become an astronaut, but the teenage years proved she sucked at Math and liked boys *way* too much. When she finally kissed the right "frog" and found her prince charming, she traded the granite snow tipped mountains for the breathtaking red cliffs of the high desert. Inspired by the blazing orange of sunset baked red rocks, she loves to create romantic tales about all the "first times" and growing pains experienced when morphing from teen to adult. When she's not writing, you can find her camping with her family, exploring trails on her 4-wheeler, or chasing her latest muse on her Harley Davidson.

COMING NEXT

THE DESIGNER GENES TRILOGY
. . . a glimpse from Book One:

"The Boyfriend Cut"

Jordan caged me against the counter, his eyes leveling to mine. He studied every laugh line, every freckle dotting my face. I stopped breathing when his head dipped and lips lingered close.

"I really want to kiss you."

"What's stopping you?" I asked breathier than intended. Our noses grazed and an eternity seemed to pass.

"You scare me," he uttered lightly over my waiting mouth. His lips barely brushed mine, but the spark in the kiss was undeniable.

"Wow," I whispered, no longer feeling my legs. "Now I'm scared."

His arm eased around my waist, pulling me into him. A seductive smile appeared, and my heart skipped a beat. "Can I kiss you again?"

"Oh yeah," I replied softly on his cheek.

His hand wrapped the back of my neck, his fingers braiding into my hair. My lips bloomed against his when
they pressed with a second, more confident kiss. When the kiss ended, our eyes locked. I worried what thoughts bounced in his brain.

Did I kiss okay? Too much? My breath?

He pecked the end of my nose.

Had he made a mistake?

"Sorry, I shouldn't have—"

Another person suddenly possessed my body. I rose on my tiptoes, tugged his collar and settled my lips on his, hushing his apology. His tongue teased and my lips parted, welcoming the delicious taste of his mouth taking mine. Jordan's arms wrapped tighter and I leaned into his curves as if by body had done it had a million times, familiar with every bend and angle.

Heat ripped through my veins like fire chasing a stream of gasoline. No one had ever kissed me like Jordan. I never *tingled* all over before. It was as if I inhaled air for the first time and my lungs wanted more. Something clicked between us—bolts sliding effortlessly through locks. I never wanted our kiss to end, or Jordan to leave my arms.

His lips tickled the spot below my earlobe and my bones turned spongy. "Marli Davis—don't break my heart.

www.ingramcontent.com/pod-product-compliance
Lightning Source LLC
Chambersburg PA
CBHW021425240626
47153CB00001B/21